A SPELL IS CAST

Fern's hand was tingling, her brain was racing, and her time was running out. Standing unknowingly before her were three women poised and ready to be guided to their destiny. Unfortunately, no fairy godmother had *ever* taken on three assignments at the same time. Could she do it? Dare she try? There was no time to send out a signal for a consultation about dealing with so many tangled tales. The door of opportunity could be lost if she didn't act now. Immediately! Fern wrapped her shaky fingers around the crystal wand tucked in the sash at her waist, and raised it above the three women. She closed her eyes and concentrated as she'd never done before. There would be some danger. Pain, too. Some hearts would be broken, but love would prevail if they had enough courage...if they would listen.

Of course—Fern smiled with just the slightest touch of chagrin—a bit of help to get the girls off to a flying start would be only wise.

Besides, she thought as she waved her wand and released a brief, glittering shower of magic over Belinda, Lilith, and Roberta, "happily ever after" was more than just shop talk. Fern Tatiana Goodwin delivered.

Other *Love Spell* books by Bronwyn Wolfe:
LONGER THAN FOREVER

Once Upon A Tangled Tale

BRONWYN WOLFE

LOVE SPELL NEW YORK CITY

LOVE SPELL®

August 1996

Published by

Dorchester Publishing Co., Inc.
276 Fifth Avenue
New York, NY 10001

The dedication in my first book was to family...so it seems right to acknowledge some special friends and mentors in my second one.

Thanks to Kay Bryant and Donna Hendricks, two talented friends who gave me the help and encouragement to actually write this story.

Thanks to Joanna Cagan, my editor, for her exquisite skills, her understanding, and for taking a chance on someone new and something different.

And finally, thanks to Madeline Baker, a wonderful, giving author who has become a treasured friend. A few books ago she mentioned my name in one of her dedications, and I can hardly believe I have the chance to thank her in this special way.

Thanks to all of you for helping my dreams come true!

Prologue

Fern Tatiana Goodwin discreetly tugged up the back of her wretched panty hose and peeked around a large ficus studded with hundreds of tiny white lights. The elegant ballroom of the Royal Arms Hotel looked more like a fairy palace than many of the real ones she'd seen over the last millennia or so.

Lacy peach swags ringed the room, and more glittering lights traced a path leading to a white lattice arbor that framed the bride and groom. Woven into the arch above their heads, like a springtime cloud of scent and color, was baby's breath, greenery, and peach roses. The theme was repeated in the floral arrangements nestled in brilliant silver bowls artfully placed around the room on linen-topped tables. Everything was perfect except for one little thing.

Someone was planning to harm the bride.

And Fern was fit to be tied.

Fairy godmothering was not the sure thing it once had been. The success rate had been declining steadily since the late 1800s, and the last fifty years had been terrible. Humans had become so blasted high-tech that they were systematically reasoning all the wonder and magic right out of their lives. Such a large population had seen so many special effects and heard so many outlandish tales that they didn't even consider real magic anymore. Even the most powerful fairy godmothers couldn't work on people who had lost the ability to believe.

In fact, sweet Cindy Ella Jones had been Fern's first assignment in over forty years who had actually sensed the cosmic mystery directing her life. Once she'd been helped to find her "life-tale," she'd followed the path all the way, dips and potholes included (which, of course, were part of the screening process). Finally she was ready to start reaping the rewards.

And nobody was going to mess that up!

Bronwyn Wolfe

Fern eyeballed Cindy Ella and her handsome groom and tried to align herself with the vibrations in the room. Ten minutes ago when she'd entered the reception, her hidden wand had thrummed a time or two, which should have alerted her immediately. However, the flush of long-awaited success must have momentarily fogged her receptors. Stars! There was so much interference. She closed her eyes and slowly began blocking all thoughts except the ones dealing with Cindy and Prince. Little by little the clamoring in her head quieted and she honed in on one distressed voice she recognized. It was Belinda Brown, Cindy's best friend.

Fern had met the sensible young woman a few times while she'd been posing as a cleaning person on the night shift with Cindy. In fact it had been Belinda who'd convinced Cindy to share her dream of approaching Princeton Chalmers, president of Chalmers, Inc., with her innovative video game. Since his office was there on the fifteenth floor, it had taken only a few well-placed words and a sprinkle of fairy dust to break Prince's computer code and get Cindy to input her idea. The single shoe—left behind at Fern's subliminal prompting—had led Prince right to her. And the rest had been, well, a storybook romance with a happily-ever-after ending. Until now.

Fern scanned the room. Where was Belinda? Aha! She was standing near the back exit with two other women. Fern worried her bottom lip and shifted on her pinched feet. Modern times might have certain advantages, like microwaves and candy bars, but the fashions were torture. High heels were ghastly, and panty hose a demonic device. Oh, she'd heard women over the years pity their sisters from bygone days. But soft, flat, slippered shoes and long, flowing dresses felt good, hid countless physical flaws, *and* one's legs could be completely bare.

Fern glanced back at Cindy and Prince now standing next to their wedding cake—the first wedding cake she'd ever seen shaped like a castle. Cindy had gotten a kick out of their names and she'd played on the fairy-tale connection right from the start. The only time Fern had really seen shadows in her gentle blue eyes had been when she'd tried to joke about having the required wicked stepmother and stepsisters. Fern had done what she could to convince Cindy that everything would turn out all right, but it was strictly against fairy godmother policy to reveal oneself to one's assignment. She couldn't *tell* Cindy that magic was on her side.

During the last hundred years, humans had become very suspicious, often labeling the unexplainable as a psychosis of some kind. Frankly, they'd grown so "cult-o-phobic" that fairies of any kind had been forced to go underground. Stars! That had made the work so much harder.

Consequently Fern had not been able to assure Cindy that dealing with problem stepfamilies was her specialty. And now it looked as though she'd let modern times dull her edge. Someone *was* out to harm Cindy, but that was about to be remedied. First-class fairy godmothers might not be perfect, but she was determined to use what power she had.

Fern took a last look. A photographer had started taking pictures, and she figured the bride and groom would be safe for the next few minutes. It was time to get invisible and get to the bottom of this. But just as a precaution, she reached into the pocket of her plain navy suit to get a pinch of fairy dust. She lifted her hand close to her mouth and chanted softly, "Doors be shut, windows close. No one leaves, till I say go."

A quick puff sent the glitter into the air, and Fern blinked herself invisible and then over to Belinda Brown. It took only a few minutes and a little mind-probing to discover exactly what was going on. And to coin a modern phrase, Fairy Godmother Goodwin was royally "ticked off." A number of selfish mortals did want to cause trouble for Cindy and Prince. But worse, one who claimed to love them wanted to destroy their marriage.

Fern closed her eyes and concentrated on the three women again. Her wand jerked in her pocket, but she ignored it. Suddenly she was flooded with insight. Thorns and brambles! The tall blonde was one of the wicked stepsisters . . . and she had just revealed the name of the villain. Lilith Smythe had confessed to overhearing a plot to kidnap Cindy. Fern floated next to her and studied the flawless face. The woman was telling only part of the truth, yet oddly enough she cared about Cindy. Nevertheless, this Lilith was lost. She was lost between who she'd been and who she needed to be. Miss Smythe would never find her life-tale if she wasn't forced to find her real self. Hmmmm.

Then Fern turned to the third woman, the small one. She was Prince's younger sister, Roberta. Ah, the name Lilith had revealed was twisting timid Roberta into knots. The poor dear was torn over the threat to her brother's happiness and the love she'd once felt . . . *for the villain?* Stars! It had been a long time since Fern had tapped into such anguish from a human. This woman was so lonely, so empty. She would have to fight to climb back on the path of her life-tale, since weakness had already blown her off it once. Interesting.

Lastly, of course, there was Belinda. Nothing was hidden in her thoughts. Even now she was forming a plan to save her friend. But her situation was actually no better than either of the other women. Belinda had been so focused on Cindy's marriage and her new business, that at this rate she wouldn't be able to find her life-tale, even if she fell over it. Loyalty was blinding her to her own needs.

Fern's wand was tingling, her brain racing, and her time running out. The spell sealing the room had to be lifted and Cindy had to be protected, but this disaster just might be the ultimate challenge of her career. While it was true that all mortals had a life-tale that could lead them to happiness, it was also true that many had lost the sensitivity needed to recognize it. Only humans willing to work could be helped by a fairy godmother. Only humans willing to open their hearts could hear her direction.

Only humans loyal enough to love unconditionally, lost enough to risk change, or lonely enough to grow and forgive, could understand the age-old truth: Everyone's life needed the healing power of love. It was the greatest magic of all.

A surge of pure power crackled through Fern's sturdy body like electricity. Thorns and brambles!

Standing unknowingly before her were three women poised and ready to be guided to their destiny. Unfortunately, no fairy godmother had ever taken on three assignments at the same time. Could she do it? Dare she try? There was no time to send out a signal for a consultation about dealing with so many tangled tales. The door of opportunity could be lost if she didn't act now. Immediately! Fern wrapped her shaky fingers around the crystal wand tucked in the sash at her waist.

What if she made sure that Cindy and Prince were not separated and she simply let the plot unfold? Fern lifted the wand and held it above the three women. She closed her eyes and concentrated as she'd never done before. Gradually four paths formed in her mind and she carefully looked down each one. There would be some danger. Pain, too. Some hearts would be broken, but love would prevail if they had enough courage . . . if they would listen.

Of course—Fern smiled with just the slightest touch of chagrin—a bit of help to get the girls off to a flying start would only be wise.

Besides, she thought, as she waved her wand and released a brief, glittering shower of magic over Belinda, Lilith, and Roberta, "happily ever after" was more than just shoptalk. Fern Tatiana Goodwin delivered.

13

Part One

"Beauty Baits the Beast"

Chapter One

It couldn't be true! She couldn't believe what she was hearing. For one breathless heartbeat, Belinda Brown thought she might faint. Why would someone want to make it look like Cindy Ella Jones had deserted her brand-new husband at their wedding reception? Yet that was exactly what Lilith Smythe, the slightly less conceited of Cindy's two stepsisters, was saying.

The tall, tanned blonde in the ivory silk slip dress did not have a good track record. Just that string of adjectives alone was enough to make most women cautious and suspicious. Perhaps once, when Belinda had been younger, Lilith's picture-perfect beauty would have swamped her with a flood of inferiority. But now it was the high-fashion model's attitude and reputation for selfishness that concerned her. Okay, maybe she was a centimeter better than the other one, Milicent, but that wasn't saying much.

If Lilith was really telling the truth . . . If some foreign-sounding man was even now waiting to . . . Belinda went up on tiptoe and tried to scan the crowded, flower-filled room. He could be anywhere, anyone!

She had to stop this. She had to do something right now. Screaming came immediately to mind, followed quickly by hailing the security guards and hermetically sealing the entire hotel. Anything to help her best friend. No, they were more than that. For years she and Cindy had been each other's only support.

Why, they'd been planning this day for three months,

using every creative trick in the book to make the ballroom at the Royal Arms Hotel into the fairy-tale setting Cindy had wanted. After all, she'd chuckled, considering the names of the bride and groom, they had an obligation to tradition. And for two young women who'd had to make their own way in the world, they also had something to prove to the rich and famous about good old hard work and ingenuity. Prince's socially conscious grandmother had been extremely concerned, but it had all come together beautifully.

And now this.

A horrible snaking fear slithered up from the bottom of Belinda's peach pumps, quivered through her legs, and lodged in her heart. Happiness could not be this easily defeated. It wasn't fair. If she just knew what to do . . .

All at once the elegant surroundings began to fade and the huge ficus next to her started to shimmer as if blown by an iridescent wind. An almost invisible shower of glittery air drifted around the three of them standing in the tight circle. Was this a stress-induced hallucination? The peach satin of her bridesmaid dress felt heavy and hot against her damp skin. With a shaky hand Belinda lifted the mass of curls she'd labored to work into her hair, and a stream of cool air against the back of her neck steadied her.

She blinked twice and the room came back into focus, and the air was just plain air once again. And she knew exactly what she had to do. Take Cindy's place. Buy some time.

Lilith looked stunned also, and Belinda wondered if she had experienced that odd moment, too, or if she was regretting her confession, her involvement. Belinda had to consider what she had observed of Cindy's stepsisters over the years. This could be a trick. But if it wasn't . . . If there was even a remote chance that someone had planned to ruin the wedding, they would darn well have to go through Belinda Brown to do it.

This was no time to mince words.

"All right, Lilith." She nodded, releasing her hair. "I'm going to trust you because I'd rather be safe than sorry. Cindy just left to finish a few more pictures and then change for the honeymoon. You go find Princeton's head of security, Frank Henson, and tell him what you think is about to happen."

Belinda watched the model's pale blue eyes widen with surprise, and a hint of something else, at her blunt order. In the space of a blink, the emotion was gone and a remote coolness fixed in its place.

"Listen, as far as I know, except for this, you haven't done one really caring thing for Cindy in the last fifteen years. Your mother and Milicent didn't even bother to come to the wedding. So if you have any feelings for her at all, you'll help now or tell me flat-out so I can take care of it."

With her last words, Belinda attempted to wave a hand for emphasis and finally noticed the tight grip Roberta Chalmers had on her arm. From what Cindy had told her, Prince's sister had lived such a sheltered life that this shocking news must have terrified her. Belinda glanced away after Lilith acquiesced with a stiff inclination of her head, and turned to the short, younger woman at her side. Ms. Chalmers's cap of auburn curls blended wonderfully with the peach satin, and Belinda acknowledged that her habit of assessing and enhancing a woman's unique looks couldn't be turned off even in a crisis. Why in the world did Roberta keep wearing those heavy, dark-framed glasses?

Strange, too, Belinda had expected those green eyes to be brimming with anxiety. Instead a flash of despair quickly changed to anger. Well, that was good. Because Roberta had a job to do, too. Wimping out could not be allowed. Not for any of them.

Gently she pried the fine-boned manacle off her forearm. "Roberta, you've got to find Prince and tell him about this as calmly as possible." She raised her hands palms-up to both women. "Look, I've got a plan, but I'm depending on the two of you to get someone to Cindy's suite upstairs as soon as possible. Let's go!"

Belinda conceded to one more moment of restraint by unobtrusively slipping out a side door. At the sound of the click behind her, she balled up a couple of yards of fabric in her left hand, scooped up her dyed-to-match heels in her right, and ran for the elevator—leaving the reluctant, mismatched duo behind to break the awful news.

Thank God Cindy's photographer was doing a thorough job. Cindy hadn't returned yet and Belinda still had time to head the scoundrels off at the pass. Belinda forced a brave smile as she locked the suite door and began stripping off her wedding finery. She'd learned to love old Westerns at her grandfather's knee. *Grandpa, I sure need you now.* Her body was weak, shaky, and she remembered how afraid she'd been all those years ago after her parents had been killed in a car accident. Grandpa had tucked her under his arm and walked her out to the barn and held her while she'd cried.

Knowing she was so loved had made all the difference; his embrace had meant safety. A little hug would have gone a long way right now.

Both he and her grandmother had given Belinda the skills to take care of herself, and a lasting belief in love, hope, and family. She loved Cindy and that love meant you watched each other's back. Fear could just take a hike.

Thanks to her grandparents, the loss of her mom and dad hadn't destroyed her life. Their love had been her safety net. Now she would be Cindy's.

As quickly and quietly as possible, she began to wedge her size thirteen-fourteen body into Cindy's size ten sun-dress—a mint-green vacation number with a matching jacket. Was it possible that adrenaline made you swell? Thank heaven there was some give to the fabric. Whew!

In college eight years ago, when she and Cindy had first become friends and then roommates, Belinda had been forced to come to grips with their physical differences or let the media's definition of beauty destroy a wonderful friendship.

It had made Belinda stop and think about all the women who constantly measured themselves against the wrong rulers. Bird bones were not in her genetic gene pool, but then again, Rubens would have tossed her back as too small for his idea of true beauty. Eye of the beholder, Grandma used to say. *You're the number-one beholder, Lindy. So get your view right and no one else's will bother you.*

Belinda's success then, of seeing the positives in her unique looks, had led to a career and her own total make-over beauty boutique. In fact, she thought, giving up on the zipper and pulling on the jacket, it had been Cindy who had convinced her to develop her concept, "Be your own kind of beautiful." They had helped each other every step of the way. Dreaming big and working hard.

A few more forceful yanks and the fit of the jacket was as good as it was going to get. Yes, once she had spent a lot of time wishing she was small and petite, but never with a reason half as worthy as the one she had now. After so much unrelenting indifference from Cindy's stepfamily, especially these past five years since her father's death, Cindy deserved this happiness. Belinda loved her like a real sister and was ready to prove it no matter what the cost.

Could she fool whoever the creeps were?

She shot a hasty glance in the mirror and saw the reflection of a wide-brimmed straw hat on the bed. Because Cindy's hair was much lighter than her own maple-syrup shade, Belinda twisted her mane into a makeshift knot and jammed the hat low on her head, covering her upper face and most of her freckles completely. She used a handy scarf to tie the most important part of her disguise into place. Even with the air-conditioning on full blast, Belinda felt a sudden hot flush of fear sweep her body.

"All right, Brown," she said sternly to her image in the glass. "Help is probably on the way this very minute. Cindy would do it for you if the situation were reversed, and you know it. So get yourself out there and stop this before the whole wedding is ruined."

It had all happened so fast that Belinda still couldn't get a fix on many details. One thing, however, was crystal clear: she had fooled the creeps. She shifted uncomfortably, wiggling her cramped hands that were tied behind her back, and reviewed what she knew again. It helped her feel less like a trussed-up victim, even though she was, and kept her from screaming like a banshee, even though she wanted to.

Belinda had decided to take a little peek down the hall to see if either Frank Henson or Prince was on the way, when her world abruptly went black. She had been covered with a blanket, dumped in a cart, and then most probably rolled out of the hotel like a huge load of dirty laundry. She knew this had to be the scenario because her one glimpse of the perpetrators had proven them to be wearing staff uniforms and ski masks.

Lilith's advance warning—that the plan was just to spirit Cindy away and humiliate Prince—had not stopped the fear from roiling in her stomach. No one was supposed to get hurt, but then she was supposed to be Cindy. After her captors had shoved her into the back of an oily-smelling utility van and tied her hands, she decided to keep that particular detail a secret as long as possible.

Except for the musty blanket the van had been completely empty, and Belinda soon felt like a ball in a pinball game. It seemed as if she'd been bouncing against unforgiving steel for twelve hours, instead of the three she thought had passed. Her concept of time in the dark wasn't very good, but she estimated that it had to be about two o'clock in the morning. She was scared, tired, hungry, mad, aching, worried . . . and she had to go to the bathroom. It was time to take some action or lose what was left of her dignity.

How ironic that Cindy had wanted Belinda to have a little adventure right after the wedding. Something to soften the change in their friendship and as a thank-you for all the work she had done. Belinda had insisted she was only doing what any family of the bride would do. But Cindy got her tickets for a weeklong cruise in the Caribbean anyway. A singles cruise. She wanted her best friend to find what she'd found in the computer rooms of Chalmers, Inc. True love. Well, the party people would be "limbo-ing" without her.

The plan for a little adventure had taken an ugly turn.

On top of everything else, she was reduced to counting on Lilith Smythe. She braced her throbbing arms awkwardly up against the cold metal side of her prison on wheels and started kicking. About thirty minutes and two shinsplints later, the driver veered to a stop, throwing Belinda painfully onto her side. A gulp of air caught in her throat, the pounding of her heart roared in her ears, and for the first time in her life she thought she was going to faint.

The grinding screech of metal doors sent her scooting on her rear end to the back corner of her defenseless space like a mouse seeking safety in its hole. Intellectually Belinda knew it was useless, but her brain was not on a rational setting.

"Okay, Ms. Chalmers, just come on outta there. We aren't gonna hurt ya. Remember we told ya that? We're just followin' the boss's orders."

Yeah, right. Like she should believe kidnappers.

A glaring flashlight beam caught Belinda as she huddled in the corner. Now that they had reached their destination, her questions boiled down to only one sure conviction. Cindy and Prince would never be free to live their lives until this *boss* person was nailed. Belinda choked down the cottony lump stuck in her throat and cautiously edged forward. Thank heavens her hat was still in place. This would not be a good time for her hosts to discover they had bagged the wrong quarry.

Pitching her voice higher to mimic Cindy's, she attempted to use reason. "I really think you should let me go now, or at least tell me what this is all about. Certainly you know that I can't be kept here forever. Someone will come looking for me and you'll both be sent to prison for kidnapping and then—"

"Let's gag her, Bart."

"Shut up, ya damn fool, and grab her!"

Belinda tried to lurch backward but the men moved too fast. Unrelenting hands dragged her to the door and she knew her own struggles would be the cause of most of her bumps and bruises. But she couldn't just let this happen. A greasy-tasting cloth was forced between her lips, and a wide strip of the hat brim tore and dangled down to her chin.

. The moment she was hauled out of the van, Belinda knew they had traveled a great distance. The oceanside community of San Leandro was nowhere to be seen. Even with the thick blanket of darkness surrounding her, she could make out trees and knew by the scent they were pine. The air was shockingly cool for the end of March, and the thin, gauzy outfit Cindy had selected for her honeymoon in Tahiti was woefully inadequate here. Where in the world was she?

"You're sure this is the place?"

"Yeah, the house is just around that bend. Let's get her a little closer; then we'll take off."

One minute Belinda was standing and the next she had been hefted over the shoulder of the biggest man. The creep grunted and she purposely went limp. Why make it easier for the scoundrels to do their crummy job?

. "Hell, this woman is a lot heavier than she looked in that picture." The man puffed out his words, and Belinda ground her teeth against the disgusting cloth. If she could only get in one good kick.

"Well, the devil's a big man. He'll handle her easy enough. Besides it won't be for long. All that's needed now is a few days. And I imagine he'll want a whole slew of questions answered before he'll come outta his den anyway."

The muffled sound of footsteps on earth quickly became a crunch on loose gravel. In an unannounced motion that left her dizzy and disoriented, Belinda was placed upright again and began staggering toward a huge wooden structure. There appeared to be one big double door with an awning of some kind, but not a single window. She shook her head, sure the rush of blood and the darkness were warping her vision. What kind of person would live in a place like this? Belinda squinted against the night and stared hard at the indistinct shapes around her. No lights anywhere. She couldn't identify another sign of human habitation.

Who in the world could want to do this to Cindy and Prince? What could they have possibly done to cause somebody to take this drastic action? Belinda was so caught up in her scrambled thoughts she failed to notice one of the kidnappers crouched at her feet with a rope until it was too late. The moment he pulled the ankle restraint taut, she tried to jump away and fell onto the gravel. A hundred tiny stinging points of pain burned across her legs and arms.

"All right, that's it. We're outta here."

The men turned to leave and Belinda was ashamed because she wanted to beg them to take her with them. Oh, they were creeps, but they were known creeps. They had been rough but they hadn't purposely tried to hurt her, and they could have. She had been completely at their mercy for hours.

"Eese, on't eeve. On't eeve ee," she managed to get out around the gag.

The shorter man looked back over his shoulder and seemed to hesitate for a second or two.

"Lady, that isn't how this kinda thing works. Just hush up till we're outta sight or I'll have to shoot you with a sleep dart—and you wouldn't want that, what with the wild animals and all around here."

No, she wouldn't want that. With a sinking quiver in the pit of her stomach, Belinda felt what little confidence she had left plummet. The night suddenly seemed as empty and ominous as a black hole, all sight, sound, and sensation collapsing in on itself, whooshing away in a vacuum. Then the man stopped one last time.

"Just get yourself up to the door and kick it a few good times like you did in the van. You'll be all right."

Belinda sat on the pincushion of tiny rocks and fought back the tears prickling at the corners of her eyes. Surely, surely if she stayed calm and tried to reach the human, caring part of the person behind this plot, there could be a safe, nonviolent solution. She blinked away the moisture in her eyes and struggled awkwardly to stand on the shifting surface.

Then, just before the inky forest swallowed up the two men, she heard the faint echo of the big one's voice in the chilly air.

"Come on now, Bart, would ya kick that door? I mean, if it was a choice between the devil or a bear, what would ya choose?"

Their voices faded away before she heard the answer.

Ultimately, however, there was only one possible choice. After twenty minutes or so of total denial, Belinda gingerly bunny-hopped forward. She fell again and knew at least one knee was bleeding by the burning sting and the whispery sensation moving slowly down her leg. Up close she could see that the monstrous house was made of logs—a giant-size log cabin. The raised porch gave her a little trouble, but she used her last ounce of strength and jumped. Next to the door was a simple split-log bench and she sank down on it gratefully.

Every muscle in Belinda's body was screaming in agony. Cindy's strappy sandals had offered little protection for her scraped, freezing toes, and her arms had lost nearly all feeling. Her abductors had referred to the man in this house as a devil, but right now heat from any source sounded mighty good. Belinda grunted as she shifted on a sore hip and positioned her feet for the first kick. If nothing else, maybe the man would untie her and let her use the bathroom before committing any dastardly act.

She hesitated for one last minute. If this were a movie, the entire audience would be yelling *Don't do it!* But this was no movie, and Belinda had run out of options. In seconds she was taking all her frustrations out on unyielding pine.

The door opened so suddenly that she had no time to stop her forward motion. Belinda rolled off the bench with a jarring thud and squeezed her eyes shut against the pain. A soft, keening moan seeped around the edges of the gag, but it was the distinctive sound of a gun being cocked that brought her head up and her eyes wide open.

"What the hell is going on here? Answer or I'll blow your head off."

A dim glow backlit the man in the doorway. If his personality had the same cutting edge to it that his voice had, she was in serious trouble. He was huge—big as a bear, and Belinda half-hysterically thought she should call back her captors and tell them she had gotten both—the devil and the bear.

"Get up! Now! Get up and answer me. I'm not asking again."

"Eese elf ee. I an't et uf."

"This gun is pointed right at your head, buddy. You'd better think very carefully about playing games with me."

Belinda slowly squirmed around until she could sit up.

Taking a long draft of air in through her nose, she made herself face the enigma in the doorway and try again.

"I haf a gag. Hans, eet, ied uf. Elf ee."

All at once the double doors slammed open completely. A golden spill of light rushed across the black boards of the porch, and Belinda found herself ringed in a pool of illumination. Her momentary blindness left her unprepared for the man's quick tug on her hat.

"Good God, it's a woman!"

She squinted up at him and focused on a set of immense shoulders descending rapidly toward her. The primal instinct for survival spurred her to twist away, but not quick enough. Not before her ankle was caught in a grip of iron.

A real bear wouldn't have stood a chance.

"Lady, I'm not going to hurt you, but I've got to be sure you're not going to hurt me."

Still holding her ankle, he hunkered down beside her and started to slide his hands up her bare legs. The panic she'd been fighting to hold at bay for the last few hours burst out of control, and Belinda's lungs expanded for the scream of her lifetime. One hand abruptly slipped under the hem of her gauzy dress and brushed the sensitive skin of her upper thigh. She went ballistic and erupted into motion with the force of an exploding volcano.

She kicked against his hold and rolled and arched, trying to break away. When that didn't work she lunged forward and butted the man with her head, taking courage from the gravelly moan it wrung out of him. But soon her ears were buzzing and her tortured arms felt nearly wrenched from their sockets. The man was too strong.

He pinned her, the considerable weight of his body forcing her down on the wood porch so hard that Belinda was sure the grain markings would be imprinted on her crushed arms and back. She could only take tiny little breaths, and her awareness narrowed down to the most bizarre handful of perceptions. The soft brush of long hair against her cheek was his, as was the spicy male scent filling her nostrils. The male chest pressed flush to hers seemed as wide and heavy as a cinder-block wall, and this time she thought she was going to faint for sure. Then suddenly he pushed himself up and straddled her. The movement chased out every aberrant thing in her head. It also changed the angle of the light seeping out from inside the entry.

And she knew who wanted to hurt Cindy and Prince.

And he was a devil. The devil stalking Chalmers, Inc. for the last five years.

Cain Devlin. Prince's worst enemy.

Belinda's eyes met his and she knew he could see her recognition and her shock. A sharp, sardonic smile slashed across his face and he held her gaze captive as he slowly turned his cheek. The shadows cast eerie patterns dancing along his skin, and then she realized it wasn't shadows at all, but the lasting legacy of something awful.

For a moment Belinda foolishly felt her heart soften at the evidence of such pain. She'd heard about the accidental explosion that had disfigured Cain, but seeing its consequences was a hundred times worse. It had turned prospective partners into bitter rivals. Devlin had never stopped blaming Prince. What had he planned to do with Cindy up here? If she could just talk to him. If she could reach him it might be the chance to end this destructive feud.

"Eese. Eese," she breathed out in a raw whisper, putting all the warmth she could into her eyes.

"Stop making promises with your eyes, lady. I have to finish the weapon check. I don't take anything at face value anymore."

To Belinda's absolute horror, he continued what he'd started. Running his big hands with obvious disdain up her sides, down her arms, through her hair, and finally, lightly over her breasts. Never once did he look away. Not even when she knew he'd seen the single tear she couldn't keep from rolling into her hair.

Somebody . . . please! Somebody help me!

29

Chapter Two

The woman was a complete mess, and Cain had scared her to death. The utter stillness of her body made him excruciatingly aware of her fear. Damn, he should be used to that particular reaction by now. Yet for some vile reason it always made him act more the monster. And God, he had. Look where he was! Sitting on a completely defenseless wreck of a woman who probably wouldn't swat a fly.

Still, Cain Devlin knew things were not always what they appeared to be. Something was very wrong here. Then he saw the tear. He cursed viciously under his breath and felt a fine tremor ripple through the feminine body so close to his. Those big eyes had just opened a notch wider and suddenly reminded him of a fawn he'd had once in his rifle sights. He hadn't been able to shoot that defenseless animal, yet here he was deliberately terrifying this woman. What kind of human being did that make him?

Maybe his administrative assistant was right. Sometimes he was more beast than man. Fool! Now she would be so afraid she'd probably faint or cry. He'd never get any answers that way. Strange, he'd just been thinking—no, make that brooding, a few hours earlier when he couldn't sleep—about the lack of any woman in his life, let alone a special one like his enemy's new bride.

If he was the kind of man who believed in that psychic garbage, this unexpected arrival at three in the morning might be interpreted as a message of some sort. But the bedraggled female barely breathing beneath him was far and away different from the one his nemesis probably held in his arms this very minute. Damn him! Love, happiness, passion . . . all denied to Cain Devlin.

Cain pushed to his feet the second he became aware of the changes in his body. Whoever Ms. Horrified, Big Brown Eyes was, she would be more horrified if she knew how her softness was affecting him. It had been over three years since he'd been this close to a woman, and his control had gone haywire. The whole thing had happened so fast, his normal walls hadn't been locked in place. Cain brushed the reaction off as a natural response to his body's deprivation and his mind's envy. It meant nothing.

But his instinctive behavior did mean something. Attack first and ask questions later. Damn! This time alone hadn't helped at all. Paul was right: he was losing it. If his mother were still alive, she would have disowned him after witnessing this scene. Whoever this woman was, and for whatever purpose she had been dumped on his doorstep, she wasn't there voluntarily. If he'd opened his foolish eyes and really looked for a moment he would have seen that. She was suffering and he had best help her or he'd never discover what this was all about.

Cain shifted and cupped a hand around each of her shoulders, then slowly pulled her to her feet. The woman swayed and he caught her with an arm around her waist. That was when he realized her arms were tied. Holy hell, he must have hurt her badly when he pinned her on the decking.

"Lady," he said, bending down a bit and peering into her tired, wary face. "Look, I know you're hurting, but I don't take chances. Ever. I've got a lot of questions, but I'll let you clean up a little before we get into how and why you appeared in the dead of the night on my doorstep."

She wasn't a tiny woman; he knew that in more detail than he should have. Still, at six foot three inches, he'd usually preferred tall women—when he'd been dating, that is. This one barely topped his shoulder. Although the light drifting out from the stairwell inside the house wasn't all that bright, he could see the red, puffy condition of her lips and felt like a world-class heel for not freeing her sooner. It was just that he *did* have enemies and it *was* the dead of night and he'd been half-asleep and still nursing a foul mood. But the glaze of pain in the eyes staring so intently at him was not faked.

Cain had learned to read people very carefully during the past five years. Many had and would lie for a link to the money and power he possessed. With that kind of incentive he'd discovered some women were willing to use every asset at their disposal, no matter how he looked. But three years ago one had almost brought him to his knees by making him believe it was more. By making him believe it might be possible to have what he'd always dreamed of. He hadn't let a female get close to him since.

He'd seen the brief well of pity in this woman's eyes, and it had turned his stomach as it always did. Maybe that was why he hadn't really seen the condition she was in. He had forced the pity away with fear. Protecting himself at all costs by intimidating the attacker using any means it took. However, he'd just sunk to a new Devlin low. He'd never manhandled a woman before. Was Paul right? Was he getting worse?

Cautiously he brought his hands up to the back of her head and gently searched for the knot in the gag. She flinched and went perfectly still, but he couldn't find the ends through the jumble of tangles. He tried to push her head forward to rest on his chest and she stiffened like a steel bar.

"Listen, I just want to get this off without hurting you again. Okay?"

There was a slow blink and she lowered her gaze to his chest, then rested her head on the firm rise of one pec. The silky slide of her hair over his fingers and its faint strawberry scent began calling up some very volatile, dormant emotions. Hell, it was happening again. It had been too damn long since he'd been with a woman, and it was becoming painfully obvious. This female shouldn't have been able to stir even a casual response, yet just her head on his chest was sending him into overdrive.

Pride had done this. His cursed pride about sleeping with a woman who didn't really care had made him weaker than he'd realized. Maybe it was time to accept the fact that he could have female companions in his life if he remembered what the relationships had to be based on. Business.

Thank God, the knot came free.

She lifted her head as if it weighed a hundred pounds. A cascade of dark, honey-colored hair covered her face, and Cain was surprised she made no effort to move it. She was either too scared or too tired. Probably both. He bent quickly and undid the rope around her ankles and then stood. The hair was still hanging there and, without thinking, he reached beneath the fall and threaded his fingers through to her scalp. He lifted the weight up off her face and pushed his fingertips deep and then back, moving from her forehead to the base of her neck, making grooves that ran like tiny furrows in newly plowed earth. Involuntarily her eyes drifted shut and he felt the stiffness in her body begin to melt away.

Cain carefully pulled his hands free, vividly aware of the fragile, vinelike tendrils clinging to his callused skin. The big brown eyes did not open. He gently began to work on the tighter knot at her wrists and registered that his arms were around this stranger more intimately than he had been with anyone in the recent past. The whole encounter was becoming more unreal by the minute. What in the world were they still doing on the porch? He hadn't even asked her name yet. This had to stop right now. He was beginning to act like some kind of idiot under a spell.

Cain's lips quirked up in a sarcastic tilt. How typical. If there really were fairy godmothers it would be just his luck to get a warped one who considered this woman his fantasy. The rope came free and she stepped away from him. The dreamy look in her eyes was gone. The fear was back and the spell was broken. Good. The last few minutes had been too unnerving.

"Ca-n," she rasped, then stopped and swallowed with visible difficulty. "Can I use the bathroom?"

Oh yeah, the spell was definitely broken.

"All right. You've got ten minutes and then I want your story. Every detail. And lady, it had better make me happy."

Cain led the way inside and then motioned for her to precede him up the stairs. Her blank expression annoyed the hell out of him, and that was a relief. He needed to feel annoyed as hell . . . and cautious . . . and on the defensive. When she paused in the doorway of the bathroom and looked pointedly at the lock, he felt the hackles rise on the back of his neck.

"I think I can manage to restrain myself, lady. I know firsthand you're not my type." He spread his palms wide and lifted one eyebrow with practiced contempt. Her answering emotion bloomed rosy red on her face. She knew exactly what he was referring to. But it wasn't until the door shut that he realized the woman hadn't moved her arms. Not once. She'd used her shoulder.

Twenty-five minutes later she still hadn't emerged. Cain paced restlessly across the glossy hardwood floor, back and forth between an entire wall of windows and a Southwestern-style sectional sofa. A creamy crescent moon was clearly visible through the uncovered glass, and Cain unconsciously lifted his hand to the ruined side of his face. Three crescent-shaped scars, the longest running from his temple to the top of his neck, represented the best repair work his plastic surgeon had been able to do.

The feel of puckered flesh dragged him back to the present. His guest bathroom was ominously quiet. The sound of running water had stopped at least ten minutes ago.

What was the woman doing in there? Cain squared his shoulders and rolled up the cuffs on the blue plaid flannel shirt he'd thrown on when the pounding had jerked him out of a fitful sleep on the sofa.

Hell! She was hiding, of course. Could he blame her? She probably thought he was going to assault her the second she came out the door. And why shouldn't she? Cain raked a hand through his shaggy hair and stared at the Navajo pattern in the large area rug beneath his feet. The subtle colors of navy, brown, and rust formed a band of woven arrows pointing in the direction his feet needed to go.

Again, reflexively, he lifted his hand . . . then dropped it. She'd seen already. He'd taken care of that with even more obnoxious finesse than usual. Well, Cain was prepared. He knew how women reacted to a man who both looked and acted like a beast. The question had to be answered even if it proved to be an ordeal . . . for both of them.

"Lady?" He spoke through the bathroom door in a moderate tone and punctuated the query with two knuckle raps. "Lady, come out now so we can get to the bottom of this. I promise I won't lay so much as a finger on you."

Silence.

"Lady?"

"No."

The brief answer was distorted and muffled, as if it were playing on a tape recorder with weak batteries.

"I won't hurt you, lady." Then he continued with a sharper edge so she knew he still meant business. "But if you don't come out, I'll come in."

"No."

Cain tried the doorknob. Damn! She had locked it. This time he pounded three times, going right back to the M.O. that worked best.

"Wait!" she choked out. "I need a few minutes."

What was going on? She sounded so strange and breathless. The window? Hell, she wouldn't be that crazy. They were on the second floor, for God's sake. Surely the little fool realized it, didn't she? But if she was scared enough . . .

Cain rattled the doorknob with considerable force.

"Wait!"

"No! Do you hear me, lady? Cover up or button up or whatever, 'cause I'm coming in right now." He stepped back a foot or two and rammed a shoulder into the golden-stained pine with punishing accuracy. The door popped open.

She was sitting on the edge of the tub with a wad of Kleenex in her hand. Tears were silently rolling down her cheeks, and the flimsy dress she was wearing was hiked up over both knees. Another wad of what appeared to be wet tissue was pressed to each of those exposed knees. Cain swept her with his first good look in adequate lighting and saw the multitude of small scrapes and bruises covering her arms and legs. Two raw spots bracketed her pinched lips. Her shoulders were hunched forward, canting her arms in an awkward manner. Those big brown eyes watched him with watery hostility.

But not revulsion. There was no mistaking revulsion. He knew that expression to the bone.

"Why didn't you open the door, lady?"

She hesitated and lowered her eyes. Cain braced himself for an outburst.

"I was crying . . . and I—I couldn't seem to stop. I don't like people to see me cry."

Cain Devlin knew exactly how that felt. He hated anyone even sensing a weakness. A disquieting pressure built in his chest at this unexpected understanding. He rarely cared how other people felt. His confusion must have shown on his face.

"Oh, you thought I was trying to escape, huh?" She pressed her mouth into a tight line and listlessly flailed one arm. "Take a good look at me, Mr. Devlin. I can't even get this jacket off, let alone climb up and out the window."

"Who are you? How do you know who I am?" he demanded, planting his hands on his hips and stepping fully into the small room. His tentative dribble of sympathy dried up like a single rain puddle in Death Valley. She knew who he was! There had to be some subversive reason for this mysterious arrival, no matter how it appeared. Cain knew his size worked for him, and the scars, too. Pain or no pain, he'd have his answers now!

"How do you know who I am?"

Rats! She shouldn't have mentioned his name. The infamous president of Devlin Enterprises had actually seemed a tiny bit concerned—for about three seconds. Well, the man had a lot to answer for, himself, and Belinda would not let him intimidate her. Show no fear!

Grandpa had first taught her that lesson when she had been about eleven and they'd found a wounded bobcat cub. Because their farm backed up to a preserve of open country, wild animals were an occasional fact of life. Grandpa had an important rule Belinda had learned very early: Move slow, talk low, and show no fear. When Devlin pulled his ruined cheek into a dark scowl, she knew the rule applied here as surely as it had on the farm.

Cain Devlin had the look of a predator about him. There was no doubt that the man knew exactly how to use his body and his face to convince his prey they faced a monster. His bare forearms were roped with veins and muscle. His mane of chestnut-colored hair brushed back and forth across the wound that Cindy said had changed his life overnight.

It was odd, though; it wasn't the scars or his size that worried Belinda now that she'd accustomed herself to them. Above everything else, it was Devlin's eyes that almost made her reconsider, those hooded hazel eyes that burned with growing hostility.

Instead she prepared to throw this man off balance. Belinda blotted her cheeks and shoved her anxiety deep inside. Her aching body was demanding rest—sleep—but there was no point in playing guessing games or putting off the inevitable. She spoke and the die was cast.

"I'm sure you must have realized by now that your men have bungled the job."

Sixty seconds of stone-cold silence froze them both into place. Those glowing eyes locked with hers in a stare so powerful that Belinda could feel a wave of goose bumps skitter up her arms. The subtle Indian decor in navy and rust faded to gray and she swallowed down the bitter taste of fear in her mouth. No! She would not let that emotion control her again.

"What in the hell are you talking about?"

"It's really very simple, Mr. Devlin." Belinda looked away for a second, hoping to distract them both by peeling her makeshift bandages off her stinging knees. "I know who you are because Cindy Ella Chalmers—as of a few hours ago—told me all about you, your injury, and your senseless attacks on her husband, your former friend. This last one however, has gone totally too far. As I said, your men bungled the job. They grabbed the wrong woman."

"Who . . . are . . . you!"

She levered to her feet, slowly maneuvering for a more advantageous position. "I'm Belinda Brown, Cindy Chalmers's best friend. When I discovered what was going to happen at her wedding reception, I had to protect her. Had to stop this if I could. Now that I'm here, I'm going to do my best to convince you to end your destructive obsession with revenge."

Belinda concentrated on suppressing the slight tremor in her legs. She supposed nothing at this moment could really make her appear all that imposing, even though she had the might of right on her side. Barefoot, bedraggled, bruised, and bleeding wasn't exactly her best look. Cain just stood there as if he were trying to translate her speech from a foreign language. One tanned hand reached out and then clamped around the doorjamb, white-knuckle tight. Maybe she'd come on too strong?

"You know, Ms. Brown," he sneered, bringing that hand against his jean-covered thigh in a series of muted thuds. "It's difficult enough for me to believe I'm standing here in my bathroom in the wee hours of the morning with a babbling hysteric. But now you tell me that I'm behind some kidnapping plot and then assert your intention of saving me from my vile inclinations."

Devlin stepped a foot closer, hooking his thumbs on a couple of belt loops, and angled his upper body toward her. Belinda hit the side of the tub with her sore legs. The plaid shirt, the worn jeans, and the wild hair made her think of an uncivilized mountain man unhappy to be dealing with a pesky human.

"Right now the only thing saving your self-righteous butt, lady, is the fact that your entire involvement in this incident proves you are dumb as mud. Until I have some verification that you're telling the truth, there's no point in continuing this conversation. Besides, you look like hell, Ms. Brown, and you won't do me any good if you collapse. You might as well grab some aspirin and some sleep. I'll wake you up for the answers I need, believe me."

Belinda realized she was straining backward and her arms were starting to cramp up again. She gritted her teeth against the darts of shooting pain, and nodded.

"Fine. Could I use your phone first?"

"You've got to be kidding. You think I'd give you the chance to pass this garbage on to anyone else?"

"I don't want my disappearance to ruin Cindy and Prince's honeymoon."

"Frankly, Ms. Brown, I hope it shoots it all to hell." He raised the flat of a hand the moment she gulped in a breath of air and prepared to speak. "I don't care if you believe me or not, crazy woman, but I had nothing to do with this. In fact it wouldn't surprise me if the whole thing had been planned to frame me somehow."

Now it was Belinda's turn to feel indignant. She

abruptly moved her arms and winced at the unexpected pain.

"You're paranoid, Devlin."

"And you're either pathetically naive or the best weapon Chalmers has come up with yet."

"Show me to my room, please. Or would you prefer I sleep in here?"

Cain narrowed his eyes and smirked, deliberately crowding her as he reached into the medicine cabinet. He offered aspirin and water, tracking every labored movement until she was finished. Then he dipped his head in the door's direction.

"Ladies first."

At this point, manners seemed completely out of character. Belinda took a deep breath, willing her stiff legs to move. No way was she going to back down. The man probably saw that behavior so much, he scented the kill whenever somebody turned around. Of course that didn't mean Devlin wasn't very good at being scary. He was. But Belinda had experienced a brief sign of compassion when he'd untied her, and she was clinging to that sliver of humanity like a starving man to his last crust of bread.

Cain had to get the woman out of his sight. He hadn't felt such a compelling combination of anger and intrigue in ages. She threw him off balance, and that could be very dangerous. Could she be working for Chalmers? She was some actress if she was. Putting up with the injuries was really taking it to the wall. Although her lurching gait was not faked, the woman had to have an agenda one way or another. He needed to know more. He needed to know what kind of person she really was.

Could this actually be about friendship and loyalty, or was it a plan to implicate him in a criminal act? That would definitely put him out of commission and leave Princeton Chalmers sitting pretty. Somewhere up on his desk he had a report from a private investigator hired to find out about the . . . bride. It seemed to him that there had been some information about her friends and family. That and a few phone calls ought to fill in the major blanks concerning Ms. Belinda Brown.

So far the woman had been pretty gutsy. Most men he knew would never have talked to him the way she had in the last hour. Now she was matter-of-factly hobbling past him with her tangled hair and freckled nose, resolutely facing forward, as if finding herself in a strange, scarred man's bathroom, in the back of beyond, was no big deal at all.

Belinda Brown needed a little more to ponder on before she slept. She'd gotten one up on him by using his favorite business tactic: Keep your opponent unsure of your next move, shaky.

It was her turn to teeter.

"Let me help you with that jacket. You don't look very comfortable."

She jumped at the rumble of his voice so close to her ear. Cain smiled behind her. Good. She wasn't as composed as she pretended to be. He watched the inner struggle play across her face and, once again, a wave of unwanted understanding intruded. Cain hated to ask for help, too. Yet she shrugged and conceded with resigned grace, turning her back to him.

Damn! She'd done it again. Made him feel a connection. Made him feel, period. One glance at the odd set of her shoulders and he could tell the woman was hurting. The flimsy green fabric had tightened like a tourniquet. He raised his hands to the collar and berated himself, with a silent litany of curses, at his momentary hesitation. Determined, he peeled the jacket back over two freckled shoulders, so absorbed in the sensation of his fingers sliding against smooth skin that it took a few seconds for her muffled moan to register.

His wince at her pain was the last straw. The ridiculous dress would damn well never come off the way it had gone on—not without torture. The hell with it! He snagged the hem of the short jacket and ripped it straight up the back.

"Aaaaahhhhh! No!" She whirled around so fast she bounced into the wall, hard. Then she immediately hunched over, gingerly cradling her arms.

Cain did not experience one iota of satisfaction at her distress. Instead he felt almost as low as he had earlier when he'd patted her down. Hell! The woman was going to do some serious damage if he didn't get his head on straight. She had all the markings of another enemy and he had to remember that. He shrugged his shoulders and lifted his hands in a calculated show of offhanded concern.

"Look, the dress obviously never fit you in the first place, Ms. Brown. You sure as hell couldn't sleep in it, so it's no great loss. I'll find you something better and bigger to wear." Her eyes narrowed, then went round. A fan of offended little lines appeared above her raised eyebrows. That got her. Petty, but effective.

"Go ahead and take the room at the top of the stairs, first door on the left. Need any help?"

"If there's a shred of decency left in you, you'll realize that's the last thing I want. Don't touch me again."

She shifted and bobbled against the wall, then slid along it and up the second flight of stairs. Cain followed and waited for her to turn and slap him across the face. Suddenly he wanted to goad her to do it.

"You know," she said in an unexpectedly steady voice, "before this, I'd heard a few rumors about your anger. I guess I thought it was all an exaggeration. But now that I've experienced it firsthand"—she lifted a dangling jacket side with each hand—"I'm more surprised that you, of all people, would take pleasure in using someone's imperfection as a weapon."

Her grave eyes held him captive. Such guileless honesty pinched in a long-forgotten area around his heart. It stung worse than any physical slap. She knew there was nothing she could do to stop him from touching her—and much more—if he chose to do so. They both knew it. But she had challenged his civility, his humanness. And although a wild, wary part of Cain urged him to push, right now, for more control, he could not play the beast again tonight.

With stoic determination she moved her battered body up the stairs and into her room . . . and he was not able to look away. Then as silently as a man his size could move, he followed and used his keys to lock the door. The beast in him needed some small victory.

Chapter Three

Cain didn't wake up until late morning. He jerked into awareness, his heart thundering in his chest from the last foggy tendrils of a disturbing dream. The woman, Belinda, had been dancing with him in a beautiful ballroom, her brown eyes gazing into his with a look as sweet as chocolate, all the bitter traces of hurt and disappointment he'd seen in them last night gone. How in the hell could he have dreamed such nonsense?

How could he have slept so soundly with this explosive situation ticking away like a time bomb? With a total stranger in his house? Although he'd thought while showering that after hearing the answers to his predawn phone calls and reading the report, he did know a number of things about Ms. Brown now. Perhaps she no longer qualified as a total stranger.

It looked less and less likely that she was personally involved in one of Chalmers's schemes. She was who she said she was—Cynthia Chalmers's best friend. Raised by her grandparents and the owner of her own quirky beauty business. And she thought he wanted Cindy Ella stolen away from Prince. So who was behind this? What was to have been the next step? He and Ms. Brown needed to talk. Cain rummaged through a downstairs linen closet until he found a pair of sweats Paul had left behind. The gray outfit had a better chance of fitting the lady than anything he owned. His administrative assistant was not a very big man.

Big. Hell! Talk about acting childish and low. Man, that woman had put him in his place like nobody had in a very long time. She hadn't backed down even though she had to have realized what a defenseless position she was in. You had to admire that.

Cain stopped dead at the foot of the stairs. It would not be a good idea to admire anything about Belinda Brown. He curled his free hand around the polished pine banister and cast a quick look up toward her door then back to his wall of windows. The broken vista of the snowcapped Sierras produced the precise effect he'd designed. The panels looked like a series of large oil paintings framed by each window's molding.

The view never failed to calm him. And it did so now. He took a deep breath and eased his grip on the stair rail and the clothes. Today needed to go much better than last night had. But the sense of anticipation and anxiety, that need revving in the back of his mind, was also alarming.

Hell, he'd never had anyone but Paul here before, and usually those visits lasted only as long as the business did. It was strange having a woman in the cabin. What would she think of his home? *What would she think!* Cain shook his head with self-disgust as he climbed the steps to the third floor. She had to hate his guts. The insult about her size alone was enough to hang a man. He had been deliberately cruel with an out-and-out lie. Belinda Brown looked fine. Too touchably fine for his own damn good.

It would serve him right if she found a way to heft a heavy object at his head the first chance she got.

"Lady, uh, Ms. Brown?" Cain tapped on the door. "I've got something more comfortable for you to wear."

"Oh? The *big* stuff? Shall I hand out the rest of my dress for you to tear up?"

She sounded much stronger than she had last night. However the tone was the real indicator. He could chip icicles off those frosty words. In the light of day, all Cain's early morning actions seemed unreasonably harsh and

45

barbaric. Irrationally, he resented her for making him see it that way. The woman made him feel too many things he didn't like.

"Listen, I'm making some sandwiches," he answered with a chilly gruffness himself. "Change if you want to and come downstairs for some food. We can talk then."

"You mean you're leaving the door unlocked?"

Cain balled a fist at his side. "I locked it last night because I don't trust strangers, Ms. Brown. No matter how innocuous they appear."

Belinda knew she was being ridiculous, but the label *innocuous* stung. She should be searching this very minute for a heavy, blunt object. Instead she pulled the steel gray sweatshirt over her head and grimaced at her reflection in the lovely prison's bathroom mirror. Gray was not her color. Wait a minute! Belinda gasped and gripped the marble counter to hold herself upright. Last week at a bridal shower, Prince's eccentric grandmother had uttered those very words about Cindy's gorgeous dress, a shade of silver smoke.

When Belinda had politely disagreed, the elegant woman had carefully backtracked and gone on to mention her fears about Cain Devlin's reaction to the wedding. At the time Belinda had been happy to see the somewhat caustic Helen Chalmers concerned for Cindy—but good gosh! Maybe she had been right. After all, Belinda had been hearing about Cain Devlin and his bizarre lifestyle and behavior for months. Maybe the wedding had caused the man to snap?

Except . . . what she saw around her in this room didn't fit with the other pieces she had to the puzzle. At dawn when she'd finally fallen into bed, she hadn't registered a single thing about the room. Now she began a careful analysis.

At this very moment her newly showered, scratched-up toes were curling deep into luxurious camel-colored carpeting. The walls were the shade of sweet cream, and the breathtaking view out the window was accented with a padded frame covered in a Southwestern-style fabric in blues, browns, and rusts. Vertical Levolors could be drawn out of sight, which was exactly what Belinda did. It appeared she was on the third floor. And as far as the eye could see, this was the only building. The motif of Devlin's house was a disturbingly sensitive choice. There was a compelling harmony between the primitive location, the masculine colors, and the Native American style. Her brain niggled over the dichotomy. It had to be a decorator's input. That would make her feel so much better; sure of her first impression and the harsh things she'd heard about this man.

Belinda harrumped and ran her hands through her wet hair. Great! Now she'd stew about this until the door was unlocked and she could ask some questions. It would probably be wise to make herself as presentable as possible. She piled her unruly hair into a listing bun and tried her best not to wash off her remaining mascara. There was a faint swipe of woodsy brown eye shadow barely visible over each eye, but not a hint of lipstick. Fortunately her arms felt tons better, but the stiffness in her knees still forced her to walk like an old woman.

Oh, well, it wasn't as if she were trying to impress the guy. Even so, as a beauty specialist it was difficult to face this crisis feeling less than her best.

And the sweats?

Well, they were comfortable and warm and exactly what he'd promised so rudely. Big. In fact if need be, they could double as both clothes and a tent. She could just pull her head inside the neck and fan the material out around her. Belinda figured she looked pretty much like a lump of gray Play-Doh. No wonder the man defined her as innocuous.

"Innocuous is safe, you idiot," she lectured her reflection. "If you hope to have any luck at all getting to the bottom of what has really happened here, you need to look and act as harmless and neutral as possible."

A few cautious minutes later, Belinda stood hesitantly at the bottom of the stairs. The spacious, airy room before her was as rich as it was simple. Numerous area rugs in varying sizes floated like colorful islands on the lustrous surface of the plank flooring. A sectional sofa in a nubby weave of navy blue created the perfect spot to relax and appreciate the sweeping view of Cain's backyard. Jagged mountains studded with clusters of evergreen pines stood as silent sentinels against the sometimes thoughtless whims of man, guarding the sparkling stream that wound into the heart of a grassy meadow.

Belinda had learned to love and appreciate nature from her grandparents. But in the four years since they'd been gone, she hadn't left the city once. She hadn't realized how much she had missed being close to such exhilarating beauty.

The rest of the room had a subtle ambience that complemented the majesty outside. Too many doodads and fussy patterns would have diminished it. A couple of small tables with pottery lamps bracketed the sofa, and a rustic stone fireplace and hearth dominated the wall to the right of the windows. A pair of deep, wing-back chairs in the same nubby navy fabric made a cozy nook for flame watchers or readers.

This didn't make any sense. Belinda had always been sensitive to the tangible, external ways people revealed themselves: from clothes, makeup, and hair, to cars, homes, and decor. So far everything she had seen in this house virtually screamed that Cain Devlin was not what he appeared to be. Maybe it would be best to get on with telling her side of the story so she could leave as soon as possible. Belinda knew herself too well and could already feel the urge to unravel this additional mystery and fix things. What was that old song about fools rushing in . . . ?

"Mr. Devlin? Mr. Devlin?"

A door past the stairs swung open.

"In here, Ms. Brown." Cain held the hinged door with his arm and waited for Belinda to enter. "Take a seat and I'll get the sandwiches."

Now she was really worried. The bedroom had piqued her interest. The living room had thrown her a curve. But the kitchen—the kitchen was an old-fashioned, bay-windowed baker's dream. Beasts did not live like this. Something was very wrong. Everywhere she looked inside the house, she saw light, perfect symmetry, and open vistas. But outside, in front—the part the world saw—the house was featureless, dark, and impenetrable.

Two very different sides to the same man, just like his physical body. The broad back she was staring at had ripples of defined muscle undulating under a snug black T-shirt. Those long legs encased in worn denim had probably stopped many a female heart . . . and then he'd turn around and what would he see on their faces? *No, Belinda, don't start thinking any wounded warrior stuff! This man should be stamped with a huge red warning sign. You are not equipped to deal with his emotional baggage.*

Did Devlin have any clue to what he was revealing about himself? *Belinda Brown, listen to yourself.* But the need to unravel grew stronger. She had to make a concerted effort to put a neutral expression back in place before he turned around. Two navy place mats trimmed in rust-colored piping indicated their spots, and she gingerly sat in a simple replica of an Early American chair. Good gosh, unless it was an original. Not antiques, too!

"Here you go. I'm not a cook, but I hope it's passable."

"I'm so hungry, Mr. Devlin, that anything will be wonderful." She forced herself to stop the wild ride her brain was spinning off on and focus on the food.

Ham and mustard on rye had never tasted so divine.

Belinda hadn't realized how hungry she really was until that first bite. It had been almost twenty-four hours since she'd eaten a thing, and weeks since she'd had a decent meal. Cain's thick sandwiches disappeared to the last crumb. She even ate a spear of dill pickle, one of her least favorite items, and all the sliced tomatoes. With an unconscious sigh of satisfaction, she sipped her frothy glass of milk until it was bone-dry.

The early afternoon sun had painted the room in generous swaths of light and shadow. A gentle breeze ruffled the Levolors and vied with the chirps of nearby birds to fill the kitchen with comfortable background noises. For the first time since Belinda had seen Lilith walking toward her at the wedding reception, she felt relaxed. She contentedly blotted her lips with a cloth napkin, fortified and ready to deal with Cain Devlin.

However, the man was scrutinizing her as if she had just sprouted a second head.

"Is there a problem?"

"I don't think I've ever seen a woman eat that way."

"What? What way?"

"I mean, as if she enjoyed it."

For a second, Belinda was almost overpowered by the pervasive and debilitating Barbie doll syndrome. A lie formed on her lips. Who was she kidding? She pushed her very empty plate away and leaned forward, resting her elbows on the smooth, white-pine table.

"Lucky for me I've got plenty of room in these sweats."

Cain choked on a swallow of milk.

"I've got a trivia tidbit for you, Mr. Devlin, that may come in handy sometime down the road. Ninety-five percent of all women involved in a wedding party have not eaten normally for weeks. Between fitting into a bridesmaid dress and my recent kidnapping, well, let's just say *starving* wouldn't have been an exaggeration."

"Would you like more?"

"No, I'm fine for now." Belinda sat back and tucked her

folded arms under her breasts. Was Cain Devlin teasing her? Had that last offer held a hint of an apology? His face was as impassive as ever, but those hooded hazel eyes had a notch more intensity, a shine. Hmmm. If she could get the stone to crack it would be far easier to reach his heart and resolve the problem.

"Have I destroyed the myth for you?"

"What?"

Yes! He was definitely off balance.

"Oh, you know. The myth that women never eat more than salads and a cracker or two. Honestly, when was the last time you had a date who ordered the works?"

Instantly the crack slammed shut. Emotionally and physically, Cain pulled away and closed up like a prodded sea urchin. What had she done? Grasping at straws, she attempted some damage control.

"I'm warning you, though, I have a sweet tooth that escalates when I'm under stress."

"Feel free to peruse the kitchen."

His words sounded as flat and deflated as an old tire. Belinda decided to push. They might as well face what was happening head-on. Her hopeful feeling had fizzled and died like a soggy sparkler.

"Exactly how free am I, Mr. Devlin? Have you decided to believe me?"

Cain was still reeling from the dating question, and he hadn't been following her last few comments. The woman couldn't possibly think he dated often with a face like his. Maybe she was giving him a little passive-aggressive hit. Damn, but he was a fool. He'd actually forgotten the whole mess for a minute and was enjoying lunch. Amazingly, enjoying the honesty and candor of Belinda Brown.

She was so completely opposite to the women he'd had in his life, soft and natural instead of hard and shellacked into place. Alissa would never have been caught dead looking like that—less than perfect. He knew now she had only tolerated his imperfection for the money and the hope that a plastic surgeon could finally repair all the damage. Cain had last seen her three years ago in the hospital when the bandages revealed his fate. It had been his fault, though. He'd known Alissa was shallow, but he'd been so lonely; too ready to believe anything.

"Mr. Devlin, I think I deserve an answer. Some decisions have to be made."

How long had it been since he'd had a meal sitting across from a woman? For a minute there, he could have sworn Ms. Brown was teasing him; treating him like a normal man instead of the usual pins-and-needles approach. How long had it been since that had happened? Of course, she had an agenda, that was a given, but this felt really different. What was it?

"Mr. Devlin? I feel it's pointless to be less than honest with you. So I'm asking you, please don't start that scary stuff again. Let's just tell each other everything we know about what happened and try to figure this out. Okay?"

Scary stuff? Cain mentally shook off his morbid fog and looked straight into the big brown eyes so earnestly locked to his. And then he knew. He knew what was different. She was looking directly at him; not at his hair, not over his shoulder, and not at his cheek. Except for that initial fleeting moment of pity, he hadn't seen any impact of his ugliness in her expression.

It moved him. And that scared the hell out of him. Yes, he'd had a physical reaction to her that had been unexpected, but he'd reasoned that away. This emotional response, however, was far more disturbing . . . and if the two came together? Damn, he'd rather take a gun to his head than go through the agony of caring again. Now that truly scared the hell out of him. But the weak chink in his armor could be fixed by hashing this thing out and discovering what it was she really wanted. Sure. That was all it would take, and then this pathetic lonely spell would be over.

"All right, Ms. Brown—and by the way, I have discovered that much, at least, is true. Let's go sit on the sofa and I'll try not to get too scary."

Surprisingly Belinda stood up, stacked their plates, and carried them to the sink. Before Cain realized her intentions she had opened the dishwasher and started to load it. He must have translated his shock onto his face, because she smiled quickly and pushed the "on" button.

He thought they took their places on the sectional sofa as carefully as the chess masters he watched on TV. Cain purposely spread out in the curve, laying his arms along the back and crossing his legs at the ankles, taking up as much space as possible. Belinda bent a leg beneath her and snuggled into the far end with folded arms, a clearly defensive position.

"Okay, Ms. Brown, you start. Tell me why you think I'm behind the plot to kidnap Cindy Chalmers."

"I know you blame Prince for the explosion five years ago—"

"It happened, Ms.—"

"Wait, let me get my side out and then I promise not to interrupt yours."

Cain nodded begrudgingly.

"Also I know that since then, on a number of occasions, you've gone to great lengths, unprofitable lengths, to win away some of his key clients."

"Free enterprise, Ms. Brown." And information from a mysterious informant who had tipped him a few times with memos signed by Prince. They had detailed plans to use those clients to undermine Cain's company. "Besides, he's done the same to me." She narrowed her eyes and frowned. "Sorry, my lips are sealed."

"I've heard Prince himself say that you're unreasonable about what happened and that you wouldn't ever talk to him. And finally, last week at a wedding shower, I was sitting next to Helen Hood Chalmers, Prince's grandmother; you remember her, don't you?"

Cain nodded again. He sure as hell remembered the coldhearted messenger.

"Well, she told me confidentially that she thought Prince's marriage and obvious happiness might push you to some drastic action. I didn't pay much attention to her at the time, because the woman has always struck me as too intense and overinvolved in her grandchildren's lives. But now . . ."

Cain had been watching Belinda Brown very carefully. He knew about body language and eye contact. At this point he could be certain of only one thing: she might be a pawn in a bigger plan, but she was not behind it. The woman radiated sincerity like the sun radiated heat.

"I just want to add that I know Princeton Chalmers and I know Cindy. If I thought for a minute that my best friend had married a man capable of what you think Prince has done, *I* would have been the one kidnapping her. Cindy deserves nothing but happiness. She wouldn't have fallen in love with some underhanded creep."

That Belinda's conviction was heartfelt, Cain had no doubt. She leaned forward, and he knew the soft hand she held out to him was an unconscious gesture.

"I can't prove this to you with facts and figures, and it may sound like magic mumbo jumbo, but I know it's true. Cindy and Prince have a goodness between them, Cain. If you could see them together, you'd know it, too."

His name on her lips sizzled like lightning through his body. Suddenly he wanted nothing more than to take the hand she offered and the loyalty and the caring and pull it all as close as he could get it. God! He was in deep, deadly trouble. This softly rounded woman with freckles and wispy tendrils of maple-sugar hair framing her face was so beautiful at this precise moment, that Cain was having difficulty breathing.

The only way to save himself was to attack. But his defensive walls didn't move fast enough, and he began to explain what had happened before they were locked into place.

"As much as I've hated Princeton Chalmers, I have never ever interfered in his personal life. Kidnapping is a felony, Ms. Brown. Even in a rage I'm not about to do something that would destroy everything I've built, no matter what my reputation is. However, business is different. When I'm hit, I hit back. In fact I owe my expanded philosophy to the man."

Cain dropped his foot to the floor and rocked forward, resting his elbows on his knees and loosely weaving his fingers together.

"Five years ago I got a memo from Prince arranging a meeting at one of the old warehouse complexes we were thinking of renovating. We were in the process of merging our companies. Did you know that?"

He shot Belinda a haunted look and her stomach cinched up tight as if pulled by an invisible drawstring. Cindy had mentioned it once, but so briefly that Belinda had thought it had just been about money. Cain probably had no idea what his clenched jaw and empty eyes were telling her. This had been far more than a financial arrangement.

"Anyway—" He shrugged his broad shoulders, rolling them forward under the black T-shirt, and stared down at the rug beneath his feet. A shank of chestnut hair fell across his ruined cheek and Belinda held her breath. Although Cain Devlin had probably never been described as a classically handsome man, for a moment she had a glimpse of what he had been.

"Anyway, I went to meet Prince. I hurried over there because the message was urgent." He stopped talking and turned his head toward Belinda. Slowly, intentionally, he sat up and raked the dangling hair back off his face, revealing the lasting reminder of that meeting.

"Here's the really ironic part. It was all for nothing." Cain absently ran a fingertip along a ridge of rippled flesh.

"I was supposed to have signed the final papers the day before, but I'd put it off. I didn't sign and then I didn't die."

This was awful! Worse than she had ever imagined. Belinda put both feet on the floor and inched closer, leaning in toward him. "But, Cain, there were never any charges. The police reports never even hinted that it was more than an accident."

"You're right. No one even considered it. Prince had an airtight alibi. The memo I'd received had disappeared. Insurance investigators found nothing unusual. And finally, there was no financial reason for Chalmers, Inc. to need control of all the money. No motive."

"But"—Belinda rubbed her forehead distractedly with the fingers of one hand, then scooted another cushion closer—"but all these years you've felt certain that Prince wanted you dead, and he has known you consider him that blackhearted."

Cain nodded and slumped against the back of the couch, dropping his head to rest on the upholstered edge.

"Did you ever once sit down and talk to him about this?"

"No."

"But he wanted to talk to you. He tried."

"That's his side of the story, Ms. Brown. Believe me, he made it very clear he wasn't interested."

"And that was it? You just left it at that?"

Cain rolled his head in her direction. "Yeah."

"But what about me? This?" Belinda asked, tossing out her arms in an all-encompassing sweep.

"You know what I think."

"That Prince is trying to do you in again?"

"Maybe he's trying to get me locked up this time around. Attempting to frame me for kidnapping would cause a lot of trouble no matter how far it actually went."

"Cain, listen. Listen to me," Belinda urged, twisting her hands together in her lap. "This is not Prince's doing. If you can't believe he's not after you, at least trust me on this. He would never, ever risk Cindy. He loves her too much. Nothing in the world would be worth that."

Trust was not an easy thing for Cain Devlin. He couldn't ever imagine trusting someone enough to feel that way. But this woman . . . Sitting so close he could see every earnest detail of her face. Sitting so close he could breathe the lingering scent of strawberry shampoo in her hair and he was beginning to think things he'd driven out of his mind and heart years ago.

She spoke his name easily, as if it felt familiar on her lips. And suddenly he wanted to taste it there, on the end of a breathless sigh. Wanted to feel the soft touch of someone who really cared. But weakness had nearly unmanned him three years ago when his ugliness had been reflected in Alissa's disgusted eyes. For one devastating moment he had almost begged her not to leave him alone. Somehow his gut-punched pride had been able to stop him in time.

After Princeton's betrayal it shouldn't have surprised him, yet he'd been blindsided once more. Never again would he put himself in such a vulnerable position. Besides, he just needed sex. That had to be why the woman was making him so crazy. He'd been both morose and abstinent too long, and that was making him see and feel things that weren't really there. Love was an illusion.

"That kind of love is a fairy tale, Ms. Brown."

She shrugged off his sarcasm, undaunted. "Well, maybe things don't always turn out happily ever after, but too much hate and anger will eat away at your health and that's a fact. Besides, maybe believing in a touch of magic now and then would make a lot of people happier, more hopeful. Maybe a few stars in our eyes would make everything look better."

Cain watched the chagrin bloom in Belinda's eyes a heartbeat after the words left her mouth. Their instantaneous watery reaction had him on his feet, hands clenched at his sides, ready to get the hell out of there. Her wide, trembling mouth pressed into a white line and he knew she was desperately thinking of something to say. Something that would only make it worse. God, he couldn't stand a pitiful apology. So he spoke first.

"No, not everything would look better. There aren't enough stars. Magic and love aren't worth the wager of one thin dime. And speaking of money, I have some business to take care of for a few hours. Things to check into. Sleep or read if you like."

Cain knew he had to leave and moved to step past her, but Belinda tipped up her face to his with such an anxious, tormented look, his booted feet stopped in their tracks. *Attack!* a distant inner voice cried. *Attack before it's too late.*

Chapter Four

"You should know I have the only phone and the Jeep keys. The car has an alarm and there is no place in a fifty-mile radius to run to. I'm willing to give you the benefit of the doubt, but if you try anything I'll lock you up again until I can discover who's behind this. I can't take the chance of tipping anyone off right now. Whether you believe me or not, Ms. Brown, someone is trying to make me the fall guy and nothing will stop me from ensuring that person pays."

All Belinda's previous perceptions were starting to shift and spin toward an entirely new viewpoint. Cain was angry and she knew his anger could be dangerous and vindictive. She had experienced a taste of it firsthand. But maybe he had good reason to protect himself. Still, he didn't seem like the kind to be so out of control that he would sever one of his own arteries in order to hurt Prince. The man felt pain. Pain she had unintentionally inflicted and somehow had to fix. It was there just behind the green-gold glow of fury burning in his eyes.

Should she do it? Was it stupid? If Belinda was wrong, Cain Devlin was strong enough to snap her sturdy body in half as easily as he would a toothpick. But her need to make amends had to be expressed. She had never been able to sit by and watch someone suffer, even when it meant putting herself in a difficult situation. Those scars must be all he ever saw when he looked at himself. In his mind, everything came back to them. Maybe that was exactly why she'd said what she had. She didn't see the scars. She saw the man. And because of that, she'd seen a brief, aching shadow darken his eyes just before he'd threatened her again.

"I want answers, too, Cain, and I'll stay, willingly, till we get them."

He nodded once, and then before he could move, she did it. Touched him. Quickly, purposefully, she wrapped her fingers as far as she could around his boulder of a fist. He jerked back, startled, but she held on, working against his strength until she was able to wedge her thumb past his and into the hidden hollow of his hand.

They might have stayed that way for seconds or minutes. Belinda had no way of knowing; she was too engrossed watching, feeling. His dark brows pulled slowly together in an expression of such distress it bordered on panic. Oh, God! Without thinking, Belinda lifted her other hand and patted his forearm. The skin was warm and she could feel rock-hard muscle tensed beneath the silky chestnut hair shifting under her fingertips.

Silence stretched between them until the very air felt tense and taut, like a rubber band ready to snap. It was as if they were caught in some kind of magnetic force field. Then, with a powerful yank that lifted her to her feet, Cain broke away, whirled around, and stormed upstairs.

Belinda slumped down on the sofa, shaking too badly to remain standing. She dropped her gaze to her tingling fingers. For a moment she had held the beast in the palm of her hand . . . and this time he hadn't hurt her.

You remember that, dearie.

A soft breeze stirred through the room, lifting the straggling hairs around Belinda's face, yet she remained motionless. Riveted. What had she heard on that breath of cool air? She finally raised her head and tilted it toward the window. Nothing. Of course, it was just her own subconscious trying to comfort her. But it helped all the same.

* * *

Two hours later, Cain was still stunned. What kind of pathetic excuse for a man had he become? A woman held his hand, just his hand, dammit, and his heart took off like a runaway train dragging his starved body toward a hopeless destination. Disgusted, he leaned back in his swivel chair and pivoted away from the desk. Cain steepled his fingers and tapped them on his chin while letting his gaze drift out the open bedroom window.

Normally he had plenty of space to think and work here. The left side of the room, close to the massive picture window, held all his business needs: desk, computer, phone, and fax. On the right was a dresser, entertainment armoire, and his king-size bed covered with a thick comforter detailed in the familiar Indian designs and the colors of the house. Layers of pillows in different shades of brown, navy, rust, and cream were piled against the simple oak headboard.

The room itself was the largest of four bedrooms, and had a spacious bath area that featured a step-up Jacuzzi-type tub, surrounded with windows. Breathtaking beauty and hot, bubbling water often helped Cain relax at the end of a long day. His mouth curved in a self-deprecating smile. Of course, that water was the only hot bubbling thing Cain *ever* had waiting lately.

Abruptly he speared his hands through his hair, tugging it ruthlessly away from his face. Idiot! Why was he even thinking this foolishness? It wasn't a brand-new condition. Celibacy had become his lifestyle. How could he let the presence of this one average woman screw him to the wall? Cain held out his hands and cursed at their fine tremor.

It was time to start acting like himself again. Time to exercise all the control and razor-sharp indifference he had a reputation for. Bottom line: solve the puzzle, end the game, losers pay. He flattened his palms on the desk and reread the scribbles on his notepad. After a few very discreet calls, he had discovered that nothing was being said officially about Ms. Brown's disappearance yet. That wouldn't last long. If this Cindy woman was half the friend to Belinda that Belinda was to her, Prince would have a wildcat on his hands demanding action.

Cain closed his eyes, pinched the bridge of his nose with a thumb and forefinger, and slammed the other hand on the desk. God, he hated it that an errant thought still had the power to make him regret the destruction of his friendship with Princeton Chalmers. If only he hadn't read that first letter in the hospital, the one that had fueled his knee-jerk instinct to fight and ask questions later. Groggy with medication, pain, and grief, Cain had called Prince, demanding to know why he had been set up; railing about going to the police; calling him a murderer. Prince had never talked with him again.

If only the subsequent information from that same mystery informant hadn't proved true every single time. Maybe Cain wouldn't have grown more certain with each passing year that the man he had begun to care for like a brother had tried to end his life.

In fact he probably wouldn't have even believed the first letter if that witch Helen Chalmers hadn't visited him the evening after his phone call and told him point-blank that Prince wanted nothing more to do with a raving lunatic, spouting libelous accusations. Clearly Cain was not familiar with a tradition of family honor, but Prince would not tolerate this affront. What kind of man was he to question anything about her family? She'd left by saying she regretted ever welcoming him into their home.

And every six months or so, the old bat continued to find a way to needle him. Usually after he'd made an end run around some Chalmers deal. Damned if she hadn't come marching in four weeks ago, in a tirade, accusing him of trying to ruin Chalmers, Inc.'s standing as the number-one business in central California. When he'd smiled and assured her that was exactly what he intended to do, the small, white-haired virago had sputtered with indignation.

In shrill, strident tones she told him he should do everyone a favor and stay out of sight. Or was he using the pity and revulsion his face caused to his advantage now?

She'd wagged a diamond-studded hand in his direction and announced it wouldn't work on her. Helen vowed he'd be stopped this time. That he'd be sorry he had ever made acquaintance with their name. Holy hell, but her ranting had brought three secretaries running into his office. Cain had waited the rest of the day for Prince to call him in a rage. But there was nothing. No response at all. Never any response.

Unless . . . He shot to his feet and paced to the window. Unless this thing with Ms. Brown was finally the response. Cain braced an arm against the oak molding edging the glass and watched the winding stream as his thoughts wound around in his head. Actually it was a very creative strategy. The Devlin-Chalmers feud was widely known in the area. Any kind of legal action would damage Cain's business, and once the story leaked to the papers . . . he'd be blackballed for a very long time.

There was only one reason to doubt it. Belinda Brown. Belinda said so. Belinda said—no, swore—that Prince would never hurt the woman he loved.

So . . . Cain moved away from the window and turned toward the door. If it wasn't Prince, who was it? His aging grandmother who wore brass knuckles under her high-society gloves? Had she been issuing a personal threat or a collective one? Who on Chalmers's team was willing to jeopardize Cindy to get to Cain? And how did Prince figure into this new scenario?

He had to see what Belinda thought about this. Maybe between the two of them they could make some sense out of it all. Cain had his hand on the doorknob when it hit him like a powerful right cross. He was thinking of her as Belinda. He was thinking of her as help. God help him . . . he was thinking of her . . . on his side. He dropped his gaze to his hand wrapped around the brass knob.

Hell! He clamped down on both the knob and the thoughts. Once before he'd acknowledged the danger of his needy body colliding with the turbulent feelings *Ms. Brown* churned up inside of him. Fool! Proving his innocence was the priority and time was of the essence. If they worked quickly he could have her out of his life by late evening or early tomorrow morning. Cain opened the door and stepped out into the wide hall. Evenly spaced squares of sunlight, from the skylights in the ceiling, lay like a path of stepping stones down the camel carpet.

There was only one thing he had to do while implementing his plan: keep the woman from touching him. One more generous, caring touch and he didn't know what would happen.

Belinda was antsy. Oh, she knew she should probably be frightened or frantic—she had been—but she wasn't now. True, she still felt strongly about calling Cindy, and had spent an hour forming a logical list of reasons for Cain to allow her to do so. She didn't want her friend to worry, but Cindy had Prince, and they could take care of each other. Surprisingly Belinda found she wasn't as distraught as she was oddly expectant. Maybe because after Cain had rushed from the room, a tiny seed of hope had taken root in her heart.

It didn't make any sense, she knew it, but somehow the man was vulnerable to her. When she'd touched him she'd felt the fight in his body. If at that moment she had been able to run her hands over each individual muscle, she knew without a shadow of a doubt that every one would have been bunched and straining to break away. Then right before he actually did pull free, his hand had tightened around her thumb. He'd held on for a heartbeat and she felt the connection all the way to her soul.

Belinda shot up off the couch, knocked the magazine she'd been reading onto the carpet, and paced to the windows. She hugged her arms against her middle and watched the twilight silently seeping into the nooks and crannies of the rugged landscape, slowly turning blues and greens to charcoal and gray. All the crisp, clear edges were beginning to feather and blur one into the other, until full dark would completely alter what was really there.

But the night's cycle of darkness hid reality only for so long, and then the dawn came again.

Cain Devlin had been lost in the dark too long without a morning. He'd forgotten the man he really was. Belinda rested her forehead on the smooth, cool glass and bit her bottom lip. There was no way she could escape herself now. She was a fixer, always had been and always would be. And evidently no extreme was going to stop the urge. Her grandmother had often told her that she had a gift for seeing the need in living things. As a child, she constantly brought in strays and injured animals to tend, only to continue that with people as she got older. Trying to fix Cindy's problem had gotten her into this trouble in the first place.

But this—this feeling that had been building in her all afternoon—was the strongest Belinda had ever had. The stern warning she'd given herself hours ago hadn't worked at all. What would it be like to have nobody? To be as alone as Cain Devlin? To be prepared for rejection all the time?

What if somehow she could reunite him with Prince? Belinda closed her eyes and swallowed hard.

"All right, Lindy, be honest. You care for yourself. Too fast and too much and probably way too naively."

Oh, God, she shouldn't have touched him because now she knew how much he needed to be touched. And . . . how much she wanted to soothe every aching muscle covering that massive frame. She opened her eyes and stretched out her hands. They shook. Good gosh, she needed to do something to get these dangerous impulses under control. Cooking? No, not now. Maybe a little exploring? Yeah. See what resources were available if she needed them.

Bronwyn Wolfe

Cain Devlin might be getting to her heart and her hormones, but her head was still working fine. The man was the perfect flesh-and-blood example of a loose cannon, and it wouldn't hurt to be prepared.

Belinda bent over to roll up the legs of her drooping sweats and headed for the stairs leading down to the first floor. Her middle-of-the-night entrance had been so hazy, she had only a vague memory of a foyer, a long hall, and doors. For a second she hesitated, tapping her thumbs together. Well, he hadn't told her she couldn't come down here. He'd only said not to leave.

She found pretty much what she'd expected. Lots of storage. A pair of Jet Skis for a nearby lake. Tools and some painting equipment. One room had a stockpile of staples, paper goods, and foodstuffs, which was smart because of Cain's remote location and the changeable weather. She smiled at the big, bright laundry room and wondered how many days she'd be wearing borrowed sweats and socks as her complete wardrobe.

Maybe Cain had some pajamas or a nightshirt or a bathrobe. He was such a tall, broad-chested man, she'd swim in his clothes. Suddenly the idea of swimming in those particular "big" clothes was very appealing. In vivid detail, a picture of her in one of his flannel shirts—tails brushing her thighs, shoulder seams hitting at her elbows—popped into her head, creating a totally different feeling than the sweats did. The image made her feel both vulnerable and protected. Dainty and doll-like and . . . and *doll-like?* Barbie doll–like?

Good gosh, no!

Belinda muffled a horrified laugh at her adolescent reaction and fidgeted with the ribbing at the neck of her sweatshirt. She was twenty-eight years old, for crying out loud. If she wanted to help the man, fine. However, these . . . these other feelings had to stop. It all had to be related to her nonexistent social life. She'd been so busy the past two years with her boutique that she hadn't been interested in dating. Had in fact only gone out a handful of times.

If she stood back and analyzed it, it made perfect sense that her underused feminine radar was having a tough time tracking the tidal wave of testosterone generated by Cain Devlin.

An earlier singles cruise might have short-circuited her problem, but her ship had figuratively sunk. So how was she going to handle this growing attraction for a cold, needy man who didn't appear to have one window on the ground floor of his glorified log house? Not one way for a single pair of unwanted eyes to look into his home or his heart.

Brother, it was nuts to be letting her emotions run amuck this way. Really, what would she tell people if anything were to come of it; they met at her kidnapping? Move slow, Grandpa had always advised her, and she nodded to herself as she stepped out of the laundry room and shut the door. Cain Devlin was as wary and distrustful of human beings as any animal she and Grandpa had ever tried to help. Patience had always made the difference then. Patience would be the key now.

Belinda dusted her hands on the seat of her sweats and reached up to secure her wilting bun. Just as she headed for the stairs she spied one last door partially hidden in the far corner. The light was dim—thanks to no windows—and she debated about staying longer. After all, it might be best if the man didn't know she'd been snooping. She started to turn away when a shiny something shimmered at the edge of her vision. Belinda swung her head back, but the gleam went out like a snuffed candle. What in the world? Curiosity got the best of her and she quietly tiptoed to the door.

She fumbled for the light switch and nearly collapsed when the darkness evaporated. This was not the same clean, well-ordered pattern she'd seen repeated in every other room of Cain's home. It smelled different, too. Musty and stuffy as if nothing, not even the air, changed in here. A large painting, half covered with an old tarp, hung crookedly on the wall. It looked as if someone had tried to block it with junk and debris, but Belinda could tell who it was.

She pushed aside a stack of empty boxes and lifted off the dusty tarp dangling from the corner of the ornate cherry frame. It was Cain. A younger Cain. Cain before. Cain smiling. And it took her breath away.

Stinging tears burned behind her eyelids, and her throat tightened up until it was all but impossible to swallow. Unable to stop herself, Belinda lifted a finger to the perfect cheek and touched it. His hair was shorter but still a rich reddish brown. His eyes were brighter, but still penetrating. His mouth showed the most telling difference. The hardness wasn't there. Cynicism had not yet carved the deep lines that bracketed his lips now.

She shifted to get closer and bumped into something at her feet. Belinda gingerly crouched onto her sore knees and shoved away more of the tarp, sucking in a harsh breath as the object was revealed. Three, then four, then countless tears plopped onto the stiff fabric. More rolled down her cheeks and she backhanded them away with an impatient swipe.

Oh God, he'd kept this intentionally. Had to have done so. Cain Devlin might act like a heartless bastard, but that was not true. Here was the proof. A beautiful hand-carved plaque that must have been meant to be a gift five years ago.

CHALMERS AND DEVLIN
PARTNERS AND FRIENDS

Belinda worked her throat against the aching lump caught there. She reached out with trembling hands and lifted the destroyed dream, pulling it close to her chest, rocking the inanimate object as if it were the man she longed to comfort.

Like a crack of a gunshot, the door crashed against the wall and Cain burst into the room, fire blazing in his eyes.

"What do you think you're doing, damn you! Get your hands off my things and get the hell out of here!"

Belinda couldn't move. The Cain she'd first met was back with a vengeance and she had no idea how to handle him. Like a mountain lion he stalked closer, deadly power in every fluid move. The color of his eyes had gone dark and glinted with the icy purpose of a predator's intentions. Belinda couldn't stand to see it. She couldn't stand to be the cause and she couldn't stand the lie. He was not an animal. He was a man.

"I'm sorry, Cain," she managed to get out while awkwardly getting to her feet and moving back to the security of the wall behind her. "I never meant to—" Belinda rolled her lips between her teeth. No lying of any kind. "Okay, I was looking around. I wanted to find out more about you and my options." Belinda paused to bolster her courage with a shaky breath. "I never, never meant to hurt you. I never meant to intrude on these painful memories. But I'm glad because I think I understand you better and I think maybe if I talk to Prince—"

"Don't you dare!" he hissed through clenched teeth and stepped forward. "Don't you dare talk about me to a single living soul. I never asked for any of this. I don't need some over-the-hill Pollyanna meddling in my life. Some things can never be fixed. I want to be left the hell alone. Do you understand me?"

Just an arm's length separated them now. Cain knew that only the force of his will was holding back the howling hurricane of emotions pounding to be free. His iron grip was slipping with every tear slipping down Belinda's cheeks. The worst of it was, all he could think about was the painting. God . . . she'd seen the picture. Seen him as a whole man, the man he could never be again. What a masochist he'd been to keep it.

"But, Cain," she whispered with a watery sob. "What if I'm telling the truth and Prince didn't betray you? What if you could get your friend back?" She turned the plaque toward him. "I know you care. I know it must be awful to be so alone. But it's not because of this." She lifted a hand and almost touched his ruined cheek and very nearly stopped the heart in his chest.

"It's because of this." Then she rested that small hand over the exact spot . . . and it did stop. "The you in the painting is still here, inside Cain. People only see the scars because I think that's all you let them see. When people really know you, your face won't matter at all."

God she was killing him. Slicing through his defenses with every word. He had to stop her. With a brutish jerk he tore the pathetic plaque from her other hand and hurled it away. A shattering silence filled the room, making Belinda's sharply indrawn breath sound decibels louder than it was. She pressed away from him, into the unyielding wall, and looked down at her empty arm.

Cain could see the red streak running up from her wrist, ending near the bunched sweatshirt sleeve at her elbow. She lifted her head and, like flower petals too heavy with rain, her tear-filled eyes widened and the tears spilled over.

Now she was ready to see. Once and for all he would make her see. Make them both see the truth.

"Open your eyes, Ms. Brown," he growled, shoving his face down next to hers. "This face has turned away every woman I've met for three years. It's changed everything! I don't believe your fairy tales about people. I don't believe that love is blind. And I don't believe in happily ever after."

Her blank expression infuriated Cain and he wrapped his hands around her shoulders and pulled her roughly away from the wall.

"Are you listening? Do you understand me?"

"Yes," Belinda managed to mumble while her mind

whirled. Oh, she heard him. But what she'd heard wasn't what he had said. The need in his touch was calling so loudly to her heart that she had no choice but to answer. No matter what happened, she had to answer the real question.

Quickly she brought her arms up between his and threaded them around his neck. She lifted onto tiptoe to reach his hard, angry mouth. How long had it been since Cain had been kissed and held? At first she moved hesitantly, rocking gently against a body that had turned to stone beneath her touch. Then she pressed and held a kiss, rubbing the tip of her tongue against the steel seam of his lips. Never before had she been so brazen and so brave. Still he didn't respond, and her resolve faltered.

Desperate to reach him, comfort him, Belinda breathed against his mouth, "I see your face, Cain." She drew one hand from the rigid muscles in his neck and felt the jolt hit him when she laid her palm over the puckered scars. "And it doesn't matter to me, not at all."

The words came straight from her heart, revealing more than even she had known. Magically, amazingly, and perhaps fruitlessly, the small seed of hope and compassion rooted in her heart had blossomed into a fragile flowering of love.

And Cain could not hold against it. The fingers tracing his scars shocked like a hundred volts of pure electricity. No one had ever touched him there. Ever. The internal battle he'd been waging from the moment she'd put her arms around him was lost. No matter how desperately he tried not to hear Belinda's words, the truth vibrated like a bell through his body, and something opened deep inside. Something that needed to be filled. So he filled his arms with her softness, and filled his mouth with the sweet taste of her lips, and filled his senses with the smell of strawberries and woman.

God help him, it had been so long. So long since he'd felt the searing rush of desire and felt a willing woman

71

tremble from his kiss. Cain flexed his knees and lifted her easily against his chest. The weight was drugging and delicious, but his starved body was weaker than he thought and he had to use the wall for support. With his arms as a buffer, he shifted a hand to the back of her neck and pushed the other up under the bottom of her sweatshirt, until it rested flush against the hot, silky skin covering her spine.

His heart pounded faster and faster, running wild with unchecked need. He had to be closer. When Belinda's hands crept up the back of his neck and tangled in his hair, Cain shuddered and instinctively moved a thigh between her legs, plunging his tongue deep into her mouth, meeting her stroke for stroke, drowning in the taste and touch of love.

Love?

No! *No!* God! What was he doing? Cain pulled his hands away as if he'd been holding live coals. He staggered back a couple of steps and watched Belinda sag against the plastered wall. Her eyes were huge pools of uncharted emotions, her sore lips shiny, moist and trembling. Cain dared not move for fear of reaching for her again. His overloaded brain and body could not compute what had just happened, could not accept it. There was always an agenda. Always. He would have to be the world's greatest fool to believe in more again. He had to protect himself.

"You've wasted your effort on me, Ms. Brown." Cain's voice caught and went ragged like silk on sandpaper. He had to fold his arms to hide the rough rise and fall of his chest. His entire body felt like it had hit a block wall going sixty miles an hour.

"Did you think the offer of your body and your pity would change my mind? You're no beauty, Ms. Brown. Not near alluring enough to make me that senseless. I won't let you go no matter what you offer."

Belinda's heart was still hammering away. Her kiss of comfort had changed to something she had never experienced before. A flash fire. Total incineration. She was rocked to her toes. He was attacking and a part of her even understood that. But the other part, blooming with the rare and delicate blend of passion and caring, began to shrivel under the blazing intensity of his rejection.

Cain Devlin was too hard. He wouldn't allow even a hint of softness inside where he needed it so badly. If she kept trying, if she let herself fall all the way in love with him and she still couldn't reach him . . . she would end up breaking herself into tiny pieces against his heart of stone.

Somehow she would have to leave. Belinda couldn't stay and let herself care more than she did already. And Cain had to learn that for once he was absolutely wrong. That it was possible for him to have completely misjudged someone. If nothing else, maybe it would force him to consider that there were some folks out in the world dealing him an honest hand.

The man needed a major reality check, and Belinda figured nobody had dared give him one for a long time. A person could never fix what was wrong until they could see it. Of course, sometimes that meant the messenger found himself in a very hostile situation.

Belinda's legs were still wobbly and she knew he was angrier right now than the first time she'd seen him. But she remembered the strange message on the breeze and she was reminded of the little, unconscious things he'd been doing to make up for the intensity of that first encounter. However, not only would Cain never believe her, he wouldn't even recognize his actions for what they were. Belinda knew she had to leave the man with the truth he no longer saw in himself.

"You're right, Cain. I'm certainly no beauty." Belinda straightened up and edged toward the open door. "And I'm probably not woman enough for a man like you, either. But unless you've forgotten a whole lot about kissing, you've got to know that was almost more than I could handle. My response didn't have a thing to do with your scars.

I've seen them from the first, you know, and they didn't stop me from, well . . ."

She stopped at the doorjamb and braced herself against the solid support. Belinda knew what she had to say, but it wasn't going to be easy. Stripping away one's pride always left such huge, defenseless holes.

"Maybe we were both hungry enough to take what we could get. Hunger and pity can make men and women fools." Cain's sardonic mask slid firmly into place with his sarcastic words.

His voice and body gave nothing away now. He moved closer, and she wondered how he'd shut down so fast. Her lips were still tingling; a foolish longing to feel it all again fluttering beneath her skin. Okay, now she had to do it.

"I can understand if that's what happened for you, Cain. You've made it pretty clear I'm not your type." Belinda glanced down at herself and tugged on a lumpy fold in the gray sweatshirt, then looked up directly into his eyes. "But I think it's very important for you to know you're wrong about a number of things. For what it's worth, I'm going to break a major male-female taboo and tell you the absolute truth."

Cain arched an eyebrow.

"My part of the kiss did start because I knew you were hurting. I did feel terribly sorry for you." Good gosh, she'd almost missed the subtle shift in Cain's indifferent stance. One dangling hand was now clamped around his thigh. *Here we go.*

"But that all changed in about twenty seconds. That kiss was the best I've ever had. It felt, well, I can't even describe it. You reduced me to the proverbial quivering mass of jelly. You, just how you are, now. And I know how you looked before." She lifted a hand to the picture on the wall and Cain briefly shot it a piercing glance.

"You know what I see when I look at that picture? What the biggest difference is?" He didn't respond, just stared with such intensity Belinda was sure he could see into her very soul.

"It's the smile. It's the missing smile I wish you could have back. Anger and revenge are not what you are, Cain Devlin. That beast inside comes out when you're hurting too much. You're not a beast. You're a man who needs to love and be loved."

Belinda's rush of words finished on a surge of an incoming tide, a driven wave of energy. But in the deadly quiet that followed, her confidence began to ebb away; undermining her courage like liquified sand under her feet. Cain rolled his shoulders as if working off the effects of a blow or a cramp. He pulled them to rigid attention and she knew in an instant her revelations hadn't changed a thing. "And you, Ms. Brown, are a pathetic rainbow chaser. Telling me I need something you don't have yourself. Don't say another word and don't tell me what I feel. You don't know anything about me."

Cain stepped past her and yanked the picture off the wall. With icy calm, he raised it over his head and bashed it against the wall. The force of his blow splintered the heavy frame into kindling.

Belinda flew by him the moment his hands fell empty. She took the stairs at a dead run and had her bedroom door locked and a chair jammed under the knob before the tears started again. For ten long minutes she sat on the corner of the bed, breathing hard, waiting to hear his heavy steps, but there was only silence. And her heart gradually slowed . . . and her shoulders slumped with exhaustion.

She fell back on the plump mattress, legs dangling to the floor. Cain Devlin had made her feel like no man ever had and he hadn't seen it at all. A last, lone tear slipped across her temple and disappeared into her hair. *Eyes of the beholder, Lindy.* As much as she wished it so, she could not make him see himself through her eyes. The adventure

Bronwyn Wolfe

was over and it was time to let Cindy know what was happening.

Her eyelids closed with a gritty drag, but she didn't sleep. Grandpa had taught his little country girl very well. She still knew enough to take care of herself. In a few hours she would leave.

Chapter Five

By the time Cain came upstairs it was almost dark. The dramatic panorama that usually filled his living room was shrouded with a foggy gray mist that mirrored his feelings. Cold. Forbidding. Lonely. He sank into one of the wing-back chairs and dragged a shaky hand through his snarled hair. In a show of studied indifference he swept the room and the stairs, looking for any signs of her. Cain let out a short, compressed breath and dropped his head into his hands. Who in the hell did he think he was kidding? He hadn't even been able to leave the storage room for two hours for fear of what he might do.

The feel of Belinda Brown's mouth and body had nearly unleashed all the need and hunger clawing away inside him. Her tears and her honesty had exposed him, left him more defenseless than he'd been in years. And of course he'd attacked with a vengeance. His legendary control, his pride, had taken a serious blow. Honesty, or the appearance of honesty, was a very powerful weapon. Innocence, too.

It was that unexpected blend of innocence, honesty, and courage that the woman wielded with the skill of a master swordsman. She'd left him scrambling and reeling from the very beginning. He fingered the damaged side of his face, and his stomach muscles clenched at the thought of the picture. Oh, God, that kiss! How could she expect him to believe the riveting things she'd said? Only a fool . . . Cain rubbed his palms down the tops of his thighs and pushed to his feet.

Only a fool would believe the words of a woman forced into a situation she'd never asked for, a woman who'd only known him a few days. He walked closer to a large pane of glass and tried to make out the well-known landscape. This view was as familiar as the back of his hand, but right now it might as well have been a piece of the moon. He felt as if the scene in the basement had transported him to another planet. Another reality where dreams were not all dust and childish wishing. Where a woman could see into his soul and find something human and noble. Without thinking, Cain curled one hand into a tight fist and brought it sharply against the glass. The reverberation startled him.

Damn! He had to let her go. Soon after first light he would take her to the small town halfway down the mountain and arrange for a car to drive her back to the city. Cain turned toward a low pine cupboard he'd made the previous winter and ran a finger along the silky, hand-rubbed patina of mellow gold. The raw wood had been so rough, so flawed, but hours of committed work had transformed it into something beautiful. A shiver of sensation ran from the tips of his finger and straight to his brain, clicking on a vivid memory. Soft fingers had touched his raw flesh with silky strokes, too. A flawed part of his body had lost all beauty, and yet Belinda hadn't let that stop her. She'd held him and kissed him with an urgency he knew she hadn't manufactured. Yes, deep down he had felt it. But to believe it? To pursue a relationship that had started so terribly? God, if this were a business deal, he'd never even chance these odds.

But his cursed body didn't seem to care. Involuntarily his gaze wandered up the stairs, and a fine tremor shot through him again. And she thought she wasn't woman enough for him. . . . Sweet Jesus.

With a strangled groan, Cain yanked open the cupboard door and grabbed a nearly full bottle of scotch. Before he could talk himself out of it, he twisted off the cap and took a long swallow. The smoky sting ran like liquid fire down his throat and sucked the air out of his lungs. Cain moved back to the chair and sat, hunched forward, dangling the bottle between his knees. He only had to hang on a few hours and he'd be rid of her.

It was good he'd acted like such a beast, he thought as he took another swig. The woman sure as hell wouldn't be coming down for another touchy-feely chat, handing out her pity and her amateur psychology and her kisses. . . . Cain brought the bottle to his mouth one last time and then prepared to wait. With a little borrowed courage he ought to be able to do it.

A dull, rhythmic pounding woke him. Cain forced open his eyes and rubbed a hand down his face. The sandpapery feel of whiskers and the tangled mass of his hair left him feeling muddled and confused. He moved to stand and abruptly the world righted itself. He knew what that nauseated pounding was all about. It was his amplified heartbeat. The horrible taste in his mouth and the half-empty bottle on the floor brought him up to speed most uncomfortably. Damn! He hadn't done this since the first few months after the accident.

Cain managed to get to his feet and head for the stairs, his stiff muscles protesting all the way. This was the last moment of weakness he was going to tolerate—period. A quick shower and the woman was a footnote. He paused for a minute at her door. Quiet. Good. He needed a little time to prepare himself to face her again. Twenty minutes later he was ready. His still-wet hair was pulled back into a hasty ponytail, but he hadn't taken the time to shave. Working around his scars took too long and he had nearly choked when he realized he'd slept the whole morning away. Man, she must be furious and . . . starving. A burgeoning smile flattened at the lurch of his heart.

And he covered the lurch with an ear-popping thump on

Belinda's door that had him grinding his teeth to hold back a moan.

"Ms. Brown? Come on out. I've decided to let you leave." He waited. The silence was infuriating. He thumped again and then tried the door. Locked, dammit. "Ms. Brown, open the door or I'm coming in like I did in the bathroom."

Ten minutes later he knew why the room had been so quiet. A chair had blocked his way and Ms. Belinda Brown was gone. She'd used the sheets to climb out the window. Cain braced his hands on the open ledge and squinted painfully into the glare of the bright morning sun. There wasn't a sign of her from here. He dropped his head and rocked forward on the heels of his hands. What had he done? How long had she been gone? The woman could get herself seriously hurt in this rough country.

Adrenaline pumped through his veins like jet fuel, rushing past the knots in his stomach and the pain behind his eyes. He knew he needed to calm down and make some plans, but he couldn't stop the horrible pictures flashing through his mind. This was his fault! The first person in years who had really tried to understand and he'd frightened her so badly she would rather face death than stay.

Devlin, you bastard! You're the one who told her she couldn't leave. You're the one who reduced her honesty to a sleazy play with her body. Now you know, man. Now you know how far gone you really are. . . .

Haphazardly Cain stuffed some supplies in a backpack and ran outside. In a few short moments he found her trail. Not once did he realize he was praying.

Okay, so she wasn't quite as self-sufficient as she had thought. There was no reason to panic. Yet.

Belinda pressed back farther into the *Y* of the pine tree she had chosen to spend the night in and tried to wrap her appropriated blanket a little tighter. Her teeth chattered uncontrollably and she rolled her lips between them to stop the irritating noise. It was cold, but not cold enough to do any real damage. She might not sleep much, but she would not freeze to death. In fact she should be really grateful she had literally stumbled upon such a good tree and been able to get up it even with her aching ankle. Cindy's impractical sandals worn over two pairs of men's sweat socks hadn't helped a bit.

In her rush to leave Cain Devlin before she lost her heart and her mind completely, she miscalculated her drop from the sheets and twisted her left ankle. And even though she been able to keep moving, her pace had been affected and she was starting to have serious doubts about finding help. Grandpa had taught her a lot, but he had also warned her plenty of times about *goin' off half-cocked and gettin' into a worse spot than you were before*.

Belinda hunched her shoulders and snaked a hand out of the blanket to rub her nose. Grandma, however, had also taught her to look for the positive, so, on the bright side, she hadn't seen one wild animal yet and would probably drop a few pounds by the time this . . . adventure was over. Certainly a technique they'd never tried at the gym.

As if echoing her assessment, a rolling rumble erupted from her stomach. *Okay, Brown, be honest. This is actually a pretty bad spot. No one knows where you are. You don't know where you are. And the only person with even a remote hope of finding you is probably thrilled to have the "over-the-hill Pollyanna" off his hands*. Belinda winced as the wind lifted a hunk of hair sticky with a blop of pine gum. So many patches of skin stung from the rough tree bark, she felt as if she'd been sanded. She had never had so many aches and pains, and to top it off, the blue-black of the night sky was growing deeper by the minute and soon she would be all alone in this vast, wild country.

That hadn't seemed like a problem at all hours ago when she'd made good her escape. But civilization was nowhere in sight, and although the stars and the sliver of moon sparkled in the velvet sky like diamonds, she could barely make out the hand in front of her face. Suddenly Belinda was sure she had only succeeded in making everything worse. Worse for her and Cain and Cindy and Prince. If she didn't get to a phone soon and start explaining this situation . . .

Maybe she could still help to fix things between him and Prince. At the very least she could try to give him that happiness, since it wasn't likely now that "they" would ever have a chance. Belinda shifted stiffly and huddled against the rising wind. Short bursts of chilled air buffeted her body while her foolish emotions buffeted her heart. It was ridiculous to have gotten so involved in such a short time. Unfortunately it seemed to be a pattern she had experienced repeatedly, only with animals and friends—not a man. There hadn't ever been so much pain and confusion before. Could she still believe Grandpa's claim that when Brown blood ran in your veins you could always trust your heart to guide you?

Well, her heart had guided her all right, and here she was scrunched up in a tree in the middle of nowhere—and it was getting just a little spooky.

Her heart began to thud faster in her chest and she swallowed convulsively. Another puffy gust of wind stirred through the trees, whooshing and shushing around her, tugging with increasing strength at her hair and the blanket, filling her nose with the scent of pine and damp earth. In the distance a long, mournful howl rose and fell on the wind. She squinted and strained to see into the darkness.

A brittle, crackling staccato of heavy snaps fired off from somewhere behind her and she gasped and clamped a hand over her mouth. With the tree trunk at her back, Belinda could not look around without exposing herself. She held her breath and felt her eyes go wide, ·frantic. *Cain! I'm so afraid.* Something was coming. Something was almost beneath her. Belinda curled into the smallest ball her body could make and started to pray.

* * *

The instant his batteries began to go dim, Cain knew he'd never find her. A wave of despair threatened to swamp him, and he stopped for a moment, bent over, and braced his gloved hands on his thighs, sucking in great gulps of frigid air. With every step he'd taken, with every hour that had passed, Cain Devlin's self-disgust had grown. If Belinda Brown had been telling the truth last night, the woman had been offering her friendship. And if his rusty male radar had read any of her signals right, she might have been offering more.

But no! Coward that he was, he'd rejected her just as he'd rejected everyone; just as he'd rejected those initial overtures from Prince. Sure, Cain Devlin would rather have his pride, the only real companion he'd had in the last five years.

He smacked the flashlight against his thigh and carefully moved forward over the rough terrain. All he needed now was to get hurt himself. Cain swore succinctly under his breath. *The beast inside comes out when you're hurting too much.* How could she see that far into him in only two days? Two damn days and she had the gall to tell him what he needed. Two damn days and she was making him consider that after Prince and Alissa it had all been about stopping any more pain. Two damn days and his heart was stuttering back to life and he couldn't stop it.

Because now he'd been forced to see the high price he had been paying to live without hurting: isolation, disconnection. Now he was very much afraid that what he needed had dropped into his life two damn days ago and he'd thrown it away. All he wanted was to find Belinda Brown. All he wanted was to hold her safe and sound, but this was like looking for a needle in a haystack. Dammit! He snapped off his useless flashlight. What had he been using for a brain when he'd left the house?

Your heart, you fool. And it hasn't been in charge for a long time.

How could one woman have gotten so far? Fear had

obviously been a very effective motivation, and he had become a master at generating it. God, he was so tired of seeing the guarded look of anxiety in people's eyes. The way they scurried out of his path like frightened mice until he'd finally stopped trying to convince them he was human. *You're not a beast. You're a man. You're a man.* Cain shrugged his shoulders as if he were carrying a heavy load. He straightened and looked up into the inky darkness that had become his enemy.

There they were. The stars. The stars Belinda had told him people should see with. The magic that would make people more hopeful. Her chocolate brown eyes and the acceptance reflected in them had been magic. Her kiss that had burned him from the inside out had been magic. She was magic—the only magic he'd ever experienced in his life. Cain slammed his eyes shut and spoke before he could stop the words.

"Please. Please. Help me find her. Help me believe."

The fierce emotion, the intense need, hung in the silence for the space of a heartbeat. Cain opened his eyes and felt a hot flush of embarrassment sweep up his cold face and warm him beneath his sheepskin jacket. Poor Belinda had been stuck with a lousy excuse for a white knight. There couldn't be a man less likely to fit the hero mold. That kind of man only existed in stories. Heroes, wizards, love . . . the childish stuff of fairy tales. And yet Belinda believed in them all. And God help him, but he wanted to believe in her—was desperate to believe that there was more to him than the man he had become.

He was her only hope and he could not stop until he found her . . . because maybe—he shuddered—just maybe she was his only hope, too.

Cain clicked the wavering light back on and swept the area ahead. The beam faltered and he shook the stupid thing. Nothing. He yanked off a glove, stuffed it in his pocket, and rifled through the backpack of items he'd thrown together. Not one damn battery. How could he keep searching in the dark? He hadn't been calling her name much because he was afraid it would make her run, but he had to do something—had to try.

"Ms. Brown!" His voice sounded as raw as he felt. The trees around him began to dance with a sudden flurry of wind like a giant bodies surging together and falling away. A coyote howled in the distance.

"Belinda! Belinda! Answer me. I want to help. Please believe me."

His words were lifted up like the leaves in the air, but nothing returned. Then, just as he prepared to head off in a new direction, an eerie, iridescent shimmer flickered off to the right. He stopped, shoved away the flashlight, and narrowed his eyes. There it was again. Some phosphorescent-type glow straight through the heart of a dense stand of pine. Cain pressed the thumb and index finger of one hand against his eyelids and looked again. The light skipped away, then jumped forward. It was like nothing he'd ever seen before.

Cain started forward and paused. He glanced back up at the sky and then once again at the unexplainable beacon deep in the trees. It seemed like days ago that he had told Belinda he wouldn't wager a dime on magic and love. But now he was going to wager a lot more. That was, if a soul as damaged as his had any value left.

As suddenly as the light had appeared, it vanished. He had followed it for fifteen minutes or more and now he had nothing to go on. He stepped forward and tripped on a dead limb. Spiky branches snapped like a string of firecrackers, and one gouged a burning path across the back of his still-gloveless hand. Cain muffled a curse and got to his feet, sucked in a deep breath and called again.

"Belinda! For God's sake, answer me!"

"Cain?"

His legs almost went out from under him for the second time. Was he hallucinating? He braced a hand against the tree next to him and tried to listen over the wind and the pounding of his heart.

"Cain? Is that you?"

The soft, hesitant voice floated to him once more. Good God in heaven. The light had led him. It was her. But . . . but where was she?

"Cain? I'm getting scared. Why can't I see you? Why won't you answer me?"

"Me? Me answer you!" he exploded in a barrage of unchecked, conflicting emotions. "Are you crazy, woman? I've nearly killed myself looking for you. Where are you? Come out now!"

"No."

"What!"

"No. I don't want to do this rage thing with you again, Cain Devlin. I'm not coming down."

"And I don't want to do this *no* thing with you again—wait—down? Sweet Jesus! Are you up in this tree?"

"You don't have to shout, Cain. I was taught that once it gets dark, a tree is the safest place to sleep if you have no protection."

"I'm here now. I'll protect you." Cain stood on his toes and felt his way up the trunk as far as he could. Yes—there. He brushed the end of a blanket or something, and a wave of relief washed through him, draining him of energy for a moment. He rested his forehead against the scratchy bark and thanked God for the first time in five years.

"I don't think so."

"What?"

"Maybe you should have your hearing checked, Cain. I'm getting a little worried about it." He felt a vibration through the trunk as she shifted somewhere above him. With tremendous effort he shut down the urgent compulsion to order her out of the tree. The woman was driving him stark raving mad.

"Belinda, I swear to you. I swear to you I won't hurt you.

I know I have before, but please believe me, I'm not the same man. I haven't been the same since you tried to kick in my door. And why in God's name are you worried about my hearing when I've acted like such a beast and forced you to run like this?"

"You're not a beast, Cain. That's not what this is about. Don't say that again."

"All right then, honey. Come down here and explain it to me."

"No."

"Belinda, it's freezing. Get your butt down out of that tree now!"

"No."

Frustration such as he had never known broke his control and powered his leap to snag a fistful of blanket. Belinda's sharp little shriek at his first tug made his point perfectly.

"Cain, please. I—I can't come down."

Instantly he eased up on the tension. "Are you hurt, honey? What is it? What can I do?"

Belinda Brown knew the jig was up the second time she heard the word *honey* come out of Cain Devlin's mouth. The first time she hadn't been sure, but his clearly unconscious repeated use of that endearment gave her courage. She took a fortifying breath and tried to cross her numb fingers. Either the man would be able to handle this now, respond in some small way instead of getting mad or pulling back or running . . . or he was just too far down the path of isolation and bitterness to bring life back to his poor, battered heart.

"My left ankle is bruised or something, but that's not the reason—"

"Belinda, let me see it. This could be serious," he demanded, jerking once more on the blanket. Then he paused, seemed to hesitate, only to continue in a somber, flat tone. "I have a gun, honey. I may have been stupid about batteries, but I came prepared to protect you. I understand what you're trying to say. Your real question is Who will protect you from me? Well, I'll give you the gun and if I get out of line or scare you, you can shoot me."

"Ooooh, Cain! For heaven's sake!"

The blanket and her right foot hit his head at the same time. Cain had barely gotten his hands in position and braced himself when Belinda Brown dropped abruptly into his life again.

They fell down in a tangle of arms, legs, blanket, and leaves. The wind made everything harder to sort out, and finally Cain got his hands around Belinda's shoulders and pulled her upright, leaning them both back against the tree. His chest heaved and he could feel the resistance in her body. But he had to see her face, had to be sure she was really all right. With a powerful lift, he pulled her onto his lap, angling her head so the silvery light of the moon gave him as much illumination as possible.

"Now don't panic. I just want to make sure you're okay and then I'll give you the gun."

"The gun? *The gun?*" Belinda grabbed the thick, woolly collar of his coat and yanked till their faces were nose to nose. "You totally insane man. Don't ever say that to me again. I'm not worried about protecting myself from you; I'm worried about protecting you from me."

"God, Belinda." He groaned, clapping his gloveless hand over her forehead. "You're not making any sense, honey; you must be slipping into some type of hypothermic delusion."

In a frenzy of motion Cain unbuttoned his coat and hauled her inside. He grabbed the end of the blanket Belinda had taken off her bed at the cabin and draped it over her, stuffing it up under her legs.

When he finally settled against the tree, Belinda could feel her body lifting and falling with each labored breath he took. His hands began running up and down her back, generating more heat than he could possibly imagine. The man had said it again.

Honey.

Maybe there *was* a chance to crack his defenses if she pushed hard enough. Somehow she knew it was now or never. *What about your fear? What about the pain?* a tiny voice of caution whispered as it had before. Well, it was too late. She had the Brown blood, so her fate was sealed. She loved him. Crazy? Unwise? Undoubtedly. But how could she not love a man who offered to let her shoot him if he got out of line? How could she not love a man who needed it so much and thought he didn't deserve it?

"Cain?" she said softly from under his chin where he had fitted her head.

"Hmmm?"

Belinda snaked her hands around to his back, pushing up under the fluffy sheepskin lining, and dragged her fingernails down the slight valley of his spine. In an instant the most powerful, masculine man she had ever known froze under her touch, and her own wavering feminine confidence rose a notch. With slow, rhythmic motion, she pressed her fingertips against the hard muscles in small circles and ducked her head free so she could look into his eyes, the dark windows to his soul. The light wasn't very good, but it seemed as if all there was had concentrated and haloed around them.

She closed her eyes and took in a steadying lungful of air. Her hands crept up higher on his flannel shirt and urged him closer so the wind wouldn't make this even more difficult.

"I don't have hypothermia and I'm not afraid of you, Cain. That isn't why I left. That isn't why I didn't want to come down."

His eyelids shuttered half-closed and his eyebrows pulled into twin slashes as if underlining his confusion and suspicion.

"This," she whispered, deftly sliding one hand forward under his arm and up lightly over his ruined cheek to weave into his hair. "This is what I was afraid of—what I was afraid I would do again. Because I have this problem with being too open and then it's too late."

Cain felt Belinda's warm, moist lips mark him like a brand. The icy stiffness of his mouth instantly changed. His entire world instantly changed. Every inch of his body that her body touched began to sizzle.

And Cain was afraid, too. Afraid because once again Belinda's honesty had voiced his exact feeling—the exact turmoil of emotions twisting around the need that was turning his body to stone. Except now, at this scorching, heart-pounding moment, he was more afraid that it would never happen again, that it would never be enough.

"Oh, God, Belinda, when I knew you were gone—" He couldn't hold it in and whispered the tortured words against her mouth before banishing the fear by sipping away her very breath and taking her lips with his own. Over and over he kissed her, unable to believe that she was safe and that she had willingly come back into his arms.

She shifted on his lap, twisting closer until the gentle fullness of her breasts pressed flush against his chest, and her hips rocked with searing accuracy over that most exquisitely sensitive part of him. Cain shuddered and ran the tip of his tongue over her lips, waiting for her sign. Waiting to see if she wanted him as much as he wanted her. Waiting to see if she would welcome him in this intimate way once more.

Her mouth opened under his and her silky tongue danced and swirled over and around, meeting him boldly and then darting away until he followed deeply into the honeyed recesses of her mouth. Cain could not hold back the moan that rumbled up from the dark, lonely place inside him—a place whose very existence he had tried to deny for so long. Belinda burrowed both of her hands deeply into his hair, drawing him closer, tracing tiny, needy patterns against that tender flesh until shivery ripples undulated through his body.

Dear God, it had been too long. Too long and if it didn't stop soon . . . it would kill him.

Chapter Six

If this didn't stop soon she would die. Belinda knew it. She would simply melt into a bubbling pool of liquid longing and cease to be. Even now it seemed doubtful that she would ever be able to walk again. The taste of him, the feel of his whiskers brushing against her cheeks, the honest evidence that he was moved by this—moved by her: less than gorgeous, less than stunning Belinda Brown. Yet Cain held her as if she were more vital than air. Never in her life had she felt more a woman, both fragile and strong.

The rough-skinned hands that touched her with such intensity and reverence made her feel beautiful and perfect. Beautiful and perfect for him as he was beautiful and perfect for her. But would he believe that when he wasn't burning?

Belinda pulled away, and Cain slowly, reluctantly opened his eyes. He looked at her as if he'd been dreaming, and she had to make sure he knew it was reality. Small white puffs of vapory air filled the space between them while they both struggled to recover. Belinda saw the old wariness steal across the face she had tried not to love. She felt a quiver deep inside her body. An aching longing threaded with fear and desire, hunger and insecurity. If, later, this turned out to be foolish, so be it. But she would always regret it if she didn't act on the magic of this moment. If she didn't put her money where her mouth was and believe in the power of love.

Cain dropped his hands to his sides as she swiveled around and straddled his lap. Belinda's sore ankle caused her leg to buckle, and she inadvertently skimmed across the hard length of him. His eyebrows jumped an inch. She smiled—she couldn't help it. This hunky, brilliant, and sometimes feared business tycoon wanted her—*her*. He glanced down with a horribly blank look in his eyes and then away.

Good gosh, she'd thought the whole thing a miracle and her smile had hurt him, embarrassed him! Well, darn it, this time when she was finished with him, Cain Devlin would never misunderstand again. The scarred side of his face was turned to her, and he rested a hand in the curve of his belly.

"Oh, Cain, look at your hand." He didn't.

Tenderly Belinda lifted it up and peered closely at the evidence of dried blood. The stubborn man who'd just kissed her into flames refused to respond, so she reached over for the backpack and rifled through it till she found some antiseptic wipes and some bandages. It took five minutes to take care of the wound. Not once did Cain glance at her. But his indifference had come a few kisses too late. Belinda had pretty hard evidence that she'd gotten to the guy—as amazing as that fact was.

She slipped off his other glove and carried his injured hand to her cheek and held it there for a moment, then cradled it in the palm of hers and pressed her lips softly in the center. A fine trembling registered against her lips. Belinda went up on her knees and accidentally brushed over him again, but the jerking swing of his head and the look on his face told her he hadn't thought it was accidental.

"Is this a game for you?" he asked low and harsh, bringing up both of his hands to grip her upper arms.

At eye level, with only inches between them, she smiled, understanding that he was asking about more than this exact minute. "No, Cain, this may very well turn out to be one of the most important moments in my life."

Before he even realized what she was going to do, it was happening. His fingers tightened spasmodically, holding on now instead of preparing to push away. Her hands threaded his hair out of the way so she could . . . she could . . . drop a butterfly kiss at the corner of his eye and brush the edge of his lashes with her tongue. She rubbed her nose along the length of his, all the while sighing with soft little catches and filling his senses with the smell of strawberries and her sweet breath.

The trembling that had begun the second her mouth touched his palm threatened to break out of control, and Cain was more afraid than he'd ever been. If she didn't mean this . . . If it was some kind of mercy . . . God help him. And then her mouth was on him, on the ugly, repulsive part of him he thought no woman could ever accept, let alone . . . Cain blinked his eyes against the sudden burning there.

With every brush of her lips he felt himself unraveling. Slowly, deliberately, she followed the path of each scar, leaving a trail of moist kisses that radiated heat in the cold night air. And the tremors became a shaking, a shaking so bad he had to—had to—haul her snug against him and pull his legs up behind her, trapping her in the vee of his body, to stop it.

Cain nuzzled his face into the crook of her neck, resting the taut line that was his mouth next to the warm, smooth skin there. He could not look into those big brown eyes— not on the knife edge of a need so great it terrified him. If she left him now—if she did not truly mean this—he would surely die.

And it was about more than sex, although his body screamed for release; it was about more than lust, although it raged through his veins; it was his heart that was bursting. It was the walls around his heart that were shaking into pieces.

Belinda held him as fiercely as he held her. She wrapped

her arms around his shoulders and moved her mouth next to his ear. Soft wisps of their hair lifted on the dying wind and fluttered against her face. Cain's whiskers prickled along her cheek, sending primal messages that reached deep into her female soul. This was her other half, the match that would make a whole. This man in her arms needed what only *her* heart and *her* body could give.

"Remember I told you I was trying to protect you from me?" Belinda whispered and felt the nod, the slide of his stubbled cheek over hers. "I was right, wasn't I? This is pretty scary."

Cain's swallow was audible and his voice cracked. "Crazy is what it is. We don't even know each other. This whole thing is—It's only been two damn days, honey. . . ."

He paused and Belinda squeezed her eyes shut, waiting for his reaction.

"Oh, God," he murmured. "I suppose you noticed that and—" He stopped and drew in a rattled breath. She could feel his lungs expand. "I suppose you've noticed the—the shaking, too."

Belinda smiled and relaxed against his body. What did the man think she was going to say? Cain Devlin needed a lot of patient tutoring. Luckily she was very willing to work for fringe benefits alone. Belinda slid a hand down into the open collar of Cain's shirt to rest against the warm flesh at the base of his throat. Her sensitive fingertips brushed across a fan of springy chest hair, and her thumb stroked the soft skin in the dip of his collarbone. His pulse pounded away.

"Cain," she said quietly, leaning back and looking him straight in the eye. "The only reason I'm not in teeny-eeny pieces on the ground right now is because you've been holding me so tight."

He groaned and tipped his head back against the tree.

"Maybe 'this' is because we're both so relieved," he mumbled.

"That could be part of it. But wouldn't a thank-you have

been enough? I mean you don't see every rescuer and rescuee on the news acting like this. And it has nothing to do with Prince, Cain."

"I believe you, Belinda, but—"

"Let's worry about that part tomorrow, okay?"

"Then maybe it's because you, you feel sorry for me."

"No way—"

"Listen," he said, running his hands up to her shoulders and drilling her with an intense look. "I don't mean to insult you, but you have to admit it's possible. You even told me so back at the cabin—"

"But wait—"

"You've been scared and we've both been strung out for lots of reasons since you arrived, and maybe we've both been lonely, so this happened. I'd like—"

"What, Cain?" Belinda asked, trying to keep the thread of panic from sounding in her voice. "What would you like?"

He dropped his hands. "Nothing. How can anything come from the way this started? In the dark it's always easier to fool yourself. You don't know what you're getting into, Belinda."

"Tell me then. Tell me what I'm getting into. Give us both a chance to see where this might lead."

He didn't speak again and she awkwardly moved off him to the far side of the tree, not touching him.

"I'm going to sleep. Without a light we're stuck till morning." She wrapped the blanket around her and curled onto her side, exhausted and battered. Patience had never been so hard for her. Proving herself to Cain Devlin was more painful than she'd imagined. He was not an easy man to love. Five minutes of thick, heavy silence passed as agonizingly slowly as a butterfly struggling through molasses. For the first time since Cain had found her, Belinda felt the throbbing in her ankle.

Then he cleared his throat. She opened her eyes and

watched the wide hands resting on his thighs curl into fists.

"I'd like to believe this is real, Belinda. I'd like to believe that it will still be real in the morning, in the light of day. But it's too soon and too damn much to expect. Talk about a fairy tale."

She sat up and gingerly folded her legs to the side, arranging the blanket around her shoulders like a giant shawl. In measured tones she spoke, praying he would truly hear her words.

"You're right; I've never felt so much so fast either. But happy endings don't just happen for characters in stories. You're forgetting I've seen you in the light of day, Cain."

"Yeah, well, not with this"—he lifted a hand and waved it between the two of them—"in mind."

"If this"—she mimicked his gesture—"means our kissing and whatever, I've done that in the light of day, too."

"But not thinking it might lead to something."

"I don't dole out charity kisses, Cain Devlin," Belinda sputtered and knee-walked to his side, pressing an insistent finger into the center of his chest. "And if you think this is about your face, let me give you a news flash, buddy. You're not the only one worried about not being perfect. In fact you've already made reference to one of my inadequacies."

"What?"

"You know perfectly well."

"I don't. Really."

"Pul-eeze."

"Belinda, I'm ashamed to say I remember you saying something about inadequacies, but . . ." He lifted his hands and shrugged, but before he could let them fall, she grabbed one and pressed it over the rise of her breast.

"Remember now? You said I wasn't your type."

Belinda's bravado faltered at the flex of his fingers, and her voice grew hoarse and breathy. "And now, if you're thinking about this going somewhere, well . . ." She swallowed and tried not to tremble. "Well, *you* certainly can't say you've seen *me* in the light of day, so what should I think?"

Cain was very grateful it was so dark. For a grown man, thirty-three years old, the feel of a woman's breast should not be able to turn him inside out like this. Yet his body had gone rigid, his eyes felt like lasers, and his hand would surely start glowing red any second. It had been over three years since he had touched a woman in this intimate manner. And not only had the woman initiated it, she was lecturing him in such a way that it should not be one bit arousing. But it damn well was.

"You should think I'm a bastard, honey. And exactly what you've heard. Then get the hell away from me before I lie and hurt you again."

His hand curved around her so gently Belinda almost missed the movement, but instinctively she leaned into his touch. He groaned and let his hand fall away. The cold air rushed into the void and she shivered at the loss, shivered at what she was about to ask. And she was oh so glad it was dark.

"Is this going to lead to something?"

Cain's long legs were stretched straight out in front of him, his hands loosely folded low on his stomach. Belinda started to sit back on her haunches, and gasped at the pressure on her ankle. Before she could reposition her protesting foot Cain had her flat on her bottom and was gently supporting her ankle with one hand and probing it with the other.

"Good God, what are you wearing on your feet?"

"The best I had, Cain," she returned, vividly aware that he'd avoided her question.

"Well, running into the woods so unprepared was not a very smart thing to do."

"Yeah, I know."

Belinda paused and registered the slow slide of her socks baring her ankle and the warm sensation of his fingers stroking her cold, aching skin. But there were other parts of her body aching for his touch in a way she had never felt before, and her heart would not let her give up. All she had was this one enchanted night. A bizarre bubble of laughter caught in her throat. This night was about as far from her childhood idea of *enchanted* as possible; nevertheless, she could not shake off the feeling that their time was running out. She simply had to press for everything and anything he would give her.

"Just think," she added, scooting forward and angling her upper body closer to his bent head. "If I'd only had sneakers you would never have found me."

Never have found me . . . Never have found me . . . Never have found me.

Cain reluctantly raised his head to Belinda. The mystic light of the moon glowed in the dark pools of her eyes. Her wind-tousled hair framed her face like ribbons of gilt and shadow. Maybe there was such a thing as magic. How else could he explain this beautiful woman cloaked in silver and velvet who had dropped into his life out of nowhere? The one woman, the only woman, who'd been able to breach his defenses and make him dream again of all he'd thought lost.

The air was still now, swept clear of clouds, revealing the heavens liberally glittered with stars and leaving no cumulus blanket to lessen the chill.

Never?

Never was a far more powerful word than all the shoulds and oughts battling inside his head. If never meant a lifetime spent like the last five years . . .

"It's cold." Cain pulled Belinda onto his lap and had to arrange her limp body into a comfortable position against his chest. Odd, as he tucked the blanket around both their legs, she seemed to be barely breathing.

"You're gonna go numb with me on you like this."

"That's what I'm hoping for, honey," he sighed against her hair with a hitch in his gravelly voice that almost sounded like strained amusement.

Belinda stayed still as a statue, afraid to break the spell, afraid to react to the abrupt change in Cain. An odd hush had fallen over the forest. The cacophony stirred by the wind had dwindled away until only faint rustles and scratches drifted through the trees. Although the temperature had dropped even lower, she felt amazingly warm. Being wrapped up in Cain's arms and the blanket was like having her own customized cocoon. She was warm, but anxious. Belinda realized she had been holding her breath, waiting for some explanation, some clue as to what this man she cared so much about was thinking.

"My parents divorced when I was seven, so it was just me and Mom from then on—"

Oh, sweet heaven, he was telling, talking. An instantaneous burn ached at the back of her throat and behind her eyes. Belinda had to move then. Had to. Cain's heavy coat was still unbuttoned so she wiggled back inside it and circled an arm around his back, just above his belt, where his torso came away from the tree trunk. She hesitantly rested her other hand on the soft flannel that covered his heart and slowly brought her head down to his shoulder, her lips close to his ear. Then to her mortification, a loud, very identifiable rumbling filled the pause in Cain's story that her maneuvering had prompted.

"Belinda?"

"Keep talking, Cain," she whispered, her lips brushing his ear. But her cursed stomach gurgled again. "Please ignore my body and talk to me." It happened again. "Oh, darn it," she grumbled, lifting her head and pulling away. "I guess this is the kind of moment designed for the salad-type woman, since they're used to long stretches without food."

Even though Belinda's eyes had adjusted pretty well to the dark, it was difficult to gauge Cain's reaction. This close, it was easy to hear a garbled, strangled sound coming from deep in his chest. The vibrations hummed into her body. Heck! The man had finally started to open up and she'd ruined it. He tipped his head back against the tree and covered his eyes with a hand, leaning completely away from her—a body-language message if ever she'd seen one. Belinda gathered herself to move.

She didn't make it an inch.

She was yanked up against the hard, wide wall of Cain's shaking chest and pressed into the crook of his neck so fast it took her a few startled gulps of air to realize the man was laughing.

Laughing.

The sound was rusty and ragged from a long period of disuse, yet it flowed over and around Belinda like the most glorious swell of a Vivaldi concerto.

"Belinda," he got out unevenly, his mouth moving against her hair. "Since the moment I first touched you I have been trying to ignore your body, and honey, I gotta tell you it's damn well impossible. I don't know where this is headed. I don't know what—or if—I can give, but I do know there is something going on here that is beyond my understanding. Having you in my arms is a miracle, every delicious ounce of you. You're honest, and from the inside out, you set me on fire. And . . . I have a surprise for you."

Cain released her and twisted to reach the backpack. He pressed a narrow rectangle-shaped object into Belinda's hand and she quickly determined it was a granola bar. With a knuckle he lifted her chin and feathered his firm, warm mouth across hers in a light, fleeting motion. She reached up to his face, cupping his cheeks to bring him back for more, but Cain palmed her head and tucked it under his chin.

"Any more of that and I'll lose it, honey. And I want you to be sure. Really, really sure before . . . Go on and eat first; then if you still want to know what you're getting into, I'll—"

Belinda turned her head to give Cain a kiss on his neck and felt his Adam's apple bob against her lips. Her heart was so filled with love, so filled with fragile hope. Tenderly she rested a fingertip at the top of each of his scars and caressed her way down their separate paths.

"I can't think of anyplace I'd rather be or anything I'd rather hear."

Cain reverently kissed the palm of her healing hand and, brick by brick, began to tear down the walls around his heart.

Chapter Seven

Cain slowly became aware of sunlight on his eyelids. The warm red glow pulled him into consciousness and he rolled over, unable to stop a muffled groan. Hell, every muscle in his body hurt. It had taken them most of the previous day to get back to the cabin, and they'd only had a couple hours of sleep that long, cold night before. He dragged a hand down his face, rubbing it over his three-day-old beard. Not one more kiss until he got rid of this scratchy thing. Well, maybe just one more.

With a broad sweep of his arm he searched for a certain brown-eyed woman's presence. He cracked open an eye, realized she was gone, and painfully jerked up before noting the sound of the shower down the hall. Cain fell back onto the navy sheets and stacked his hands behind his head. What was she thinking after a night and a day of almost nonstop revelations—his and hers?

Well, she'd stayed the night in his bed; that had to mean something. Cain glanced down at his forest green sweatpants with a rueful smirk. No, they hadn't made love. They'd been too exhausted and too wrung out emotionally and physically. But in some ways what they had shared had been more intimate, more fulfilling.

That night in the forest, Cain's talking had started like a hairline crack in a dam that grows wider and wider with the incredible pressure building behind the fissure. Once he began, he could not seem to stop. The lonely years after his mother died and his fight to work his way through college poured out, and he worried he would drown Belinda in boring details. But her eyes spoke silent words of compassion, understanding, and encouragement. She, too, had lost her loved ones. She, too, had felt lonely and adrift. She, too, had rejoiced in finding a true friend.

Cain still couldn't believe he'd told her everything about the catastrophe with Prince, including the mysterious information he'd received over the years and the last tip that had led to the buyout he was about to make—the deal that had sent Helen Chalmers into his office a few weeks ago in a rage. He'd even confessed the information he'd gathered on Cindy and the fragments of Belinda's life he'd been able to garner. She'd stopped then, in midstride, and stepped away from the arm he'd been supporting her sore ankle with.

For a moment, a surge of gut-twisting dread had roiled in his belly, and then she'd lifted those sweet, candy-colored eyes to his and proceeded to tell him that now she could tell less and he could tell more. And did he realize it only proved, that after all he'd thought, he was still looking out for Prince? Cain had not been able to make her see that he'd had a less than noble motive. She simply would not believe it. He simply could not believe her. The woman was totally without guile—someone to trust at your back.

When they had finally reached the cabin, it seemed like they'd been gone a month. They had relived their entire lives in little more than a day, and he'd never felt so close to another person. With every fiber of his being he wanted to take them the last step, to bring their bodies as close as their thoughts, but one look in Belinda's weary, pain-rimmed eyes and he knew neither of them was ready. He'd given her some aspirin and she'd showered and gone to her bed.

However, after he'd showered and collapsed onto his king-size mattress, Cain had not been able to relax. The space he used to crave was too empty; his arms felt too empty. His body had been next to hers for so many continuous hours that now something seemed to be missing and he could not sleep. It was at that groggy, irrational moment that he realized he loved her. Loved her so completely and so unexpectedly that he'd lain frozen on his back, incapable of any movement.

But while his mind and heart were still stunned, his body had responded to the revelation, and he found himself lifting Belinda into his arms and carrying her back to his room. She was wearing one of his T-shirts and it left very little to the imagination. He'd trembled as he curled her along his side. Without opening her eyes, she'd wiggled her nose against the hair on his chest, and a feathery sigh had ruffled over his skin. Finally it felt right and he began to drift off.

"Don't look," she'd surprisingly breathed in a thready whisper.

"I just need to hold you, honey, that's all," Cain had answered to reassure her that he was not about to make love to her under these conditions.

" 'Kay, jus don look. Wannabe beautiful first."

"You are beautiful, sweetheart."

"No. You'llsee. Makeup . . . shavemylegs."

Cain had laughed again then. It came from deep inside where he had always hurt the most. He'd gathered her limp body up in his arms and knew not a woman in his past could hold a candle to the one he held now.

Cain blinked back to the present. He realized the shower had stopped some time ago and he sat up, swinging his legs over the side of the bed. He clasped his hands between his knees and stared at the door. They still had this mess with Prince to get through before they could really concentrate on what had happened between them. He stood and ran both hands distractedly through his hair. It was midmorning. The glorious spring view out his picture window sparkled with the rich jewel tones of nature. Sparkled with sunlight.

The unrelenting light of day.

A swift swirl of nausea spun in circles in his stomach. What in the world would his honest, candid beauty have to say after last night?

Belinda had been up cooking for an hour and a half before she slipped into the shower. She hadn't wanted to wake Cain because she just wasn't ready to face him yet. They had both revealed so much that now she was worried he would regret it. Regret trusting her. Really, she thought as she blew-dry her hair and pulled on her freshly washed haute couture gray sweats, they'd only known each other a handful of days. Of course, that handful had been incredibly intense and more than enough time for her to fall head over heels in love.

She tiptoed down the stairs to the kitchen and took a long, satisfied sniff, letting the yummy blend of smells and the charming room soothe her. Belinda grabbed a quilted pot holder and checked the cinnamon-apple cobbler in the oven. She winced at the pot of stew on the stove and the pan of corn bread covered with a dishtowel. Well, he had offered her the use of the kitchen, and cooking destressed her. Boy, had she needed some destressing.

Belinda walked over to the bay window and followed the tree line at the base of the mountains that circled the grassy meadow. What in the world would he think after last night? She'd vaguely recalled being carried into his bed, however, the memory played in her head as if it had been filmed underwater. Belinda rubbed her hands up and down her arms and bounced her forehead lightly against the window. Could she have actually mentioned shaving her legs? A mortified shudder ran up her back. Well, he'd been the one to wonder about seeing things in the light of day. The good old light of day that would soon reveal Belinda Brown au naturel. Had she really pointed out her dependence on makeup? She prayed with all her heart that the fragile fiery bonds forged between them were as

105

real as they'd seemed deep in the night. If only he would laugh again.

But just in case things didn't work out, Belinda had gambled on making sure that one thing would. Right after she'd woken up, she'd made a short phone call. She patted the inside pocket at her hip and hoped he would forgive her for breaking her promise. Prince's grandmother hadn't wanted to give her the number where the couple was spending their honeymoon. But Belinda had insisted she had to have it. It was crucial. Helen Chalmers had asked lots of odd questions. She'd kept demanding until Belinda agreed that there really had been a plan to kidnap Cindy and that it had strangely involved Cain Devlin.

But before she could explain, Mrs. Chalmers hung up. Which was just as well because Belinda knew she had to get off the phone before the man sleeping upstairs discovered what she was doing. She would give him the number and let him decide what he wanted. No more pushing.

"Ummm, something smells good. I'm starving."

Cain came through the hinged door with a smile pasted on his face and his heart pumping double time. Was the dream going to end and the nightmare he'd been living about to begin again? Belinda swung around at the sound of his voice. Her big brown eyes were watchful and waiting. A sexy, tousled pile of shining, maple-sugar hair crowned the top of her head, with scattered tendrils caressing her neck and whispering along her cheeks. Cain moved closer and saw a warm, peachy flush spread over angel-kissed cheeks. The woman looked good enough to eat . . . and he was starving.

So hungry that he did exactly what he'd promised himself not to do. He had her in his arms and his mouth open over hers in seconds. Asking in the most elemental of ways if this was real, if they were real. The sweet and spicy flavor of cinnamon and apples drove him wild. This was the taste of his woman; the one he would always crave. He lifted her up against his desperate body and braced her on the counter, moving into the space between her legs. He gloried in the feel of her curling around him and in the welcome of her response.

Those soft, healing hands wove into his loose hair and sent arrows of desire pulsing through him. Cain's hands cupped the back of her head and angled it so he could fit their mouths together more closely. The sound of rough, ragged breathing echoed in his ears. Sweet, sweet strokes and sips, tongues and lips. It was real. It was!

"Well," Belinda puffed, collapsing back against the pine cupboard doors. "That . . . answers my . . . question . . . I guess."

Cain tipped his head back for a moment and drew in a harsh breath. He raised his gaze to hers and, for the first time in ages, smiled openly, without reservation. He leaned closer until he could whisper next to her damp lips, "Mine, too."

Belinda couldn't hide her tears, but it didn't bother her. She didn't know if Cain was ready for them, but her heart was too full. If she didn't release a little of the emotional pressure building inside her, she might burst wide open and tell him she loved him before he was ready to hear it. Cain Devlin had made a lot of changes in a very short time, and it was just as she'd told him: the beast's roar came from pain, and love could heal it. Belinda traced his smile with the tip of a finger and she knew by the look in his eyes that they were both thinking the same miraculous thing: His smile was back.

"That was unbelievable, Belinda." Cain grinned as he pushed back from the table. "Do you always cook like this?"

"Are you kidding? You'd have to crane me from room to room by now if I did."

His laugh rolled out like a well-oiled machine, and Belinda's happy heart hitched and stuttered like a rusty one when he chuckled about the honesty of his woman. His big, calloused hand stretched across the smooth pine, open-palmed, waiting.

And the phone rang. Sharp. Shrill. Insistent.

Cain didn't move a muscle. The steady look in his hazel eyes never wavered, but the persistent ring slowly flattened his mouth into a straight line. Belinda's heart stuttered again, but this time with fear. *Yes,* his eyes silently spoke. *The world hasn't gone away. Does it make any difference?*

She answered with a wide smile and rested her fingertips on his, then slowly slid them over his warm skin until she could rub her thumb across the heel of his hand. *No, my love. It makes no difference.*

His fingers tightened like a vise, but Belinda didn't pull away from his punishing grip. Instead she lifted her thumb and pressed it against the corded tendons in his wrist.

"Come with me. Let's go for a walk," he said in a low voice. But it was not a question. It was far more than that.

It was a choice between Cain and the world. And it was the easiest decision she'd ever made.

Belinda was hiding in the kitchen and she was bugged with herself. Being mealymouthed was just not her style, but then, she had never been in love before. She dried her hands on the dishtowel and put the leftover sandwich fixings back in the fridge. They'd had a long, relatively silent walk. After the first few minutes Cain must have realized he was crushing her hand. He'd murmured his apologies, kissed her crumpled palm, and then slipped his arm around her waist, supporting her still-unsteady gait.

When they had returned she'd tried to feed him and even joked about him keeping his strength up since he had to cart her around so much. He smiled, but just barely.

Okay, so fine. They had some explaining to do and some people to straighten out. Belinda squared her shoulders, resolved to be herself and meet the problem head-on. Cain Devlin simply wasn't used to having someone by his side in hard times and now was the perfect moment to show him the difference it could make.

She hesitated in the doorway. Although it was only midafternoon, dark clouds had rolled in, casting an unnatural grayness over the room. Fingery shadows crept through the windows. Cain sat on the sofa facing the fire, the only light in the room flickering red and gold. He looked at her for a long moment. Looked hard, the intensity etched on his beautiful, imperfect face. Then he opened his arms.

Belinda went straight to him and he pulled her close, wrapping both arms tight around her. He cradled her head in the curve of his shoulder and caught her chin on the edge of his hand. Something just a little wild leaped and fell with the flames reflected in his eyes.

"You do know that you are the most honest, most beautiful woman I have ever known." She grinned in protest and he carried her back against the couch, lying full-out alongside her. "Beautiful inside and out. Every inch of you perfect." Cain lowered his face and kissed her tenderly. "Believe me, honey. If nothing else, believe that."

"I will, but only if you believe you are, too." His long, dark hair fell around them like a sable veil. Cain's eyes narrowed, then went round. "You see." She laughed quietly, bringing her hand to his ruined cheek. "Beauty is truly in the eye of the beholder. When stars are in your eyes things look different."

He clenched his jaw and willed away the ache in his throat. "I—" He swallowed hard. "I think something led me to you in the forest, Belinda. I think maybe we were meant to find each other. I want—"

The pounding on the door downstairs was so loud Cain stopped in midsentence. He surged to his feet just as a medium-built man with a crew cut appeared from the stairwell.

"Why in hell haven't you been answering your phone, Cain? Two police cars are about twenty minutes behind me with a warrant for your arrest!"

"Paul, what in God's name are you talking about?"

"Dammit! The woman *is* here! Man, we've got to think of something to say and fast."

Cain grabbed his assistant by the arm. "Look, the phone was unplugged for a while and we"—he glanced at a white-faced Belinda—"we haven't been here. Is this about Ms. Brown?"

"Listen, Helen Chalmers has been screaming for two days about a botched kidnapping of Cynthia Jones. She pointed the finger at you and must have called in all her markers with the authorities. The office has been crawling with cops, only they didn't really have anything but hearsay to go on until yesterday." Paul broke Cain's hold and sagged onto the couch. "Yesterday afternoon Mrs. Chalmers brought a letter to the station with your signature and some demands. And then"—Paul turned his head and stared at Belinda with a look of such disgust she stepped back—"she told the police that a Ms. Brown, Cindy's best friend, was helping her prove your involvement and that she was just waiting for a call with your location. Helen Chalmers got that call this morning, Cain. It was traced back to here."

Oh, no! What had she done? "Cain, look at me." Belinda took a step toward him and tried to reason in a low, strained voice. "You know that isn't true. *You know that isn't true.*"

"Boss, for gosh sakes, come on, let's leave the woman and get out of here!" Paul latched on to Cain's shoulder, ready to steer him to the stairwell.

Belinda watched with growing panic as the man she loved metamorphosized before her eyes. His face went blank, set, hard. He shrugged off Paul's hold as if he were nothing more than some annoying gnat. A cold, razor-sharp expression she hadn't seen since the beginning cut through to her heart like a laser. They hadn't had long enough.

Oh dear God! She could hear a siren. Paul ran down the stairs and started to yell. Belinda couldn't catch her breath, couldn't get any air, couldn't feel her arms or legs.

"Cain, please." She lurched forward, her words ending on a sob.

He held up a hand to stop her, to keep her away.

"Just tell me, yes or no." He dropped his head back on his neck and then raised it again. "Did you call?"

Heavy bootfalls thundered on the stairs, but Cain never moved. How could she explain in twenty seconds?

"Yes." He flinched as if he'd been slapped. "But wait! It's not how Mrs. Chalmers says. It's not. Please believe me. I'd never do that. Not even if we'd hadn't fallen in—"

"Stop!" Cain exploded with such quiet force Belinda's heart jumped to her throat. "For God's sake, don't make it more than it was. Cindy is your best friend, your family. I understand you had to protect her. I can understand revenge. But don't ask me to believe. No more stories."

"Boss!" Paul broke in. "Do something!"

"No," Cain said, still holding her gaze. "Let them come."

That was the last time Belinda saw him clearly. Uniformed men and detectives in dark suits suddenly appeared and surrounded Cain. She staggered back against the wall trying desperately to gain some composure, but the spine-chilling clank of metal scraping metal broke through her stupor. *Oh help, help, help.* They'd handcuffed him. They were taking away the man she loved. Her stubborn, novice love who was protecting himself the only way he could: by becoming the beast.

Belinda went ballistic, but no one would listen. They thought she was having some posttraumatic breakdown. One policeman, the one they'd ordered to take her statement, even suggested she was probably suffering from that captive-captor syndrome.

No way was she going let this happen. Her heart was

being ripped out of her body and preparing to trail down the stairs after her beloved beast. She sat huddled on the couch watching for an opening. There had to be a way to get to him. A detective walked over to the windows to use the phone and gestured for her guard.

Belinda was down the stairs and out the door before she heard them sound the alarm. Cain's wrists were shackled and two uniformed men stood on either side, waiting for him to duck into the open patrol car.

"Wait!" she screamed, but the window was closed between them by the time she got there. Belinda pounded her hands on the cold glass until he turned his head. The empty look in his eyes killed her. "I'm coming, Cain! Do you hear me? I'm coming. Believe me! Believe me—" Tears splashed down her cheeks, the words broken with sobs.

A heavy hand fell on her shoulder to tug her backward. Desperately she flattened a palm on the glass as the engine roared to life. Cain turned his face away and she saw the scars. They were nothing compared to the wounds he carried inside. Wounds she could heal. She would heal.

"Please, love," she pleaded under her breath. "Try, try to believe." Then, just as the car began to roll forward, Cain moved. He never even glanced at her, but for an instant his hand lifted to the window and met hers. Perfectly.

A sharp succession of door slams cracked like a spray of gunfire and two of the cars sped away. Belinda stood very still, her burning palm dangling at her side. She'd been hit. Hit everywhere. There just wasn't any blood yet.

It had taken Belinda four hours to get back to San Leandro. After she'd pulled herself together with steel bands of control, she'd finally gotten through to the police and explained her version of the story. No, she was not pressing charges. She had only one purpose: to reach Helen Chalmers and get Cain out of jail. Paul Johnson had gone ahead, gone with the first group, so she had mechanically locked up the house and forced herself to be calm on the long ride back to the city with the officers.

However, just before leaving, she'd made one more short phone call, praying it would repair the damage she'd done with the last one. Miraculously, Cindy had answered and quickly gotten Prince on the other line. Somehow Belinda coherently explained what had happened, including Helen Chalmers's bizarre accusations and the informant who'd been tipping Cain. The silence that had boomed from their end had chilled her to the bone. They hadn't heard a thing about Belinda's disappearance. Nothing. A wooden-sounding Prince assured her they'd be on the next plane.

But she hadn't been able to wait.

Belinda screeched to a halt at the very doors of Chalmers House, the huge Greek revival mansion built by Prince's great-grandfather at the turn of the century. She slammed the door of her Geo Prism and marched toward the alabaster marble columns that stood at attention like giant sentries guarding the castle. She was not about to be stopped.

With a balled fist, Belinda pounded on the oak-and-beveled-glass door that had probably cost more than her car. She couldn't help but catch a glimpse of her reflection. A wild-haired, battered Joan of Arc in baggy gray sweats storming the citadel at eight o'clock at night. It was undoubtedly a social faux pas; however, it was the most minor of her upcoming offenses. Calling the grandam of San Leandro society a liar was not going to go down easy.

The door finally opened, but the prune-faced butler hesitated at her request to speak with Mrs. Chalmers. Belinda pressed, claiming she had an urgent message from Princeton, and since the man had admitted her a number of times with Cindy, he reluctantly directed her to a private sitting room.

Belinda paced. She couldn't sit and think of Cain behind bars, believing she'd betrayed him. With complete disregard, she tracked over the Oriental carpet and its pattern of blue and mauve flowers edged with two lines of gold. An elegant cherry desk and a chair upholstered with needlepoint were arranged at the curved end of the room to take advantage of the large-paned window. It was draped with Irish lace from molded ceiling to polished hardwood floor.

The room shouted of money. Screamed of money and privilege, and fear pooled in Belinda's stomach. How could she fight this? *Prince, Cindy, hurry!* She wrung her hands and clasped them tightly. Somehow she felt that with every minute slipping away, Cain was slipping farther away, too.

Belinda stumbled to the small cherry-trimmed settee and purposely ran her sweaty palms over the blue and mauve brocade. Where in the world was Mrs. Chalmers? Seconds later, the diminutive white-haired woman swept into the room. Belinda slid to the edge of cushion, her back ramrod straight. Prince's grandmother sat in the small, matching wing chair and smoothed a heavily jeweled hand over her cream-colored linen slacks.

"My, Ms. Brown, this is a most unexpected visit at a most uncivilized hour." Her tone was pleasant, but her eyes were assessing and narrow. "You certainly look as if you've been through an ordeal."

"All thanks to you, Mrs. Chalmers," Belinda challenged, tossing her social graces figuratively out the window. Helen abruptly pressed a palm to the base of her throat in an agitated manner. "Why did you lie to the police, Mrs. Chalmers? Why did you tell them that I was working with you to trap Cain Devlin? It's all completely ridiculous."

"When Roberta told me what was happening at the reception, I—I naturally assumed you'd expose whoever was behind this despicable plot to hurt your dear friend. It's possible I exaggerated our connection a bit." Helen Chalmers raised the fine-boned hand to her chin and rested the curve of her knuckles beneath it. "But perhaps the vile, beastly Mr. Devlin had found some, shall we say, earthy way to obscure what he's done."

Anger flashed through Belinda like a brushfire. How dare this old biddy say that about Cain! About her! She forced her trembling hands flat on her knees. "I love Cindy like a sister and I would do anything to help her, but Cain Devlin is not—Wait a minute. I just realized. . . ." Open-mouthed, Belinda shook her head. "They were on their honeymoon. I—I was so worried I missed it. You never told Prince, did you? You didn't let Roberta tell Prince?"

"Roberta? She went off with a friend before the reception was even over. And there was no need for Prince to know. Besides, it all worked out anyway. It's a matter for the police now."

"No need to tell him that there was a kidnapping of his wife planned and that I had been taken by mistake? Are you out of your mind?" Belinda shouted. "Thank heavens I called and filled them in on what was happening here. Did you know that Prince had no idea about the information leaks Cain Devlin had received over the years? There are just too many unanswered questions, Mrs. Chalmers. Too many things pointing to Cain that don't make a bit of sense. Maybe Prince can get to the bottom of it all once he arrives. Then I'm going to the police station and tell them you and I never had a plan of any kind. So be prepared, they may want to know why you lied and didn't bother to inform your grandson."

"I want to know as well, Grandmother." Helen Chalmers's face went as white as her hair as Princeton and Cindy walked into the room. The old lady's shoulders rounded and her eyes clouded with confusion, then darted to the faces of the beautiful blond, tanned couple.

"I love Cindy more than my life, you know that. How could you keep this danger from me? We hadn't heard from anyone until Belinda called. Frank Henson must be a wild man by now. Has he been trying to reach me?"

"Please, Prince, dear," Helen chided in a disturbingly childlike voice. "No one was going to be hurt but that awful man. Now I suppose the others will be disappointed because you didn't come to your senses, even though I told them I was most concerned about him. He had to be stopped, my boy." She braced her hands on the arms of the chair, rose to her feet, and stepped close to Prince. "Grandmother has taken care of it, dear. You know he never did belong with us, don't you?" She patted his cheek and left the room with slow, careful steps.

Belinda slumped back against the brocade, dumbfounded. This Helen Chalmers was completely different from the one who had entered the room such a short time ago.

"Oh, Prince." Cindy sighed sorrowfully, snaking her arm around her shell-shocked husband. "Come on, sweetie." She tugged him over to the chair, pushed him down in it, and sat on the upholstered arm, holding one of his hands between both of hers. Belinda felt sick. Everything had gone crazy.

"All right, Lindy," her best friend said while patting her husband's hand. "Tell us all you know."

And she did. Except, of course, for the intimate moments between herself and Cain. Oh, she waffled for a moment over revealing Cain's real feelings about Prince—his side of what had transpired. But not knowing and not talking had caused a big part of this mess. Besides, she hoped that if she could get him out of jail and cleared of all charges, he'd believe her. There was, however, the awful possibility that because he was so new at having someone on his side, he might interpret this as another betrayal. Yet Belinda had no choice but to risk it. Thirty minutes later the three of them sat in stunned silence.

Princeton lifted his free hand and raked it through his hair, then brought the back of Cindy's hand to his lips for a soft kiss. "What has my grandmother done, love?" he asked with his eyes closed, his head leaning on his wife's shoulder. A moment passed, and then he got to his feet. "All right, ladies, I've got to go talk with her. Something more is going on here. Belinda," he said, looking at her with sad resignation in his eyes. "My lawyer should be here soon and then we'll go see about Devlin."

Cindy crossed to sit by Belinda as soon as Prince was gone. They hugged each other tight and when they drew apart, their eyes were brimming with tears.

"I'm so sorry, Cin. Sorry about Mrs. Chalmers and your honeymoon. Sorry about everything."

"I'm just glad you're all right, Lindy," she said, shaking her head back and forth. "This is all so bizarre I can't begin to process what it all must mean. Do you really think Helen planned to frame Cain Devlin?"

"Yes, Cin," Belinda whispered and caught up her friend's hands. "I've got to go to the station, okay? I'll wait for you guys there. I have to see if he's all right."

As Belinda started to stand, Cindy pulled her back with a firm tug. "Lindy, you love him, don't you? You love my husband's worst enemy?"

"Cin, please trust me. Please hear it all out before you make a decision about Cain. Help Prince do that, too. There's so much healing possible if we'll all just give this a chance."

Belinda walked out the door, wishing with all her heart that everyone had an emergency, one-use-only magic spell that would suspend pride and let people really listen to each other. A few minutes later, as she pulled onto the freeway, the most profound thought just popped into her head out of thin air: *Love is all the magic you need.* It sounded right. It felt right. Belinda clenched her fingers around the steering wheel and prayed the words could really be true. She was about to stake her future on them.

Chapter Eight

Belinda had been sitting in the San Leandro police station for over an hour and a half. One would think that at nearly midnight, the waiting room would be pretty much deserted. But that was not the case. Crime clearly flourished in the dark. She was exhausted, wrung out and hollow eyed. Her entire identity as a beauty and fashion consultant had been obliterated. The all-purpose sweats would definitely have to be destroyed if this night ever came to an end. A couple of times she had the creepy feeling that a few of the other people waiting had pegged her as an inmate of some kind. Gray was a far too institutional color.

But worst of all, she hadn't been able to get a message to Cain. Belinda could only imagine how terrible it had to be, being treated like a criminal and locked up somewhere in this dismal building. Just waiting in it was bad enough. She shifted in the hard plastic chair and checked the clock on the wall for the five hundredth time. An officer she hadn't seen before walked into the room holding a clipboard. When her name was called, Belinda felt a dozen pair of assessing eyes watch her stiffly get to her sandal-shod feet and leave.

In seconds she was ushered down a stark cinder-block hall and into another room with bland beige walls, a folding table, and some of the ubiquitous plastic chairs. Its only redeeming feature was the fact that Cindy Chalmers was sitting in one. She had a pinched, bleak look on her face, and Belinda's heart sank to her toes.

"It's worse than we thought, Lindy," she said with a shrug, notching a shank of chin-length hair, the color of spun gold, behind her ear. "Come and sit. I'll fill you in until Prince gets here."

Belinda moved gingerly, afraid one bump would shatter her. Cindy took her hand and instantly they were stronger. Together they had always been stronger. The right kind of love worked that way.

Helen Chalmers had admitted to a plan to damage Prince's marriage and destroy his enemy. The broken woman had claimed it was all for love. Clearly the wrong kind. Cindy added that Prince was probably talking to Cain this very minute, explaining that the explosion years ago had been a desperate attempt by his grandmother to stop the merger. Prince believed she'd never meant to hurt anyone, just create enough suspicion to scotch the deal.

Belinda was reeling. What was her stubborn love thinking? Would he—could he hear the truth from the man he'd thought of as his enemy for five years?

"What about the kidnapping and Helen's strange reference to others being disappointed?" Belinda asked.

"Helen isn't in her right mind about this, Lindy." Cindy's gaze skittered away and she fiddled with the hem of her oversize island top, then slumped forward, elbows braced on the table. She seemed like a living rainbow slowly being drained dry by the colorless surroundings. "She was so upset about Devlin Enterprises moving ahead of Chalmers, Inc. that she and some others decided to take care of a number of problems with one devastating blow. Luckily it didn't work."

"What else was this about?"

"Listen." She looked up and Belinda saw a shadow of raw pain there that she hadn't seen since Prince had come into Cindy's life. "Any minute that man—Sorry, Lin. I'm trying to change the way I've thought of him, now that we know the truth." She fashioned a sincere smile and for the first time since Belinda had entered the room, a little light came back into her sweet friend's eyes. "The man you love is due through that door momentarily and I want you to know I hope it works out between the two of you. Truly, Belinda. Your happiness is so important to me."

"But the other—"

Cindy squeezed her hands. "Later, hon. Later I promise we'll all have to talk about it. Right now just deal with this."

It was ironic that after the countless hours she'd endured, frantic to see Cain, she suddenly wished for a few more minutes to prepare herself. However, the door opened . . . and he and Prince were . . . there. A jolt of heated testosterone zapped into the room like a power surge. Clearly a lot had passed between these men, and a quick glance at Cindy confirmed her awareness of it, too. For a moment Belinda just stared at him, at them. Cain looked as haggard as she felt. And she supposed his disheveled state along with the scars made him appear even more dangerous. But to her he was beautiful and so compelling that her heart began to beat faster.

The men seemed awkwardly at ease. It sounded crazy, but she detected it in their expressions. No hatred visible. Please, she prayed silently, please let them rebuild what was lost. These two friends, both so tall and strong. Cain the perfect image of a renegade, with his long, dark hair pulled back from a face that had seen too much pain, both physically and emotionally, his powerful body clothed haphazardly in jeans and a rumpled collarless knit shirt. And Prince the exact opposite side of the coin: golden, razor-cut hair, a leaner build, and clothes that created the look so often glorified on the cover of *GQ*.

Prince sought his wife's face, and Belinda could see the impact of that unspoken communication reflected in his body language. His shoulders relaxed; his drawn forehead smoothed and cleared. "Are you all right?"

Cindy nodded with a wobbly smile, leaned over to buss

Belinda's cheek, then went straight into her husband's arms. Belinda blinked back an unexpected rush of emotion as Prince wrapped Cindy up close and spoke against her hair. "Nothing and nobody is going to take away what we have, love."

She could not stop herself from glancing at Cain. For one second she swore she saw naked longing in his eyes. Then, as if he felt her gaze, he turned his head until his eyes held her captive. The inscrutable set of his features gave nothing away. She had no idea what he was feeling.

Prince shifted Cindy and held his free hand out to Cain. "I've gotten an urgent call from the house, so we must head back there right away, but I'll be expecting you soon. Once I track down Roberta we'll have her side of the story, and Frank Henson should be calling anytime with a report from his lead." He paused and waited until Cain's palm settled next to his. "We've got a lot to resolve, Cain, and I'm going to need your help to unravel this disaster. I've . . . I've missed that analytical mind of yours."

Belinda held her breath and chanted silently: *Love is the magic, love is the magic.*

"I've missed you, too, Prince," Cain answered, his voice as firm as his grip. "And I'll be there soon. Don't worry if it takes a few hours."

Cindy only had time to send Belinda a quick wink and then they were gone. The door clicked shut and the room suddenly felt much, much smaller. Belinda knew she should speak, say something, but she couldn't make her mouth work. She was stunned by Cain's admission, and cheering wildly inside her head for his courage and growth. The man was unbelievable, and she loved him so much it hurt to hold in the words. Her tired, emotion-ravaged body was on the brink of flying to pieces, and she desperately needed Cain Devlin's strong arms to hold her together.

If he had already rebuilt a tentative bridge between himself and Prince, would he do so between them? Could he trust enough, believe enough, love enough? Only love had the strength to span the chasm of fear and pain he'd had been surrounded with for so long. Could he believe that some determined, committed people really did create lives with fairy-tale endings?

Cain took in a slow breath through his nose and forced his hands to hang open at his sides. His anger had faded away hours ago, and bitter self-recriminations had rushed in to fill the void. Prince had told him what Belinda had done and about her vigil here at the station. He closed his eyes. The first real test of his love for this woman, who had more than demonstrated her integrity, and he'd attacked her instead. Acted the part of the beast.

He'd let his initial shock and pain wipe out all they had shared. But with each passing minute since he'd left her wounded and rejected, he'd ruthlessly exorcised his pride and vowed to turn his life around, even if he couldn't prove himself worthy of what Belinda had offered. These last few godforsaken hours he'd experienced more fear than he'd ever felt in his entire life. The fear that he had driven her away. That his brown-eyed beauty would not come as she'd promised.

He lifted his head, stepped forward, and stopped. She hadn't moved a muscle; only her eyes spoke. And they pierced him with shimmering flashes of pain and joy, longing and sorrow. He had failed her once, but he would not do so again. She was here; that said all he needed to know.

"I'm free, Belinda. Prince has straightened everything out."

"That's great," she said, getting to her feet and punctuating her words with a too-bright smile. "I'm really glad you and Prince seem to have come to some kind of understanding. I'm not sure what all is involved in this whole thing, but it's wonderful you're willing to help. I . . ." She hesitated and glanced down, suddenly occupied with smoothing the wrinkles out of the sweatsuit he'd so callously announced she needed days ago. "Maybe later, after everything's settled, we could meet for lunch and talk?" She gifted him with a brief moment of eye contact and then solemnly pushed her chair up to the table.

"I don't think that would do it, Belinda."

She blanched and Cain mentally kicked himself. His erratic thinking was twisting his words into knots. If he could just touch her, she'd know, and that horrible bleak expression on her face would disappear. He walked around the table and she shuffled back until she bumped into the wall, then extended a hand, palm up.

"Cain, I didn't make that call to hurt you."

"I believe you, Belinda."

"And I didn't know a thing about Helen Chalmers and her psychotic plan," she blurted in a rush.

"I believe you."

"I know you haven't had a lot of reasons to believe people, but Cain, you can trust me. I—"

"I know I can, honey. I do believe you."

Belinda went owl-eyed and slumped against the wall. "You believe me? But I thought you'd hate me and—and never want to see me again and I . . . I—" Her voice grew thick and soggy and her eyes took on that liquid sheen Cain was fast becoming used to.

"Ah, honey, please don't cry." He lifted a hand and brushed a limp strand of hair off her cheek. "I don't want to make you cry ever again."

"Well," she sniffed, dashing away her tears with the backs of her hands, and, summoning a stern expression to cover the tortured one he'd been watching so closely. "You know I don't like to, but it keeps happening. And you will make me cry again, Cain Devlin, if you don't figure out what's really going on between us and stop acting like a stubborn beast. If you ever misjudge me again I'll give you a swift kick, buddy."

"This time I really think I deserve the gun." He couldn't help it. He had to say it just to watch the face of the woman he loved. Besides, he deserved more than a swift kick for almost letting his pride destroy this miracle, the magic that this indignant, candy-eyed lady, glaring through her tears, had brought into his lonely, cheerless life. The dark cloud that had been Cain's constant companion for five years began to break apart as hope and laughter started to build deep inside. This was not the right time to laugh, but damned if this woman wasn't as fun to tease as she was sexy to kiss. Her outrage on his behalf soothed his aching heart like a healing balm.

"Ohhhh! Don't ever mention that gun to me again." She lunged away from the wall and he caught her at the shoulders, trying to hold her still.

"Stop, now, Belinda," he ordered, his mouth next to her ear and her struggling body moving like fiery licks of flame against his. He rested his face more heavily into the lee of her neck, breathing in the scent of his woman. Sweet Jesus, she was back in his arms! And he was hit by a need so powerful and elemental that he went weak in the knees. Yes, they had a lot of crucial issues to deal with in the next few days, but there was only one imperative thing Cain needed to hear and needed to say in return.

"Honey." He tightened his hold and managed to seat himself in a plastic chair and haul Belinda onto his lap. "I think I've figured out what's going on between us." She froze and Cain flattened a palm on her rigid back and slowly began to rub in small circles. "I asked you a question at the cabin I never even should have considered."

He felt a fine tremor rack her body, and it stung to feel what just the memory of that scene did to her. Cain lifted the hand that had been resting on her knees to cup the side of her face and press that tousled head onto his shoulder. "I want to ask the right question this time, Belinda. The one I should have asked then, okay? And you tell me yes or no." He paused and knew by the stiff feel of her muscles that she was uncertain and preparing herself.

Cain shifted his shoulders and used a knuckle to nudge

up her chin. Hazel eyes into brown. He would not let her look away, and his heart thumped almost painfully in an irregular rhythm. What if he was wrong? No! He trusted this woman. If it hadn't been for her belief in him he wouldn't have had the courage to face Prince and open his heart.

"I've not an ounce of pride left when it comes to you, woman. I want to hear how you really feel. Do you love me?"

Belinda heard the words, the magic gift she'd wished for, and she answered without a moment's hesitation. "I love you, Cain. I love you so much."

He smiled then, a breathtakingly beautiful smile on the face of the breathtakingly beautiful man of her dreams. Belinda lifted a hand to Cain's scarred cheek and touched him there with tender reverence, then pressed her mouth to his, imbuing the kiss with all the love and passion she felt for him. He groaned and pulled her snug against his chest, a hand right in the center of her back pressing her breasts closer until they burned to be closer still. Cain opened his mouth over hers and Belinda felt it seeking for more than words.

"Oh, God, honey." He broke away and whispered harsh and low, "I love you, too. So much—so much. Marry me now. Now, before we face another thing. Come on." He kissed her again, coaxing her tongue deep into his mouth. "Let's go to Reno and then we'll help Prince."

"Yes." He sipped her breath away for a few seconds and she tried to speak again. "Yes, Cain, I'll marry you, but it's the middle of the night and maybe we should wait till—" His hot mouth covered hers once more and Belinda felt all her reservations melt the way her body was melting. "But these sweats, Cain? How can I . . . ?"

He drew back and fixed her with a look of such intense need her protest died on her tingling lips.

"I have never seen a more perfect bride. You are all that is beauty to me, honey, every freckle on your face and

125

every delicious inch of you." He ran the tip of a finger over her cheeks, down her neck, and onto the gray fabric, trailing that branding finger between her breasts until he rested his palm low on her stomach.

"Woman," he growled and pressed his hand against her urgently, "I want you to be mine and I want to be yours in every way possible and as soon as possible. You only need to wear these clothes until I get you in a hotel room, honey. I promise to get you anything else you need later."

"You know, Cain." She gasped, unable to calm her breathing or the rush of love and happiness racking her body, "I think there might be a place, every now and then, for a . . . modified version of the beast."

For a second, Belinda's meaning was lost in Cain's haze of desire. And then he understood. And he threw his head back and roared. Laughed until the dingy, barren room disappeared and a vision of the rich, full life waiting for him was all he could see. A home. A family. A friend and a lover.

"You, my beauty, are a dream come true."

And then the strangest thing happened. As Cain sent her soaring with another sweet, savage kiss, Belinda heard the voice that had come to her once on the breeze, and she smiled against her soon-to-be husband's lips. *True hearts . . . true love . . . Happily ever after, my dear . . .* And she knew it was a promise and a blessing.

Part Two

"The Nerd Prince"

Chapter One

Lilith Smythe estimated she'd known Belinda Brown for nearly eight years. In all that time she had never once realized how little the woman thought of her. Perfect—another one! She held herself as regally as possible and decided she should have started a list some time back. Such bad form, you know, to lose track of social cuts. And since three months ago she wouldn't have considered the opinion of her stepsister's friend at all, this newest revelation stung with surprising and disturbing intensity. Even more disturbing was that as Belinda continued delivering her pointed ultimatum about informing this Henson person, Lilith felt a traitorous urge to cry. She never cried. That, too, was an alarming change!

Then, before she had herself completely under control, an odd, low humming seemed to fill the air. The insistent expression on Belinda's face shimmied, wavered, and began to fade. Was she passing out? Lilith stood riveted to the vanishing floor, and all at once she was looking through a glittery cloud—not the elegant wedding party crowd. She saw an icy wall that formed part of a castle; a fairy-tale castle from her childhood memory. She slowly moved closer, each step pounding more loudly in her ears. Someone was in that wall of ice! Some poor person was trapped and suddenly Lilith didn't want to see.

She tried to back away, but the fear she'd worked for years to hide climbed up her throat and made it hard to breathe. *No!* Showing that weak emotion was unacceptable, had always been. But lately she'd been losing her ability to hold everything in. She was feeling so alone, so cold and untouchable. Ever since her thirtieth birthday and the awful night of Cindy's engagement party a week later, something weird had started happening in her head . . . and she couldn't seem to turn it around again. She couldn't go back to who she'd been and she didn't know who she was becoming.

She blinked, and just for one second she saw the bluish face in the ice. It was hers.

Every muscle in her body tensed to run, and then the image vanished. Lilith blinked again and managed to stay on her feet. Belinda was still clipping out orders to both her and Roberta Chalmers as if nothing had happened, nothing at all. For a moment she longed for some Valium, but Lilith had ended that scene years ago. She needed to leave. It wasn't supposed to have gotten this complicated. But before she could even conjure up a response, Belinda was gone, weaving her way through the room full of laughing, dancing people who had no clue that something really, really weird was going on.

Lilith had to get a grip. After all, she had opened this Pandora's box by opening her mouth. She summoned her practiced aura of emotional detachment, shut off her feelings, and concentrated on externals. With gritted teeth, she held back the words pressing to get out and assessed the room while considering her options.

Cindy had actually done quite well. A tuxedoed string quartet was playing a lilting piece by Mozart, and the tables sparkled with silver, crystal, satin ribbons, and baby's breath. The peach and cream colors were soothing, and roses scented the entire Royal Arms ballroom. As she silently acknowledged that the reception had turned out much better than she'd thought, an alarming mix of happiness and envy for her stepsister bubbled to the surface again.

She pushed it down. Too much was bubbling to the surface. Mother and Milicent would have been surprised, if they'd bothered to come. But then, they'd clearly been plotting their stupid, wretched plan all along and had left Lilith with no choice but to do something to stop them. An icy chill crawled up her bare back. The awful coldness left behind its usual spill of nausea.

She unconsciously tossed her hair over her shoulder and rigidly held on to her aloof facade. Years of strict control as a top model had taught her that eyes were always watching, and when beauty was your entry ticket, beauty was what they'd better see. Every time.

So she used every centimeter of her slim, five-foot-ten-and-a-half-inch frame (six feet in her low, ivory silk heels) to her advantage. Long ago she'd learned that her face and figure made a perfect shield; intimidation kept people in their place and out of her space quite effectively. Lilith intuitively struck a flattering pose and tried to decide how far she should go. Perhaps just passing on the name of Maximillian Wolfe would be enough to stop the whole thing. She thoughtfully ran a fingertip along the diamond choker clasped around her neck.

If only she hadn't accidentally stumbled upon Mil and Prince at the engagement party. Her sister had shamelessly thrown herself at the man, and when Prince had grabbed her by the shoulders and told her he loved Cindy—really loved Cindy—well, Milicent had not been able to understand that. She screamed that he'd be sorry, that one day he'd pay for humiliating her and leading her on.

Lilith dropped her hand. Prince had never made any promises to Mil, and when she'd tried to point that out to her sister, things had begun to fall apart between them. Now she was about to destroy what was left. Lilith took several quick breaths, the only indication of her inner turmoil. She was crazy. Why else would she be doing this? Contemplating the destruction of the only life she'd ever known? Too many years of calorie deficiency must have finally withered the part of her brain that triggered self-preservation.

But ever since Cindy and Prince had gotten engaged, it seemed things had been pushing her—almost forcing her to move in a new direction. She'd had more and more bouts of melancholy and more and more arguments with Milicent. In fact, Lilith had begun to find her sister so caustic and so shallow it was frightening. Because, of course, previously they had always seen eye-to-eye on just about everything.

Initially they'd both refused to be in Cindy's line. They'd both refused to help with any of the preparations. They'd both talked trash about their stepsister. They'd both laughed with their mother about Cindy, the naive bumpkin, getting a date with the bachelor of the decade. But only one of the Smythe sisters had accidentally come across Cindy crying after their ridicule. Only one had seen the proof of Prince's love for Cindy. Only one had come to the reception. Only one had heard the sensuous French voice confirming a plan to ruin a woman who'd never done an unkind thing in her life.

Only one was standing on the edge of a mile-high cliff on her tiptoes. Could there be a way to get out of this dangerous spot without plummeting past the point of no return?

Lilith turned to the short woman standing motionless at her side. She and Roberta Chalmers had exchanged surface pleasantries on a number of social occasions. Although they barely knew each other, she suddenly realized they were indirectly related now. Perhaps Prince's terminally shy redheaded sister could relay her information.

"Look, Roberta, since Belinda ordered you to find Prince, I really think you and he should go together to the authorities and tell them about that gigolo lowlife Maximillian Wolfe and—"

A mournful, mousy squeak from Roberta cut Lilith off and pulled her up short. Gads, what was she doing speak-

ing so familiarly about that snake, Max Wolfe! Vague . . .
she had to be vague if she hoped to get out of this and—
All at once, the diminutive bridesmaid in peach satin was
slumped against Lilith's ivory silk slip dress. Just for a second, Lilith wondered if Cindy had any clue that she'd chosen the color of her own dress very specifically. Matching
the wedding colors and coming to the reception had been
her unspoken way of showing support. But who would
believe that? Even she had doubted her own sanity. She'd
been doing that a lot lately.

"I think you'd better sit down, Roberta. This is the second time in five minutes that you've almost fainted." Another squeak, this one in a negative tone, drew Lilith's gaze
down to the green eyes nearly hidden behind the thick-
framed glasses. This young woman wasn't going to be able
to stay upright long enough to find Princeton, let alone
Security Chief Henson. Gads!

Lilith closed her eyes with resigned frustration and was
totally unprepared for the fierce tug that almost rocked her
to her knees. Tiny, trembling Ms. Chalmers was suddenly
hauling her toward an exit door in one of the most ungra-
ceful displays of her life. It was all Lilith could do to regain
her balance and her composure. Luckily the champagne
had been flowing long enough to desensitize most people,
and they uninterestedly watched them lurch by.

They came to an abrupt halt in front of a tall, thin man
who was also wearing dark-framed glasses, and Lilith
couldn't help but think how ridiculous the two of them
looked as a couple. Why, Roberta would need a stool just
to reach the man's shoulders. But what was that saying
about birds of a feather? The disparity in their heights was
so great and the room was so noisy that the formerly timid
Roberta grabbed his lapels and yanked his head down to
hers. The two obviously knew each other because the man
didn't seem at all bothered by this extreme greeting. Lilith
stood uncomfortably to the side, watching the odd
exchange, and was surprised to hear a deep, smooth voice

touched with a hint of magnolia blossoms. Roberta responded in a lower-toned mumble, then nodded, and Mr. Poindexter the professor curled an arm around her and patted her back. Truly, all he was missing was a name tag and a white lab coat.

But the man had riveting hands.

Lilith felt ridiculous for even thinking that when she should be concentrating on getting out of this explosive situation as quickly as possible. However, she'd done some hand modeling in the past and she couldn't help but notice physical perfection when she saw it. After all, that focus had dominated her life for years.

Whether it made sense or not, the "professor" had to-die-for hands. Surprisingly tanned and long fingered with smooth, healthy-looking nails clipped short, but not too short. A fine dusting of silky, golden hair gave him just the right touch of masculinity. These were strong hands, but not broad and hammy. Perfect for the camera and perfect to turn this entire nightmare over to before she said more than she should.

"Listen, Roberta." Lilith leaned in toward the pair. "You know all I know so I'm just going up to my room now. Keep me posted. I'm not flying out until tomorrow morning." Right! She'd done all she could reasonably do to help Cindy, and now she had to get away. Tonight if possible. Time to look out for number one.

Lilith didn't make it a full step. She was stopped cold when one of those perfect hands clamped around the bare skin of her upper arm. A quick tug was fruitless; he just held tighter and pulled her closer to Roberta. The faint Southern flavor in the man's voice did not mesh with his nerdy-professor look and his major-league power hold.

"Robbie, you'd better go find Prince and your grandmother. Check back with me as soon as you can."

Lilith pointedly cleared her throat and wiggled her arm. The man's head suddenly turned in her direction as if he had just become aware that she was attached to his hand. The light wasn't all that bright, and the shadows from his glasses made it difficult to read his expression. Lilith took a carefully concealed deep breath and tried to relax. This could be handled very easily if she kept calm and waited for the right moment. This poor excuse for a man would be the one in trouble once she had a little time to work on him. Men weren't that hard to manipulate. She'd been doing it all her life.

"Now, Ms. Smythe," he said, after watching Roberta hurry away. "You are coming with me for some questions." Unexpectedly, he shot her an ominous glare.

Time to start the salivating—and quickly. Lilith rolled a shoulder, purposely causing the light to shimmer across the snug silk bodice of her dress. She fixed an innocent, trusting expression on her face. A little dash of sophistication mixed with naivete was always a winning combination. This poor man could probably only take a very small dose of vamping without blowing a gasket of some kind. Obviously he wasn't used to interacting with women at her social level, maybe women at any level. He didn't look like he could possibly have had much romantic experience.

Lilith calculatedly blanched and wet her lips. His eyes widened behind the frames. Bait taken, hook in place.

"I'll be glad to answer a few questions, of course. But my emotions are so ragged I may only have a few minutes of composure left." She smiled tremulously, bravely, and hunched her shoulders as if bracing for an ordeal. Those mysterious, shadowed eyes dipped to the neckline of her slip dress, and Lilith was certain the man was a goner. One could not wear a bra under such an evening gown. And if Mr. Inexperience hadn't been aware of it before, he was now. Lilith knew exactly how much honey-brown cleavage she was revealing. One never went into battle without knowing precisely how to use every weapon.

His gruff voice was a good sign. "This way, Ms. Smythe."

He didn't let go either. Excellent.

In a few minutes they had walked down a deserted hall and entered a small, simply furnished room that must be used as a hotel office. The color theme played out in the light blue wainscoting and the striped mauve wallpaper. A Scandinavian-style desk and two chairs stood against one wall, and a small love seat in a complementary pattern was opposite them. A nice print of a flowering meadow was hung above the love seat and Lilith thought it would make the best backdrop for her next scene.

But just as she was about to break away and strike a pose, the professor surprised her by snagging the straight-backed chair next to the desk. He whirled it out and whirled her into it with more strength than she had expected. A shank of hair swished onto her face and she lost her composure for a second. A niggling spark of anger ignited beneath her wide-eyed facade. She smoothed back the platinum tumble that had helped to create her trademark California look and decided to make the impertinent man suffer just a bit. Yes, she wanted to help Cindy, felt oddly compelled to, really. But this peasant obviously had no idea who she was or whom he was dealing with.

"My, but aren't you a powerful man." She cocked her head and fanned herself with one of her pampered, acrylic-nail-tipped hands. Lilith knew the diamond-and-gold bracelet circling her wrist reflected every light in the small room and sent a message of wealth and significance. The professor's eyes jumped from her face to her fluttering hand, and his mouth flattened into a thin line. The nostrils of his aquiline nose flared. Perfect.

"I'm sure you're just the one who can help my stepsister." Lilith willed a few tears to her eyes and quivered her bottom lip. Its fullness was ideal for this effect and usually generated fast results. She knew she had to get this lanky wannabe warrior to let her go before the big boss, Henson, arrived. As skilled as she was, Lilith was too tired and worried to try to bamboozle another male right now. It was imperative that she make her getaway while the link between Milicent and Wolfe was still unknown.

And the continued state of that deception was growing more tenuous by the minute. What would her mother and sister do when they found out what she'd done? If she could help Cindy, but put all the focus on Max, then maybe she could warn Mil and make some sort of compromise before all hell broke loose.

"I'm sorry," she quavered and carefully blinked, sending one mascara-free tear rolling down her cheek. "Let me tell you what I know so you can take all that—that strength and save Cindy. I would be so grateful if we could do this quickly so I can go rest in my room." Ego. Men were slaves to it. Lilith deliberately hugged herself, using her arms to plump her breasts until they were straining against the thin fabric.

The professor abruptly backed away and shrugged off his dark blue suit-coat, revealing a surprising set of broad shoulders. She'd thought him to be more gangly and thin than he really was. He sat on the edge of the desk and lifted his empty hand to pinch the bridge of his nose. The dark frames bobbled with the movement, and then he dragged that same hand down over his face and the square line of his chin. Perfect. The man was rattled.

"I must warn you, Ms. Smythe, if you're offering me something, ah, personal to avoid adequate questioning, I'm really not interested. In fact"—he straightened up a bit and extended his coat to her—"I insist you put this on so you don't develop a chest cold over the next few hours."

Lilith's mouth dropped open for a millisecond—she was shocked. Instantly she recovered and sneered. Her eyes narrowed into slits and she bared her perfect white teeth in a sharklike smile. "How dare you, you pathetic excuse for a man. How dare you imply that I would offer a pocket protector like you even so much as the time of day. I have information about my stepsister and I will give it only to your superior, Frank Henson. I suggest you tuck your tail between your legs and pray I don't tell your boss about your ridiculous accusations."

The insufferable nerd squared his shoulders and tightened his jaw until Lilith saw a muscle jump beneath the skin. One blond-brown brow arched above his glasses and he sneered right back at her. That wasn't right. His type wasn't supposed to react this way. It took all Lilith's resolve to hold her position and not back down.

"Ma'am, I have only one concern at this precise moment, and that is the threat to Princeton and Cindy Chalmers. How dare *you* imply that I have a drop of interest in a plastic mannequin like you. You may be under the impression that your body is the dream come true of every red-blooded male in America, but you've struck out with me, lady. So let's solve this problem. You think I'm looking at the breasts you've been trying so hard to *cover up,* and I frankly don't want to see them. Put on the coat and preserve your offended modesty, Ms. Smythe."

How could she do otherwise when he'd put it in such an insulting way? Lilith glared, snatched the offering out of his hand, and shrugged into the voluminous jacket. She was a tall, long-limbed woman, but still she felt dwarfed in his coat. She was furious and only cooperated to throw him off guard.

"Fine. It's done. Your testosterone surge for the next month has been satisfied. Now get me Henson."

He rested an elbow on the thigh propped up on the desk and leaned forward, laying his other hand loosely over the crisp white cuff covering his dangling wrist. "I am Frank Henson, Ms. Smythe, head of Henson Security. And I must disappoint you, because I have no intention of tucking anything you suggest between my legs. In fact, there isn't a suggestion you could make that would interest me."

Lilith blanched, unintentionally this time, and pressed back against the hardwood frame of her chair. It was a weak move, a vulnerable move, but she couldn't stop herself. Gads, but her messed-up thinking was wreaking havoc with all her instincts. She'd felt this Henson's physical strength from the first, but had totally ignored that factor and misread all his other reactions. How long had it been since a man had rocked her so severely with her own weapons—confidence and sensual intimidation? Her brain was scrambling for a killing response.

"Look, Henson, this is not helping my stepsister. While you're wasting time flexing your macho ego, Cindy could be in trouble." This time he raised both eyebrows.

"All right then, Ms. Smythe, if you're ready to stop the adolescent theatrics, so am I. Let's get to it. Tell me everything you heard."

It took twenty minutes to relate her story about leaving the reception for a break and wandering toward a little side room. No way was Lilith going to mention she'd been so depressed after seeing the love that radiated from Cindy and Prince that she'd had to find some privacy to pull herself together. She wouldn't give a single living soul that kind of weapon to use against her.

Then just as she'd been about to push through a door standing ajar down the hall, she heard Cindy's name and froze, listening. A man with a light French accent was demanding some answers. He wanted to know why the plans had changed. He hissed that they were to have waited for his call. What in the hell was going on? Cindy was supposed to be observed leaving the reception willingly with another man. Where was she? A brief silence followed and the man's identity slammed into Lilith's head.

He was Maximillian Wolfe, a rich playboy with a dubious reputation of whom Milicent had been enamored in Monaco last New Year's. Of course, she didn't tell that to Herr Henson, but it was at that moment that she knew exactly what was happening. Milicent had made good on her threat to get even with Cindy and she had found a capable partner. With a horrified crash, the emotions that had been seesawing inside of Lilith for the last few months teetered and pushed her to action. Before she had time to reason through the consequences, she was rushing toward Belinda Brown.

However, she only told Henson that after the brief silence, the unknown man had cursed and warned the party he was speaking to that they'd be sorry for double-crossing Maximillian Wolfe. He would have satisfaction even if he had to follow them to St. Thomas.

Frank Henson listened without a flicker of reaction. He sat back and folded his arms, and Lilith had the distinct impression that somewhere behind those Clark Kent glasses, a computer was clicking on and processing her story. If only what she'd just told was enough, maybe she could be out of the country before any connections were made to her mother and sister. Maybe—she closed her eyes and prayed, knowing none of them deserved a moment of heavenly intervention—maybe it really had been that smoke-and-shadow playboy who had masterminded the whole thing. Maybe her sister hadn't really become so terrible. And maybe if she kept saying it was so, it would be.

A series of sharp knocks reverberated on the door, and Herr Henson shot her an assessing look as he moved to answer the summons. An exchange of low rumbles drifted Lilith's way. She couldn't make anything out but the word *flight*.

Henson swung around to face her. "I have to take a call, Ms. Smythe. Why don't you review what happened and make sure you haven't left anything out? I'll be back as soon as possible."

By the time Frank Henson returned it was almost 12:30 A.M. After discovering the door was locked and fuming for a good hour, Lilith had curled up in a ball on the small sofa and reluctantly dozed off. But the snapping click jerked her out of a frantic dream and she slumped against the rolled arm of the couch, her heart pounding and her surroundings smeared, hazy. Although her hands were freezing, her face was hot and moist. Lilith blinked and focused on her tall, rangy captor. Oh, no. He'd been in her dream.

For some bizarre reason she had dreamed of the ice castle she'd imagined hours ago. Lilith tried to shake the images away, but Frank's sudden appearance re-created the sensation of the frozen prison pressing in on her body, cutting off her air, smothering her. In the dream she had panicked, sure that if she didn't break free soon, she would remain trapped forever. Then she'd seen Cindy and Prince approach the cold, crystal prison and, just as she had earlier, Lilith felt their warmth seeping into her brittle bones.

One frozen finger on one hand had moved a fraction, and dripping rivulets began to roll down the walls, puddling on the ground. Lilith had wanted them to come closer, to warm her completely, but suddenly a black, oily cloud snaked up around Cindy's feet. Lilith saw it tugging her hand away from Prince and he could not hold on— could not stop it. Cindy disappeared and the liberating drips instantly froze, like a broken string of diamond beads. Prince fell to his knees and a freezing wind swirled around the castle, sealing every weakened spot with a new layer of ice. Lilith's tears stopped halfway down her cheeks, solid as stone.

Then, in the distance, she saw a light shimmering like the cloud that had surrounded her in the daydream. The dancing light floated closer, and Prince stood and extended his hand to the iridescent mass. Frank Henson stepped through, dusted with glitter. Prince gestured toward the castle, toward her. Lilith was saved! She knew it. Soon she'd be free. Even though Frank didn't like her, he worked for Prince, and Prince was signaling for his help. The two men came closer, and Prince held up a palm to stop Henson. He turned to Lilith and mouthed the words *Where is Cindy?*

Lilith couldn't answer. She couldn't tell! She was trapped. Couldn't they see that? Couldn't anyone understand? Prince tapped Frank on the shoulder, and Frank stepped to the very spot where Lilith waited, suspended in a wall of ice. She felt his warmth like a blazing fire. It stung and burned, an exquisite pain because it meant she was alive—feeling something. His eyes were glowing embers and he asked her silently *Where is Cindy?* He stretched out his hand, but after long moments of waiting he shook his head, raised his arm, and . . . turned away, leaving her in the cold once more.

But it wasn't real. It wasn't! Lilith's heart was beating in her throat and she struggled to control her choppy breathing. She was losing her mind; this—this dream thing was getting creepy. One awake, and now one asleep. What was happening to her? She must look like a fool. Gads, how she hated to be caught off guard, exposed. Her life in the public eye had taught her that most people could not be trusted and would stab you in the back if given the opportunity. This was a major opportunity.

Lilith swung her rubbery legs to the carpet and pushed herself up. She was still wearing Henson's coat and it reminded her of the ugly exchange that had culminated with her putting it on. All right, her behavior might have been too extreme, outrageous, but Mr. Professor Perfect wasn't walking a tightrope of annihilation. It irked her that her stupid subconscious had put him in her dream, and it irked her that the man had been right in a perverse way. It had gotten cool in the room and she pulled the synthetic-silk-lined wool more securely around her. It was a wrinkled mess. Good.

"Can I go now, Mr. Henson?" Lilith asked as evenly as possible. With every passing moment the jittery effects of her eerie dream were fading and she was feeling more like her old self. "Surely I have a right to sleep in a real bed at some point tonight." She smoothed her tangled hair away from her face and held it clumped at the base of her neck for a second. "I'll even agree to your posting a guard outside my door."

The professor wasn't rising to the bait. He stood stock-still, his shirtsleeves rolled up to his elbows, his tie gone, and his short, sandy hair swirling in opposite directions as if he'd been tunneling his fingers through it. His face was pale, and looked even more so because of the fluorescent lighting and his unfashionable glasses. Things must not have gone well during his absence. The man was tired and worried. She could see it in his haggard expression, the thin line of his mouth, and the slight droop of those incongruously broad shoulders.

"There won't be any bed for a while, Ms. Smythe, but if you can sleep on planes, you will get part of your wish."

"What?" she stuttered, teetering on the edge of the cushion. "What are you trying to pull, Henson?" She gathered momentum. "I'm not going anywhere with you! Don't you dare—"

Frank had her by the arms and standing on tiptoe before she could finish her sentence. Even though she was six feet, he still topped her by three inches, and every one of them was rigid with fierce emotion.

"Listen, Sleeping Beauty, I'm too tired to deal with your continued 'daring' rhetoric rationally, so I advise you to back off. Things have gotten very strange and you may have to be inconvenienced in order to help your stepsister. Of course," he said with a sneer, "historically, you stepsisters haven't done too well in that department. But this time, Your Highness, I'm going to make sure you do your duty. Somehow Cindy and Prince never got the message from Roberta. They've already left for their honeymoon, and Helen Chalmers is tracking them down.

"In the meantime, Belinda Brown is missing. The police don't think finding her bridesmaid's dress in Cindy's suite is enough to start a search yet. That damn twenty-four-hour waiting period has left me no choice but to follow my only lead." He shook her once for emphasis and bent his head until they were almost nose to nose. "You are the lead, lady.

"My men have just confirmed part of your story. Wolfe

was booked on a flight that left for Florida thirty minutes ago. He had a woman with him, Ms. Smythe. If he was after Cindy, but has taken Belinda Brown anyway, who knows what the bastard could be planning? That woman has put herself on the line like few people I have ever known. And nothing," he said, vowing with such conviction that Lilith briefly wondered what it would feel like to inspire such regard, "nothing will stop me from doing everything I can to help her and protect Prince and his wife. I owe the man, Your Highness, and you, I believe, owe your stepsister."

Chapter Two

Lilith's mouth had gone dry as dust during the security chief's passionate outburst. Frank Henson had not seemed to be a passionate man. After all, he hadn't responded to her diversionary tactics in the least. But now she saw the strain and emotion in his eyes. Eyes suddenly so close that even behind his lenses, she could see their clear amber color and the thick brown eyelashes that seemed to be tipped in gold. Eyes that glowed just like the embers in her dream . . .

She shuddered and dropped her gaze to the two deep lines bracketing his mouth. The pressure of each finger digging into her shoulders bordered on pain and forced her to face a very alarming fact. This man was not going to give up. Under his distant, controlled surface was bone-deep commitment. Bone-deep honor. And seeing it this personally made Lilith feel small and ugly. And then it got worse.

"Roberta told me that you've never had a warm relationship with Cindy. She said you don't even treat each other as friends, let alone family. How anyone could not like Cindy Chalmers is beyond me. But frankly I don't care how screwed up your sibling rivalry is. Deal with that later. If you are not a completely plastic person, you won't fight me; you'll be human enough to do the right thing. But I should warn you that we're going—easy or hard. We're following Wolfe. You and me, right now. You're the only person who can link the man to what's happened here and I *will* have his answers and your personal identification!"

Lilith blinked. Blinked again. Oh, God. This overbearing, self-righteous man would have her head if she was anywhere near him when the whole truth became known. What should she do? Maybe she could slip away from him once they got to St. Thomas. After all, she knew it like the back of her hand. For a moment Lilith felt the trapped sensation she'd experienced in her dream. She wasn't going to win, not either way, but she was stuck for now. She'd just have to play along with him until she could get away, until she got some definite word on Cindy and Belinda. Lilith glanced up at the stranger who had abruptly entered her life and taken over. The line of his jaw was set, his expression cautious, his eyes holding hers. Waiting.

She could see that he wasn't sure which way she'd go. He wasn't sure she could be human. It stung, that suspicion. It stung just as it had with Belinda. Nice, passably pretty Belinda Brown, whom Frank Henson had praised and admired. Lilith's flush of envy was disgusting. When had she ever envied anybody anything other than the biggest magazine cover of the year?

But those days were behind her now. Younger models had taken her place. And there'd been too much time to fill. Too much time without the travel and the work to break up the meaningless swirl of parties and sycophants. That was what had finally started to drive her and Milicent apart. Mil thought only as far as next week, while Lilith was beginning to wonder what she was going to do for the next fifty years.

Spending that time envying women like Belinda Brown had never even occurred to her. But she could not deny that suddenly she wanted to hear Frank say noble, honorable things about her. *Gads, Lilith, that's so absurd.* But what was worse, she couldn't bear the thought of looking into his golden eyes once he knew how much she hadn't told him. She'd have to be long gone by then.

"All right, Mr. Henson," she agreed, straining against his hold until he let her go. "Let me grab some clothes and I'll—"

"No time, Ms. Smythe," he interjected matter-of-factly, all signs of his emotional outburst wiped away. "I just want to dump your jewels in the hotel safe. You're going to be trouble enough without them. A car is waiting and if we speed we may just make it."

"B-but wait! My bags! I can't go like this!" she insisted, waving her hands and flopping his coat like bat wings.

"Of course not," he agreed, once again latching on to her abused upper arm. Lilith let her shoulders droop and sighed with relief.

"I have a disguise so you won't be recognized. We'll get the rest as we go."

He stopped at the door and handed her a dark, lumpy bundle. A knit cap and a pair of sunglasses? Lilith stared slack-jawed at the nerdy professor who had proved to be smarter and stronger than she had ever imagined. Maybe a large part of her was out of whack and maybe her old instincts had gone haywire, but there were still some absolutes. Thank God! For some reason it helped to know that in at least one area, Mr. Perfect was as clueless as all other males of the species. It gave her hope for her escape plan on St. Thomas.

Lilith closed her mouth and forcibly kept it relaxed. Laughing at a time like this, at a man like this, would definitely be a sign of deranged behavior. But inside, where she'd learned to hide her feelings, she was laughing. Only a man would think that a woman wearing a silk evening dress, a huge man's dress coat, a ski hat, and a pair of Blues Brothers sunglasses would not be noticed. Of course, in L.A. her chances *were* better.

And as they were whisked toward the airport and most probably the end of her life as she had known it, the thought of his typical male cluelessness was somehow comforting and encouraging. Maybe she could handle him after all.

Frank Henson felt as though he'd been run over by a truck. Make that two heavy-duty semis. He was exhausted, feeling guilty as hell about letting Prince down, and stuck on a red-eye with a world-class witch. That wasn't precisely the word he wanted to use, but because of the little girl a seat away, he had to improvise. If *witch* slipped out under his breath he could face her mother without guilt.

Frank shifted his long legs awkwardly and smiled at the nine-year-old who was flying to visit her grandparents in Florida. Shannon Shamblin was a quiet, well-behaved child with big, soulful gray eyes and wispy light brown hair only a few shades darker than his. She didn't look the least bit terrifying, but Lilith, the plastic princess, had been hiding from her in the bathroom since the seat-belt light had gone off.

She'd glared at him as if he were a monster when the stewardess had informed them that the last two seats were next to a child. And Frank should have known. True to form for her kind, women like Lilith Smythe never wanted to be bothered by children. Hell, they were still too much like children themselves: wanted all the attention all the time.

It had been his fault, though. And truthfully Frank was a little embarrassed about it. They'd been walk-running down the converse when out of the corner of his eye, he caught an odd shimmering reflection coming from underneath the jacket of a burly man wearing a cowboy hat. The image of a gun flashed so insistently in Frank's head that he'd taken a few precious minutes to alert airport security to watch the guy. He knew "her highness" was still blaming him for being the last to board and ending up with the seats of terror.

Frank stretched one leg discreetly out into the aisle and twisted around to check the bathroom cubicle. Occupied.

Well, she sure as hell couldn't stay in there the whole five-hour flight. He knew just the line to use to get her out, but debated the pros and cons. Even pretending to be married to the woman made him queasy, yet it seemed he had no choice.

He took a deep breath, ran a hand over the top of his head, and stood, moving his big body carefully through the small space and toward the narrow bathroom door.

"Sugar?" he said as he knocked lightly. Holy smokes! He hadn't called a female *sugar* since he'd been in high school back home in North Carolina. Frank made a quick scan of the area and put his mouth right up next to the metal door. He nodded, assuring himself the ruse was necessary. "Sugar, are you all right in there?"

"Who are you?"

She sounded distorted and alarmed. Frank frowned. Worldwise witch-women didn't usually let weakness show. Never let them see you sweat, unless it'll get you something, was their general rule of thumb.

"Sugar, it's me, Frank, *your husband*. Do you recognize my voice now?"

"No!"

"Ma'am?" Frank said, turning to a stewardess. "I think my wife may be having a panic attack. Do you have something I can use to open the door?"

He used a screwdriver-type tool and spoke through the crack and over Lilith's startled shriek. "Now, now, sugar, let me in here." He forced the words and the door. "No need for false modesty, woman." He got his head inside and zeroed in on the ridiculous sight of elegant Lilith Smythe trying to wedge herself into a tiny, stainless-steel corner. The two of them looked like giants in the land of Lilliput.

"What in the hell are you doing?" he hissed.

"How dare—"

Frank shot out a long arm and clamped his hand over

149

her mouth, then crammed in and shut the door behind him.

"Don't get high and mighty on me and act all offended, Your Highness. We both know you aren't the modest type, so cut the routine and get the hell out of here!"

For a moment Frank thought he saw hurt well in the ice-blue eyes framed above the edge of his hand. Unexpectedly he felt her lips move against his palm, and the feathery motion sent a shiver racing up his arm and down his back. He dropped his hand and analyzed the response. Lilith Smythe was a beautiful woman. So beautiful his body couldn't help but notice. But her kind of beauty was deadly. Deadly because all she had to offer was on the surface and all she wanted was the same thing in return. Once the surface changed, once the image wasn't "hot" . . . there was nothing left.

Oh, glamour and money were addicting, Frank knew that only too well. In fact, he'd been so addicted to that life, he hadn't even realized how he'd been changing and what those changes had been doing to his family. His little brother in particular. Frank had only started to deal with that when he'd blown out his knee in a play-off game at the Pond. The king fell from grace like a lead balloon.

Not one of the women he'd been dating had even called. Not one of them had wanted a thing to do with him once the parties and the notoriety and the money stopped coming. If it hadn't been for his forgiving family and his friendship with Prince that had stayed constant since college, Frank didn't know if he would have had the confidence and strength to turn his back on all of it and build a new life, a new career, and a new image. One that would keep the vamping vampires away for good. For good measure, he had changed his style of dress, changed his hair, and stopped wearing contacts.

If a woman wasn't interested in the package she saw, he sure as hell wasn't interested in her. It hadn't been a very social four years, but if it kept women like Lilith Smythe away, it was worth it. A little loneliness was a small price to pay for weeding out the poison apples. Frank almost smiled at that. Here he was with a storybook beauty who seemed to be more like a wicked witch. If he only had one of the magic tests he'd read about as a child, maybe he could decipher Lilith Smythe's flip-flopping behavior.

His mother had warned him about keeping make-believe and the real world straight, but magic and wizards had always intrigued him. And then his own dream had come true and he'd won a place on an NBA team. But the fairy-tale life had brought out an ugly side he hadn't thought existed in himself. And when the magic had abruptly ended and the real world slam-dunked him, he'd survived and found that making an honorable life with real people had a quality and a depth that lasted long after "happily ever after."

Beauty was only skin-deep and he would never let himself be fooled again.

"Frank?" His ears pricked and his warning sensors honed in on the plaintive note in her voice. Lilith had braided her hair in some intricate way that accentuated the fine-boned structure of her face and the purple shadows smudged under her eyes. Begrudgingly, he felt a flicker of conscience. Even the rich and famous got tired. This had been a hell of a night for both of them. But what did she want? Really?

"Let's talk about this in our seats, Ms. Smythe. It's ridiculous in here."

"What's ridiculous, *Frank,* is continuing to call me *Ms. Smythe* now that you've stupidly made people think we're married."

"Fine. Let's go, Lilith."

"Will you change seats with me?"

The unexpected question and its completely childish content blew his cork and forcefully reminded him of the type of woman he was dealing with. "Is that what this is about? Your damn seat?"

Lilith recoiled and clasped her hands, almost as if she were trying to decide her next move. She licked her lips and Frank narrowed his eyes. The woman was at it again.

"I-I need more room. I-I've never flown in coach before and I feel claustrophobic."

Frank bared his teeth. "So you decided to stretch your legs here in the bathroom?" A rosy flush stained her honey-toned cheeks. So she had some small particle of conscience after all.

"Frank." She squared her shoulders as much as possible and looked him in the eye. And he saw it again, that little flash of hurt mingled with fear this time. But indifference blinked it away and arrogance took its place.

"Children hate me. I can't sit next to that little girl for the next four and a half hours. I'll go crazy."

She almost made him believe it, but something was a fraction off kilter. High-society debs generally didn't like children, true. Kids read through bull too easily and drew away all the attention. Hmmm. This just might be a good way to test this unknown quantity. After all, once they got to St. Thomas he would have to count on her at least a little. Maybe he'd better see how thin this beauty's skin was.

"Shall we measure our legs, Ms.—Lilith?" He arched an eyebrow. "Just come out and go to sleep, for God's sake. I'll talk to the kid. You won't have to be bothered."

Suddenly the plane jerked and dropped as if it were being manipulated by a mad puppeteer. Frank slammed back against the door and bounced again when Lilith flattened him. Her arms, swaddled in the sleeves of his coat, shot up around his neck, and another dipping impact smashed them together. He could feel her trembling and the pounding of her heart drumming against his own. He'd never held such a tall woman, and her body lined up perfectly with every dip and ridge in his. Her face was buried in the crook of his neck, and he could feel her short gasps sough across his skin.

Time stopped. Nothing else existed but the fear and the adrenaline thundering through her body and into his. It felt as if he were in an old movie running in slow motion. Nothing around him seemed real. The woman quivering in his arms was his only anchor. Instinctively Frank wanted to comfort her. He wanted to comfort himself. He didn't want to die alone and unconnected. A sharp-edged, peppery tingle blasted through his chest and out to his straining limbs.

In that moment of breath-stealing awareness, he knew her thoughts; her deepest fear was *living* alone and unconnected. Their mirrored feelings swamped him. Without processing one rational thought, Frank pulled Lilith closer.

Three sharp raps exploded next to his ear.

"Sir, please come out and take your seats immediately. The captain has ordered all passengers to use their seat belts."

Frank did not glance down at Lilith as he peeled her arms away. He did not want to look into her eyes. He did not want his first impression of the plastic princess altered. He wished this had never happened. He didn't want to hold her for even another second for fear he'd sense something real from her again. Not for a brand-new knee would he let himself feel more than disgusted pity for a grasping socialite.

But was he as immune as he thought? Dammit! Maybe it wouldn't seem so terrible if he could blame it on her gorgeous body. Except her long legs and willowy curves hadn't moved him before. The hell of it was, that wasn't what had just gotten past his better judgment. Fear had torn away her mask and his defenses and for a bleak moment he'd felt her despair and lonely need. And he'd recognized it.

Frank shouldered around, wedged the door open, and shut off his reaction. He stood in the aisle until Lilith swayed next to him and fell into her seat, buckling the seat belt with shaking hands. The plane dropped again, and Frank angled away, using his back as a wall to block her harshly indrawn breath. He clenched his hands in his lap to keep from reaching for her. Good God, he had never let fear drive every drop of common sense out of his head like this before. Danger was part of his business, dammit! Why was he being so stupid about some rich witch? Why should he care if a plastic princess was scared to death? Maybe because it meant she wasn't quite so . . . plastic?

The plane intercom buzzed on in the cabin. A deep, confident voice assured the passengers that the turbulence was over. Just a few more minutes and they could resume normal cabin activity. Frank rubbed the bridge of his nose and then his eyes up under his glasses. He was rattled and it bothered him more than he cared to admit—let alone think about. Okay, he'd just toss off something impersonal and reassuring and then sleep or feign sleep until the plane landed. No more interaction for a while would be best.

He swiveled in the small seat and froze with his mouth open. Lilith and Shannon Shamblin were holding hands. Oh, yeah—and he'd been so disgusted by her highness's attitude toward this little girl—as if he were so superior. Damn! Not once while the plane had been dribbling across the sky had he thought of this child's welfare.

But Lilith had, no matter what she'd claimed in the bathroom.

The light flashed on the instruction panel and a synthetic bell chimed three times.

"There, you see, lady." A small, dainty hand wearing a Pocahontas ring patted Lilith's arm through his wrinkled coat sleeve. "It's all right now. I told you it would be."

Frank nearly swallowed his tongue.

"So, Shannon, what do you and your grandparents do for a whole month?"

"We play and go camping."

"That sounds fun. Tell me what you like best."

Lilith could not believe she was having such an easy conversation with a child. It really wasn't hard at all. She simply listened, really listened, and then asked questions as if Shannon were a real person. Children were people: that mind-boggling fact had somehow escaped her all these years. Lilith supposed she should be humiliated for acting as she had. Maybe three months ago she would have been. Gads, three months ago she would have been so out of it on Valium she wouldn't have even known she was flying. *Show no fear no matter what the cost. Always protect yourself.* She would have been in first class in a seat as far away from children as money could buy.

For that matter she wouldn't have even consented to go on this trip of doom. Lilith sighed and leaned her head back against the headrest, carefully avoiding any possible eye contact with the witness to her real humiliation. The safety she'd felt in those strong, soothing arms was absolutely horrifying. Horrifying because she hadn't wanted to let go. She briefly closed her eyes against the memory of her hero the nerd, peeling her clinging arms away and then leaving her as quickly as possible. Leaving her! Men never wanted to leave and only did so when she insisted. Frank Henson hadn't uttered a word since.

She shuddered as she remembered his accusations back at the hotel. Gads, had he thought she was making the moves on him in that sardine can of a bathroom? Lilith lifted a hand to her flushed cheeks and accidentally bumped his arm. She held her breath. He didn't move. Good . . . or was that bad?

"Lilith, did I really help you feel better?"

Two baby-fine brows puckered and the dove gray eyes they framed would not let her fudge one iota on the truth. For the first time since the battle of her opposing sides had begun months ago, Lilith felt a surge of tentative joy at this oh so vulnerable desire to let someone see her real feelings.

"You sure did, sweetie. In fact you made me feel better

than I have in a long time." She smiled a wide, natural smile and winked. The little girl beamed back and Lilith felt another jolt of insight.

It seemed to take so little to please this child. Maybe people who didn't have dollar signs or ladder-climbing shadowing their eyes when they looked at her could also be pleased so simply. Maybe she could find a way to connect with some of them, since her world was fast losing its appeal and even faster going to dump her completely.

The gnawing anxiety she'd been living with since the night she'd overheard Prince and Mil had eased only twice and only from the touch of honest, human compassion; no strings attached. One had been when sweet Shannon had grabbed on to her hand during the plane's rodeo ride. And the other—she swallowed and didn't dare let herself look—was when Frank Henson had held her.

For a moment Lilith's old, instinctive need to fend off emotion welled again. Fear was her worst enemy because giving in to it could expose her as the fraud she'd always been. Her pattern was to avoid it, buy it off, or medicate it away. But not this time. She drew in a deep breath through her nose and prepared to give this generous sprite a sincere thank-you. Her cursed pride be damned. By rights she should have been comforting the child, not the other way around.

"I was really afraid, Shannon, and you helped me feel like I wasn't so alone." Lilith struggled to keep a watery sound from her voice. Tears? Absolutely no way. She blinked and swallowed. "Hey, tell me what it's like camping. I've never done it."

"Really? But you're so old. Don't you have a grandma or grandpa anymore? Are they dead?"

"Well." Lilith hesitated. "Yes, I guess I am pretty old, and my grandparents are dead now. But I wish they had taken me camping like yours do." As if her grandparents would ever have left their servants. "You tell me all about it, Shannon, and it will be almost as good as going."

"Okay. And when you get your own little girl you can take her and teach her everything I said."

Stunned, Lilith quickly called upon the skills she had honed to perfection as a cover model. She set her face in stone, holding the interested, attentive expression in place as if it were the last Calvin Klein original in the world.

She hadn't thought of having a baby for over fifteen years. Once, shortly after Cindy and her father had become part of their family, Cindy had talked excitedly about maybe having another brother or sister. Barbara Smythe-Jones had ranted and raved the day Lilith had mentioned that possibility and her own dream to have a baby when she was older. Her mother had called her an idiot and a fool for even thinking about ruining her body with a pregnancy and her life with living millstones. In fact, it had been having the two of them so close together that had ended her own chances for a stunning career.

Six months later, Lilith had landed her first modeling job and started the endless journey of trying to make it up to her mother.

But the little girl who shyly took her hand and began talking about sleeping bags and tents didn't look at all like a millstone. She looked like an angel . . . or a fairy come to life. So Lilith closed her mind to all the doubts, fears, and questions that lay ahead and just let herself enjoy this guileless gift. Someone liked her.

Chapter Three

"I'm not leaving her, Frank, *darling!*" Lilith bit out, then leaned around him and wiggled her fingers at Shannon, who was standing at the airline information desk. "Airports are creepy so early in the morning, and our flight for St. Thomas isn't taking off for an hour and a half. I'm not leaving!"

Frank paced back and forth on the institutional-style burgundy carpet, his hands fisted in his dress-pants pockets. Suddenly Miss Keep-the-Child-Away had become the surrogate mother of the year. Okay, so the Miami airport was a little skeletal, but there were proper authorities in place and they needed to check their luggage—Damn! He raked a hand through his hair and rubbed the back of his neck. They had no luggage and, truthfully, seeing Ms. Smythe in the unforgiving light of day, he had to wonder what in the world he'd been thinking with the hat and the rest. She looked worse than bizarre. Frank felt for his wallet and approached the two so engrossed with each other.

"Listen, *Lil.*" He smirked very, very faintly at her indignant owl eyes. "Since you're waiting, I think I'll get us a few items for the island." He stepped quite close and put a hand firmly on her shoulder. "I expect to find you right here. You're not the kid's mother, so don't get carried away. In fact I'm surprised the novelty didn't wear off a few hours ago. You're not exactly the mother type."

Lilith drew up her wilted shoulders and spoke through clenched teeth, a mannerism he was becoming familiar with.

"Listen yourself, *darling*. Thanks to you, I have never before been so uncomfortable, tired, hungry, and unfashionable. I also know quite clearly that I am your definition of pond scum. And although I may not strike you as the motherly type, neither am I a murderer. So give me a break here."

She lowered her fierce gaze to the small head of sandy curls and Frank winced when he saw real regret flicker in her eyes and pull taut across those photogenic cheekbones. Just as quickly, the emotion passed and her face softened. All her brittle, practiced affectation smoothed away. When she lifted those topaz blue eyes to his once more, he could not deny the change. He could not deny the hurt he saw either. And he could not deny the fact that he'd callously thrown that mother crack at her, not even thinking she'd care. He wanted to like hell, but he couldn't.

"You're right, of course. I would be a terrible mother. I don't know the first thing about children."

Lilith reached out and slipped a plastic butterfly barrette from Shannon's hair, then deftly wove a French braid sideways across the crown of her head. Frank realized she was completely unaware of what she was doing and how naturally she was doing it. Why couldn't he have left well enough alone? He did not want to see this. The woman was a selfish manipulator and he'd best not forget it.

"Besides," she continued quietly, turning to look him full in the face, "mothering is just so endless and I'm not good at endless commitments. But I mean to see this through, Frank. I mean to see Shannon safe with her grandparents and Cindy safe, too."

"Don't forget Belinda Brown," he added, not sure exactly why.

Those perfect white teeth clenched again.

"Certainly. Belinda, too." Frank had the distinct impression that Lilith did not like Cindy's best friend. She dolefully fingered a limp strand of hair and pushed it behind her ear. "Look, if you can't believe me about this, then just

handcuff me now and get it over with. Either we have a truce and agree we're working together or forget it."

Frank rubbed his bristly jaw and debated with himself. After four years, here he was with his worst nightmare for a partner. The woman's face was probably in the dictionary under self-serving. He looked at her and saw the kind of beauty that even terrible clothes and twenty-four hours without sleep couldn't diminish. As beautiful and deadly as a sea anemone. Still, she hadn't actually complained much, for a witch. In fact, she seemed to be fitting that stereotypical mold less and less perfectly. And that had to be his lack of sleep talking for sure.

"Okay," Frank spat out. "We've got a truce as long as we both tell the truth and put the assignment first. I'll be back in thirty minutes."

He race-walked toward a souvenir area, but stopped before turning the corner and glanced back over his shoulder. Lilith was there. She and Shannon were hugging and laughing, their two heads close together, platinum blond and beach-sand brown. The calculating, hard-edged Ms. Smythe had vanished and instead he saw what his own words had declared to be impossible: a mother and daughter . . . with his color hair in a shimmering circle of light.

Frank sucked in a hiss of air through his teeth, snatched off his glasses, and cleaned the lenses on his shirtfront.

He needed a hit of caffeine and he needed it right now.

This was awful. One of the worst feelings Lilith had ever experienced. She clutched a small sheet of paper in her hand and slumped on a gray-and-burgundy brick planter near the spot where Frank had left her. No wonder she'd stopped caring so much about people. It sucked! Shannon's name and address were printed in a listing childish scrawl and Lilith couldn't stop looking at the paper. The grandparents had seemed wonderful, like storybook models, and they'd been so grateful for Lilith's kindness to their sweet Shannon. After a brief, cheek-to-cheek hug and a promise to write, the little girl was gone.

Against her will, Lilith felt the corners of her mouth pull down as if they had weights attached. Why did it seem that the fariy-tale endings in some people's lives came at the cost of others? She blinked. Gads, people had probably thought that of her life for years. Agents and photographers had called her "Princess" since she'd been a young teen, and she had childishly thought what others probably thought, too—that it meant her life would be magically happy.

Wrong. She plunked her elbows down on her thighs and tugged at a loose button on Frank's coat. Lots of folks would hate her for this, but it was true nonetheless. Just because she had everything that a princess ought to have, it hadn't guaranteed a happy ending. Every time Frank called her "Your Highness" or "plastic princess" it only drove home what an empty shell her life had become. Sure, you could live a long time in such a privileged shell, but when it cracked . . . there was nothing left. It was hollow. You were hollow.

Her mouth trembled and the corners dipped again. This would not do at all. Fine, she had had a good experience for once with a child. At least she and the child thought so. Clearly Frank Henson did not. Oh sure, when they'd been in danger he'd shown compassion, and she supposed that was the most she could expect. He was the kind of man who would do that for anyone. But he didn't like her.

Lilith carefully folded the precious paper and rubbed her stinging nose with the back of her hand. What kind of torture was this? She didn't even have a purse or a Kleenex or a comb or moisturizer. And passersby were beginning to stare—the kind of look-at-that-weirdo stare she had never, ever gotten. She felt dejected and friendless and so emotional she feared she would not be able to sustain her aloof front long enough to finish this hellish trip.

With a self-deprecating grimace she wondered what would happen if she suddenly jumped up and marched around the terminal like Lucy Ricardo, singing "Friends of the Friendless." Of course, lucky Lucy had a party full of friends that eventually proved her wrong. Lilith would only have a party full of friends if she guaranteed the most exclusive caterer, the most expensive champagne, and the most A-list of guests.

And then those friendships would last about as long as the party and linger or flourish in direct relationship to her current popularity. That message had been driven home quite ruthlessly ever since she'd slowed down on her jobs. Even Milicent had complained she was becoming a bore and a hanger-on.

Now, looking like a freak and sitting all alone in a cold airport, Lilith had finally discovered how precious uncalculated friendship really was. But one needed to offer something meaningful to build that kind of friendship on and she was fresh out of redeeming qualities. With hunched shoulders she twisted away from the main thoroughfare. Gads, it was pure idiocy even to think of Frank Henson liking her! Why the heck should he? The man didn't have a drop of respect for her. A painful image of Prince and Milicent formed in her mind, and Lilith vividly recalled Prince using those very words to her enraged sister.

Do you know how I knew I loved Cindy? That it was so much more than desire or sex? She made me laugh. She could laugh at herself. She made me want to be better just by being around her. A man will never truly love a woman he can't respect.

Never love?

Lilith sprang to her feet, stalked over to a trash can, and stuffed in the cursed black hat. She rubbed hard, small circles in the center of her forehead and took a cleansing breath. Okay, she knew she had problems. And she knew she needed to sort through them and figure out why, at this time in her life, the value of so much seemed to be changing. Things were probably going to get very ugly, and that had to account for some of the weird stuff churning away inside of her.

But given all of that, she had to be really, really sick to have even connected the word—she swallowed—*love* with Frank Henson. The man was a self-righteous nerd and any further thoughts of wanting him to like her were more than stupid. They gave a whole new meaning to the expression *psychotic episode*.

A heavy hand fell on her shoulder, and, startled, Lilith lurched forward. Gads, she was losing every ounce of poise she'd ever possessed.

"Hey! It's me."

She whirled around, determined to remain aloof and competent at all costs. At the very least she could cling to her dignity. Closing her eyes for a millisecond, Lilith silently vowed that she would rather shop from a rack in a discount store than give this man another reason to belittle her. But when she opened her eyes she nearly lost her resolve and . . . her sight.

Her immediate impression was that only a bad LSD trip in the sixties could have produced the pattern and colors of Frank's ensemble. The shirt was beyond loud. It was a screaming yellow, orange, and green splattered in a bird-of-paradise motif. The pants were solid lime green, gathered at the ankles with deep side pockets. Never had a pair of black-framed glasses looked more out of place. Only the moppish hair fit the stunning picture.

Lilith pressed her lips together. Although Frank had somehow shaved, he'd been transformed into the consummate caricature of a gauche tourist. Suddenly Lilith regretted trashing part of her hideous disguise. She didn't want a living soul to know she was traveling with the Caribbean clown.

"I see she got off all right."

"What?" Lilith shook her head and dragged her throbbing eyes up to Frank's face.

"Shannon? You know, the child you couldn't leave?

Bronwyn Wolfe

Wow, have you got a short attention span, woman. I see what you mean about the *endless* issue. Things don't move you for long, do they?"

Lilith gritted her teeth. It was pointless to defend herself because it had been true . . . before. And truthfully she didn't know if it had really changed for good. But if feeling pain and loss was an indicator, well, time would tell. "She got off just fine. Her grandparents are wonderful people."

"Great. Here's some stuff I got for you." He shoved her a tote bag screen-printed with huge red hibiscus blossoms and checked his watch. "You've got about twenty minutes to change and take care of whatever. I'll be waiting outside the ladies' room door. But hurry; I want to grab some food before we board."

A quarter of an hour later, Lilith studied herself critically in the mirror. The black hat would not be missed at all now. She felt confident that she would never be recognized by any of her acquaintances. What was it about being with this man that caused all her most dreaded scenarios to materialize? Oh, to take back the words that moments ago had fallen so glibly from her tongue. Never before had she worn a one-size-fits-all dress. If one could call this scoop-necked, puffed-sleeve explosion of color a dress. Lilith had a horrible feeling that it was, in fact, a *muumuu*.

She, who had modeled some of the most glamorous and glorious clothes in the world, reduced to this. Oh, Mr. Fashion Impaired must be laughing it up, waiting for her to appear. And she'd thought he looked bad! Lilith shuddered delicately and plucked at a fabric poof with the tips of two acrylic nails. Move over, Bozo. Thoughtfully he had provided a pair of lovely purple plastic sandals and a shocking pink-and-violet scarf to accessorize her outfit. Couldn't the man have had enough common sense to pick something that, dare she say, blended with his own outfit? No! The only color they had in common was a splash or two of fluorescent yellow.

To his credit, Frank had evidently scraped enough common sense out of his superinflated brain to secure and provide a few basic toiletries. With a rueful shake of her head, Lilith washed her face and brushed her teeth. This at least was heaven. She quickly rebraided her hair and paused, furrowing her brow at the one truly beautiful thing that had been in the tote bag: an exquisite enameled butterfly in rich, beautiful shades of the garish colors she was wearing.

It didn't seem like the kind of thing Frank Henson would ever buy, let alone consider so carefully as to match it to her muumuu. Perhaps the saleswoman had done it? Of course.

A few minutes later she was as ready as she was ever going to be. Her ruined silk dress and shoes were stuffed in the bag, and it felt like weeks had passed since she'd put them on. Fourteen hours had never lasted so long. The only remnant left of her wedding finery was her diamond studs. Frank Henson would probably scoff and belittle this, but diamond studs were an excellent fashion investment. They went with everything and made a woman sparkle.

Lilith wrapped the brilliant scarf around her head and stuffed the ends into her drooping neckline. The voluminous skirt could be dealt with, but the shoulders in a one-size-fits-all were a few sizes too big for her. And since she hadn't been wearing a bra under the slip dress and since Frank hadn't gotten one for her—heaven forbid—Lilith was stuck being a bit more "free" than she liked to be. But not one word of complaint would pass her lips.

She eyed her reflection and leaned forward. If it killed her she would not give that perverse man the satisfaction he was anticipating. If nothing else, she would hold fast to her dignity, and perhaps he might come to respect at least that.

* * *

An hour and a half later they were flying over the sapphire sea of the Caribbean, looking for all the world like a pair of crazed limbo callers.

Frank was too confused to sleep. He was faking great interest in the plane's emergency escape instructions while sneaking furtive glances at the woman out of the corner of his eye. Lilith had drifted into a doze and her head looked to be bent at an uncomfortable angle. How did a female with hair the color of moonlight have such naturally dark eyebrows and eyelashes? He may not have been close to many women over the last few years, but he knew makeup when he saw it. Lilith Smythe wasn't wearing a drop.

Frank shifted in his small coach seat and tried to wedge an ankle up on top of his other leg. Before he realized what was happening, he'd accidentally snagged the hem of her muumuu and dragged it up over her knees. The tent was so big that she didn't feel a bit of resistance and had no reaction. Unfortunately the same couldn't be said for him.

Her legs were the shade of rich coffee mixed with a good dollop of cream—smooth, brown, and bare. He swallowed and unhooked the skirt, letting it fall back in place. Even her knees were beautiful, and Frank suddenly wondered if she had ever struggled with her physical appeal as he had. He knew lots of women irrationally disliked someone like Lilith. They were often jealous, and so they attacked until they found something negative to destroy that beauty with.

He flattened his lips with the side of a fist and mentally wandered down a dangerous path. Had Lilith Smythe ever experienced betrayal or disappointment like he had? No! They were nothing alike. Their circumstances and family life had been totally different. That was why he'd picked the muumuu: to drive their differences home and to make the woman look as ridiculous and unappealing as possible. He eyed her again, twisting his mouth with disgust. It hadn't worked.

Add that to the fact that she hadn't argued or been petty or sulked or whined either. Frank didn't like it, any of it. It didn't fit. She'd been cool and calm, waltzing out of the bathroom as if she were draped in satin and furs. Striding up the runway and into the plane like she was the pièce de résistance of a spring show in Paris.

He didn't like her. She reminded him of everything he'd grown to loathe in his old life, everything he'd grown to loathe in himself. And it should be as easy as shooting one of his famous three-pointers, to swish any feelings for her right out of his head. But, dammit, he'd seen her fear and felt her tremble in his arms. He'd seen a completely changed Lilith in the presense of Shannon Shamblin. And worst of all, he knew exactly what it was like to have the fates dish out something beyond your control, then force you down another path not of your choosing. Exactly the way he was forcing Lilith.

Whoa! Hold up there a minute. Frank shook his head and reared back in his seat. What in the hell was he thinking? This woman had tried to vamp him from the very start. Roberta had urgently warned him about her manipulating and her decadent lifestyle. It was just his hormones causing this reaction. Of course, his hormones were turning his logical mind to mush because it had been so long since he'd been attracted to a woman. Attracted! Hell, he hadn't actually thought that, had he?

Idiot! Maybe her beauty went a hair deeper than the skin, but she'd never be able to live a normal life and he sure as hell wouldn't go back to her world. A world that had more false fronts than a boomtown in the Old West.

Lord help him, what was he thinking? Her—a normal life? Him—back to that other world? Damn! As soon as this mess was over he had to start dating immediately.

Frank uncrossed his legs and spread his hands wide on his thighs. Attraction be damned. Literally dammed up with disciplined resolve as effective as a twelve-foot-thick wall of steel-reinforced concrete. Good. This little mental talk had straightened him out and alerted him in time. He would be civil, but that was it.

Businesslike, distant, remote—

A soft sigh and a gentle nudge derailed his speeding train of thought as fast as a caboose jumping the tracks.

Frank dropped his chin to his chest and looked down through his eyelashes. Her head was suddenly resting on his shoulder and the neck of her dress had gaped and pulled, revealing a polished, butternut shoulder and the gentle rise of a smooth breast. Frank could feel his heart start to pound and saliva pool in his mouth. He swallowed and shifted his own wire-taut shoulders, only to cause Lilith to lean in further. Her ruffled neckline dipped and the shadowy, velvet valley between her breasts made him break out in sweat.

Damn, how long had it been since he'd had a serious date? Six months? He couldn't remember. But Prince had dogged him lately about his ludicrous appearance and the fact that maybe he was looking for a perfection that didn't exist. That in his own way he was presenting as false a front as the women he despised. Frank scrubbed a hand down his face and turned his head away. How could he let a woman like this get to him? ·

He couldn't. He wouldn't. With an abrupt move of his arm he tried to shove her head over. Frank swiveled with the motion, and instead of the movement making it better, she slid halfway down his chest. One long-fingered, long-nailed hand crept up the buttoned placket of his shirt, and he sucked in a deep breath, trying to pull his body back away from her touch. What kind of woman made a move like that in her sleep? He froze. Maybe she wasn't sleeping. . . .

"Hey, Lilith." He reached over with his free arm and tapped her on the head. She nuzzled. It figured! "Woman, your con isn't working. Get off me."

"Frank," Lilith whispered in a husky, wavery voice that narrowed his eyes and prickled the hairs on the back of his neck. "You came back." She laid a warm palm on his arm and tipped her head back against his shoulder. Was she as foggy as she seemed or was she trying to mess with his mind completely?

And then the plane dropped. And her half-closed eyes went round as silver dollars and almost as gray with fear. Frank didn't even have time to speak before her arms were knotted behind his neck and she was moaning softly into his collar. Sensations just like before poured through him, wiping out control and reason. He could not stop his hands from closing around her shaking body and hugging her tight.

The plane bobbled twice more and Lilith went rigid, then yanked herself away trying to surge out of her seat.

"Stop. Stop that," he ordered, unfastening his seat belt and using the weight of his upper body to pin her flush against the corner created by the seat and the plane wall. The pressure seemed to calm her. She stopped struggling and went very still. Frank lifted her face with a knuckle.

"Are you awake, Lilith? Are you all right?" He nudged her face higher so he could see her eyes. The pupils were so black and so big that only a thin circle of blue haloed them. Now *he* was getting a little scared. He unfurled his fingers against her cheek and patted firmly. "Wake up, sugar. You're okay. I won't let anything hurt you."

"Kiss me, please—I'm so cold. Ice in here."

She pulled his hand down from her face and pressed it high on the curve of her breasts, flattening his palm on the expanse of skin left uncovered by the gaping muumuu. A strange roaring filled Frank's ears and he felt the scraping slide of her fingernails riding around his waist and then digging urgently into his back. Her heart hammered beneath his palm, sending shock waves of desire pulsing through his reawakening body.

He knew he should pull away, but his tingling hand slid up instead and curled around her neck. He knew he would regret this, but his other hand pushed its way between her body and the seat, pressing into the small of her back. He knew he was a goner when she arched into him and whimpered against his mouth.

"Ahhhyes soowarmmm."

Frank ignited like a summer-brown field of dry grass. Lilith's lips moved against his in a frenzy that caught him up and hurled him somewhere he'd never been before. Almost instantly, the pulse throbbing in her neck had his lower body throbbing an echoing rhythm. She kissed him in rapid, frantic pecks, as if her need were so great she couldn't stop. He pulled her closer and slipped his hand around to cup the back of her neck, spreading his fingers wide and kneading the base of her fragile skull.

His nose brushed alongside hers, back and forth across her icy skin. Fanned by the heat of his ragged breath, her faint, exotic scent filled his senses, and Frank captured her rooting mouth, trying to slow the wild pace she was setting.

She bucked against him as if in protest and he tightened his fingers to hold her head still. Frank opened his mouth over hers, wanting more than this frenzied touching; wanting to reach her and calm her and soothe the panicked something that was racking her body. The moment his tongue rubbed against her trembling lips she opened and he swept inside . . . his fiery breath shockingly surrounded by the icy-cold cavern of her mouth. Pinpricks of strange images and urges stung like tiny darts against the primal force that drove him.

He had to warm her. He had to save her before she froze in the castle. The woman he held was turning to ice in his arms, her body chilling his. His nose burned as if he were breathing frigid air. She moaned desperately into his mouth and shivered violently against him. Instinctively he swept inside with his tongue, flickering over the tender flesh as if he were a living flame coaxing her to burn. Over and over he slipped in deeply and then pulled back to pluck at her lips, nipping and sucking the soft little pillows until they felt hot and full. All he could think of was setting her free . . . melting the ice . . . saving her.

She opened wider under his insistent tutoring and finally met his tongue as if the ice had disappeared and she was free to move at last. Scorchingly slow, steady strokes; relentlessly rubbing smooth against rough; heat against heat. Sweet and wet and sizzling and—

"Excuse, me, sir?"

The crystal castle shattered.

"Ummm, sir?"

An abrupt shake broke the searing seal, and a cold rush of reality poured over Frank Henson like water from a glacial stream.

Dazed, he blinked and looked over his shoulder into the beet-red face of a young stewardess wearing mile-high eyebrows and a wary smile.

"Seat belts, please," she singsonged as if he'd just been awakened from a little nap. "We'll be landing soon."

Frank stiffly pressed his shoulders into the upholstered seat as if fighting the pull of a g-force and fumbled for his seat belt. Damn. He let out another few inches and folded his hands discreetly. He didn't speak and he didn't look. But after maybe three agonizing minutes he angled a peek out of the corner of his eye and locked straight into Lilith's stunned gaze. Her eyes were so wide and so shocked he thought she might be preparing to scream. She was staring at him as if he were a two-headed monster.

"I have never been treated like that in public."

Frank curled the hands in his lap into fists. He'd fallen right into the witch's trap. Hell, maybe she'd even cast a spell on him. Where in the world had all those impressions of ice come from? He lifted a hand to his forehead and pressed against a suddenly aching temple. His glasses were cockeyed and he realized he must look even more foolish than usual. Not at all like the white knight he'd just had a waking delusion about.

Oh, yeah, he'd done a terrific job of it, too. His diva damsel in distress looked ready to call for a disinfectant. No way was he going to let her accuse him of something sleazy.

"Listen, lady. You were terrified and freaking out." He raised a finger and shoved it at her face. "You begged me to kiss you and you went right along with it. You were clawing right through my shirt, babe, so don't act the offended virgin with me. We both know there's nothing farther from the truth!"

Lilith's outraged expression went abruptly slack, as if she'd just flicked off a switch somewhere in her head. She turned away from him and scrunched herself into the corner, while Frank began an intense, psychologically unsound internal dialogue to deny the most devastating kiss he'd ever shared. It was imperative. He had no other choice. He didn't like her.

Chapter Four

Lilith didn't know how things could possibly get worse. She'd had about two hours of sleep in the last thirty, looked like a reject from the Cirque du Soleil, and was now ensconced in a dingy, plebeian motel room, or "guest house," as the low-priced accommodations on St. Thomas were called. She both felt and looked like a limp noodle.

But by far the most disastrous development had to do with the man sitting at the laminated desk talking on the phone. The man who looked like a nerd and kissed like . . . like no man she'd ever kissed before. Lilith pulled the scarf from her head and dropped the sunglasses on the passably clean, but worn, multicolored bedspread. That cursed dream, the turbulence, and the stress had all swirled together in her sleep, and then when Frank was suddenly there, she knew he'd come to save her, help her, warm her. For a few breathless moments she'd felt all that and more.

Lilith leaned back against the metal bed frame and rested her head on the stark wall. The "more" part was what really scared her because the hard cold facts had quickly intruded and still buzzed in her cottony head. She had never begged for a kiss until now. She had never needed a man so much until that moment in the plane. She had never had a man remain so unaffected by her, ever.

Frank had acted as if they just exchanged insurance in-formation after a car accident instead of the most bone-melting kiss she'd ever experienced. Or had it been? Now, after the initial humiliation had abated somewhat, Lilith couldn't help but wonder . . . hope? She hadn't felt much of anything for so long; maybe her dream had enhanced the whole thing.

It had been months since any of the men she knew or met had caused so much as a ripple of awareness. Lilith closed her eyes and sighed deeply. Perhaps it was time to go back to a therapist. Actually, she should probably make an appointment, because over the next few days she was most likely going to have what was left of her waning self-esteem stomped right out of her. Her dwindling career had been the first blow, then Milicent's criticism and selfishness, and now this horrible debacle.

Belinda Brown thought she wasn't human; then Frank Henson accused her of bartering with her body, which she really hadn't been doing. It was just that men were so much easier to control once their hormones were involved. But he'd never see that. And that was even before the kiss. She rolled her head and raised a hand to tug the butterfly barrette and her braid out from behind her shoulder blade. Heaven help her, once he discovered she'd left out a huge chunk of information, and her mother and sister discovered she'd tipped the authorities, and Cindy learned Lilith could have warned her weeks ago . . .

Thwap! A deflated pillow hit her in the face.

"Don't you dare go to sleep now, Your Highness. We don't have days to gentle you out of jet lag. You'll have to tough it out till at least eight tonight."

Lilith flapped a hand at the hair in her face and tossed the offending missile away. Frank swiveled in the mismatched desk chair and held the receiver against his ear with a cocked shoulder. "As soon as I make this call we'll head out and do some preliminary scouting."

He reached behind his back and grabbed a can of soda she hadn't known he had. "Here. A good dose of caffeine should help." Frank tossed it without a word of warning and Lilith's drugged reactions were too slow. The can hit her square in the chest. Her lips formed a surprised *O* and she gingerly rubbed the aching spot between her breasts. Her nemesis abruptly looked at the phone and busily pressed in a series of numbers. The clod didn't even care that he'd hurt her.

Lilith felt a disgusting sting at the back of her throat. Gads! This was becoming pathetic. How stupid had she become? Where was her pride? How could she let this one man's disdain—this, this *nerd*—affect her like this? The last three months of conflicting emotions had left her too drained. She was too tired. After all, no one had *ever* really cared when she was in pain. Her mother never wanted to see it and Milicent was too concerned with herself. What was so different about this time? Besides—Lilith grimaced and closed her hand tightly around the cold can—princesses were never supposed to hurt, or cry, or be unhappy. Nobody thought they had a right to be.

"Don't tell me you never open your own cans?"

Oooooo! She hated him! That kiss had been the dream, all right. No way did a man like Frank Henson have enough experience to deliver what she'd felt. Lilith gave him one of her haughtiest looks and jammed her long thumbnail under the pop-top. Thank God he had turned away and started talking at the precise moment her champagne-colored nail flew through the air and bounced on the faded teal carpet. She'd show him if it killed her!

"What do the police say? Oh, sure, the woman's just disappeared and left her clothes behind, but that's no cause for alarm. Ms. Chalmers still insists Prince hasn't returned her messages? I don't know. . . . Let's see, it's about three in the afternoon here. Okay, I'll call tomorrow morning at eight o'clock St. Thomas time. Yea, it'll be Tuesday. We'll make a decision then. Fine. Bye."

Frank hung up the phone and stood while glancing at his watch. "Okay, let's go."

Lilith gritted her teeth, set her half-empty cola on the

175

scratched end table, and swung her legs over the side of the bed. Just as she was about to stretch across the spread to snag her scarf, Frank unexpectedly stepped forward, scooped it up, and dangled it in front of her nose. She reached for it, but when her fingers closed over the wild fabric, he abruptly twisted his fist and turned her hand, denuded thumb up.

The moment his amber eyes kindled with sardonic glee, Lilith completely lost it. Before either one of them knew what was happening, she'd formed a fist and punched him hard in the solar plexus. A gust of compressed air hissed out between his lips and she reared back, shaking her pulsing hand.

"I guess I had that coming, Ms. Smythe."

"Right from the beginning, Mr. Henson."

"Damn his black, beady eyes," Frank exclaimed as he slammed open the motel door and stalked across the carpet. He threw the keys down on the desk and pinched the bridge of his nose. "I know that Dejong knows something. I could smell it—and it wasn't easy. The man reeked of booze and tobacco."

Lilith wobbled in behind him and shut the door. She hadn't truly thought it was possible, but now she knew exactly how things could get worse. She'd spent the last five horrendous hours proving it.

Her legs felt like Jell-O and her hair smelled of stale smoke. Exhaustion and shock were making her punchy. She would never have believed that after all the winter seasons she'd spent on St. Thomas, and knowing what a small place it was, she could have totally missed the existence of such an ugly underbelly. The lush, beautiful island with its exotic smells and tastes had disappeared as the sultry, sullied night had snaked in around them.

She cast a listless glance at Frank, who was sitting on the edge of one of the double beds, his head in his hands. He straightened up and glared at her. "If I don't get some answers in the morning from my men I'm gonna lean on that guy. He thinks he's some big-time operator owning that sleazy little bar, but I'll find a way to get to him. The fool has no idea how personal this is. I'd do just about anything for Prince Chalmers. Are you sure you didn't hear anything else? Have you ever been here?"

Lilith sank down on the lumpy mattress and had to hold back a pitiful sigh. This place was a dump, but for the first time she understood how grateful one could be for the most basic comforts. She curled on her side, got comfortable, and then she lied. Straight-faced and deliberately she said, "No and no," toed off her purple sandals, and continued, "I'm going to sleep now and if you try to stop me, I'll hit you again."

Frank narrowed his eyes as if just seeing her for the first time. Well, she knew she looked awful. One couldn't ride on the back of a motor scooter up hills and down, driven by billowing trade winds and a madman, without doing serious damage to one's coiffure and ensemble. In fact there had probably never been another time in her life when she'd looked worse. And that included the night of her emergency appendectomy. But even more amazing, she didn't give a flying flip.

Two more nails had bitten the dust when Frank had taken one sharp curve too many and Lilith had slid right off into a hibiscus bush on the side of a ribbon-thin road. And she had scabs. Scabs on knees praised by some of the most elite judges of beauty in the world.

"You can take the bathroom first," he offered in a half-argumentative, half-tentative tone.

"I'm sleeping!"

"Hey, look." Frank palmed his lime-covered knees and leaned forward, his glasses reflecting the dim light from the one yellow ceramic lamp. "For a woman used to the lifestyle you normally live, this must seem like a trip to the Stone Age. I know you've had a rough couple of days. Hell, I'm tired myself, but this has to be done. Don't act like a spoiled brat and think you're going to make me feel bad about any of this. I didn't purposely dump you off the bike, and your damn nails can be glued back on. End of disaster." He finished with a wide sweep of one hand.

"I have nothing clean to sleep in."

"Well, hell, Your Highness," he gritted out through clenched teeth, a mannerism she was becoming familiar with. "I thought I made it clear that you have nothing I'm interested in. So wrap up in a sheet for all I care."

"I can't tell you how happy it makes me to know I'm sufficiently repellent to a man like you."

"Fine!" Frank surged to his feet and began to unbutton his shirt. Lilith closed her eyes . . . almost. "Suit yourself."

A pair of surprisingly broad shoulders that tapered to a slim waist suddenly came into her limited line of vision. Frank whirled around and chucked his rainbow-colored shirt at the desk, and Lilith traced the generous triangle of light brown hair that covered the hard rise of his chest and trailed down the lean contour of his stomach. A ripple with the power of a tidal wave rolled through her body and she flashed back to their kiss and the comforting, delicious feel of those long, corded arms tight around her. She squeezed her eyes shut and wished she hadn't seen anything. It would only make things worse. How much worse— Oh, God! Don't even think it!

The sharp crack of the bathroom door signaled the all clear and she jumped up to crank on the air conditioner, then scurried back to her bed. At the very least she could be cool, and suddenly she desperately needed to be cool. Then in the morning, if the news back in California was good—if Cindy and Belinda were accounted for—she was outta here. She'd go to the Riviera and live it up until she was able to straighten out her thinking and put the opinion of a certain nerdy professor into perspective.

The thrum of the shower bored into her ears, but she refused to let her mind wander. Instead she covered her head with a pillow and concentrated on the message she'd mail Shannon tomorrow.

"No! Noooo! Frank, help me! Help!"

Frank rolled onto his knees, one hand reaching for the handgun he hadn't brought and the other tossing off the sheets tangled at his feet. It was freezing. His heart was pounding and he couldn't see a thing in the coal black room. Adrenaline zapped through him like a bolt of pure electricity. Good God, he could hardly breathe.

"Frank! Hurry!"

He damn near broke his neck doing just that in a blind effort to reach Lilith—once he realized it was she who was screaming like a banshee.

"Lilith," he croaked, stumbling onto her bed and frantically patting the mattress to find her. He connected with something, a chilled, bare ankle, and shimmied right up that conduit of skin until he could pull her close. She fought him just as she had on the plane, and he struggled to hold her with one arm while he strained with the other to reach the lamp on the small table between their beds.

Instantly a pool of yellow light spilled across the hills and valleys of Lilith's bedding, making it look like a giant relief map. A relief map of another world peopled with only the two of them. Frank squinted against the disorienting glare. He was sprawled nearly on top of her, and her rapid breathing perfectly matched his own. The ragged sounds filled the room, competing with the hum of the damned air conditioner. She was scared to death. And she wasn't awake.

Hell, she'd been dreaming on the plane, too.

"Lilith. Sugar?" he murmured low and soft, watching her wide, wide eyes. "You're all right. It's me, Frank; I won't let anything hurt you."

"Yes—youwill," she whispered with a razory edge. "You leave—meinthe—iiiice."

"Lilith." He moved to kneel beside her and then wrapped

his hands around her shoulders and pulled her up. "Wake up, woman. Come on, now."

Dammit, he'd pushed her too far. He hadn't let her sleep, purposely set them up in the crudest accommodations; and then hauled her all over the island on that cheap scooter. All to take the royal pain in the butt down a notch or two. Prince was right. He was being as manipulative as the bloodsuckers he hated. Frank shook her once, twice; the blank look in her pale eyes was creepy as hell, as if there were nothing behind the clear glass.

Then her eyelids fluttered and her soul came back from wherever it had been hiding and those round eyes filled with horror. He was caught so off guard that with almost no effort she was able to yank out of his grasp and scramble to the corner of the bed against the wall.

"Bad dream, huh?" he managed to get out, hoping she'd answer with a rational response. All at once Frank realized he was sitting there in nothing but his boxers and goose bumps. He got up, turned off the cold air, and then sat back down, slowly pulling a corner of the sheet across his lap. Wide, blinking eyes followed his every move.

"I-I didn't—I wasn't trying to get y-you in my bed," she stammered, tucking her loose, tangled hair behind her ears with trembling hands. "I believe you—you aren't interested—really."

Frank raised his eyes to the ceiling and shook his head. "I know that, Lilith. I'm not trying to protect myself from you." He gestured at his covered lap and grimaced with self-disgust. *Henson, you arrogant bastard.* "In fact, I think I more than deserved that right cross you gave me earlier. You were dreaming on the plane, too, weren't you?"

She nodded but didn't move, and he felt like an even bigger bastard because he knew exactly what it was like to have a nightmare and wake up scared and alone. The first few months after his injury he'd dreaded the nights. And that reminded him of the man he'd worked so hard to change.

"Listen, I know how it is to have frightening dreams. I had an accident a couple of years ago that pretty much screwed my life to the wall. For weeks I relived it when I slept, only to wake up like a crazy man. It wasn't till after I talked it out with a good friend that it started to happen less and less. Wanna tell me about yours? It has something to do with ice? Right?"

"Was it Prince?" He knew she was evading his question, but maybe it would help her to know why this search for Wolfe meant so much.

"Yes. Prince has been a good friend since college. He got me interested in a new career after basketball."

"I don't have any good friends."

Frank tried desperately not to acknowledge the twinge he felt at her flat words. Perhaps she wasn't fully awake. He leaned closer. The witch type almost never revealed such truth. But Lilith had and she was completely coherent now. She was a paradox, this woman. He didn't want to see that or feel it, but he did.

She'd never believe him for a second if he told her that crammed against the wall in a shapeless tent, wearing no makeup, and sporting hair fashioned like a haystack, she almost paralyzed him with her beauty. And paralyzed him with dread because the beauty he was beginning to be moved by was deep inside, trying to find its way out.

Oh, yes, dearie . . . Frank reared back at the strange voice echoing in his head. What? Then on its very heels the most bizarre memory started playing in his mind.

He and his little sister, years ago, reading her favorite stories over and over. At the time, he'd come up with a theory that heroines like the ones in "The Princess and the Pea" and "The Princess Who Couldn't Laugh" were far inferior to the women he'd dubbed "blue-collar royalty," like Cinderella and Snow White.

He and his mother had had quite the absurd conversation about fairy tales and the fact that perhaps the message was that those particular princesses, like some of us, needed a nudge or direction to do the right thing. After all, how could they be expected to act like real people when they'd never lived a real life?

He'd completely forgotten that. Frank swallowed uncomfortably and shifted on the bed. How did a woman so famous and privileged end up with no friends? Fool! He knew exactly how. You believed your own hype, and your so-called friends were friends with *it*. When that changed, everything changed. Maybe Lilith was really trying, but no one cared enough to help her. If Prince had given up on him and the stuck-up snob he'd become for a while, where would he be now?

Damn! This was weird. From the moment they'd been thrown together at the reception things had begun to spin out of control. But there had to be a reason. That was one thing he'd learned after basketball was lost to him. If you hung in there, things had a way of working out. Maybe he was supposed to do for Lilith a little of what Prince had done for him. Well, he sure as hell hoped he wouldn't live to regret it. No matter what, Prince had to come first, not his sudden urge to be a Boy Scout.

"Lilith." He stopped, then started again. "I know we're not good friends. I know I've given you a pretty hard time, but I want you to know I respect your willingness to help me and I really do understand about nightmares. Why don't you lie down and try to go back to sleep? If you want to talk, I'll be right here. And if the darkness doesn't bother you, I'll turn off the light so you can have some privacy."

Lilith went completely still, and then she nodded. She never took her gaze off him while she uncurled beneath the covers. Frank waited until she settled. Their eyes locked and her wary longing was as easy to see as the ocean floor beneath the crystal clear water of the Caribbean. At that moment Frank felt such a powerful need to comfort this vulnerable woman that he had to turn away and flick off the light.

For fifteen tense and silent minutes he waited on his

bed. Finally, out of the safe cocoon of darkness he'd spun for her, Lilith began to speak, to tell. The dream had only happened a few times. She was always imprisoned in a castle of ice, but this time it had been worse because she'd seen her mother and sister there, too, lifeless and blue—beyond help.

"Every time I dream, I'm colder, I'm less able to feel. Isn't that stupid?" Her husky, self-deprecating voice wrapped around him in the darkness and he clenched the sheet in his fists, stunned. He hadn't made the connection before. But on the plane he'd experienced it. Felt the deadly cold. When he'd kissed Lilith he'd seen her dream.

What was going on between them?

Damn the fact that the high season was in full swing and not another room in the seedy motel had been available. Otherwise he'd never have known. Never have known she could make him feel this way. Never have known about her dreams and never have been about to ask the question that was forming on his lips.

"You said something about me leaving you in the ice. Am I always in the dream? Does anyone else come to help you?"

He held his breath.

"Ummm . . . You weren't in the first one, but the second and third, yes. And no. No one else comes."

Not even for an instantaneous, direct line to Princeton would he ask the next question burning on the tip of his tongue. Not tonight. Maybe not ever. Instead Frank said, "Think you can sleep now?"

"Yes. Thanks."

He waited for another heavy, uncomfortable silence, but it didn't materialize. The darkness seemed intimate and soothing and lapped away at the last twenty-four hours of tension in warm, rolling waves. His body relaxed and his mind let go of the "ifs" and "mights" that waited in to-morrow. It drifted back to the one thing that still kept him from giving in to exhaustion, and he spoke before he could edit himself.

"I'm sorry about that can, sugar." Oh, man, was he out of it. Maybe she was asl—

"Issokay . . . doesn't hurt anymore."

And he smiled and slept.

"Hey, Lilith, wake up now. You've been zonked out most of the morning and I've gotta make the rounds again. I'll be back and fill you in."

Lilith moaned and pulled her toes out of her tormentor's grasp. Hadn't this just happened? Was she repeating the same dream sequence over and over? No. No. This wasn't the dream. This was real. Frank was leaving? *Wait!* "Wait!" she croaked, struggling to sit up and open her bleary eyes. "What have you heard?"

Her bare-chested, midnight confessor was gone and the neon professor was back and poised at the door. A swift fiery blush stained her cheeks. What had happened between them last night? What did it mean in the light of day? No. Don't think about it. "Have you gotten any word on Cindy and Prince?"

"It's still status quo, but I'm going to rattle a few chains and see what turns up." He shifted and planted his hands on his hips, staring for a second at the toe of his scuffed loafer. "I want you to take it easy today, okay? Last night was—was screwy as hell and I need you to be in good shape when we corner Wolfe."

"I'm not a wimp, Frank. Models put in grueling hours."

"You don't have to convince me; I have the bruises to prove it. Makeup must weigh a lot more than I thought."

"Oh, my gosh!" Lilith lurched onto unsteady legs, but Frank stopped her with an outstretched hand.

"Hey, I was joking. You're denting my fragile male ego. Just take it easy and I'll be back in a couple of hours." The door was almost closed when he suddenly stuck his head back in, his tousled hair and Clark Kent glasses alarmingly appealing.

"I left you a few things on the desk and some money. If you feel better later, see if you can find a store and get us some food. Just do me a favor and forget the caviar and go for peanut butter and crackers, stuff like that."

He paused and Lilith had the most curious impression that her starchy professor was trying to keep from smiling.

"You do know what peanut butter is, don't you?"

"Of course. I had it once in a soufflé."

"Figures. Try to keep your nails on."

Lilith wasn't sure she heard it. She couldn't be positive it had really happened. But the rest of the afternoon as she shopped and put Frank's gifts to good use, she savored the thought that he had helped and teased her and she had made him laugh. It was something friends would do.

Well, she was ready, but should she do it?

Lilith let the faded curtains fall and turned away from the crimson-and-turquoise sunset. Frank had been gone for over four hours and she knew that probably meant he hadn't had much luck. She eyed the black telephone as if it might metamorphosize any second into a huge tarantula. One call and she could deliver a truckload of information. Lilith shuddered and rubbed her hands up and down her bare arms. At this very moment, just miles away, her mother and sister were probably getting ready for the evening's entertainment.

Oh, she didn't know positively they were on the island. They could have gone to Switzerland. But Max had mentioned St. Thomas, so probably . . .

"No! Do you hear me, Smythe?" Lilith yelled at her reflection in the bathroom mirror. "It's time to be ruthlessly honest. You know darn well they're here and you know you should tell Frank."

Her shoulders drooped and she sadly scanned the pretty, ankle-length sheath dress. The subtle pattern of

Bronwyn Wolfe

gold and purple reminded her of the butterfly again. Was it another coincidence? A soft, elastic shirring around the neck made it perfect for wearing off the shoulder, and Lilith had nearly collapsed when she'd unwrapped it after Frank had left.

Somehow the man had found it, shampoo, lip gloss, a bottle of coconut lotion, and a fluffy white terry-cloth robe. In truth the presents were some of the least expensive she'd ever received, yet they touched her as nothing else had in years. But his words . . . Those sweet, simple words that made her feel valued and understood. Words that made her think of Prince and Cindy and her longings back at the reception. Frank had actually said he respected her for helping. He hadn't ridiculed her after her stupid dream. He'd even acted sorry about the mistake on the plane.

And she didn't deserve any of it. She *was* a conniving, spoiled, plastic princess and she couldn't stand herself. Lilith glared at the beautiful woman in the mirror. Still in better shape at thirty than most women in their early twenties. Still rich. Still able to mingle with the elite and famous. And all she wanted was what Cindy had.

"Admit it, Smythe. You want love. You want friends. You want real people that really care. And you're scared to death because now that you've said it out loud it will hurt twice as much if it never happens." She leaned closer, almost nose to reflected nose. "You can't keep pretending things don't hurt. You can't keep faking, period. No pain no gain, Lil. Heck, it worked on your thighs; it's bound to work on the heart."

She thoughtfully fluffed her hair one last time (the lack of mousse had taxed her skills), and made her decision. If she could get the information Frank needed . . . If she could prove herself by taking the initiative . . . If he really respected her, maybe he would give her a chance to explain. . . . And if he came to like her, maybe he would understand the horrible position she'd been forced into.

Lilith had watched Frank and that creep Dejong from the shadows last night and she knew she could wrap the burly man around her little finger.

A sick, queasy feeling swirled in her stomach. That kind of manipulation used to be par for the course and now it made her ill. No wonder Frank had been so insulted at their first meeting. But she could do it one last time for a good cause. Thank heavens Dejong hadn't seen her. Frank had insisted she stay in the background, and Lilith had readily agreed to keep her identity a secret.

She scrawled a hasty note and propped it up on her pillows. Luckily she had been a very careful shopper and had enough money left for a taxi. Lilith Smythe on a budget! She pursed her lips in a silly smile. No way would she ever admit to the fun she'd had analyzing every item for its ability to prove her capable and competent. They now had a tidy, balanced assortment of snacks. She knew food value, after all. One couldn't make a living off one's physical appearance, as shallow as it was, if the appearance in question wasn't in excellent shape.

Lilith stopped abruptly at the door. She'd almost forgotten her butterfly. With expert efficiency she swept up one side of her heavy hair and clipped in her talisman. It made her feel safer. It made her more determined to crawl out of the old Lilith and become someone better. It made her feel as if Frank were with her. And even though this feeling was something Lilith knew she shouldn't indulge, she simply couldn't go it alone now.

She had to prove herself. She had to prove she was truly human.

Chapter Five

"You stupid woman! You rich bitches always think you can come slumming to find a little excitement, then skip out when it's time to deliver."

Oh, God, how had this happened? Lilith was struggling to breathe and fighting against a pair of cruel hands. She hadn't done more than smile and ask Dejong if he'd seen a man that matched the description of Maximillian Wolfe. She confessed she'd met the Frenchman a week ago at a nightclub and then accidentally given him the wrong directions when he'd suggested they meet in a more discreet spot. Had there been a man in the bar the past few nights trying to find her?

Dejong had nodded and asked her to come to his office where he could answer her questions privately. Then without any warning he'd backed her up flush against a wall and began demanding she give him something in return. Dear God, she had been about as stupid as a woman could be! A couple of times in the past men had made passes at her, but they had generally been good-natured, and stopped the instant she got angry. Lilith knew anger would only make Dejong more excited.

"You'll have a much better time with me than that Parisian pansy. Besides, he had two women already. No need for another blonde."

Lilith choked in a sharp-edged breath and reeled from the foul odor that emanated from the big, slovenly man. His greasy black hair and beady black eyes made her think of a weasel toying with a mouse. The pig had seen Max and maybe Belinda! Oh, God! The blonde could have been Mil! But her frantic thoughts screeched to a ghastly halt when Dejong began to force her legs apart and one ham-sized hand pushed between their bodies to cruelly squeeze her breast.

Lilith screamed then. Screamed bloody murder. She kept screaming until he moved his putrid hand and slapped her hard across the face. It was worth it.

Frank burst into the dim, smoky bar like the madman he'd become forty minutes ago when he'd found Lilith's note. *I can get what you need, Frank. I'm not a plastic princess anymore.*

Where was she? Where the hell was she? He rammed straight into the crowded room, heedless of the bodies in his way. Over in a shadowy corner he spotted a bouncer eyeing him suspiciously. Frank topped the man by three inches, but knew his appearance gave him a distinct disadvantage. There was no time to prove how wrong that assumption was; he had to find Lilith. He skirted the room, desperately looking for a clue, when a brief burst of iridescent light caught his eye. Frank blinked and it was gone, but a narrow hall was in its place.

Without further thought he pushed toward it through the calypso rhythm of steel drums and loud, raucous voices that reverberated in his head and pounded along with his heart. Now which door? That same shimmery light suddenly appeared beneath the middle door and Frank knew immediately that Lilith was on the other side. He ran to test the knob, but it was locked. And then he heard her screaming.

Seconds later the door was kicked in and Frank had a stranglehold on Dejong. He pulled the piece of slime off his woman and hurled him onto the hardwood floor.

Frank took one wild-eyed look at Lilith's red cheek and trembling hands as she tried to pull the elastic neck of her dress up over her nearly bared breasts, and he had to turn away. Fear and fury were raging in him more fiercely than any natural storm he'd ever experienced, and he was battered by his feelings, overwhelmed by the magnitude of his reaction.

He had to get her out of here before he killed Dejong or said a hundred macho, arrogant things that were way out of line, but true! Dammit to hell! Some places, some jobs were not for women. Not ever. Not ever *his* woman! Oh, God!

When Frank had himself in check, he pivoted back toward Lilith and poured every last ounce of reasonable control into his smile and the hand that cupped her elbow and supported her quivering body as they left the bar.

He managed to sit and wait for ten minutes after they arrived back at the motel. They hadn't exchanged one word when Lilith had grabbed the white robe and gone straight into the bathroom. Frank straddled the desk chair and laid his glasses on the local phone book. He wrapped his hands over the smooth wood and rested his forehead on top of them. The creak of an opening door brought his head up and his heart into his throat.

She looked so fragile all bundled up in white, her hair streaming over her shoulders and her bare toes curled against the carpet. One side of her face had gone a dark, angry red, and Frank's fingers tightened on the slat of pine.

"What in the world did you think you were doing?" he demanded, giving each word the same intense value.

"I'm thirty years old, Frank. I'm not a child, but I was naive. I-I've been in difficult spots before and I thought I could handle this." She hesitated and cleared her throat. "We agreed to each carry our share of the load, and at the time, it seemed like the best way to help. I'm sorry my mistake put you in danger. I can only say I-I accept the blame for what happened and I thank you for coming to find me."

Lilith fiddled with the cloth belt tied at her waist and moved closer to her bed. She seemed amazingly calm for what she'd just been through. Too damn calm, and it was starting to bother Frank. He stood and leaned his hips against the desk, then folded his arms.

"Well, that was a very nice little speech. You delivered it with such polish that I have to wonder if being attacked is some kind of routine for you."

"No!" Her voice cracked and her eyes went round and watery. Frank could literally see the effort she marshaled to relax her body and continue, her tone evenly modulated. "Because of my work, I-I have always had to be careful. I-I guess I'll be better prepared now. That's what my mother used to tell me after after difficult experiences. And she was right. No point in carrying on or upsetting other people. Just put the knowledge to good use."

"In case it happens again."

"Yes." She pulled back the colorful spread and loosely clasped her hands. "De—" She coughed and cleared her throat again. "Dejong has seen Wolfe. I think it was Monday night. Wolfe was with two women. I was only able to find out that at least one was a blonde."

Was this reaction for real? What was going on with her? He'd have to push harder.

"That's too bad." Her confused gaze darted to his and danced away. "I mean if you could have stood it a few more minutes you might have gotten names." Frank shrugged and nonchalantly unbuttoned his shirt, all the while watching the emotions flickering across Lilith's pale face. Her lips trembled and she pressed them firmly together.

"Well, looking ba-back on it now, if I had known you were outside . . . or if—if I had waited for you and made a plan . . ." She stopped and sat on the mattress, pulling her knees up to her chest and circling her arms snug around her legs. "I suppose that would have been the thing to do. I-I can see what you mean."

Frank shoved his hands deep in his pants pockets and forced himself to take a hard look through the ugly window he'd just discovered in Lilith's life. Sweet Jesus! She didn't expect a drop of sympathy, not an ounce of comfort. She matter-of-factly accepted the fact that he would have sent her to be hurt if it had served his purpose. How many times had she been used over the course of her life to have imprinted this kind of acceptance?

"I'm going to sleep, okay?" She scooted down and curled away from him onto her side.

"Sure. Hey, Lil?"

"Yes?" She didn't turn back.

"It was a crazy thing to do and you should never have done it without backup. But you've got guts, woman."

Her answer was so slow in coming Frank almost started over to her. Then he heard a soft, muffled, "Not quite enough, though, huh?"

He shrugged off his shirt and snagged his own robe. Hell, he was a total jerk. Now this poor, hurting woman was berating herself for not enduring even more abuse. He'd only been trying to fire up her old smart-ass attitude. Why hadn't she charged him and socked him right in the kisser? If she had, maybe he'd feel better. A good verbal sparring match might have drained off the rest of the frustrated energy still racing through his body. The frustrated energy that was demanding he pull this dangerous lady into his arms and make sure she really was all right.

Why in the world had he been celibate for so long?

Frank stood under the hot water and knew time had run out. He was going to lose it if he didn't get Lilith Smythe out of his life, ASAP, because, dammit, she got to him in spite of everything she represented from his old life. His celibacy had evolved soon after that shallow time period when he'd been sick of empty relationships that were going nowhere. Hell, what was he using for a brain? This wasn't even a relationship.

Time to put first things first. Sure things first. Tomorrow

was absolutely the last day he could stay on St. Thomas without any news or a lead. He had to reach Prince and he had to get away from Lilith before something happened that couldn't be taken back or quickly forgotten.

Frank slumped back against the shower wall, letting the spray pound away, and raked his hands through his wet hair. How was he ever going to take back or forget the truth he'd been denying since that kiss? He'd thought of her as his. It had come without hesitation from somewhere in his foolish heart. In his clumsy effort to draw out her real emotions, he'd stumbled onto the real truth about cover model Lilith Smythe. She didn't think she deserved anyone's concern . . . and he had moved way beyond that.

Lilith thought her lungs were going to explode before Frank got out of the room. She released a muffled sob an instant after hearing the snap of the bathroom door. Against her will, hot tears leaked out of her squinched-up eyes. It had been so long since she had really cried, it felt like her chest was collapsing under the weight of years of suppressed emotion.

Being noble was not easy. She hadn't done it well and Frank had been furious and disappointed with her efforts. Maybe she should have tried to stand it a bit longer but—but it was so horrible, so disgusting. She'd been so afraid she was still shaking from it.

Lilith backhanded her wet cheeks and started taking ragged drafts of air in through her nose. She had to get a grip before he came out. No way she could deal with one more confrontation and hold her practiced front in place. So she wasn't as perfect as Frank was; at least she was trying. No matter what else he thought, he had said she had guts, and that was worth much more than being a plastic princess. Actually—a fresh rush of tears threatened to spill—it had been the most meaningful compliment she'd received in years.

Lilith went taut when the bathroom door whooshed

193

open. She became excruciatingly aware of the tiny wet trails wending their way down her face and into the pillow. A huge lungful of air stuttered in her chest and she determinedly held it, prepared to handle her fear and hurt alone. As always.

She didn't quite make it.

"Lilith? Are you all right?" Frank stood stock-still with his hands in the terry pockets of his robe, straining to hear that odd hiccuping sound again. Was she crying? He waited in the dark, and slowly drew up his arms and folded them. "Answer me, Lil. Right now or I'm turning on the light."

"I'm fine." Her breath hitched and she sniffed.

"Dammit to hell! Can you please drop the plastic mask and admit you're crying? I don't care how rich or how famous you are! Underneath you're a regular human being, no matter how much that bothers you!"

"No." Her voice wavered and wobbled. "I'm not! I'm not a regular hu-human being at all. And I-I don't know how to change and I don't know how to make people like me and I don't want to be afraid and I don't want to cry!"

Lilith's anguish drowned out all the warning bells ringing in Frank's head. Here was the pain at last and he could not stop himself from going to her. Once again, in the dark, he felt for her across the mattress and found a bare ankle, but this time he crawled up next to her and tugged her resisting body into the curve of his own.

"But that's just it, Lil," he murmured against her silky, flower-scented hair. "You have every right to be afraid and cry after what happened tonight. Your feelings make you human, sugar. Let them go."

He held her rigid body awkwardly in his arms. She wouldn't relax against him; she wouldn't melt. . . . And the image of an icy prison came again so swiftly he acted before thinking out the ramifications. Frank lowered his face into the vee of her neck and brushed his freshly shaved cheek along smooth skin that smelled of his coconut lotion. The sensation was electrifying and she must have felt it, too, because her body shivered and quaked.

"And you're wrong, Lilith. You are changing. I've seen it since the plane and little Shannon." Even as he said the words he realized how true they were. How different she was from their first encounter. It was something she needed to see, needed to believe. And it was very possible that he was the only person in the world who could tell her. "You've put up with all kinds of guff from me without quitting, worn some truly hideous clothes, even lost your—"

Frank patted down her side and found a fist and tugged it up. From the tight curl of her fingers he suddenly realized *all* her pretty fingernails were gone. "Aww, Lil. Ask yourself, a few months ago would you have put up with any of this to help your stepsister?" He pulled her balled hand to his lips and slowly kissed each knuckle. He couldn't stop himself.

"Of all people, sugar, I know how hard it is to change, to find the real you again. Putting somebody else first is the very best way to start. You willingly risked yourself at that bar, Lilith Smythe. You can't do more than that." Frank moved her fist to his cheek, his fingers wrapped around her wrist. With his thumb he stroked over the back of her hand. "Just don't stop now and you'll make it."

It started so slowly Frank held his breath to be certain. Yes, she was softening, melting. Centimeter by centimeter, Lilith uncurled her fingers until her soft palm lay flat against his cheek. Frank took a deep, desperate gulp of air. God help him—he was standing on the edge of something he might not be able to control. . . .

And then she spoke and he started to fall.

"I-I-I'm so scared, Frank. Scared it's too late."

His hands were shaking and he rubbed them up and down her stiff spine as much for himself as for her. Gently he rolled to his side, tugging her along, and ever so lightly she rested her free hand at his waist. He splayed his fingers

195

along the side of her slender neck in order to guide her ear close to his mouth. "Remember I told you about my accident?"

"Uh huh."

"Well, I ruined my knee in a play-off game and it ended my professional basketball career."

"Oh, Frank!"

"No, it was the best thing that could have happened. I had become an arrogant bastard, Lil. So insensitive to my own little brother that the kid just about destroyed his health practicing to get my approval. But I was lucky because Prince and my parents helped me get my inflated head back down to size. I would have lost a lot more than basketball and my fifteen minutes of fame if I hadn't taken a hard fall. It wasn't too late for me, sugar, and it isn't too late for you."

Lilith abruptly turned her head and Frank felt, more than saw, her eyes find his in the murky darkness. "How can you be sure?" she whispered.

He knew what those vulnerable words cost her and he could not equivocate any longer. Frank cared about this woman. There was a connection between them. A connection in their life experiences and, amazingly enough, in Lilith's dreams. A bond that seemed as mystical as the fairy tales he used to read to Janna. And damn his traitorous body . . . but he wanted her so badly even his teeth ached.

What would come of it all was uncertain. But suddenly, almost urgently, he felt compelled to reach her tonight in every way possible. Bind her with the honest depth of his feelings. Because time was so short, had been from the start, and it was running out. Frank had no idea why this thought was spinning in his head, but it was. Laying open his heart after so long wasn't easy, but he could do nothing less. They both needed to discover what it was between them.

"I'm sure because I can see you're winning the battle

you're fighting inside yourself and I admire that. I admire you, Lilith Smythe. Tonight, when I saw that jerk touching you, I wanted to kill him. I'm so sorry that slime hurt you."

Dear Lord but it was awful to feel the effort she was exerting to silence her sobs. Her whole body was fighting the release she needed desperately. Damn! Had he just made it worse? He shifted again until Lilith lay flat on her back and he had one arm circled beneath her and his torso angled over hers. His eyes had adjusted to the faint glow from the lights outside their room. The vague contours of her face and form could be seen, and he threaded his fingers deeply into her hair and gently massaged her head.

Eyes like dark, liquid pools watched him with fathomless need and fear and loneliness. And Frank knew it was more than the night's trauma still haunting her. It was this excruciating, exquisite feeling blossoming between them, and she felt it, too. A brilliant flash of heat and hope surged through the last of the old pain he'd been holding on to. He felt like one of Janna's heroes. A prince so powerful he could touch Lilith in the deepest, coldest part of her—and melt the ice.

"You know, when my sister was little and she got hurt, she liked someone to hold her until the pain went away, and she always asked for a kiss to make it better. Let me do that for you, Lilith. Let me."

He leaned down and brushed his lips so lightly over hers it felt like a kiss of air. She didn't move a muscle. Nothing. But silent tears began to roll down her temples. He kissed her again, this time pressing his mouth against her unresponsive lips and murmuring, "You don't have to do this alone, sugar. Let me have some of that pain and fear. I should have protected you. Trust me to protect you now."

Frank cupped the back of her head and lowered his chest until he rested on the soft fullness of her terry-cloth-covered breasts. Her tall, willowy form fit against his so perfectly. Her sweet, minty breath feathered his face, and his poor, deprived body began to tremble with need, both physical and emotional.

Fierce waves of desire were starting to build in him and rush to every point they touched. The effort to hold himself back burned up the air in his lungs. With a ragged exhalation he softly rubbed his nose next to hers and nuzzled her lips, coaxing them to open so he could sip the moist, tender flesh he wanted to devour.

"There's a connection between us, Lilith. I don't know what it means. But I'm telling you it's there." Frank drew back and pulled his fingers from her hair and held her chin in the vee of his hand. "This isn't a line, sugar. I want to help. I have to help."

There was a moment of hesitation, a taut silence. He heard her swallow and take a deep breath before she said, "Then kiss me and make it better."

The instant his mouth opened fully over hers, Lilith knew the kiss on the plane had not been her imagination. That everything happening was real, and a miracle. Warm, wet, fevered meetings of their lips mirrored what she had felt once before. But oh so much better, because this honorable man had found something worthy in her and she gloried in the way it made her feel. Her hands climbed up the rigid muscles in his back and she both heard and felt a groan rumble in his chest and echo from his mouth to hers.

She was on fire and needed to feel him closer. Needed to wipe away the memory of the ugly hands that had hurt her earlier. Lilith drew her hands from around him and wove them up between their bodies, pushing at his robe's lapels until she touched the mat of hair covering his chest. Frank's heart pounded like a drum against her palms, and she sucked on his bottom lip, laving it with her tongue, letting go of her fear and trusting—trusting as she had never done before. She kissed him with her whole heart and it translated into sweet, desperate flurries of her tongue until she took him deep into her warm mouth.

Frank went wild. Her impressions of an inexperienced, bookish man were blown completely out of the water. He covered her cheeks, eyes, nose with moist, urgent kisses. The undeniable evidence of his need pressed against the top of her thigh, burning like a brand through both layers of cloth. Lilith had never felt anything like this. No matter what the public thought, she was not a floozy. There had only been two men she'd ever been intimate with and they had been brief, empty affairs. Neither one had ever really cared about her. They had only wanted a disgusting claim to fame. But this was everything she had dreamed of as a young, innocent girl. This was her Prince Charming come to life and lying in her arms. A strange kind of music filled her spinning mind, and then one of Frank's beautiful, healing hands covered her breast. Deep inside her body she felt a white-hot, melting joy.

He knew it was too much. The minute his hand tunneled through her robe and cupped one soft breast he knew he'd barely be able to make it back from the edge. Everything was happening too fast. There was still so much to be resolved and he didn't want any old baggage left between them when they made love for the first time. Some tiny reservations still tugged on his heart. Settle this thing with Wolfe and then . . . Frank groaned and dragged his lips away from Lilith's mouth and his burning hand away from her tender flesh. His face rested in the crook of her neck and his whole body shook with need.

"Nooo, Frank. Please. Your touch makes me feel so good. It makes the—other better. You make everything better."

"Aww, sugar. I'm glad." He panted and kissed her satiny skin, grinning at the still significant pressure she was able to get out of her new, stubby nails. "But we need to slow down. I want Prince's problem behind us before—I want this settled so we can concentrate on what's happening between us." Frank swallowed down the rest of the words. He wanted the meeting he had set for tomorrow night over with first and he wanted to talk about his own little deception—his nerdy disguise.

Oh, God! Lilith froze with her arms around Frank's back. How could she have forgotten? Even experiencing the most wonderful feelings she'd ever known, how could she have forgotten? A swift, sickening wave of nausea swept through her and she closed her eyes with dread. *Oh please, please don't let this happen. Please, please don't take it away now that I finally know what love is.* Love? Heaven help her, it was true. She loved him. Lilith loved Frank. How could she ever tell him she had lied from the beginning?

Cindy would tell.

"But, Frank, I need to—" She stopped, petrified.

"Sugar, I need to, too. Believe me." Frank moaned and then chuckled as he rearranged their bodies and drew the spread up over them. "Tomorrow we've got lots to talk about, and then if you feel the same . . ." He tucked her head under his chin and rubbed against her hair. "We may have something very special here, Lil. Magic. I want us to be very careful and very sure."

Lilith tightened her arms around the man she loved and lay in the dark recording every breath he took, just in case this was the only night she ever had. She should make him listen right now. A strange whisper kept repeating it. Her recently awakened conscience, no doubt. But being noble was too new and Lilith was only sure of one thing. She was a coward.

Chapter Six

Frank had been called from the front desk about mid-morning. The shrill ring had woken them to startled confusion and a tangled jumble of legs and bedding. In moments the cool, incisive professor was in complete control and rushing to get to the message waiting at the office. Lilith had been painfully unsure of the change in their relationship and hesitated a heartbeat too long, missing the chance to confess her lie. Before she could stop him, Frank had abruptly scooped her up in his arms, kissed her long and hard, and promised they'd have all the time they needed in a few hours.

Initially Lilith had felt a spill of relief and euphoria at Frank's show of affection, but that had waned as the afternoon wore on. Her new effervescent feelings of love and jittery desire began to pop and go flat. Where was he? If he found Wolfe before she could tell . . .

Eventually, as dusk forced its shadowy presence into her consciousness, Lilith concluded that was what must have happened. The gut-wrenching conviction cut her heart to ribbons. Sitting rigid on the bed she suddenly flashed back to the memory of not wanting to see his face once he knew what she had done.

Lilith jumped up and scrambled for her tote bag. Gads! What had she been thinking? Storybook happiness for her? She grimaced and rushed to the bathroom to stuff her toiletries inside. Her frantic features loomed out at her from the mirror and Lilith had the most hysterical urge to laugh at her childish stupidity. She studied her image. Face it, when had a wicked stepsister ever gotten the prince?

She had to leave. Had to run. Had to escape before he returned. Had to prove herself to be exactly what Frank had thought in the beginning. Breathing hard, Lilith slumped onto the end of the sagging mattress and let her hibiscus bag fall at her feet. She dropped her head into her hands and felt the swish of her loose hair feather over her fingers. In thirty minutes she could be safely locked behind her family's doors, safely beyond any pain. In a prison of ice.

She did laugh then. High and harsh until the sound hurt her ears and her throat felt raw. Poor, poor little Lilith Smythe. How many people would spare even a second of sympathy for her and the life that had brought her to this point? Not a one. Most would think that her moment of revelation had come too late and justly so. Lilith stood and walked in her purple plastic sandals to the desk chair. She angled it to face the door and sat.

There was perhaps a slim hope that she could still have what she'd held so briefly last night. That sweet spark of feeling that flickered against the winds of fear churning in her heart. But that was not what kept her in the uncomfortable chair. She glanced down at her feet and pressed her mouth into a brief, aching smile. For once in her life she was going to face the consequences of her actions— of who she had been—by being the person she wanted to be.

Cindy had shown her it could be done.

And she was praying that wherever Frank was he might remember the magic he'd talked about last night. That maybe she could convince him that his plastic slipper was a perfect fit. And if not, she would pay the price because now she knew what the dreams had been trying to tell her. She had chosen the icy prison all along.

Lilith folded her shaking hands in her lap and waited.

Once Upon a Tangled Tale

* * *

An hour later the door opened and Lilith's fragile thread of hope broke, letting her heart drift away from her body. Which was just as well. Holding such pain inside would have doubled her over and left her unable to meet the stark glare in Frank's eyes. To see such disdain on the face of the man she loved hurt. God, it hurt so badly.

But as he came inside and kicked the door shut, the far side of his face moved further into the lamp's imited range and she gasped. "Frank!" she cried, surging to her feet, her concern overriding everything else. "What happened to you?" His bottom lip was split and her gaze darted around, cataloging a tear in his shirt and the dirt streaking his pants. "Oh, your knee! Frank, is your knee—"

Frank immediately stepped backward, away from her. Lilith froze, stunned at the rejection. Gingerly she sat back down and forced herself to take the bull by the horns, like bare hands around a double-edged razor. "It looks like you found Wolfe."

"You mean your sister's ex-boyfriend, don't you? Funny you never mentioned that, isn't it? And Wolfe's relationship with Milicent wasn't the only one you left out of our conversations, was it, Ms. Smythe?" Lilith flinched and he stalked closer until his body and anger trapped her in the chair. "Old Max and I had quite a little chat after we realized we were both on the same side." She audibly inhaled and Frank bared his teeth in a parody of a smile. He lifted a hand and pressed two fingertips over the swollen part of his lip.

"Yes. Amazing, isn't it? It seems he'd played along with your sister's scheme in order to buy some time to convince Prince of her sick jealousy, but things spun out of control. By the way, he was certain you had to have known about it. In fact, he asked rather pointedly just what part of my body I was using for a brain. Given the fact that if you were really helping me we could have confronted both Milicent and your mother at the home *y'all* have here on the island. Since that minor detail managed to slip your memory, Max was kind enough to tell me they were both in residence and that Milicent was categorically denying any involvement."

Frank bent down until his face was a hairbreadth from hers. The dark frames of his glasses outlined his beautiful amber eyes, and Lilith felt such a piercing stab of loss she couldn't think of a thing to say in her defense. *I love you* would ring hollow and empty, just as the life she'd so ignorantly lived. He would toss back her declaration without a moment's hesitation. How much could those words mean coming from a hollow human being?

A faint woodsy smell of aftershave drifted from his overheated body, and she wished she could close her eyes and lean against him. That she could will the night back. But it was gone. All the magic vanished as if what they'd shared had never been. And of course, it had all been an illusion because Frank hadn't known about the lie.

"Maybe you are trying to change, Lilith, but I don't care anymore. Blood is thicker than water. That's what this has been about. Period. I won't forget that when you had to choose, you stuck with your own kind. And just as soon as you get me into your home as a houseguest and I get what Prince needs, you can waltz right back to your plastic world and your plastic friends."

Frank hadn't thought he could ever feel so betrayed again. But here he was, an inch away from a woman who'd turned him inside out and left him bruised and bleeding. Dammit! It enraged him to look into her eyes. Eyes that he would have sworn were tormented and grieving. Hell! The woman's entire career was about faking and feigning and making people believe an illusion. She had damn well better do the real thing now! Frank wrapped his hands around her shoulders and pulled her roughly out of the chair.

"There's a taxi outside and you're leaving in five minutes to set the stage for my arrival tomorrow morning. Drop a few hints about my money and connections with Hollywood. That ought to grab your sister's attention. Don't you dare think of warning your family or you'll be slapped with accessory charges so fast your head will swim. And don't be fool enough to think last night will make a bit of difference now." He lowered his strident voice and finished in quiet, dismissive tones. "I thought you were someone else. I won't make that mistake again."

"Frank! I didn't know how to tell you. Didn't know where to start." Her shredded pride allowed the plea to escape before she could stop it. The old smothering fear that she would never be enough as the person she really was hammered in her chest, threatening to break her down completely. *Please listen!* "Every way I turned people were going to be hurt."

Abruptly he spun around and snagged the flowered tote off the floor. "Save it. It's done. I've spoken to Prince and the whole thing has gotten a lot more complicated and, dammit, I have a job to do! So we're back to our original agreement. All I want to know now is, can I count on you?"

"Wait! How's Cindy?"

"She's fine and they know where Belinda Brown is. Under the circumstances, I think it's best to leave it at that."

"You mean I'm not to know."

"Take it however you want. Just get ready to leave."

Lilith bit the inside of her cheek and reached for her bag. Too bad she hadn't given in to her weak principles and run. Being noble was the pits and it hurt like hell. Besides, where had it gotten her? Frank despised her and now she was heading out to set up her mother and sister. Gads, in a few days there wouldn't be a safe place left on the planet. Yet as she walked to the door she simply had to tell the hardheaded, letter of the law, ex–man of her dreams what to expect. She swung to face him and found him right on her heels. Frank opened his mouth as if to beat her to another argument, so Lilith spoke quickly.

"Listen, Frank, you need to know that Mil is very picky

about men. I have to warn you that if your plan hinges on my sister becoming interested in you . . . Well, she's going to get one look at the whole picture and probably ignore you completely." Lilith watched a sardonic smirk curl his puffy lip and he shrugged.

"Lucky for me, I've recently had some experience with plastic princesses. I'll just have to improvise."

"O-Okay," Lilith fought to keep her voice steady. "Think whatever you want, Frank Henson. But remember I'm the one who started all of this in the first place. I could have left the reception without saying a word. I chose to get involved and I chose to stick it out here when I could have escaped a hundred times. But then you're Mr. Perfect now, aren't you? Except it seems to me that all those pretty words you told me about changing were as empty as you think my character is."

Lilith grabbed hold of the cheap metal doorknob and leaned into it to keep her legs from buckling. "If you really look at it closely, we're not all that different, Mr. Henson, and I hope that sticks in your self-righteous craw."

"Oh, darling, your hands look dreadful."

Lilith froze for a surprised instant, her hands still poised in midair after finishing her French braid. She quickly schooled her features into a neutral expression that belied her battle-ready state. Barbara Smythe-Jones almost never came directly to her daughters' rooms, and Lilith had discovered years ago that anytime she was the focus of her mother's attention, it behooved her to tread very carefully.

She wasn't prepared for the skilled grilling Barbara was capable of. She felt shell-shocked and bone tired. Lilith had barely slept a wink after dodging all possible conversation last night and leaving strict orders not to be disturbed until morning. Obviously her reprieve was up.

"With our party tomorrow night I'm sure you'll want Maria to come to the house and repair the damage."

Lilith watched her elegant mother float up behind her and preen in the heavy, brass-framed mirror. Its beveled edges made bizarre angles of their bodies and she couldn't help but think of all the distorted "edges" between the three of them. Barbara had Milicent's gold-blond hair, but it was cut in a short, wispy shag that feathered around the stunning bone structure and the blue eyes she had passed on to her daughters.

A rich amethyst silk blouse and flowing silk slacks made her skin glow like that of a woman half her age. In fact at the moment Lilith felt years older than her own mother. And she wondered for the very first time if Barbara had ever really loved anyone or been willing to sacrifice or risk it all for—

"Darling, are those crow's-feet I see?" She gasped, taking hold of Lilith's chin and pulling her around. "Oh, my, you've aged so since I saw you last, and your cheek is discolored. You'd better call Dr. Burton, dear." Her mother's face was a perfect picture of horrified shock. As if she'd just discovered Lilith had an incurable disease.

Lilith blinked. Three months ago she would have already made an appointment with her mother's plastic surgeon. *Plastic?* She shuddered. *Take that, Mr. Perfect— wherever you are.* She had changed, was changing, and it felt good. It felt real. It felt—lonely. As shallow as her mother and sister were, as her whole world was, it was all she had ever known. And now? Now Lilith was a square peg and she knew she would never fit in again.

All at once the silence registered. She hadn't answered and her mother had actually narrowed her eyes in an assessing look. Barbara never narrowed her eyes. Crow's-feet were her pet phobia. Lilith scrambled. "I'm trying a new regimen, Mother. If it hasn't improved in a few weeks I'll do something." Sink out of sight, most likely.

Barbara arranged herself in a plush white velvet barrel chair and wove her hands together, clicking her long nails. Lilith took an expertly concealed deep breath.

"So, how did Cynthia's little affair turn out? Truthfully, Milicent and I were quite taken aback at your decision to attend."

Her mother's beautifully made up face didn't show a flicker of honest emotion. Lilith realized she was a fool to expect more, but she was compelled to try; she knew she had to give both Milicent and Barbara one last chance. Gads! Being noble could be a truly masochistic urge. One she apparently could not turn off, now that her eyes had been opened.

"Mother . . ." She paused and sat on the edge of an identical white velvet chair. "Cindy and Prince are right for each other. And I think if Milicent will just accept that and stop, stop whatever might be—"

"I'm surprised at you, Lilith. It's not like you to stab your sister in the back this way. Though I suppose that her continued success may have driven you to take a disloyal stand." Barbara lifted one perfect winged brow and tsked in refined tones. She stood and walked to the door before delivering the rest of her discreetly veiled command.

"You've been quite strange the last few months and it's time you knew that many of our friends have commented on it. Now you've brought this mysterious man here, whom I assume you're attached to in some way, although you certainly wouldn't know it by his behavior. And I'm warning you, I will not tolerate any fuss at the party tomorrow night. Try to keep your dignity, Lilith. If the man prefers Milicent, accept it. Things have—have not been easy for her lately and she needs extra attention now. Besides, your time in the spotlight is over."

Lilith's hands pushed down the sides of the velvet cushion, hidden by her legs and the fine, peach-colored muslin of her sundress. The carved mahogany door swung closed and she was still hanging on for dear life, gripping the cushion as if it were the only thing keeping her from running screaming from the room. And it was. He was here.

Already! Frank was here and Milicent was . . . interested? What in the world had he done?

Lilith hesitated on the top step leading down to their large sunken living room. The pale green marble floor seemed to spill like a waterfall from beneath her feet and form a small, still pond that flowed out toward the three walls of French doors. The entire room was open to the paradise of St. Thomas. Their home sat on one of the hills that comprised the spiny ridge running down the center of the island, and the view of lush greenery, blue sky, and even bluer water was spectacular. As she breathed in the fragrant air and felt the soft, balmy breeze whisper over her skin, Lilith had to wonder if she would ever stand in this spot again . . . after it was all over.

"Why, Lilith, darling, you look positively haggard."

Lilith didn't move. Milicent's brittle greeting and unexpected appearance from the veranda shattered her reverie and took a moment to assimilate. She watched her sister saunter to an overstuffed rattan chair and knew immediately that Milicent was still angry about their most recent argument over Cindy's wedding. Well, it was about to get worse and Frank was going to get caught in the middle of more than he bargained for. Where was he?

"Come sit. I wondered if you were trying to avoid me, but it seems Bernard was right to insist on letting you sleep."

So trusty Bernard had kept them away. The man deserved a medal for staying all these years. How had he ever tolerated the games? How had she? *I really have changed.* Would Frank see it? Probably not. His mind was closed to her now, and besides, she would have to play enough of her old part so nobody grew too suspicious. However, Lilith was in no mood for the put-down game. She'd already gone one round with Barbara. Maybe if she just conceded, her sister would lose interest.

"Well, I'm past thirty now, Mil, and travel takes a greater

209

toll. I'll just have to accept it." Lilith held back a self-deprecating smile. Her gorgeous, golden sister, who had always been the more vibrant of the two of them, was speechless. A very uncommon occurrence.

She moved to the rattan sofa-and-chair grouping, all of which had been newly upholstered to achieve a sand-colored Banana Republic look, and sat opposite Milicent. Her younger sister wore a tightly wrapped sarong that barely restrained her ample breasts. The white fabric made her look even more tanned and sleek than usual. Every long curl was skillfully arranged on her bare shoulders, and delicate, white leather sandals crisscrossed her pedicured feet. What could she see in Frank Henson? Barbara must have gotten it all wrong.

"Wow, Mil! You look fantastic." Flattery always softened Milicent. "I bet you have half the Riviera eligibles here and dancing on your string. You haven't by any chance had to deal with Max what's-his-name, have you?" Whether Frank trusted her or not, Lilith was going to get some answers.

Milicent cocked her head abruptly and used one gold-polished nail to tap her chin. "You know I dumped him months ago, Lil. Frankly, everything about him was overrated and I really don't think the man would dare cross my path—especially now." She smiled with a purposeful show of teeth, and Lilith was uncomfortably reminded of a barracuda. Exactly what had gone on between Wolfe and her sister?

"He was another waste of time."

"I hope you're referring to Prince Chalmers, too."

"Prince?" Milicent choked out, her whole body leaning forward with tension. "I don't know why you bring him up, Lil. He and Cindy are such fools. But maybe one day he'll know how wrong he was."

"That's not up to you, Milicent. You need to let this go and—"

"Speaking of letting go, sister dear," she pointedly interrupted. "I'm afraid Franklin has fallen for me." Milicent splayed a hand over the full curves of her breasts and idly stroked the bare skin.

Lilith shook her head, confused. "Franklin? Franklin who?"

"Oh, wonderful! You're detached. Perfect. It's all happened so suddenly and I hoped it wouldn't upset you. You were sleeping and Bernard asked me to receive him and even though I was irritated at the bother—well, Franklin more than made up for that. He's like some kind of Prince Charming. I'm so glad you're okay with this."

Uh oh! An ominous clamoring began in the pit of Lilith's stomach. Milicent stretched out a hand and patted her knee.

"He *did* tell me there was absolutely nothing physical between the two of you. It must have been another blow for you, Lil, but he insisted he was just using you to meet me and talk about a movie—" She gasped and dramatically covered her mouth with her palm. "Sorry, darling. It just slipped out. But there's no harm done, after all." Her eyes widened and fixed over Lilith's shoulder.

"Why you naughty, naughty man! How long have you been standing there?"

In a dumbfounded daze, Lilith turned her head . . . and it nearly kept spinning.

One of the most drop-dead gorgeous men she had ever seen stood waiting on the very steps she had just descended.

And it was Frank! Franklin was Frank!

"Oh, just long enough to know y'all have answered the most important questions, Milicent, sugar."

Sugar? Lilith thought she might heave. The slight Southern flavor of Frank's speech was suddenly as thick and gooey as molasses. Sugar? *Her* sugar? It took all Lilith's force of will to swallow down the broken pieces of her heart that were threatening to spew out of her mouth.

Frank moved down the steps and over to her sister with

the grace of a dancer. His long legs were fashionably encased in beige linen slacks, and a pair of cordovan Italian loafers shod his sockless feet. She swallowed again as he took Milicent's hand and kissed the palm before sitting next to her.

Siamese twins could not have been closer.

His shirt was silk, for God's sake! A subtle blend of gold, cream, and brown that accentuated the breadth of his shoulders and chest. The cuffs were rolled back with casual elegance, and the hair dusting his arms had taken on a burnished cast. A slim gold Rolex circled one wide wrist, and a diamond pinky ring circled one pinky. Both of which caused her to focus on the only thing she recognized. His hands. Those beautiful male hands had been her one clue and she'd missed it completely.

Who was this imposter and what had he done with her nerdy, fashion-impaired, limbo-bedecked professor?

The imposter settled back against the rattan sofa and rested an arm around Milicent's shoulders. "You see, there's absolutely nothing between your sister and me."

Frank might have been talking to Milicent, but Lilith felt the concentrated force of his amber gaze down to her toes. Where were his glasses? Oh good gosh, he was beautiful! The wild hair was brushed back and waved just a bit at his temples. Chiseled cheekbones and a perfect nose had all been distorted by chunky lenses and the heavy black frames. And now she could see that those flame-colored eyes were thickly lashed.

How could she have been so blind? Even with the glasses and clothes—even with her preconceived prejudices—even in the dark . . .

A wave of horrific longing suddenly swamped her, drowning out the delighted laughter of her sister and even the searing pain of betrayal. How could she still love him? Her wretched mind was quick to supply a reason and began playing back a blurry scene full of razor-sharp feelings. Those arms had held her and that slightly bruised mouth had, had—

"So we're off to tour the island now, Lil. I suggest you get some repair work going posthaste. You know how people love to talk when someone's had a turn of bad luck."

Lilith blinked and Milicent and Frank seemed to materialize on the steps. She desperately focused her eyes and slowed her breathing, sure that if they moved a foot closer, the pounding of her heart would be audible.

"And dump the butterfly, Lil. It looks ridiculous in the hair of a woman your age."

For one excruciating second Frank's cold eyes met hers over Milicent's head, but Lilith didn't flinch. She held his impersonal gaze. Held it. Held it—until it wavered and opened the window to his old self. She felt Frank see her. And just like that, Lilith knew exactly what he was thinking. Almost as if someone were whispering it in her ear. She knew the "why" of the butterfly.

"Maybe so, Mil. But I love butterflies. Their whole life is about changing and I—" She stopped and lifted her hand to the clip at the end of her braid, pulling it over her shoulder. "I met a little girl who had one and she helped me learn a lot. I think someone wanted me to remember that sometimes the most improbable things are possible. I only wish he could truly believe that."

"You and a child? Please, Lilith. You really have gone delusionary. Ask Mother for her therapist's number, and get some psychic repair, too."

Milicent raised her hands, palms up, and shrugged as if there was nothing more she could do. "Come along, Franklin. I know an exclusive little club with divine margaritas. Maybe one or two will make that nasty split lip you got wind-surfing feel better."

Frank didn't respond. His and Lilith's eyes still held with a current of feeling so consuming neither one heard Milicent grumble. Neither one could look away until Lilith closed her eyes and the break released them.

But not really.

Chapter Seven

They still weren't back. They still weren't back. They still weren't back!

Mil and *Franklin* had been gone for hours. It was almost two o'clock in the morning and Lilith felt like an idiot hiding out in the shadows of the veranda. Yep, that therapy appointment couldn't be made too soon. She tugged an ivory cashmere shawl more securely around her shoulders and leaned against the wrought-iron railing. In the vanilla-cream light of the Caribbean moon, the intricate white metal looked like a delicate border of lace circling the property, gathering it up and away from the long slopes of hillside that fanned out beneath it like an old-fashioned skirt.

Or a tent.

Lilith let out a shaky sigh. Gads, she was seeing that hideous muumuu in topographical foliage. She was in a bad, bad way. This would not be a good time to face either Frank or Milicent. Suddenly she didn't want to know the slightest detail of how he was getting her sister to feel comfortable enough to confess the facts about the plan to kidnap Cindy.

But just as she moved to step out of the shadows and past their large, Italian tile spa, a French door swung open and yet another worst nightmare began playing out before her. Once again compliments of Frank Henson. Arm in arm, the only man she had ever loved—the only man who had ever rejected her—strolled into the romantic, garde-

214

nia-scented darkness with her sister. Lilith pressed back into the rough stucco and behind a potted palm. The grating surface of the wall poked through the shawl, sanding off little spots on her back and arms. Her sundress wasn't much protection.

She closed her eyes, but that wasn't much protection either.

"Franklin, darling. Kiss me."

Milicent was using her Greta Garbo voice, and Lilith bit her bottom lip. Men fell at her feet like slavering dogs when she used that routine. In all the years they'd dated Lilith had never, ever cared much about who got whom. And in the last three years or so, she had grown so bored with the privileged few that she'd virtually taken herself out of the running. But this was different. She didn't think she could bare to see Frank slaver.

It was awful. First the Adonis transformation, then the "sugar" thing, and now this! Please! Even the most terrible of stepsisters shouldn't deserve this kind of payback. And she was trying to change, gosh darn it! She was trying to claw her own way out of that prison of ice and be a real person.

Days ago when Shannon left, Lilith had wondered if the pain and loss had meant she was feeling real emotions that wouldn't fade away. Well, Shannon's memory was still vibrantly teary and she was fast becoming an expert on pain and loss.

"Franklin, I know you want me. Let's go upstairs."

Lilith shot her head through a spray of palm fronds. Milicent was wrapped around Frank like a boa constrictor, her hands at his neck, his hands at her waist. He once said he'd do just about anything for Prince, but this was too much. It was supposed to be an act. Frank detested women like Mil . . . like her. And what about *their* kiss and all his talk about magic? A spurt of tears stung her eyes and Lilith blinked them back. Okay, so her lying had abruptly altered their potential relationship, but if Frank

Henson was really this fickle, he darn well had no room to criticize.

"Now, Milly girl, I just can't let myself treat a lady like that. A few of those scoundrels you told me about tonight would have rushed you, sugar, and I don't want to be confused with that sort. Let's take our time."

Milly girl! Yuck! Milicent hated being called Milly.

"Oh, Franklin, you're the kind of man little girls dream about when they read fairy tales." Mil tittered like a nitwit and then went up on her tiptoes and laid one on the man till Lilith thought her own lungs would burst. With another burst of giggles she broke away and ran into the house. Greta Garbo had turned into Shirley Feeney and it was not a pretty sight. Any man who could fall for that deserved to get a head injury from the tumble.

"You can come out now, Lilith . . . Yeah, I know you're over there." Frank sighed and stepped closer to the white railing while running a hand roughly through his hair. "I don't know how I know it, dammit! But I do."

Slowly Lilith inched into the dim circle of light created by the moon and the dancing flame of a gas tiki torch. She was wrapped up in something soft and fuzzy the color of the moon and her hair, and Frank thought she looked as if she'd been gilded in silver. Different as night and day from her brassy sister. A day ago he'd never have believed it, let alone seen the distinction.

Frank closed his eyes, opened them and tried again, but Lilith still looked the same and so damn beautiful—but she'd lied to him! He had to remember that. Even so, she wasn't the kind of woman Milicent was. The last hellish hours had left him no room for doubt on that subject, no matter how much he would like to deny it.

"I do declare, it looks like *y'all* had a very profitable evening, *Franklin*. Why, who in the world would have thought you were concealing such a powerful secret weapon?"

He grimaced at her pointed sarcasm and wearily pulled his unused glasses from his jacket pocket. "She bought the package, Lilith. For some people that's all they want to see. It's all that ever matters." Frank swung his head around to gauge her reaction. "You should know how that feels." Why was he doing this? After all he knew, why was he still grasping for connections to this woman?

Because he, too, had been less than honest. Because the hell of it was, he'd thought about her all day, wondering how he could stop himself from remembering. And because he felt physically ill from the act he'd been playing and the people he'd had to gush over. He was exhausted and needed to feel like himself again. Needed someone who could understand what he was talking about. How it felt to be a commodity, a status symbol, and not a human being. The whole awful night had been an eerie reminder of the path he'd been mindlessly careening down.

"You're right, Frank." She paused, shrugging her shoulders as if giving in to something, then gave him a sad smile. "I know exactly how that feels. I guess that's why you changed your own wrapping. I'm sorry you had to play the part for Milicent. I could tell how much it bothered you. And whether it's possible for you to believe me or not, I've recently come to know exactly how demoralizing that is. How hard it is to hold on to the real you." She spoke without a drop of artifice as she moved a few feet closer and took his glasses from him. Her perception stopped him cold.

The breeze billowed and he couldn't say a word, just watched her cradle his protection, his lie, his disguise, and ship it unconsciously into her pocket. Her dress against her legs, lifting tiny wisps of hair from her braid to dance around her face. Her eyes shone like twin candles in the darkness, and Frank had to curl his fingers tightly over the iron beneath his hands. God, he remembered how she tasted and how she felt, and he fought against the need to wipe away Milicent's memory with this woman who'd once been so like her. This woman who'd had the courage and strength to try to change all alone.

Yes, she'd lied. And at first he'd hardly been able to keep his mind on maneuvering Milicent and off his betrayed emotions. But now he had to ask himself, in her place, would he have done any different?

Frank traced her strained features and thought about his struggle when his career had ended and he was no longer the golden boy. He'd made his way back to humanity because he'd had a family and a friend who really cared. Lilith was going it all alone. He knew now that she pretty much always had.

"I want you to know I've . . ." He paused and sought her eyes in the flickering shadows. "I've had a chance to think about the other night and how difficult it would be to betray family. I will protect Prince regardless of the cost. I can't let my feelings jeopardize that, but I have thought about your side. One thing I do know after today; you are not like Milicent." Frank swore he heard a catch in her breathing, and its meaning tore at his weakening resolve. Did his opinion affect her so much?

"She finally told me about paying Cindy back, and later, when she'd had one drink too many, she said something about being set up and lied to. But whoever that person is, it's not Max. Oh, she hates the guy almost as much as she hates Prince. It seems the Frenchman lied to her, too, about helping her make Prince look like a fool at his reception. But even drunk, that's all Milicent owned up to. Max told me himself that she'd vehemently denied anything about a kidnapping, and I have to admit I believe her."

Frank fisted a hand and thumped it against an iron loop. "There's a missing link here, Lilith, and I only have until tomorrow night to find it; then I've got to fly home. It's that other name I need. The name of someone so determined to cause trouble for Prince that it looks like they've involved his most ruthless business rival, Cain Devlin. I just don't know if I can keep up the act with your sister. It's getting mighty hard to hold her off." Frank looked out toward the ocean and expelled a tight breath.

Lilith pressed against the decorative iron until she felt the pattern boring into her back. "You once said you'd do just about anything for Prince, Frank, but please, even Mil doesn't deserve to be used that way. And don't think I'm standing here forgetting how I tried to—to physically side-track you. I admit that technique has worked for me in the past, but it was always wrong; I just didn't realize it. Please don't make my mistake; you're too good a man. Even though I never did more than act . . . encouraging, it wasn't right. Nothing meaningful can come from that kind of thinking, and it's taken me a few lonely years to finally figure that out."

Lilith lifted a beseeching hand toward him. "Let me get the name, Frank. You don't need to be twisted up in my family's problems anymore. I swear you can trust me. I'll have it before the party ends and you can do whatever you must, then. I-I need to be the one that confronts her with the whole truth. I don't want to make the same mistake that I made with you—" She froze, the words suspended in the air between them.

Frank tried desperately not to hear her appeal. He hadn't really given her a chance to explain that night, but he'd sure as hell passed judgment. Lilith's proposed scene with Milicent was doomed. How easy would it be to destroy the only family you'd ever had? And how much would it hurt to discover that family didn't really care?

Hours ago Mil had laid out a crystal clear picture of her disdain for Cindy and her pity for Lilith. Her hands had slipped suggestively over his body and she'd asked him to tell her again that he'd only used Lilith. Under her liquor-scented breath he'd heard her whisper, *I'm the most beautiful sister. I can take their men anytime I want.*

He'd mumbled something that sounded approving and then very neutrally probed her groggy mind. Milicent told about Prince's alleged promises, Cindy's trickery, and Lilith's defection. Frank had been forced to suffer an unexpected, bitter kiss before Mil had laughed and announced how lucky he was that she had rescued him from her conscience-ridden prude of a sister. In fact, they could really put the screws to old lonely Lil by laying it on in public. After all, Milicent had giggled in his ear, her sister had been living like a nun for ages. That alone should prove how weird she was.

Frank watched Lilith and let the silence spin out between them. Could Milicent have been telling the truth? Had Lilith and he both found the same emptiness in trophy relationships and surface sex? Could they really share this, too? Yes. He'd just heard the truth of it. Frank looked away, unable to move another muscle in his body. Hell, they'd nearly set the bed on fire and she'd only seen him in his *disguise,* as Prince referred to it. His altered appearance hadn't affected her response at all.

But would she let go of her past the way he had? Could he even ask that of her? God, he wished he could just leave tonight! He wished he wasn't standing here in the tropical moonlight burning for a woman who might be an illusion. At that aberrant thought, he almost laughed. Hell, he was screwed up but good! Most men probably had fantasies of being in just such a sultry spot with a modern-day fairy-tale princess like a cover model. The externals would be more than enough. But Frank's fantasy was about the real woman he'd discovered inside the princess.

Because, God help him, he loved that woman, and he had the strangest impression that only he could rescue that part of Lilith and set her free.

Could there be a bigger fool?

Frank leaned into the cool metal and felt the rough drag of a soldered seam beneath his fingertips. What should he do? He turned his head and stared into the face that had haunted him all day. The delicate breeze suddenly began to sweep and sigh around them and a feeling—a thought— started to swell down deep inside. *Tell her how you feel. Tell her. Tell her.*

But the words stuck in his throat and he pressed hard

against the intricate barrier as if he could force the metal to give as he could not force his heart to trust. Dammit, he'd seen evidence of how far Lilith had come. Frank saw her eyes widen and two tiny lines form between her brows at his silent stare. God help him, but he was a hypocrite. What would he have done if no one had been willing to believe he was capable of changing? His love was useless and hollow without total trust. He couldn't tell Lilith a thing.

"Listen, Frank," Lilith blurted. "Obviously you'd rather not talk, but you need to know I'm going to deal with Milicent and help Cindy no matter what. I have to; it's the only way to start my new life. I'm changing for me even though I'm probably not going to be too good at it for a while." She hesitated and glanced down at the rippling hem of her dress.

"I guess after the last few days you know that. Anyway, you can take back or regret all the things you said—all of what happened between us—I can't stop you. But I won't give back the butterfly and what it means. I believe in butterflies now. It's all I've got."

Lilith's legs trembled and she leaned against the wrought-iron fence, shoving his glasses in her pocket as she wrapped her hands around the flapping ends of the shawl. Frank stood stock-still, buffeted by the wind, as if he hadn't heard a word she'd said. And somewhere deep inside a feeling, a thought, swelled. *Tell him. Tell him how you feel.*

But fear choked off the words and an unexpectedly harsh gust suddenly caused Lilith to rear backward at the exact moment the tiki poles rattled and began to wink out. *Stuuuuuborrrrrnn.* The sound or word or *something* tumbled and danced on the wind, strung out in a pained whine that had Lilith's eyes straining into the darkness and her feet struggling for purchase. Then, without any warning, the support behind her snapped and she fell headfirst off the veranda.

"Frank!"

The man moved like a flash of lightning—fast, powerful, illuminating. She was falling and then she was caught, caught close against a hard chest and a hammering heart by strong, desperate hands that moved almost roughly over her back and shoulders. They were both kneeling on the deck, and Frank's stricken features were washed with a ghostly white. For an instant they looked into each other's eyes and held nothing back. In that moment of near loss, the fullness in their hearts could not be denied.

The stinging bite of the wind gentled and warmed, blowing softly off the water, and Lilith felt it wrap around the two of them like an invisible length of gardenia-scented silk.

Tell him.

She opened her mouth to speak . . . but Frank covered it with his own before she could utter a word.

His arms pulled her into the curve of his body and anchored her like bands of steel. Bands of trembling steel. Lilith could not even process who had started shaking first. Frank's lips surrounded hers, demanding a response, and she opened to him and let him deep inside. For one glorious moment she allowed herself to feel the joy and passion only this man could ignite. She had thought she would never have this again. She had thought he would never forgive her.

A sharp burn burst behind her closed eyes. No words of forgiveness had been spoken. No words of anything but duty and leaving. Lilith shut off her thoughts and ran her hands up the muscled wall of Frank's chest, spearing her fingers into the wavy hair at the back of his head. With moist, clinging lips she sipped and sucked his slightly swollen mouth, careful of Max's handiwork, until Frank groaned and sent his tongue sliding urgently over hers, heedless of any possible pain. He pressed his palms high against her sides, those beautiful long fingers wrapping around her ribs and his thumbs resting snugly under the curves of her breasts. Lilith felt the magic again.

This was the moment. Now. Now she would tell him. Now she would say the words she had never, ever spoken before.

"Dammit! What am I doing?" Frank panted as he jerked away and heaved them both to their feet. "I shouldn't have let that happen. Too many complications." He stepped back and bent over at the waist, bracing his hands on his thighs. "Go ahead and try for the name of the setup person. But whether I get the name or not, I'm leaving tomorrow night."

He was gone. And it looked like the words would never be said.

Lilith was powdered, perfumed, coiffed, and adorned. She was draped in a sheath of ice blue satin, dripping in diamonds, and about to ruin her mother's party. But it had to be done. Frank's plane was leaving in two hours and he hadn't gotten the name he needed. Lilith hesitated at one of the doors leading out to the veranda. This was her moment of truth. Ties would be broken now, maybe forever. She took a deep breath and lifted one finger to the butterfly unobtrusively nestled in a loop of her hair.

Originally she'd wanted to prove to Frank that she had changed. But now it was far more important to prove it to herself. Lilith stroked a small, smooth-enameled wing and hoped Bernard had done his job and gotten her mother and sister out there.

"Lilith! What's the meaning of this?" her mother demanded the moment the paned door closed.

"Really, Lil," Milicent chastised, carefully balanced on the arm of Barbara's patio chair. "The guests are about to arrive. What was it that couldn't wait?" Her exquisite face was distorted with anger, and the gold sequined dress she was wearing winked and sparkled with the light of dozens of tiki torches.

Lilith mentally braced herself and plunged in.

"I want to know who helped you set up Cindy and Prince."

"What?" the two of them demanded in unison.

"None of your games will work on me, so don't even bother. I know you both too well. And I know exactly when you're lying." Lilith folded her arms and walked toward the outraged pair. "Max has spilled the beans, Mil. I know everything but the name of the other person involved. If you want any hope of keeping this out of the hands of the authorities, you'd better cooperate."

"Max Wolfe is a rotten, conniving turncoat! He—"

"Milicent, hush!" Barbara abruptly interjected before turning to Lilith. "Be reasonable, Lilith; you wouldn't do anything to your own family. Don't be foolish," she finished condescendingly, fussing with one of the CZ-studded cuffs on her flowing gown of white organdy. "Besides, whatever hurts us would hurt you, too, daughter! Wait—this display doesn't have anything to do with Franklin, does it? I warned you about him and Milicent. Do grow up."

"For God's sake, Lil," Milicent spat out as she stood. "You're never going to get a man like Franklin, so don't think you can threaten me away from him."

Lilith felt herself go rigid and cold. She wasn't asleep and she wasn't dreaming, but the ice castle was most definitely closing in around her. Her heart ached because for so much of her life these two people had been her only definition of love. And now she knew they didn't have the slightest clue about what it meant. The revelation hurt, but it was also liberating. She wasn't responsible for them. She couldn't be. Lilith knew what love was now and she was going to build her new life around it no matter how long it took. But she had to start with the truth.

"First, I want you both to know that I consider Cindy my family, too. We've been terrible to her and that will end now. Second, Mother, I could care less how our image fares in the press, so don't think that will stop me. And third, you're right, Mil. I'll never get a man like Franklin and here's a news flash, sister dear—I don't want that kind of man anymore. Of course, a plain old Frank would be a whole different thing, but I digress. Think it over, ladies. I want a name and I want it now!"

"Milicent, you'd better answer your sister."

"Mother! Are you crazy? Don't say anything!"

"I won't have your obsession ruin my party. I tried to be tolerant, but really, Milicent, Helen Chalmers is not worth a moment's inconvenience." Barbara got to her silver-slippered feet and faced Lilith with her implacable mask in place. She might as well have ice water running in her veins. Lilith briefly glanced away. She had come so close to following in her mother's unfeeling footsteps.

"It was Helen who approached Milicent. She thought it might bring her grandson to his senses and, frankly, Milicent wanted to stir up a hornet's nest. I suppose I could have said something, but I assumed that if this *feeling* between Cynthia and Princeton was strong enough, no harm would be done, and Milicent could have a bit of satisfying revenge and then get on with her life. She is negotiating for a *Cosmo* cover, did you know that? Besides, it's certainly not our fault if Helen went too far."

Lilith didn't even try to close her mouth. What could she possibly say to counter such convoluted thinking? Her mother and sister and Prince's grandmother were twisted, warped human beings, and suddenly all the anger and outrage drained out of her. Lilith felt battered and exhausted and barely had the energy to muster some pity.

"All right. I'm going to take this news to Cindy and Prince myself. I'm sure they'll probably keep it quiet, but I'm warning you, if they'll let me, I'm going to be in touch with them often. And you will hear me screaming all the way from California if I ever get wind of anything like this again."

Milicent was vibrating with fury. She pushed past Barbara and yelled in Lilith's face, "You're a traitor! I was going to offer to share that cover and help your pathetic career, but you can forget it. One day you'll be sorry, Lilith, and we won't care, do you hear me?"

Before Lilith could react, Milicent reached out and snatched the butterfly from her hair. "I told you this looked ridiculous!" She flung it into the hot tub and jabbed a finger in the air. "You'd better run, sister, because I plan to paint you as a pathetic has-been the moment our friends start arriving. You'll never work again."

Lilith could actually feel the hatred dissipate as the French doors slammed behind her mother and sister. She staggered back to her spot behind the palm and leaned up against the wall, trying to take one steady breath. She was alone now. In a few minutes this familiar house would begin to fill with familiar people, and in hours it would all be strange and they would be strangers and she . . . ? Lilith rubbed her hands up and down her bare arms.

"Milicent was lying, you know."

She slumped into the scratchy stucco. Mercy. Had Frank heard everything? Lilith couldn't speak. There was nothing to say except the words that choked her with fear. The words that still tingled on her lips along with the taste of his kiss. Perhaps they were her only chance of reaching him, of rebuilding his trust. Did she dare risk it?

"Lilith? Did you hear me? Milicent was lying about working. She told me *Cosmo* only wanted the deal if you were part of it. You can have everything back again. I'm sure a call from Prince could straighten it all out."

Frank drew in a deep breath and lifted the thick palm leaves that hid the woman he loved. Sweet Jesus, but she was beautiful. As lovely and rare as a blue diamond. He registered her wide, round eyes, the jewels at her ears, throat, and wrists, the satin gown that would have pleased any honest-to-God princess in the world. How could he ever have thought seriously about asking her to give this up? Why would Lilith Smythe ever want to leave this behind for him? Just because this world had chewed him up and spit him out didn't mean it affected everyone that way. Damned if she hadn't been right. He was on some kind of

Mr. Perfect, self-righteous bandstand.

"Oh, Frank," she whispered, cinching her arms around her waist. "This is going to hurt Prince and Cindy so much. How could Helen have done it?"

Frank shook his head in disbelief. "Lilith, your family just hurt you pretty badly, too."

She waved a hand dismissively. "But Cindy doesn't deserve this."

"And you do?"

"I-I don't think that a wicked stepsister is usually a candidate for 'happily ever after.'"

Frank stepped closer and felt the feathery fronds brush the back of his tux. Lilith's eyes sparkled with tears, and the dancing light of the torches glittered in them. The balmy night had stretched long, dark fingers across the gold-and-burgundy sunset as if slowly gathering up the colors in a giant hand. Frank had a desolate feeling that what little color he'd had in his own life was going to be lost to the night, too. Because, God help him, he was going to walk away and leave his princess in the enchanted land she'd been born to. Neither one of them would be happy living in the wrong world. And it would kill him to see regret in her eyes. Best to end it quickly and cleanly.

"You're a brave and beautiful woman, Lilith Smythe. And I was wrong; you are not a wicked stepsister at all. I admire you for doing what you just did."

Lilith still wasn't used to seeing straight into Frank's eyes. His handsome face had moved close to hers, and the steady amber gaze, coupled with his low, sincere words, shot straight to her heart. She was about to do the bravest thing she'd ever done and voice her deepest feelings. It was time to start being the real Lilith, no matter what happened.

"I love you, Frank."

There was a ghastly silence and Frank pulled back. Lilith fought to keep the corners of her mouth from turning down. All right, maybe she didn't have his love, but she did have his admiration. She clasped her hands and determined to say it all. For herself, at least.

"I-I'm sure this is a surprise. But I want you to know I mean it, Frank. I love you."

"I don't belong in your world, Lilith, and I couldn't ask you to give it up. It would never work between us."

"But I don't want to belong to that world anymore, Frank. Give us a chance. Please try to trust me." She swallowed and curled her hand around the one he held clenched at his side. "You're everything I've ever dreamed of."

"That's the hell of it, Lil. I think your feelings may be tangled up with those bizarre dreams of yours. How can you be so sure of such a huge change in so little time? Frank broke her hold and lifted his hands wide, looked down at himself and then back to Lilith's bewildered face. "This isn't me, sugar. This isn't what's real. Maybe all you want is the package."

"Oh, Frank, don't do this. Don't put me back in the ice I've been clawing my way out of."

A sudden smattering of taps rained against a pane of glass in the French doors. "Excuse me, Miss Lilith," Bernard apologized with a slight bow as he stepped onto the patio. "Mr. Henson has a call from the States."

Frank managed a determined move toward the little man.

"Frank, wait!" Lilith called breathlessly. He stopped and looked back over his shoulder. The motion triggered an instantaneous flashback of the airport scene with Lilith and Shannon. He rapidly blinked the memory away.

"Please don't leave without saying good-bye."

He nodded once. He didn't dare speak.

Once in Monte Carlo Lilith had watched a man risk his entire fortune on a single roll of the dice. The room had become so quiet that heartbeats seemed audible, every breath an explosion of sound. She would never forget the looks of dread and exaltation on the faces that ringed the gaming table. Some had seen a man of vision, some had called him a fool. But at this precise moment, Lilith thought she knew what he'd truly felt.

It was about putting it on the line. Wanting something so badly that you could do nothing less than go all the way. Frank didn't think she meant it about leaving her old life, and she had to show him she did. He had a point. It had been a very short time for such a huge change. Lilith took a long look at her reflection in the full-length mirror in her bedroom. This was her one shot, her one roll. And if it didn't work? Well, Lilith Smythe was not about to slink out of sight. Oh, no! This little plan would guarantee her life as major topic of gossip for quite some time.

She turned a bit to the side and pressed a hand to her queasy stomach. If she had truly changed, then she had to prove it. On such short notice, she couldn't think of a more effective way. Talk about a clear statement. Cindy wouldn't hesitate, and suddenly Lilith felt very sure that her stepsister would welcome the new her. It was the emotional boost she needed.

In a few quick moves, Lilith had her hibiscus bag packed, and she'd tucked her secret weapon into her pocket. She would not be returning to her room. A rhythmic squeak sounded as she walked to the door. One last time, Lilith glanced back at the mirror and adjusted the vivid scarf she'd had to tie around her hair. She had to go back to the hot tub. She was not leaving without her butterfly. Perhaps it was ridiculous, but she felt like the beautiful little thing had become her magic talisman. And if ever in her life she needed a touch of magic, it was now.

Love is all the magic you need.

Wide-eyed, Lilith whirled around, her hand splayed over her heart. Gads, was she stressed! Hearing things was not a good sign—particularly when no one was there. She'd better just get on with it before she hallucinated something really crazy, like a fairy with a magic wand.

Although . . . the words did give her another surge of hope.

She took a deep breath and squeaked out the door. Okay, plastic shoes had some drawbacks, but they'd get her in and out of the spa in no time, and maybe her prince would recognize the perfect fit . . . in more ways than one.

Frank had stashed his bag out on the patio to avoid the crush of dazzling, diamond-dripping phonies. He glanced at his watch. Damn, he had to get to the airport. The call he'd taken from his office had been a recorded emergency message from Prince asking him to meet his plane and help track down Helen Chalmers. The crazy old woman had escaped and was presumed to be headed to St. Thomas. He needed to leave, but where was Lilith?

Part of him wanted to sneak out now, but he'd made a promise. A promise to a woman who'd said she loved him. Frank could feel his heart accelerating at just the thought. He ran a finger around his snug collar and black tie. This whole charade was making him crazy, and with a couple of jerky moves he pulled off the noose and freed a few buttons.

Across the packed room he saw a sleek, sable-haired woman with bloodred lips giving him a disgustingly thorough once-over. Frank felt his blood go cold. How could anyone stand to live this way? He turned around and walked out behind a caterer and nearly stepped on the biggest butterfly he'd ever seen. He froze in his tracks as the pink-and-yellow phenomenon fluttered up from the floor and lit on a small service table next to the back door.

Something that beautiful and rare shouldn't be trapped in this house, of all places. Hell, every minute inside was a death wish. The second the poor thing was spotted the rush to profit from it would probably guarantee that very end. Frank couldn't let that happen. He slowly edged toward the door, praying the innocent insect would fly out and not farther in. This was one beauty that would not be

vied for as a showpiece or treated as a commodity or—
Oh, God, Lilith!

Frank braced an arm against the doorjamb and watched the delicate creature dip and lift on the evening breeze. The woman he loved was exactly like this butterfly. She didn't belong in this house either. She wouldn't survive here. All his pontificating about their differences had been a smoke screen for the hurt he'd experienced so long ago. The hurt he'd been judging Lilith with. He'd let his fears blind him to what they both really needed. Dammit, Prince should have kicked him in the butt instead of talking.

He'd almost walked away from the love he'd been looking for all his life. Thank God for little, magic miracles. He snapped the door shut and hurried down the hall, tugging on his silk cuffs and tossing the tie over his shoulder. Lilith loved him and he loved her and she wasn't going to go another five minutes without knowing it. Hell, the whole damn party was gonna know it. He had let her take all the risks, then left her hanging, and if it took every day for the next ten years, he'd make up for that.

The moment Frank pushed into the edges of the room he knew something was wrong. The crowd was even more tightly packed and they'd all gravitated toward the circular staircase. A swell of mocking laughter rippled around the room, and with growing alarm Frank saw Milicent climb up on a stool. She caught his eye and gave him a conspiratorial wink while circling her index finger near her temple and then pointing at the human knot between them. Obviously Lilith hadn't revealed his involvement. What was going on?

Then, through the shifting sea of humanity, he saw what the commotion was about.

Lilith, the limbo queen, had come to the party in all her gauche glory. And Frank had never seen her look more beautiful. God, she was so brave, so determined to prove what she'd told him was true. A loud, ugly comment from Milicent quieted the vultures, and Frank saw the stoic mask on Lilith's face slip. He had to get her out. Now. For once his face and his size made things easier. The women didn't mind him moving them out of the way and the men took one look at his shoulders and held their tongues.

The sable-haired woman tried to stop him when he brushed past her, by dragging her fake nails up his thigh, and Milicent clearly thought he was making his way over to her. She pursed her bronze-colored lips as if she were kissing the air and beckoned him with a waving hand.

But the hand went still in midwave and the crowd went pin-drop silent when Frank scooped Lilith up from behind, tossed her over his shoulder, and whisked her down the servants' hall.

"Stop fighting me, woman," he grunted, trying to control her swinging legs and open the side door at the same time.

"Frank?" she screeched. "What are you doing?"

"Listen," he huffed, sliding one hand up under the generous fabric and clamping it around a smooth, bare thigh.

"Frank!"

"Okay, okay, sugar. There you go." He took a few more hurried steps and then purposely slid her down his body, hoping to keep her off balance long enough to tell her how he felt. It didn't work.

"Don't Frank." She flailed a hand at him and moved backward. "Don't you dare call me sugar. I thought it meant something and then you—"

"Ah, Lil, I know. I remember that exact moment sitting on the couch by Milicent." Frank winced when he saw the shadowy pain in the blue eyes he loved so much. "The second that word left my mouth I knew how much it did mean. I was in deeper than I'd realized and hurting, too. I just couldn't believe that what we felt was real."

"All right, I've had it!" Lilith shouted, stalking over to the spa with her hands on her hips and then spinning to face him in a swirl of fuchsia-and-yellow cotton.

"Now, sugar—"

"Wait! For your information, Frank Henson, I may not

be there yet, but one day I'll be as real as you. Only you'll be sorry if you wait that long to believe me." She waved her hands at him and continued. "I love you, you stubborn man. I loved you before I even knew you could look like this."

"Lil—"

"Wait!" Lilith blinked back her tears and tried to hold on to her composure. If this didn't work . . . if he couldn't . . . She fished a hand deep in her pocket and pulled out Frank's dark-framed glasses. With two sharp snaps she popped out the lenses and looked straight into his surprised face. She moved to stand in front of him and felt her throat grow thick with unshed tears.

He never moved a muscle as she slipped them on him and gently ran her fingertips down the sides of his face.

"I don't care how the package is wrapped, Frank," she whispered, laying a hand over his heart. "It's what's here inside I'll always love. It's what you see in me."

"Lil?" Frank stopped and curled his fingers around the feminine hand on his chest. "You are finished, right?"

She nodded and drew her brows together, perplexed.

"Remember when I told you days ago that I couldn't do this job without your help?" She nodded again and Frank slid his thumb into the hollow of her hand. He could feel her pulse in that soft, tender spot and he wondered if Lilith knew she he held his entire future in her small palm.

"Well, I don't think I can do the rest of my life without your help, sugar. So I have to tell you we can do this easy or we can do it hard, but you're stuck with me. Marry me, my beautiful butterfly. I love you."

"Oh, Frank," she whispered with a watery sob, and he tugged her close, running his hands up and down her spine and pressing his lips to the coconut-scented skin behind her ear.

"Lil—"

"Frank, wait!" She jerked away from him. "My butterfly! I've got to get it, please. I can't leave without it and we don't have much time. Milicent is furious."

"I'll get it, sugar."

"But I have the plastic shoes, Frank, and you're in an Armani tux and—"

Frank stepped into the water, Bruno Magli shoes and all. He could see the gift he'd not been able to stop himself from buying. Even then, somewhere deep inside of him, he'd wanted it all with Lilith. Her protestations stuttered to a halt and he flashed a big, macho smile.

"Of course, love, now that I've rescued your precious butterfly you owe me a boon." He extended the vibrant enameled barrette, heedless of the water sluicing off his jacket sleeve. "I know all about such things because of those fairy tales I used to read to Janna."

Lilith laughed and stepped to the tiled edge of the spa.

"Ask for anything you want, my valiant hero."

"You haven't answered my question, sugar. Will you marry me? Will you let me sleep with my head on your pillow? Will you kiss me every day of forever and have babies with me? I have to warn you, though, I have something endless in mind."

Her eyes went dark and then shone as brightly as the flames of the tiki torches. Lilith didn't hesitate; she stepped into the water and lifted her arms around his neck.

"Yes, Frank. Yes to everything. I promise."

"All right, then." Frank grinned and gave her a quick peck on the lips. "We've got to get to the airport to meet Prince, but then we're getting married; I don't care what time it is."

"Prince is here? What happened—Wait!" Lilith sputtered. "You mean we're getting married tonight? In our wet clothes?"

"Yep. Your muumuu and my dripping Armani. But don't fret; by the time we finish with Prince I should be close to a damp-dry. And sugar, it would take a lot more than clammy clothes to keep me from making you mine. I want you, Lilith. I want you permanently. You know"—he waggled a finger close to her nose—"there were a few stories where the princesses tried to sidle away and I'm not about to let that happen. We'll have to have a honeymoon later, after the Chalmerses' problems are resolved."

"I-I'm a little bit scared, Frank. I don't want to let you down." She swallowed and tried not to shake. Everything she'd ever wanted was within her grasp—love, respect, laughter, caring—but she had to be honest. This was real and she had to be more than she'd ever been.

Frank cradled Lilith's face in his hands and looked deeply into her eyes. "There's nothing we can't handle together, sugar. Besides, I've discovered you're a blue-collar princess; just look what you've done in the past week. Hell, woman, you can do anything. You have the magic touch."

"What?"

Frank laughed, lifted her out of the water, and kissed her until the confusion turned into passion. "See what I mean? Why, that kiss just turned me into something I thought I'd never be . . . a married man."

And it was odd, but as they grabbed their bags and sneaked around the side of the house, Lilith thought she heard a tinkling spurt of laughter from that strange voice that had scared her earlier. She glanced around for a moment, and Frank tugged gently on her hand, his golden eyes sending her a smoldering message. No more ice. His warm, firm grasp was real. And the voice? Well, it rang with such joy that Lilith let the words comfort her as they had once before.

Ahh, you found the magic. It's about time, my dears. . . .

Part Three

"Little Roberta Hood Gets Even With the Big Bad Wolfe"

Chapter One

Roberta Hood Chalmers knew she should let go of Belinda's arm, but she was swamped with a dizzy, nauseous feeling. Dozens of shimmering lights had just flashed wildly in her field of vision and she was terrified of sliding to the floor in a dead faint. She closed her eyes and took a deep breath. A small eddy of steadying strength flowed into her wobbly legs and she gripped Belinda a little tighter. Max was here. *Max was here!*

Max was here—and if what Lilith Smythe had just said was true, he was involved in ruining yet another Chalmers wedding. Two years ago it had been their wedding he'd destroyed. Tiny, razor-sharp pricks of pain ran up and down her spine. Oh, God! She'd been fooling herself. All these months she'd thought it was over, that this man who'd so callously tossed her aside was old business, boxed up and thrown away.

But the therapist she'd secretly seen a few times after Max had dumped her had tried to tell her that too much had been left unresolved. That there was too much in her life she was simply not confronting. Stubbornly, Roberta hadn't listened. That had been a new side of her that Max's cruelty had uncovered. Actually, his desertion had forced a number of changes on the obedient, mousy Roberta Chalmers.

Her secret dream of being a painter had died with his lies, and sometimes she still wondered if his dream of leaving business and making wine had all been a lie, too. A way to win her trust, since she'd told him in the very beginning how she felt about the sharks that plagued the world of Chalmers, Inc. She'd also stopped attempting to make herself more attractive. What was the point? After all, her efforts had been a dismal failure. Roberta dressed for comfort and for herself. Contacts hurt her eyes, and she was too short to ever look devastating. It was past time to accept that.

But she did have things of value to offer: willing hands and a quick mind. She threw herself into volunteer work and started back at school against her grandmother's wishes. Roberta hated being at odds with her grandmother, especially since she hadn't listened about Max, but Prince had been in her corner and so she'd kept going.

Looking back on it, she was convinced she would have gone nuts without another focus. Now she had a degree in business, and Prince had given her a job she'd earned—not been born to. Grandmother was having trouble with that, too. But then—Roberta grimaced—at least she was family and not at all like Helen Chalmers's favorite target, Cain Devlin. Grandmother hated that man with a passion.

Maybe unreasonable feelings for certain men was a weakness in the Chalmers blood, because here she was—after just one glimpse of those dark eyes and that strong, lithe body—and both her courage and her control were shaking to pieces inside of her. Was she a sham? Was everything she'd tried to change in her life that easily undone? Roberta was scared to death. She wanted to run, to hide. Confronting this man who'd left her without a moment's regret filled her with ice-cold horror. It could be the second most humiliating moment in all her twenty-five years.

But how could she let this sleaze of a sweet-talker stand her life on end again? How could she stand by and let him kidnap Cindy?

The happy noise in the Royal Arms ballroom faded away. Roberta glanced at Belinda and then Lilith. Neither one of these very different women would have fallen for such practiced manipulation in the first place. Neither one would be pathetically wishing even for a moment that it wasn't true. That a man they had once loved wasn't capable of hurting them even more.

But then only a shy, mousy wallflower would have bought his whole line of bull in the first place. That he could talk to her, that she could detect his real emotions no matter what attitude he assumed, that she cared for more than his good looks. Mercy! That one should have set off a number of alarms. But oh, no. She allowed herself to believe the lies that had left her waiting at the altar with a short, blunt note and five hundred guests to break the news to. If Grandmother Chalmers and Prince hadn't been there, Roberta knew she would have simply curled into a ball and disappeared.

Roberta looked up at Belinda. Cindy was so lucky to have such a take-charge best friend. Even if that friend had just ordered her to jump right in the middle of this impending disaster. Okay, her job was to find Prince, and Lilith's was to find Frank Henson. Fine. But her stomach began to roil. What would Prince do when she told him Max was involved? That maybe her poor judgment had brought this devious man back to haunt her family again? After years of handling the business, her jilting, and Cain Devlin's betrayal, Prince had finally found such happiness with Cindy that it made Roberta sick to think of telling him anything that would ruin this day.

But what if she could get all the answers before she had to tell her brother? What if, this time, she could save the Chalmerses from Maximillian Wolfe?

Belinda suddenly peeled away Roberta's hand and demanded they all take action. In a swish of peach satin she was gone, leaving her alone with Lilith Smythe. The willowy beauty made Roberta very uncomfortable. Here was the kind of woman who *would* have the power to tie a man like Maximillian Wolfe into knots. Roberta tipped back her head and pushed her glasses up on her nose. Grandmother was right. She'd never had what it would take to hold a man like Max. Not even close. His lack of desire might have been the clue that saved her if she hadn't been so inexperienced.

Roberta shuddered at the humiliating memory and then squared her shoulders. Yes, it had been horrible, but she hadn't let it defeat her. She'd had two years to see herself more clearly, to find a Roberta Hood Chalmers she could be proud of, and darn it, she was not going to lose all that! She was not going to slink away and lick her wounds in the dark, even though her grandmother had insisted once that she do so. This time she was going to exorcise the man from her soul. This time he was going to pay for even thinking about hurting her family. This time she was going to get even!

Anger felt wonderful. The red-hot rage bubbling in her veins was liberating, invigorating, and for a second she could have sworn even the air around her shimmered with it. The cold tendrils of fear that held her rooted to the Royal Arms ballroom floor disintegrated, and Roberta grabbed Lilith by the arm. She knew she had to act on this miraculous burst of courage quickly. She couldn't waste a moment of righteous wrath. Lilith seemed to stumble for a second, but Roberta didn't stop. She spotted Frank and zeroed in on him.

Frank was her friend and only raised an eyebrow when she tugged on his lapels to drag his lofty height down to her level. She knew she should tell him she'd seen Max. But deep inside Roberta realized this was her chance to finish it once and for all. If she were ever truly going to be able to move forward, this old pain had to be dealt with head-on and alone. At long last she understood how true that advice had been.

She had to speak loudly over the noise in the crowded reception hall. With tremendous effort she masked her growing urgency, and outlined Lilith's story.

"Wait a minute, Robbie," Frank rumbled. "You come with me and this Smythe woman. I can tell she's going to be a royal pain in the butt."

"No, Frank. I've got to find Prince. I'm going to do it right this time." She smiled and stepped away. Yes. She was going to find Prince and tell him everything . . . just as soon as she got a few supplies and cornered a certain snake in wolf's clothing.

Roberta was mad as hell, and darn it, she wasn't going to take it anymore. Wasn't there a story about a mouse that roared? Well, she was about to create a whole new version.

Maximillian Wolfe was furious—although not a single guest could tell. No, he'd spent far too many hours learning to conceal his emotions, learning to give nothing away. Such control had been the only thing that had helped him survive two years ago when the full scope of his father's duplicity had been so cruelly revealed and his dream for the future had been torn away. With great skill he allowed the world to see only what he wanted it to. And so he'd become a formidable international businessman with no one the wiser about the scars that marked his soul.

Frankly, his reputation for coldhearted indifference had worked to his benefit. He was wanted at every party, wanted in every big deal, wanted by countless women. Wanted because he represented controlled wildness and acceptable danger. He was the perfect example of a modern-day gentleman pirate. A titillating blend of the forbidden and the desired.

And since his mother's death a year ago, he'd become even emptier and more remote, thus playing the part yet more effectively. Perversely, the less he cared, the more he gained. It was such an absurd irony, and there wasn't a person in the world to share his twisted humor with.

Max discreetly straightened the diamond studs on the cuffs of his handmade linen dress shirt. His black tux was tailored to fit him like a glove, and he knew that many a female gaze was trailing him across the crowded room. What a priceless joke that he, who could have perhaps any woman with a mere snap of his fingers, wanted none of them. His body, his mind, his heart, simply would not respond. Max scanned the elegant throng and cursed silently. The legendary Maximillian Wolfe was actually starting to get concerned about his lack of interest. Would he ever feel desire again? How long could his mystique keep women from comparing notes, and what difference would it make if they did?

Perhaps he'd played his part too long. Perhaps he didn't feel because he wasn't really there anymore. Perhaps that was the reason no one could reach him and no one could see who he was. There'd only been two who had. One was dead and the other . . . he might as well have killed. God, he prayed he wouldn't see her.

But that selfish, maudlin wish was neither here nor there. Right now he had a debt to pay. A debt that had been eating him alive for two years. A purpose that had finally made him care about something again. Max curled the corner of his mouth in a self-deprecating smile. If he survived a meeting with Princeton Chalmers about his demented grandmother and if he managed to discover what that self-centered shrew, Milicent Smythe, had put into motion, perhaps he might redeem a portion of his blackened soul and break the curse over his heart and body: the curse he'd sealed with a promise more than two years ago.

The soft strains of Mozart seeped into his tumbling thoughts and soothed him. He nodded to a few dowagers and wondered what Helen Chalmers would do if they suddenly met face-to-face. *Mon Dieu!* How she hated him, and the old witch thought she had him over the coals still. But she would have a rude awakening if she tried put him to the guillotine this time. He was prepared for her devious mind and her underhanded tactics. But then, her precious granddaughter was not at stake, so it was possible his concern was unfounded.

Ah, but there was a debt to be settled there, too. For, as unbelievable as it might be to the world at large, Maximillian Wolfe had once cared desperately. He had once loved with his whole heart. He had once dared reveal his real self and his real dreams. What foolishness to think of that! The very last thing any of them needed at this moment was the past intruding into the present problem. If he was careful and stayed out of sight there would be no need. . . .

A tight knot of silk and satin suddenly unraveled in front of him, and his eyes naturally flowed over the gleaming parquet floor. Max felt the blood drain from his face. The onlookers vanished and he sucked in an audible gulp of air. He saw her. Roberta. Robbie. The woman he'd hurt so unforgivably. The woman he had loved and tried to forget. The woman he'd hoped not to see.

With the force of a hard fist to the gut, the truth swelled and burst free of the dark place where Max had buried it. God help him, it all rushed back in a twisting torrent of feeling and it took all his control to withstand the pain that exploded inside his chest.

He loved her. He loved her still. Had never stopped. Just grown slowly more numb with each passing day until he'd become a living mannequin. But she had every reason to hate him with each breath she took. His sweet, intuitive friend who'd become so unsure of herself when he'd started to change their friendship into something more. And he had so blindly thought he could handle his father's mistake and still make the woman his. That he'd have all the time in the world to bring her out of her shell and prove how much he loved and wanted her. Prove how much her understanding and acceptance meant. Instead he'd inflicted a mortal wound. His betrayal had plucked the bud too soon and he could see that she had never blossomed.

God's curse was just. He deserved to suffer even though he'd been caught in a vicious trap that had promised great sorrow no matter what he'd decided. No matter which love he protected.

Max cautiously moved back into a camouflaging wall of people. There were two things he owed the Chalmerses that he vowed to deliver, whatever the cost. One was the information Prince needed to keep his new wife safe, and the other was to spare Roberta from having to see his face.

And unlike his father, Maximillian Wolfe always paid his debts.

Dammit! He couldn't find them. Max had been discreetly looking for Prince and his bride, Cynthia, since he'd run fr—left the ballroom. *Think only of the present, Wolfe!* Right. He needed to tell the couple to be alert. Yet delivering that message successfully would depend on whether his former friend knocked him senseless in the first two minutes. Either way the man would want facts, and Max didn't wish to reveal too much until he'd confronted Milicent face-to-face. There was no way Prince Chalmers would take his word carte blanche, so a warning and the promise of more information was the best he could do.

After reading the smug, threatening letter Helen Chalmers had sent to his chateau, there was no doubt that somehow she'd had a hand in this. But only Milicent's confession could finally prove what the old witch had been up to all along: controlling her grandchildren's lives at any cost.

Once Max had arrived in California and discovered that Milicent hadn't come to the wedding or the reception, he knew she must have changed his bogus plan. All his safety valves had been short-circuited and he was feeling his way through this mess as best he could.

He turned down a narrow, empty hall and discovered he'd gone in the wrong direction. *Mon Dieu!* He'd wandered into a service area. The Chalmerses would never be here. In frustration, Max slammed a palm against the wall. He didn't have time for this. His plane was leaving in an hour. If he couldn't find Prince, he'd just have to call when he landed. His only proof had to be cornered.

Max stopped at a slightly open door and disappointedly registered the cleaning supplies. Damn! He had to get to Milicent, but what would be the best—

Max crashed forward against the door, stumbling into the small storage closet and onto a pile of mops. Towels fell off the shelf over his head, and a number of metal poles flailed at him as he tried to right himself and whirl around to face his attacker. What in God's name?

"Don't move, Max."

Max pulled a dingy piece of toweling off his head and tried to prepare himself. He knew that voice. Its soft, husky tone had haunted him on many a lonely night . . . and it was so close that his entire body vibrated as if it were waking up after a long sleep. He opened his eyes, and Roberta was standing just inside the room, her back to the closed door. His gentle, trusting Robbie, all peaches and cream, with a cap of shining copper curls and a delicate heart-shaped face she always thought too round. His gaze moved back to her hair. She'd cut it. Right before everything had fallen apart he'd been teasing her about doing something really different.

Shoving him like a linebacker was different. Holding him at bay with a . . . a weapon? . . . was different. Max leaned back against the mop handles and tried to compose himself, but he was completely unprepared for this confrontation, and he was losing it. The closed room smelled strongly of disinfectant, yet he swore his poor, deranged senses could detect the fresh, lemony scent she loved. The urge to laugh like a madman bubbled in his throat. For the first time in years, Max wanted to act exactly the way he was feeling: crazy.

The woman hated him; she literally had him in her

sights and his body did not care in the least. Just a short time ago he'd been lamenting his physical and emotional disinterest. Well, now he had proof that his promise *had* been a curse, because it seemed the right woman made all the difference. His heart had never been free and somehow his body had known it. *Mon Dieu*, but his punishment was to be even more excruciating than he'd imagined.

Max tossed the towel he had clenched in his hands to the floor and moved to step forward.

"No! Don't move, Max. I mean it and I'll stop you if I have to."

He froze at the hard edge in her voice. All the softness had vanished, and he really looked at her. Roberta held her body in a taut, ready stance, and in the small, hesitant hands, whose touch he'd desperately longed for, she held a palm-sized canister. Max blinked and stared fully into her eyes for the first time. Behind those dark frames he found the green eyes that had last glared at him with pain and then hatred. Those emotions were burning there again. He wondered how long she would last before she ran and if he should stop her.

"I want some questions answered, Wolfe. And I promise to make it very unpleasant for you if you try to leave before I have them."

Max's stunned brain suddenly came up to speed and he recognized what it was she held. The woman was serious and he didn't know what to think. How had he been so careless, and how was he going to get away and reach Prince with this pint-sized enforcer blocking his path?

"Is it Mace or pepper spray, Roberta?"

"Pepper spray."

"Were you following me?"

"Of course I was following you! You weren't invited, Mr. Wolfe. You would never be invited to any Chalmers function. Surely you couldn't be that dense. But that's just the point, isn't it, Max? You aren't at all dense and you never do anything without weighing out the personal advantages."

Roberta pressed her pale pink lips into a straight line and stared him down as thoroughly as anyone ever had. *Gentle* didn't seem to be quite the right adjective anymore.

"I know why you're here, Maximillian. A very reliable witness overheard you talking on the phone about a plan to kidnap my brother's wife, and make it seem like she was leaving him. The authorities are being informed at this moment, but I couldn't take a chance on you slipping away. It's something you do far too well." Roberta wrapped her free hand around her elbow to steady her arm and hiked the can up higher. *Trusting* was wrong, too.

"Now I want to hear your confession. I want to know how hurting Prince and Cindy this way could possibly benefit you. You don't even know her, for gosh sakes! Haven't you done enough? Isn't there a woman or six waiting for you on a beach or a ski slope somewhere? Isn't there a business deal you're finagling? Why can't you leave my family alone?"

Max concentrated on feigning an indifferent shrug, but spoke the truth burning in his heart. "Ah, *chère*, I wonder if you truly want to hear my answer to that question."

Roberta pushed back against the door, and her mouth formed a perfect little O. "Don't ever call me that again, Max. I'm warning you. What happened between us was all just an act on your part, anyway. So please don't insult my intelligence by using those empty words. You can *chère* yourself to death as soon as you leave. Just tell me what you've planned for Cindy."

"I think this would be best discussed with Prince, yes? If you can take me to him, I'll explain what I know."

"As if I'd trust you that far, Wolfe. You're lucky I haven't had you chained."

Max narrowed his eyes at that. Yes. Why hadn't she simply told the security people? In fact, the old Roberta would never have followed him in the first place. She was much stronger now. He could see it in the set of her jaw and the intensity of her gaze. Although her slight body was probably still too child-sized for her liking, Max had just experienced her new physical prowess and agility. She was a far more confident woman than the one he'd left behind. Even in satin, lace, and seed-pearl buttons, he knew she meant business.

Perhaps she was strong enough to hear the truth about what had happened between them.

Max curled a hand into a fist. No. Still loving her was agony enough. Such a dangerous thought had no place in his head. He was here to pay a debt, not risk the chance of incurring an even greater one. Princeton would kill him if he got so much as a hint of Max's feelings for Robbie. But . . . what if he could finally clear his conscience and make some kind of amends? What if Robbie learned for herself that her grandmother was part of Prince's problems? What if he then dared ask his lost love to believe that Helen Chalmers had ruthlessly blackmailed him and told him in explicit detail exactly how he had to leave her?

But that would mean he'd have to reveal his father's tragic mistake and the true depth of his own feelings. Pride would have to be painfully torn away and there would be no guarantees. At this precise moment, he couldn't see a sure bet in his corner. Nevertheless, Max very consciously relaxed his hand.

Maximillian Wolfe was a gambler. A shrewd, knowledgeable businessman who won big because he wasn't afraid to risk everything. Since the innocent person that had kept him from her in the first place was gone, what was there to lose? How could his life possibly be more empty? Now that he'd seen Robbie again—now that he'd had a glimpse of all he'd missed, it would drive him mad to walk away without trying. The chance of winning her back was worth it—worth the biggest gamble of his life.

Max shifted slightly and began to formulate the response that would force his little mouse to play into his hands. His mother had often teased him about his good looks. That women saw in him the daring pirates and mysterious princes they loved so in certain fables and fairy tales. *I hope,* ma mère, *that this once, your silly observation proves to be true. Because I will need all the magic I can conjure, to make my love believe.*

And if, after his best efforts, her heart remained cold to him, well . . . At least he could leave her with the freedom to find love again, without fear of Helen Chalmers poisoning it.

But such nobility would have to wait. Now he would begin to weave his spell.

"How brave have you become, Robbie? I wonder . . . how far would you go to find the truth? What would you be willing to do to help your brother?" Max slowly stepped forward and sank one hand deep in his pants pocket. "I know where to find the answers, but they cannot be reached without courage. And you can't run away, no matter what we discover."

Roberta felt the trembling begin in her wrist. She drew in a breath through her nose and willed the tremors away. The small can of pepper spray was growing incredibly heavy, but Max had just challenged her at the weak link she'd worked so hard to strengthen over the last two years. In small, steady steps she'd stood up to her grandmother and made Prince acknowledge her as a contributing adult. She had carved out a new life and she was determined to hold her own. No matter what Max said or did, she would have to meet his challenge. Then, at long last, her heart might be truly free.

No running. Not physically. Not verbally.

Even though her poor, deranged senses seemed to detect the subtle scent of sandalwood he loved. And even though he stood so close she could see the thick black lashes she'd once laughingly wished were hers . . . and the silky mustache that felt like feathers brushing her lips . . . and the broad shoulders that . . . Roberta closed her eyes.

She needed to prove herself, not lose herself.

"I'd do anything to help Prince, and I've regretted running that night in the garden, Max. I've regretted not hashing the whole wretched thing out. It would have been better to see your face and hear your decision than to read it. But everyone seemed to think I was too fragile, too emotional to bear up under your rejection. Now I know they really thought I was too weak. I think Grandmother actually thought I might give you another chance. Can you imagine that, Max?" She sighed, shaking her head. "After your actions clearly told the world what you thought of your wallflower fiancée, she feared I would make an even bigger fool of myself and beg you to come back.

"So I suppose I did run that one time, but you never tried to see me again and that seemed to say it all. However, this situation is different—and now I'm different. I want everything between us, between you and my family, resolved once and for all. I won't sit back and let others direct my life this time. Especially you. Even Grandmother has had to accept that since I started working for Prince. So tell me what you have in mind, and I'll tell you if it's worth it."

Max answered with the slightest of smiles. A mere curve of his lip that sent an absurd dart of satisfaction to Roberta's heart. *Oh, be careful, Robbie, my girl. Don't want to please this man. Don't want to see his reaction to the older and wiser you. Don't want anything but straight answers.*

"I want you—"

"Wha-what?" she stuttered with a telling squeak.

That lip curved again. Not good.

"I want you . . . to come with me to St. Thomas. Milicent Smythe has some very revealing information about this problem and I think you need to hear exactly what it is."

"Oh, my gosh!" Roberta flung out her hands, shocked. "What will Cindy think? Her family's involved? How could they do something like this? I don't care how cold their relationship is, it's unbelie—Oh, mercy, Lilith! Frank will kill Lilith if she's lied. She's the one who told—"

"Ahh, so she's the one who gave my name, *n'est-ce pas?*"

Roberta gestured with the pepper spray as if it were a pointer. "Tell me the truth, Max. Really. It was you she heard on the phone, wasn't it? You *are* involved."

Chapter Two

Max reared back a bit. *Mon Dieu,* a blast of pepper spray wouldn't be as damaging as this confession. But he had no choice; the context would crucify him, but he had to start earning back her trust somehow . . . and he had to buy some time.

"Yes, I was on the phone. But there's much more to it and certainly no time for me to be detained here with questions. Do you dare come with me and discover the truth?"

He watched the emotions flicker over her face. The fear and suspicion were well deserved, but it hurt nonetheless.

"You can smuggle your spray onto the plane and use it if there is a need. But whatever your decision, I'm leaving for the airport in"—he glanced down at his slim, platinum watch—"twenty minutes."

Roberta unconsciously gnawed her bottom lip.

Max lifted his free hand and stroked a knuckle along the edge of his mustache. He concentrated on unhurried, even breathing and cautious, restrained movements. The vibrant woman he'd had only tiny glimpses of two years ago had struggled against great odds to find her footing. And although it wasn't initially visible, she had indeed blossomed in very difficult circumstances. And Max wanted to hold her, touch her. Wanted to touch her more desperately with each passing minute. Would it be the same? Would her kiss still taste as sweet . . . ?

Sweet heaven! Should she do it? A mouse traveling with

a Wolfe didn't seem wise, but if anything would prove she was no longer the Roberta she'd been, it would be this trip. She could help Prince and Cindy and she could answer every question that still bound her heart to Maximillian Wolfe.

And she wouldn't be rattling around Chalmers House all alone waiting for word. That sentiment would probably offend her grandmother, yet it was the truth. Most of the time Roberta felt terribly alone. But if she were finally able to shake Max off for good, that just might change a whole lot of things. For the first time in two years, she felt a spark of tentative hope.

"All right, Max. I want the truth and I have to help Prince. I'll go."

He took a harsh breath and tried to relax. She wasn't going to run. She was taking his bait. He would have the small gift of time he so desperately wanted.

And by God, when the moment was right he would touch her again. Touch her as he'd never allowed himself to years ago. Tell her everything he'd kept locked inside and show her that what they'd once shared had been real. With the softest caress, he would cup her cheek and trail his finger over those auburn brows so delicately framing the glasses that protected her from too much intimacy. Too much self-revelation.

They'd dated a month before she'd even taken them off. Clothes had been out of the question. Once, in the very beginning, she'd told Max with unexpected candor that if he were waiting for some kind of quick score, he should just move on to the next name on his list. She was only interested in sex if it came along with true love and a wedding ring. She might sound ridiculously naive, believing in such fairy tales, but that was her stand and he ought to know before he wasted any more time.

Max had never before engaged in such a conversation with a woman and he hadn't known what to say. He'd never been one to indulge in meaningless physical relationships, but even so, he wasn't used to living a celibate life. He'd tried to stay away from Roberta after that, but her earnest face and her honesty had haunted him. Haunted him until he'd had to return. Somehow she could read through the screens that normally kept his real emotions hidden.

He supposed that at the time, many had wondered about the two of them. They couldn't have appeared more different. He, a sardonic European, always dressed to the nines, and she a soft-spoken, understated woman with a generous heart. Max vividly remembered the first time he'd met Robbie. It been about a month after his father's unexpected death from a heart attack. A very exclusive business party was being held at Princeton Chalmers's home and Max had had no choice but to attend, since he'd just recently discovered the extent of his father's . . . *debts*. He was desperate to generate some business and see if any rumors had started.

For a few hours he'd been able to hold his urbane, incisive persona in place. But inside he was falling apart. One too many men had mentioned his good sense about not letting his father's death get in the way of a timely deal. And damn his soul, Max had agreed. Cultivating their interest and their money was the only way to save his mother, and time was of the essence.

Eventually, though, Max had had to escape and so he'd wandered down to what turned out to be the library. And there she was, reading a book in a big leather chair that made her seem all the smaller. He'd blurted out his name and his apologies, which proved how close to the edge he was, since he never blurted. She had looked at him oddly, then smiled and pushed at her glasses.

"Too much time with the sharks, I bet," she'd said thoughtfully. "I'm Roberta Chalmers; come in out of the water for a minute."

To this day, Max did not know how they'd ended up talking. But before he could stop himself he'd mentioned his father's death and his mother's illness, and Roberta had become very still.

"Don't let the sharks drive the heart out of you, Mr. Wolfe. I-I know they say you don't have—" She'd flushed then, the way only redheads can, and got to her feet, holding the heavy book across her chest like a piece of armor.

"Listen, this is none of my business, but I do know how it hurts to lose someone you love. Just let yourself feel it. All of it, really. Find a safe place out of deep water every now and then till it gets easier. Eventually the good memories will come through and it will help. Honestly."

She'd stopped then, shrugging her shoulders as if asking his pardon for saying too much. Before he could manage to speak she was gone and he'd just sat there, stunned.

Falling in love had not been wise. He'd tried to stop it from happening, but the woman was magic. In a matter of weeks, their relationship began to unfold as if it had always been meant to be. Roberta found his hidden heart and he found her hidden beauty many had missed. He'd been enchanted and moved and it seemed more than right, two months later, when he and Robbie promised to give each other the gift of their bodies after they had legally pledged their hearts.

Dear God, but she would never know how severely he'd had to clamp down on any physical contact to keep that promise. Then he'd betrayed her and the promise became his curse.

For long, silent moments, Max held her serious gaze and wondered if she still remembered. He wondered what she would say if he told her he still kept that vow. And he wondered if he had the courage he was demanding of her. This was his only chance to win her back. This was his only chance to bring the magic back into his life. This time would he die if he lost her?

"I'll have a cab waiting at the front door in fifteen minutes. I won't wait," Max finished raggedly, realizing full well how many people and things could stop her from leaving.

"Yes . . . I know."

Five seconds after she backed out the door, he sank down on his haunches, his face cradled in his shaking hands. In a few days he'd either be in heaven or hell. It was, indeed, the gamble of his life.

It had been impossible to sleep or feign sleep once the plane landed in Miami. Luckily there hadn't been a layover or any time to talk as they'd rushed to board the flight for St. Thomas. After a mad dash, Max had gotten her to their seats and then left to check on something before they took off. Roberta looked out her first-class window and watched the twinkling lights of the runway.

A new dawn was just creeping over the Florida horizon, and she wished she could appreciate the watercolor wash of pinks and grays. Once she'd dreamed of painting just such a scene, but that fanciful wish had died a quick death with Max's desertion. Now she worked with numbers and sales quotas for Prince, her feet firmly on the ground of reality. Chasing the sun sounded so romantic and adventurous . . . and so unlike her.

It was good she had a moment to gather her thoughts. Everything had happened too fast, and then she'd escaped facing what she'd done by sleeping nearly the entire trip from California to Florida. Somehow in her burst of assertiveness, Roberta had failed to really consider the fact that she would be spending hours and hours with Maximillian Wolfe. Once she had him explain all he knew about Cindy and her stepsister, what in the world would they talk about?

She rubbed her sweaty palms on her black, corduroy pants from thigh to knee. Could she actually confront him about their wedding day? Deep inside she knew her life wouldn't get back on track unless she did so. Somehow Max's desertion had blown her off course, and as far as she'd come on her own, she still wasn't there. It sounded crazy and she'd certainly never mentioned that odd feeling to anyone else, although Cindy seemed to be someone who just might understand. Maybe, after this was all over, she'd talk with her new sister-in-law and lay out the whole tragic story for her. It might help to hear an objective perspective.

She glanced up the aisle and absently noted other early morning passengers, most of whom were headed for a vacation of a lifetime to the Caribbean islands. *Islands? Tropical islands?* Roberta felt a cold knot form in her stomach. How could she have forgotten? She and Max had been going to spend their honeymoon in Tahiti. They'd spent weeks planning the trip, since Roberta had never, ever visited any tropical spots. Not even Hawaii. Max had been incredulous.

About a week before the wedding, he'd startled her one night by pulling her a bit roughly onto his lap, something he'd never done. Max had always been affectionate, but never very physical. His normal, even voice was a hoarse whisper in her ear, promising that were many things his little mouse had never seen . . . or done . . . or felt . . . that he would show her very thoroughly and very . . . very . . . slowly.

His silky mustache had brushed against her ear and he'd kissed her neck and then abruptly left. The next time she'd seen Max had been the aborted attempt in the garden, after he'd deserted her to face all her friends alone. He'd once told her the islands were created for lovers, but it had been a lie. And she had been alone ever since.

Try again. . . .

Roberta lurched forward and whipped her head from side to side. Her heart was beating in her throat as she scanned the area. No one was talking to her. No one. No one had spoken but her own masochistic subconscious. She pushed her glasses up off the end of her nose with a shaky sigh and sank back in her seat. Heaven help her, but she could not start dredging up all those torturous memories again. Look what one little slip had done. Now she was hearing things!

Being physically close to Max again had to be the reason and she would have to fight it. There was no possible way she would ever let that man know he still had any power over her. Roberta pressed her fingertips against her mouth and took in a calming draft of air through her nose. Okay, she had legitimate, rational reasons to be jumpy, and those emotions could be controlled by facing them head-on. She was traveling out of the country with her ex-fiancé to track down a possible kidnapper.

Traveling was the most normal of the three factors, and for her, even that was unusual. Oh, she supposed she could have seen the sights on many occasions; money wasn't a problem. It was just . . . there hadn't been anyone to go with. Her one really big trip to Europe, a gift for high school graduation, had been with her grandmother. And then, after the debacle with Max, she wouldn't have set foot on the European continent for a million dollars. She didn't want to see the breathtaking beauty he'd thought she should paint. She didn't want to see his beloved wine country.

Now Roberta shrugged, smoothing the wrinkles in her forest green camp shirt. She really didn't have any people with whom she was close enough to vacation. Grandmother Chalmers had become so critical, constantly reminding her of her faulty judgment, that Roberta could barely stand to be around her. And Prince? Well, he was too wrapped up with being in love to notice his little sister's nonexistent social life.

Consequently she hadn't told either one of them she was leaving. There was no time to argue and she would not be stopped. So she'd nabbed one of Frank's men and sent him to warn Prince, then left her grandmother a note in her hotel room. She'd written that she was going to spend the weekend with an old school friend she'd met again at the reception. Helen would tell Prince where she'd gone, and if they didn't compare the facts too closely, neither one would worry too much before Roberta could get some answers. Her plan had more holes in it than a slice of Swiss cheese, but it was the best she could come up with in five of the frantic fifteen minutes Max had given her. This was all about protecting her family and, for once, it was her job to do it.

"Hear that, Rob, my girl?" she mumbled. "Be honest; the man is devastating and he uses it like a weapon. All your memories were an act. Remember that. An act for a wallflower."

Roberta ran a hand through her short, curly red hair and fluffed her fringe of bangs. Okay, maybe it was closer to rust. And face it, what man with the dark looks of a Valentino or a swashbuckling pirate would ever see something sexy in a woman who could pass for a grown-up Annie?

Max would be back any moment, and now that she knew how unstable her subconscious was, she would be prepared. Roberta detested women who lost all mental capacity around a good-looking man. And she was not about to become one—again. Yes, she had succumbed once, but Max had caught her off guard. Oh, they'd started out as casual friends and then unexpectedly found a deep core of understanding. Roberta had never really experienced a friendship like that before and she loved having an intelligent man to talk to. But never once had she even considered there being more to it. She may not have been the most experienced of women, but she knew when two people did not suit. So his dark eyes and his sensuous accent hadn't intimidated her. But then Max began to change the rules and she . . . ? She'd been blindsided. She'd turned into an idiot.

Well, not this time. She'd be tough, cool, indifferent. She'd just deal Mr. Wolfe the same inscrutable card he dealt everyone else. All at once the engines whined to life and startled Roberta out of her pep talk. She snapped her seat belt in place and leaned over into Max's empty seat in an effort to see up the aisle.

The unique lilt of his musical laughter hit her at the same moment her darting gaze honed in on him. A slow burn ignited in the pit of her stomach. Fear was cold and anger was hot. Fear froze, immobilized. Roberta knew that very well; too well. But anger cut through the ice like a smoking blowtorch and fueled assertive action. Her brother's happiness was hanging in the balance and he was off making a conquest.

The beautiful stewardess had jet black hair, a tall, curvaceous body, and her arm linked through his. Max was, of course, the perfect picture of casual elegance in chocolate brown dress pants, a crisp white shirt open at the throat, and cuffs folded halfway up his forearm. He wasn't a big, blocky man, but about average height, maybe an inch or so under six feet, with the body of a true European who fenced or played polo to stay in shape. He was all lean, ropy muscle and regal bearing.

Roberta rubbed her damp palms on her black corduroy pants once again. This was what she would have been dealing with if they'd gotten married. A beautiful man whom women simply couldn't stay away from, and he reveled in it. For the first time, she considered that perhaps the awful pain of two years ago had saved her from something even worse. Well, fine! This was exactly what she needed to see.

Roberta abruptly sat back and turned to face the window. She continued to focus on that thought while Max settled next to her.

"Now, Mr. Wolfe, you just call if there's any little old thing you need." *My, my. What a conscientious employee.*

"*Merci*, Ms. Johnson. A thousand thanks for your help."

If they kissed, Roberta was changing seats.

Okay, she was overreacting big-time. Best to press right into business. She twisted a bit to face him and he flashed her a warm but cautious smile.

"I see you've managed to stay awake. How nice."

"I won't play mind games with you, Maximillian. I slept because I was tired and wasn't ready to deal with this problem, but now I'm ready. Tell me everything you know about Milicent Smythe and why she would do this."

The plane began to taxi down the runway, picking up speed, and Roberta lost her train of thought. She felt a brief spill of anxiety and tightened her grip on the armrests. Taking off was not her favorite part. Suddenly Max's hand was over hers. Her eyes widened, then narrowed into slits.

"For luck, *chère*. Nothing more."

"Max . . ." she warned.

"Ah, your pardon. I forgot."

The plane quickly leveled out and Roberta pulled her hand away. "All right. Tell me, Wolfe."

Maximillian Wolfe rarely missed the subtleties in communication. But he was missing something now. Maybe because for a few brief moments she'd let his hand remain over hers. Damn! He'd never get anywhere if he lost focus like this. Max wove his fingers together in his lap. The woman was on the attack and not softening at all. He suddenly wished he had a cosmic pair of loaded dice. What if there was really nothing left of her feelings for him? God! Why should there be, after what he'd done?

His brief flare of hope suddenly went as dark as the sky was growing light. He might as well tell her the basics of what he knew; but this was no time to go into the *hows* of it all. Romancing information out of Milicent wasn't a topic for discussion.

"I became acquainted with Milicent Smythe last year, and around New Year's I was at a party where she got a little drunk. She started spouting off about her sneaky bumpkin of a stepsister marrying a man she didn't deserve. Someone completely above her social standing. In a few minutes I realized the man she was talking about

263

was Prince and that she was planning to do something to humiliate him and his bride."

Max hesitated, trying to gauge Roberta's mood. Her green eyes, made even greener by the deep color of her unadorned shirt, stared into his with a growing storm of emotions. For a second he considered revealing the probability of her grandmother's involvement, then decided it would be too much to hit her with too soon. But would she buy the abbreviated account of his connection?

"But how did you get involved, Max?" Roberta demanded. "Lilith Smythe never said a thing about her sister. She said it was you giving the orders on the phone."

Max cleared his throat. Damn, what was wrong with him? He never hesitated like this. "I had to do something to help, Robbie." He didn't miss the slight stiffening at the use of her nickname. "Proving this is impossible, but I wanted to spare your family any more pain. So I told Milicent I'd be willing to help her, since . . ." Max looked away before he continued to verbally drive the nails into his coffin. ". . . since she knew I already had an unsavory link to the Chalmers family. It gave me all the credibility I needed, and she believed I was telling the truth.

"Unfortunately, I thought I had everything arranged so I could arrive in time to notify Prince and allow his bride to take care of her family problems out of the public eye. I had to make the phone call when I realized Milicent had changed the plans I was supposed to be the only one to deal with Cindy. I was going to guarantee that nothing happen to her."

"So." Roberta paused, trying to line it all up in her head. "You've only acted the part of the bad guy in order to help Prince, my brother. The man who once treated you like a trusted friend, before you stabbed—"

"Why, Mr. Wolfe." The Dixie twang oozing from Elvira the stewardess abruptly broke the charged moment. Roberta nearly bit her tongue when the woman bent over and brought her face right next to Max's—so close that one surge of turbulence would smash them together. She curved a hand over his shoulder and he just sat there with a pleasant expression on his two-timing face.

"I was just wonderin' if you might want anythang. I'd be happy to get it."

"Oh, she'd be happy to get it, all right!" Roberta mumbled under her breath. Max shot her a startled, puzzled look and slowly turned to answer Miss Honeysuckle.

"I'm fine right now, Ms. Johnson, But I'll let you know if something comes up."

"I just bet you will!" Hell's bells, she couldn't stop that one fast enough. Max cocked his head and eyed her again. Roberta smiled with clenched teeth.

"This airline certainly has devoted employees."

"Roberta?" He stopped as if weighing his next words. "You don't think that I'm encouraging—"

"Max," she interrupted, using her hand as a stop sign. "There's only one thing I can think about, and that's helping Prince and Cindy. They've had enough problems. Even my grandmother was a bit cold and resistant in the beginning. Besides, some people in this crazy world have to get a 'happily ever after' or we'll all just want to give up hope."

What his little mouse *hadn't* said was deafening him. She'd lost her own happy ending and now her brother's meant everything to her. Max curled his fingers into a fist. Damn. He'd been a big part of ruining both of the Chalmerses' happy endings.

How could the truth ever heal that much pain? *Mon Dieu*, but the dice had been rolled and the game had to be finished. Truth was the trump card and he would have to play it.

Roberta folded her arms. "It's hard for me to believe your story, Max. If you'd said it straight out like this at the reception I don't think I would have come. I guess I was just so upset that I jumped at the chance to take action."

"Roberta." Max swallowed, despising the dread that snaked through his body at her words and the words he was about to say. "I know I've acted without honor. I hurt you and—"

"That's all over now."

"Please." He raised a hand, palm up, to stop her. "Let me finish. I'm saying I realize you have no reason to believe me, but I ask you to listen to what Milicent has to say. Just a few days, Roberta. We're almost there anyway."

She glanced away, then back to his face. Max could see the uncertainty in her eyes and he held his breath. "At this point, I-I suppose it would be the sensible thing to do. Now I think I'll rest till it's time to land."

Roberta lifted a hand and rubbed her temple. "Headache," she mouthed, before turning toward the window. Hopefully the man would remember that she occasionally suffered from migraine headaches. And that sometimes they could be controlled without medication if she went to sleep quickly enough. Max didn't speak. Her ploy had worked in the nick of time, but it wasn't her head that was hurting.

Roberta inhaled as evenly as possible, working her throat against the painful tightness there. Mercy. He'd done it. The man had breached the chasm of silence and opened the agonizing door to their past. She was shaken, but determined to use the next days to purge her soul of Maximillian Wolfe and the dangerous effect he still had on her. Yet oddly, after such nail-biting emotion, Roberta felt a heaviness grow in her eyelids and her body. Sleep slowly stole her conscious thoughts and she slipped away on a soft, lilting wave of *Try again . . . try again . . . try again.*

A jarring thump slammed against Roberta's arm, and her eyes flew open. She was groggy and disoriented, and her gaze skittered around until it fixed on Max and—He was holding Miss Kudzu on his lap. Her arms were tangled with his and her generous bosom was about to smother the man. Just the way he'd like to go, no doubt. Roberta shook her fuzzy head and winced. Nope! It was probably his second choice. Max had pulled her on his lap once, too. Maybe it was his forte. God, it hurt so bad to actually see what she'd imagined him doing with other women. Too badly for a man who was supposed to mean nothing to her.

She had darn well—No! She had damn, damn, damn well had enough. "May I get by, please? You seem to need some extra room."

Max was still struggling from the shock of one moment noting Ms. Johnson moving toward him and then the next, seeing a shimmery, miragelike wave ripple through the air. He'd blinked and she had dropped onto his lap.

"If you two could just hold that thought for a teensy second. I'd rather not feel like the odd man out."

"Wait a minute," Max hissed, grabbing the wiggly stewardess by the arms and thrusting both her and her impressive chest out of the way. She giggled as she got to her feet and suggestively smoothed her hands over her breasts and down her thighs in an obvious attempt to *tidy* her uniform.

"I'll be on St. Thomas a few days at the Outrigger Hotel. Call if you're lonely."

Lonely? Lonely? The deep, dark vortex that word sliced open in Roberta cut to the quick. What clearer picture of their lives could she have been given? He had never and would never lack for . . . companions. While she . . . God help her. This had all been a mistake. Grandmother had been brutally correct. She would never have been able to satisfy Maximillian Wolfe—in any way.

"Roberta, I'm not sure what you're thinking, but I had nothing to do with that." He shifted toward her, blocking her exit with his long legs. Already halfway out of her seat, Roberta had no choice but to sit down.

"Oh? Is it your magnetic personality that pulls women to you without your control? What a burden. And how odd that it almost never worked with me." She rolled her lips between her teeth to stop them from trembling. Thank

267

heavens her glasses camouflaged her eyes fairly well. They stung and Roberta knew what that meant.

"It must have been such a relief for you when I so stupidly announced my feelings about sex. Talk about a task above and beyond the call of duty. But you rarely had to suffer much that way, did you, Max? Luckily for you, I thought your lack of interest was courtesy and respect. Isn't that a laugh on little Roberta Hood Chalmers."

Max was stunned. Angry and stunned. All this time, all this damned time she'd thought he hadn't wanted her. That he'd been so uninterested he'd had to force himself to touch her. God! For the second time in less than twenty-four hours, Max wanted to laugh like a loon.

And he wanted to shock her speechless, act like the big, bad, testosterone-driven animal she obviously thought he was. He narrowed his eyes and leaned forward, crowding her into the corner, using his back as a wall between them and any prying eyes.

"You think I want that woman? I don't, Roberta."

"Spare me, Max."

"This trip is about truth," he rapped out in low, clipped tones. "Do you still seek the truth? Do you dare? Surely, Roberta, you know the one unmistakable sign that proves a man wants a woman."

The green eyes behind the black frames went round as the lenses themselves. Max snagged her hand and pressed it against him before she could react.

"You see, I have no interest in Ms. Johnson. None. But she, like many others, never thinks a man will turn down an invitation."

The hot burst of anger began to cool and Max realized that Roberta was still as stone. He let her hand pull free an instant before his sure proof would have condemned him. Hell. He'd scared her to death. But as his brain began to process all she'd said, Max felt his wilting hope surge back to life. If she knew how much he wanted her, past and present, perhaps she would believe his love had never died?

Ahh! An idea. It was a deliberate manipulation, but if it worked . . . and if it opened a door, Max would beg her forgiveness later.

"You can help me straighten the woman out, Roberta. And I can show both you and Ms. Johnson that I never wanted more than pleasant, efficient service." She tried to speak, but only managed a squeak of protest. Max determinedly held his mouth in a straight line. This was not the time to smile at his little mouse.

He glanced over his shoulder. "Quick, she's coming, and probably with her room number." Max turned back to Roberta. She was immobilized with confusion. That would make things even easier. "This is a truth, *chère*. A lesson to learn about men and women," he murmured, moving closer and wrapping his hands around her shoulders. Max felt her mouth tremble against his as he whispered, "A certain kind of woman may pointedly try to interest a man, but once she knows he truly, passionately, desires another, she will go. Help me make her go, *mon coeur.*"

Max had never kissed her like this before. It was the only thought in Roberta's head. His mouth captured hers and with soft, sweeping passes he drew his lips over hers until she wanted to moan. The silk of his mustache tickled and tantalized a quiet gasp from between her lips, which immediately allowed Max to press deeper and harder into the dark empty hollow of her mouth. The dark empty hollow that mirrored the one in her heart.

His warm tongue invaded, making smooth, rhythmic passes against hers as if coaxing her to join in the dance. Heat suffused every pore of her body and for the first time in her life, Roberta understood passion. In the months they'd dated—been engaged—he'd never shown her this power. *Why? Why? Why, Max?* What did it mean? What did any of this mean?

His hands tightened almost painfully on her shoulders and Roberta felt him prepare to pull away. Three moist, clinging kisses ended the suspended moment and she found herself staring into the eyes of the—the man she loved. Her heart sank like a stone.

"Now, Robbie," he murmured, his mouth moving on hers. "Now, do you dare see who it is I really want?"

"Excuse me, Mr. Wolfe." A terse, irritated female voice jolted her back to reality. "We're preparing to land. Please get your seat belts on."

Max stiffened, then gripped the armrests on either side of Roberta and pushed back into his seat. The sweet-as-pecan-pie Ms. Johnson was gone, and a hard-eyed ice queen had taken her place.

"You see," he said in a broken whisper. "I spoke the truth. Remember it is possible." Max winked and closed his eyes.

Truth? What truth? Both? Neither? Roberta's head was spinning and her ears ringing. She couldn't help but notice the distressed set of Max's features, and a similar look surely had to be stamped on her own face, too. This should never have happened. Oh, God, what she'd give to go back and erase the last few minutes! Her foolish heart had betrayed her. What should she do? How fast could she muster up the denial she needed to keep Max from seeing the damning truth in her eyes? A hysterical giggle tickled the back of her throat. The kind of laughter that ended in huge, racking sobs.

The pilot's voice abruptly buzzed to life in the cabin, and Roberta just sat there shocked, scared, and—heaven help her—sizzling.

Neither one said a word until they arrived at the hotel.

Chapter Three

Her kiss had nearly killed him.

The chemistry between them was even more powerful than he had remembered. Which explained his half-taunting, half-serious dare. *Mon Dieu*, he was losing his mind, his finesse, and his control. Max followed Roberta to their table in the hotel restaurant and tried to focus on the profusion of scarlet hibiscus blooming from each centerpiece . . . and not his aching body.

The contrast of this garden setting and his shy mouse could not have been greater. Ah, but things were not always what they seemed. For he had seen the fire in her eyes and tasted the sweetness of her mouth. And yes, after countless cold nights, it had almost killed him. He was fortunate to be walking.

Be that as it may, round two was about to begin and Max wasn't backing down an inch. Occasionally his business associates jokingly bemoaned the fact that his name gave him sharper, mystic instincts, and so, unfair advantage. It was absurd, he knew it was, but back at the reception he'd hoped his mother's fairy tales would bring him luck, and now he hoped those associates were right, too. After his slip in the plane, Max would take any help he could get, magic or otherwise.

He draped a rose-colored napkin across his lap and attempted to make some small talk while he read the menu. The terrace restaurant of their hotel was one of the most famous in the one city on St. Thomas, Charlotte Amalie, capital of the Virgin Islands. So named for the Danish king's consort by the sturdy settlers from Denmark who'd settled there in the 1700s. Roberta nodded slightly behind her own menu. Damn! The glory of the Caribbean was spread before them with surrealistic clarity. Blues and greens so intense that the wipsy white clouds and the white, latticed wood crisscrossing the terrace seemed to glow. This was the breathtaking beauty he'd once dreamed of showing her.

And not once, since stepping off the plane and into paradise, had she reacted to it at all. He wondered if she remembered Tahiti.

Max tightened his hold on the menu. He couldn't believe he'd just been spouting the history of the island like a tour guide, but he had to try something to reach her, to soothe her. Roberta wasn't talking and his time was running out. Max felt his tentative footing falling away like sand under a swimmer's feet.

An hour ago, as they checked into their rooms, he'd taken one look at her closed face and shuttered eyes and known she was planning to barricade herself behind the gilded door, preparing to pull back as fast and as far as possible, after his demonstration and baiting. But Max couldn't let that happen. He'd insisted they go over their plans for the next few days before sleeping off the effects of jet lag. The "sleeping" dig had done the trick.

Max signaled for the waiter and unobtrusively studied a wary, slightly frazzled Roberta. She did look tired, even more so because of the dark clothes that leached away all her color. She was the embodiment of winter in a roomful of perpetual summer. And no doubt Robbie wanted to sleep away the emotional bombardment that had climaxed with that kiss far more than her jet lag. Max curled his lip at his unfortunate word choice. *Mon Dieu!* He'd upped the ante painfully and for very little insight. How did she really feel? Roberta had responded, but barely.

Now he was tortured, wondering if her stillness had been shock or disgust.

Max shifted with unfamiliar anxiety on the cane-bottom chair. He had the duration of this lunch to come up with a logical, buyable reason to keep his little mouse from scurrying away. Challenging her courage seemed to be the only sure lure. So be it. He recited their orders and proceeded to bait the trap.

"I'm going to try to set up a meeting with Milicent for tomorrow night."

"Why wait, Max?" Roberta insisted with more animation than she'd shown since before the kiss. She fidgeted with her napkin, finally laying it on the pale green tablecloth. "I want to get it over with. Try for tonight."

Max ran a finger around the rim of his crystal water goblet, considering. "We need to be rested when we take on Milicent Smythe, Robbie." Once again he purposely used the verbal reminder of their former intimacy. It made her brows arch and her eyes just a bit panicky. Now that he'd tipped his hand, he might as well keep the pressure on. They both needed to know what was left between them.

"You promised a few days. Surely you're not changing your mind because of that kiss? If there are no feelings for me in your heart, it shouldn't have bothered you at all."

Roberta pushed up her glasses with a finger. "Don't flatter yourself, Wolfe. I'm bothered because you used me. You wanted to send a message to Ms. Johnson and grabbed the most convenient female to make your point with. And then made me suffer through some adolescent need to make me squirm. Was there supposed to be any more to it?"

"Only you can say, *chère*. But squirm? Really?"

The waiter materialized with their lunch, cutting Roberta off in the middle of an indignant huff.

She had to get back to her room as quickly as possible. She was too tired and far too aware of her disastrous feelings for Max. Did he always kiss women that way? Oh, mercy, it was worse now that she knew. Now that she could imagine what he'd been doing the last two years. If she ate, she could leave! Roberta forked up a bite of an avocado, papaya, and chicken salad that looked like a work of art and tasted divine. The exotic blend of flavors triggered the hunger she'd been ignoring for hours. For a few delicious moments she blocked Max out.

But there was a downside, she realized too late. The salad, the colors, the tastes were suddenly so real . . . she couldn't keep everything gray. She couldn't hold on to the numb, this-really-isn't-happening fog she'd been in since getting off the plane. Roberta blinked and in a spilt second the tiny, vivid spot centered on her plate exploded, drenching everything around her with color and sound.

She looked at the room and the kaleidoscope of objects and people. She looked at breathtaking vista of sea and sky. Then she looked down at herself, her clothes. She didn't belong here and she didn't belong with Max. And if she didn't get away from the *chères* and the kisses and the man, she might weaken and let her heart lead. Lead her back to that dark place she'd barely crawled out of before. Roberta shot to her feet.

"Set it up as soon as you can, Max. No later than tomorrow. Ring my room when you've got the time. I'm going to sleep now and—"

"Wait," Max said, his brain scrambling. "Would you like to see some of the sights in the meantime? Blackbeard and Captain Kidd have left their marks here, and so did Francis Drake. We could—"

"What? No more helpful man-woman chemistry lessons? No suggestions of romantic walks on the beach? No moonlight dancing?" Roberta heard the shrill pitch edging into her voice, but she couldn't smooth it out. "See, I caught you! Your first thought was to offer me the pirates, me bucko. Not a hibiscus-filled hot tub. Set up the meeting and forget any tours or any more games like the one on the plane, Captain Wolfe. Look at me. I don't belong in this world. I never did and I know it."

Max was utterly speechless. He sat at the table and watched her walk away, a wren in a room of peacocks. Dammit, she was right, but only up to a certain point. He'd offered the pirates because they fascinated him and he thought she might feel the same as they once had about so many things. And yes, he did see that, dressed the way she was, she didn't exactly blend in here. But that was all it had to be—clothes. Only Roberta didn't see that. Change the feathers on a wren and you still had a wren unless you changed the attitude, too. And who was she trying to convince with her *I don't fit* rhetoric? Him or herself? She could belong anywhere if she just gave it a chance. If she tried something different . . .

There had to be some way to make her her see a side of herself that had always been there, but hidden. A Roberta that had been covered up and protected with layers of fear and insecurity. *Mon Dieu*, if nothing else, he had to show her how beautiful she was, inside and out, and how much of life she was missing. How much of *herself* she was missing.

Ahh, beauty disguised . . .

Disguised? Max bolted from his chair, nearly colliding with one of the poor waiters. God! It seemed even the breeze was echoing his very thought. Yes, of course, he knew exactly what to do! First he'd show Roberta Chalmers that she was a beautiful woman; then he'd get Milicent to confess so he could at long last tell the truth. And if luck was with him . . . if loving someone counted for anything at all in the cosmic scheme of things . . . he'd have a chance to prove to Robbie just how desirable she was.

The breeze actually whirled and whistled at that, but Max missed it. He'd already rushed off for a serious night of scheming and dreaming.

* * *

"I'm telling you, Max, I don't understand why we have to go to such extremes. I told you last night that I don't fit in here, so let's not overdo for such a short time. Besides, to my knowledge, Milicent has only seen me once when she tried to crash Prince's engagement party. She stormed out the door so fast I was probably just a big blur."

Max cupped Roberta's elbow and guided her into a posh, very hip island shop in the Royal Dane Mall. She'd been reluctant and suspicious when he'd phoned her room two hours ago, but here they were. Round three was about to begin and it all hinged on his new approach. For right now, and as long as he could stand it, he was using his distant, unemotional mode. His "wanting" had scared her off.

It had taken about thirty minutes before she stopped casting him covert, assessing glances and hugging her arms to her sides. Gradually he'd felt her relax as he blandly presented the need for a disguise. His logical, matter-of-fact explanation was what she expected and felt comfortable with. And it was making it easier to accomplish his goals: Protect Robbie and open her eyes. The disguise in and of itself was a good, solid defensive measure. But it might also blow her narrow, restrictive picture of herself to smithereens.

Late last night he'd finally understood that for Roberta, it was more than just feeling he'd rejected her—heavens knows, that had been enough. But as Max sat on his balcony watching faint fingers of light stretch and yawn across the sky, he realized that Roberta Chalmers, the love of his life, could not even conceive of the fact that she was desirable. That was why she'd been so upset by his actions on the plane. She thought he was mocking her.

Max signaled a blond saleswoman and tugged Roberta farther into the rainbow riot of a room. Up to this point, everything he'd tried to do to change that misconception had only made it worse, à la last night's pirate debacle. As important as helping Prince was, Max felt the deepest distress over Roberta's bleeding self-perception, a wound he'd unknowingly cut deeper than he'd ever imagined.

He wanted desperately to make amends, but his little mouse—no, his little *tiger* was making it very difficult. She was literally dragging her feet all the way.

"Listen, Roberta." He swung her around to face him and spoke in his no-nonsense business tone. "We're meeting Milicent tonight in a rather shady bar. You need to blend in, remember. But more important, it would be a disaster if she recognized you. We can't take even the smallest risk of that happening. Besides"—he crooked his finger at the saleswoman and whispered out of the side of his mouth—"the faster we have the proof for Prince, the faster you can leave." Roberta perked up at that and Max ground his teeth.

Three hours later they staggered back to the hotel. The world-renowned Maximillian Wolfe's international powers of persuasion were as depleted as his poor body. And most men thought shopping with a woman who loved to shop was bad. Ha! Try being the enthusiastic one. Try being the one who actually had to shop. Nevertheless, he had risen to heretofore unknown heights.

By trying to recreate the sexless tenor of their early friendship, he'd been able to steer away from the undercurrents that had made Roberta jumpy. And in that delicate process, he'd finessed her into getting two dresses, two pairs of shorts, two blouses, and assorted shoes and accessories. She'd even thrown in a couple of things Max hadn't seen.

The coup of the day, however, was the trip to the optometrist and Roberta's new disposable contacts. It might not be fair, but money pulled strings—and on this bright and balmy Monday, Max had pulled every string he could reach in his pockets. And he wasn't finished yet.

"At last, Robbie, deliverance," he dramatically huffed, setting her bags down next to her door. Max waited, but she didn't so much as bat an eye. Either she was suffering from an exhausted stupor or she'd grown accustomed to his use of her nickname. They didn't call him a high-roller for nothing. "Remember I'm sending a hotel hairstylist up here at six-thirty. That should give us plenty of time to get to the club by eight. Meanwhile I'll just go collapse."

Roberta couldn't help it. She tsked with a scolding smile and a wave of a finger. Yes, the man had been charming, disarmingly so. But he was playing a part—again, to gain her cooperation—again, and she knew it. And yet he had been very pleasant and patient, and in a few hours they would have the truth. Then she'd be able to leave and put this all behind her.

The past night had given her the time and space she'd desperately needed to get her heart back under control and face reality. An adolescent part of her would probably always love the suave and dashing Maximillian Wolfe. Hell's bells, it had to be tough toting that much male ego around. He was the kind of man women like her fantasized about from afar. A rogue, a pirate, a bit of a cad. But things were finally back on an adult level and she could not falter now.

Max had said he was sorry about their past, and he was helping with Prince, and, most important, Roberta had had a chance to see the man without stars in her eyes. He hadn't made one suggestive comment or sexual innuendo all day. And so it was more than ridiculous to feel a tiny twinge of disappointment looking at that mobile mouth curved into a dazzling grin or those midnight eyes crinkling at the corners. Roberta quickly fumbled for her keys, and at her determined twist, her door came open. The beautiful room was so empty and she was all alone.

She shook the nonsense out of her head and turned back to Max, nervously running her hand up the plain placket of her green camp shirt and running the tip of her tongue over her dry lips. Then, as mildly as possible, she spoke.

"Should I meet you in the lobby at seven forty-five?"

Max abruptly stepped back and stuffed his hands in the

pockets of his white chinos. Roberta drew her brows together. Darn, what had she done? His smile had vanished along with his teasing air. Suddenly Max seemed stiff, cold. She waited for some explanation.

"Yes. Fine." He'd turned, walked a few paces to his own door, and stepped inside before Roberta could close her mouth and do the same. Well, the man had spent hours with her. He'd probably just reached his wallflower tolerance level.

"All right now, Miss Roberta, you just have to remember to let the hair curl the way it wants to. Fluff with your fingers, girl, and use the makeup just the way I showed you."

Roberta looked at herself in the vanity mirror and couldn't believe her eyes. Oh, she was still short, and she'd never have the curves most men prized so highly, but she was, amazingly enough, pretty. Without her glasses and enhanced with a subtle touch of brown eye shadow and mascara, her eyes looked so big and so green. A peachy glow highlighted her cheeks, and a coppery lip gloss defined her mouth. Was it really her? Roberta blinked, surprised once again at how little the disposable contacts bothered her. She glanced at the clock on the dresser. 7:40. Mercy, it was time to go. Self-doubt barreled down on her like a runaway train.

"You know . . . I'm not sure about this. I feel like a magic wand has just been waved in my direction, but this isn't me, Lucinda. I—"

"Now, missy. You listen to me." Roberta watched the statuesque, middle-aged woman lift her finger and waggle it at her in the mirror. Lucinda's hair was hidden by a rich purple-and-gold turban that framed her exotic face and made her coffee-colored skin look smooth as melted chocolate.

"Why, of course it's you. And the only magic you need worry over is the magic that's been inside you all this time with no way out. You gotta love yourself, Miss Roberta. Love is all the magic anybody needs. Lord, but it can do what a hundred spells can't begin to touch. It's what this poor old world needs in the worst way. But ya see, honey, sometimes we have to change to find that powerful love, search mighty hard and not give up. 'Cause what we think is so just might turn out to be something else entirely. And if what you see isn't quite right, why, you try again."

Lucinda gathered her things and gave Roberta an encouraging pat on the shoulder. "Get that dress on and let yourself be happy, missy. But no panty hose, eh, dearie?"

The door was closing before Roberta could move. Magic? Love? Try again? Why did she seem to be hearing that every time she turned around? She spun on her chair at the sharp snap and thought she saw a trail of sparkling light seeping under the door. She blinked and ran her tongue over her teeth. Nothing. Just nerves. Which weren't helped at all by Lucinda's coincidental refrain. Add that to her new look, the meeting with Milicent, and being with Max, and bingo: frazzled nerves.

Roberta walked to the rattan armoire and fingered the long, silky, island-style dress: a swirling concoction of leaf greens and white, shot with silver. It was so beautiful, and she remembered thinking how disappointed Max would be when he saw it on her. But now? Roberta glanced over her shoulder at her reflection. This time when they parted she would have this memory. This time she would hold her head high and be proud. Every woman deserved to feel like Cinderella at least one night in her life. And this was her night.

Try again? Maybe she would.

Fairy tales were a cruel hoax. How many little girls, albeit foolishly, held on to an image of a brave prince on a white charger racing to the rescue? How many big girls had just listened to someone blather on about the magic of love? Roberta studied her five-dollar glass of Perrier and smirked. Boy, had Lucinda's island mumbo jumbo been a crock. Try again? Change? Well it hadn't been change enough. Oh, sure, Max had been more than complimentary, offering his arm and his evenly modulated, French-accented congratulations on her lovely appearance.

Roberta ground her teeth. She was a perverse woman. What had she expected? The man falling to his knees in awe? Raving on about the pearl beyond price he'd mistaken for a chunk of gravel? She plopped her glass back down on the small table and squinted through the smoky haze. Her Cinderella night had ended up in a noisy, seedy bar with her newly discovered good looks affecting only suspicious-looking members of the less-than-stellar clientele.

Max had taken her unveiling, as it were, in stride. Although, for one brief moment, when she'd first walked into the lobby, Roberta could have sworn the man looked faint. But then he'd reeled off his impersonal acknowledgments and rushed them on to the rendezvous. So much for her psychologically twisted desire to make the man suffer for downplaying the ugly duckling transformation!

Roberta took a gulp of cold water. It was probably not a good sign that her brain kept making these fanciful analogies. Pirates, princes, magic, fairy tales? She crunched down hard on a piece of ice. It was common knowledge that people who spent too much time alone could become eccentric. This might be a warning sign, but there was no time to worry over it now. Max was checking with the man at the door yet again, and he'd be returning any second to drone on about Milicent Smythe.

"Roberta," Max murmured, his mouth suddenly next to her ear. Roberta lurched and turned, excruciatingly aware that without her glasses she could get much, much closer to people. His thick sable lashes lowered for a second, hiding eyes so dark they seemed to pull at her like a black hole, and his normally straight black brows were bunched and drawn. Max spoke her name again and his silky mustache captured her gaze. She couldn't stop herself from staring at the chiseled lips she stupidly longed to feel again. Oh, she was one sick puppy.

"Roberta! *Mon Dieu!* Don't do this now. Please, I can't take it."

What? She blinked and felt her own eyebrows hike up under her wispy bangs. Mercy, she hadn't heard the man at all. Did he think she was freaking out? Backing out?

"I'm ready, Max," she promised over the ringing steel drums.

"You're killing me, Roberta Chalmers," he nearly moaned, snagging her hand and pressing the palm hard against his lips. Roberta was instantly alert. What in the world was going on? She opened her mouth to ask and Max dropped her hand.

"Here she comes, Robbie," he warned without looking at her, his gaze locked on the tall, breathtaking blonde floating toward them. Roberta closed her eyes. She'd seen Lilith; she should have been prepared. Her fingers stabbed at the bridge of her nose before she realized her defensive reflex, but there were no lenses to shield her now.

"No matter what she says or does, don't speak. Let me handle her." Max's voice was low and urgent, and for the first time since leaving California, Roberta felt tendrils of dark foreboding snaking through her chest, squeezing the air out of her lungs.

"Hello, Max, darling," the cover model oozed, completely ignoring Roberta and sidling into the chair next to Max. Her strapless dress was made of a shiny fabric in teal blue and it looked as if she'd been wrapped in a length of the Caribbean sea. Small sprays of delicate white shells dangled from her ears and circled her neck. Cindy's stepsister wound an arm around Max's neck and spread an acrylic-nailed hand flat against his chest.

In a weird, stomach-twisting way they looked good together: a mermaid siren and her pirate captain. A mermaid siren apparently prepared to send out her lures regardless of the insignificant onlookers. Long, gold-tipped fingers restlessly ran up and down the tiny pleats in Max's collarless beige dress shirt, giving Roberta the distinct impression that Ms. Smythe resented its presence.

"Max, I thought we were going to be alone."

Those accusing ice-blue eyes cut to Roberta and pinned her. But Max subtly leaned back in his chair until his head moved out of Milicent's line of vision and caught her attention. While Roberta watched, his face seemed to take on an almost feral, wolfish intensity. She knew he was demanding her unquestioning compliance and she started to nod, then stopped in the nick of time. Somehow she knew Milicent was looking for just such communication between them.

The blonde held her assessing stare for a few more seconds, then turned away, and Roberta blew out a shaky breath as silently as possible. Luckily a rollicking calypso melody stuttered to life at that exact moment, and luckily Lilith Smythe had been the only member of Cindy's stepfamily involved with the wedding.

"Hey, Red, go get me a drink."

Roberta rested her folded hands on the edge of the table. The command in his expression belied the casual tone of his request. Of course she was going to do it. But *Red?* It sounded like the name of a gun moll. Oh, well, lights, camera, action. She got to her feet and almost asked what he wanted, then decided the night had already gotten way too bizarre. No point adding strong spirits to the mix. Besides, Max would need every sharp little edge in his brain to fend off that barracuda.

With one eye Max watched Roberta wend her way through the crowded room. Too many of the patrons huddled at tables and lining the walls were questionable, to say the least. But Milicent knew that full well—which was exactly why she'd chosen this spot and exactly why she was studying him so closely and exactly why he'd sent Robbie off. The witch wanted to know how much he cared. His answer was perfectly clear. She smiled and scooted closer.

Damn! Max just wanted it all over with—wanted to be able to hold the woman he loved, show her how beautiful she was, and finally explain everything. He lost sight of Roberta at the bar, and Milicent must have realized she'd lost his attention. She slowly ran a fingertip around the shell of his ear. Max looked into her cunning, glorious eyes and felt his skin crawl. He held her gaze while he captured her hand and pulled it away.

"So, you *have* come because you're angry. Mother thought that might be it."

"What happened to our plans, Milicent? You've left me in a very vulnerable spot and I want some answers." Max caught the green-and-silver pattern of Roberta's dress out of the corner of his eye and slowly uncurled the fist resting under the table on his thigh. Soon—soon she would know.

"Here's your drink." Roberta shoved it toward him and scooted into her chair. He didn't dare spare her a glance. It was time to get what he'd come for.

"My name has already been tied me to this, Milicent, and I'm not going to take the fall alone. So you better tell me exactly who and what's involved here. Did somebody else change your mind?"

"Now, darling, please," she cajoled, her gaze dancing to Roberta and then back to Max. She leaned even closer, purposely pressing her unbound breasts against his arm and side, making silent promises. Max saw Roberta's eyes go wide and her nostrils flare. It wasn't right and it was god-awful timing, but for a second he hoped she was the tiniest bit jealous.

"If you have nothing to tell me, so be it. But be warned, Milicent," Max threatened, imbuing the word with all the disgust he felt for this woman and the whole damned situation. "I am calling a contact in California in a few hours and if anything has happened to Cindy Chalmers, I'm turning in a detailed anonymous tip." He wrapped a hand firmly around her wrist. "I won't risk my future because you had some kind of temper tantrum."

"All right, dammit, Max! All right," Milicent spat. "I was willing to do exactly what we planned. It wasn't me who changed everything." She yanked her hand away and absently rubbed her wrist. "It was that crazy old woman. I'm telling you she's bonkers." Damn, he was right! Helen Chalmers *was* tied up in this.

"Go on."

"She called two days before the wedding raving on about fixing everything in one blow. I told her that I didn't care who else she was trying to punish, I just wanted Prince and Cindy to pay for what they'd done to me. Only she wouldn't listen. I couldn't reach you and I wasn't about to be close by when it all fell apart. I figured that once you arrived you'd catch on, so I washed my hands of the whole thing. I'm completely out of it, Max."

Because Max kept his face toward Milicent, he couldn't see Roberta's—couldn't read her reaction. The only thing this angle allowed him to glimpse were her hands, clenched together on the table, knuckles white.

"Listen, Maximillian, I didn't start any of this. It was Helen Chalmers's scheme from the beginning. And yes, I know I didn't tell you that detail, but there was no need. I wanted a little revenge, and remember, you went along with it. I had no idea the woman would suddenly go too far, so you can't blame me. The old loon has flipped out and my worst nightmare is she'll show up here. I mean, how many people would guess Prince's own grandmother would do this?"

Max heard the gasp and saw it register in Milicent's narrowed eyes. He had to get rid of her before Roberta broke down.

"So your hands are absolutely clean? Well, I'm going to make those calls anyway, Milicent, and I suggest you don't leave the island. I'm not going to let this happen again, and if things blow sky-high, I want to know where to reach

285

you. You'd be wise to contact me if you hear anything. Here's my number." Max got to his feet, which caused her to do the same. He extended one hand with the card and discreetly reached down with the other to cup Roberta's shoulder. God, he could feel her shaking. This was not the place for her to fall apart.

Max tugged her up and turned his back on Milicent. Damn, it had all sounded far worse than he'd expected. Roberta's head barely topped his shoulder and she suddenly seemed so fragile. He curled his body around her and propelled them through the human maze, trying to get then out the side door before she started crying in earnest. *Mon Dieu*, what had he been thinking? He'd known the truth about Helen Chalmers for so long that his horror of it had been dulled to a blunt, cold anger. But Robbie?

Even if she and her grandmother had argued, had struggled with some problems, Roberta had no idea what jagged feelings lay beneath her family's picture-perfect surface. And he—he had been so consumed with love and need that all he'd considered was the possibility that the truth would give them another chance.

Max swung open the heavy door to the warm night air. In one deep breath, the scent of stale smoke and stale bodies was replaced with the spicy, sweet perfume of greenery and hidden blossoms. Palm trees, silhouetted against the navy blue sky, dotted the parking lot, their feathery fronds lifting gently on the breeze. Stars beyond number glittered overhead, making the very heavens seem alive with thousands of blinking eyes. Max tightened his hold around Roberta's waist, wishing that were true. Wishing someone who really cared was watching. Wishing the stars really held magic.

But magic was for children, and the beauty surrounding him only made the ugliness he'd just subjected Roberta to a hundred times worse. Damn, but he'd been blind to everything but the chance to redeem himself. Max looked down at the bent head of his love. He swallowed hard against the lump of fear in his throat. As awful as Milicent's revelation was, at least they were together. He could hold her through the pain. "I'm so sorry, Robbie," he crooned, his cheek against the satiny crown of her head. "Something like this is hard to believe and—"

His silent, devastated Robbie snapped her head back so fast she clipped him on the chin.

"Believe? Believe!" she cried, jerking out of his hold and whirling to face him. "You think I'd listen to that . . . that woman in there"—she stabbed a finger toward the bar— "and buy her story? You want me to believe that Milicent Smythe was double-crossed by my own grandmother?" Roberta suddenly dropped her arm and went very, very still. Her voice became very, very soft. "Oh, my God. You do, don't you, Max? This is what you brought me all this way to hear."

Max fisted his hands at his sides in despair. Everything had gone crazy and somehow he'd betrayed her again. He could see the truth of it aching in her eyes. Damn, but truth was highly overrated, a wild card. Truth hadn't healed a thing, because she didn't believe it. Hell, she couldn't believe it. He'd been so fixed on what the truth might give them that he hadn't realized what it would take away.

Max raked a hand through his hair. He didn't know what to say. He didn't know what to do. Roberta's life would never be hers if she didn't learn what Helen Chalmers was capable of. But heaven help him, to convince her of it he would have to hurt her as deeply as he had two years ago. Love, honor, dread, and fear twisted in his gut.

Lies had ruined his life. They'd stopped the beating of his father's heart, forced him to walk away from the only woman he'd ever loved, and left Max's mother to die without her husband—unasked questions burning in her eyes. Their bitter, damning taste rose up Max's throat. Merciful God, but the only way to free Roberta was to wound her again. A wound that would surely kill anything left between them.

It made him sick. It was bad—and he'd have to be a bastard to force her to see it. But she had Prince. They really loved each other. She wouldn't be alone. Max would call him as soon as it was done and tell him everything.

"I want to go back to the hotel, Max. I need to arrange a flight home."

Max forced himself to set his jaw and harden his gaze. "I promised you the truth, Roberta . . . and you promised not to run. Too bad you're still so much the mouse and too bad your brother will suffer for it." The shock and disbelief he'd verbally slapped onto Roberta's face almost brought him to his knees. Damn him to the very depths of hell, but he had seen too much pain on the faces of those he'd loved. Max held his shoulders rigid against the shudder trying to climb his spine.

"I'll tell you what's too bad, Maximillian Wolfe. It's too bad you ever came into our lives," Roberta rasped, folding her arms tight against her chest and visibly swallowing. "All right, you obviously have something else to throw at me. Fine. I love my brother and no matter what you think, I will do anything to help him." She closed her eyes for a second, pressing two fingers to her temple, then drilled him with a defiant glare. "I'll give you till tomorrow night to deliver something more reliable than some spoiled brat's sour grapes. Do your big, bad worst, Wolfe, but beware—I may be small and insignificant to you, but I'm a mouse who recently discovered she has very sharp teeth."

Max watched her stalk toward a line of taxis, the last of all his hopes crashing around him like angry waves pounding the shore. He shoved his hands deep in his pants pockets and dropped his head back on his neck. An unusual burn stung behind his closed eyes. Somehow the most hellish, wrenching thing was . . . he'd never told her how beautiful she looked.

Damn his cursed French blood—his romantic impulse

to wait until the confession was over with first. He'd wanted to take her in his arms and stand together in front of a mirror and say, "See yourself as I see you, love. Everything about you makes me want you . . . your head, your heart, your taste, your scent. Your body speaks to mine as none other ever has. Ah, *chère*, come, let me love you."

But his dreams for the night had turned to ashes in his hands. And tomorrow would be worse.

Chapter Four

Roberta sat on the bed, staring unblinkingly at the hotel clock on her dresser. She'd hardly slept all night, and between that and her battered emotions, she was feeling as fragile as one of her grandmother's expensive Lladró figurines. *Grandmother*. She started to rock, shoulders hunched, arms tucked tight against her stomach. It was true that in the beginning Helen hadn't been very happy about Prince and Cindy. But surely, surely she couldn't have . . .

It was too awful to even consider. In ten more minutes she'd leave to meet Max and, once she heard him out, she would be free to go home. Very soon she could put all this behind her. Roberta stopped moving, wove her fingers together in her lap, and willed herself to be calm.

Her room was neat as a pin: the rattan furnishings empty, the green-and-brown, vine-patterned bedspread perfectly in place, and her lone bag resting on the sandlike Berber carpet. How clever of some interior designer to bring the beach inside, too. It was really too bad that all this paradise had gone to waste.

Paradise lost. Mercy, she was maudlin, but she had reason to be. How many women were fool enough to let the same man break her heart twice? Roberta cringed and felt a heaviness in her head at the involuntary movement. She plucked at the crease in her pale peach Bermuda shorts and stopped in midpluck when she realized that, on top of everything else, she hadn't even checked her message service to see if Prince or her grandmother had been trying to get in touch with her. She'd been too busy discovering she still loved the wrong man. Thank heavens she hadn't let him know.

Roberta stood and walked over to the window to drink in a last look at the picture-perfect beauty, ignoring the dull ache starting behind her left eye. Yes, she could see why pirates and princes alike had loved and fought over this jewel of an island. The warm sun felt good on her bare arms and the vee of skin exposed by the open collar of her new shirt. She curved her lips ever so slightly. Oh, she'd almost thrown all the new clothes away, but that would have been childish and stupid. And if nothing else, Roberta thought, she'd finally learned that facing reality was the only way to resolve a problem. Max would never have still had a hold on her heart if she'd had the guts to do that two years ago.

Which was, of course, the exact reason she was meeting him. No possible tie would be left uncut this time. No possible question unanswered. Besides, the only really positive aspect of this whole gut-wrenching experience was her new look. Being forced to finally try so much that had petrified her had taught her a profound truth: Even in the worst of times, there could be a silver lining if one would look for it. The time-worn adage about dark clouds and finding hope wasn't just an old wives' tale.

Roberta knew the dark clouds were building above her again, but she had a hold on at least one hopeful thing. Her new view of herself. Max had promised he'd reveal the truth, and in a strange way he had.

Mercy, she thought, rubbing her forehead hard. It hurt and she was so tired. Maybe she should take a pill? No, she didn't want to be groggy with Max. She'd wait just a little while longer.

Roberta checked the clock. It was time to go. Max had insisted she meet him at three sharp at a new room on the eighth floor. He'd punctuated the cool demand with an-

Bronwyn Wolfe

other dig about running. His evenly modulated attack was far more effective than ranting and raving, and Roberta knew that he knew it. He was every bit as ruthless as she'd heard. And even though she was playing right into his hands, she would not give him a reason to label her a coward again. For herself—for the long way she'd come—she would face Max for the last time and show him.

Roberta dropped her card key into her pocket and took a quick look in the mirror. Peach flowers bloomed on the white background of her sleeveless shirt. It tied at the waist for a jaunty island look that made her legs seem longer than they really were. The deep, open collar showed the barest hint of cleavage, and for the first time in years, Roberta didn't wince at the size of her chest. Her hair was a riot of copper curls that framed a more defined, glowing face. Yes, she still felt a bit naked without her glasses, but she also felt more powerful, too. Her new confidence in the way she looked made a difference, and that was what she needed right now. Strength. Because Max was determined to prove something. Something horrible.

Roberta squared her shoulders and headed for the door, her strappy white sandals nearly soundless on the carpet. No matter what the next hours brought, she would not run. It was the promise she'd made to herself days ago. Max had dared her to face the truth and this was the moment. She'd hidden from disaster once before and she had never healed. Too late she had discovered that wound was still her greatest weakness. For Roberta, love had become a two-edged sword.

Max barely heard the knock. Then it came again, stronger, firmer. He took a breath and scanned the darkened room, grimacing as he looked down at himself. If Roberta didn't laugh, or run, or sock him in the nose, he just might have the chance to tear her heart out. But first he had to explain what was about to happen and make sure she cooperated. A picture of a pair of dice formed in his head and as he grasped the doorknob he knew this was it. Heaven or hell.

"Ah, Roberta. You're right on time," Max murmured, at a loss for something more meaningful to say. Instead he stood half hidden behind the door, hoping the dim light would make it hard for her to see what he was wearing. He, however, could see her, and his hand tightened on the brass knob; his mouth pressed into a thin line. God, she took his breath away. But it was much more than just the physical beauty she'd so recently learned to enhance. Max saw her courage in everything she was wearing, everything she'd done to her face and hair.

He'd half expected to find her once again barricaded behind her glasses and sober clothes. And how could he have blamed her for retreating after all he'd done? Hell, intimidation was a tool of his trade, and he'd learned how to wield it like a master swordsman or one of his pirates of the high seas. *Mon Dieu*, he was so proud of her.

"Max?"

"I'm sorry, *chè*—Roberta. Come in," he said, quickly catching himself. He stepped backward and waited for her to enter, then shut the door. She stopped in the middle of the room and turned to face him. Her gaze darted down to his feet and then over to the poster bed curtained with layers of light yellow netting.

"What's going on, Max?"

"Robbie, I don't want to hurt you." He couldn't hold the words in. The harsh way he'd been treating her burned like acid in his stomach.

"Yeah, right. Why are you wearing that nightgown?"

Max rolled his shoulders and rubbed a hand down his face. Fool. She was right to protect herself. Lord knew he wasn't going to be able to.

"I'm going to be pretending to be someone. All you have to do is stand over there"—he pointed to the far corner opposite the bed—"behind that screen." He pushed up his long white sleeve and checked the time. "We'll have to wait about ten minutes, and then I promise if everything doesn't come clear you can leave today."

Roberta inched away from him. "This whatever it is, is really weird, Max. You've been yammering about Prince's welfare, but I"—she raised her hands and shrugged—"I have no reason at all to trust you."

Max pulled an envelope out from a voluminous pocket. "Here's your ticket home. Nine o'clock tonight."

He handed it to her and watched the confused surprise register on her face. Roberta absently lifted a hand and pressed her fingertips low on her forehead over her eye. Then she nodded and without saying another word, she walked behind the screen. Max blew out a relieved breath and got into the bed, tugging the netting into place. The lacy cap was the final touch and he laid back, praying he was doing the right thing.

Ten seconds later a rapid tattoo sounded on the door.

Roberta froze, clutching the ticket in one hand and pressing the other against her mouth. As a child, Prince had sometimes played hide-and-seek with her, and this queasy rush of adrenaline always swamped her when he'd been about to discover her hiding place. She held her breath and tried to swallow her jittery nerves.

Someone fumbled at the doorknob, and in the stilted silence Roberta heard the whoosh of it opening.

"Helen?" a low, throaty voice whispered. "Helen, are you in here? Dammit, what in the hell do you think you're doing? Why didn't you just call me?"

The voice grew louder, and Roberta dropped her hand from her mouth and pressed it against the erratic thumping in her chest. It was Milicent Smythe. Oh, God. The dull ache in her head began to sharpen. A soft click signaled the closing door, and muffled footsteps shushed on the carpet.

"Wait—are you in bed? Are you sick? For God's sake, if you've come here sick something terrible must have gone wrong. I told you to leave me out of it, old woman. I told you I only wanted to ruin Prince and Cindy's reception, not hurt anybody, and I won't take any blame that isn't mine. I've already got someone breathing down my neck because you changed all the plans."

Roberta knew she couldn't move and she couldn't make a sound. But inside she was screaming and howling her rage and pain. Sweet heaven, it was true. What had her grandmother done? And in the agony of the moment, her only release was the trail of soundless tears rolling down her face.

"Who?" a high-pitched, quavery voice weakly asked. Roberta rolled her lips between her teeth to keep from gasping. Exhaustion and a full-blown migraine were clouding her thinking. The nightgown. The netting. *Max was pretending to be her grandmother.*

"Maximillian Wolfe, Helen." A garbled, questioning grunt followed Milicent's perfunctory revelation. "Look, we became very, shall I say, close, soon after Prince and I stopped dating. So when you called with your little plan I thought he'd be the perfect man to play Cindy's secret love interest. What sweet revenge to have the man that had jilted Prince's sister appear to steal away his bride. But then you had to go crazy. And I'm telling you, Max knows you started this whole thing."

Roberta couldn't contain a soft exclamation.

"You'd better get your ducks in a row, Helen, because the man was furious, and you know the reputation he has. He told me he won't let this rest if something has happened to Cindy—" Milicent stopped cold and Roberta gingerly leaned back against the wall. Her body had started trembling and she had to have some support or crumble to the floor in a heap.

"Wait a minute." It sounded as if Milicent snapped her fingers. "That's what's been bothering me. Why was the man so upset, Helen? I mean I can understand not wanting any legal problems, but this was far more than that.

He warned me not to leave. He ordered me to call with any more information. He said he wouldn't let this happen again—" A soft, crude curse spiked the palpable tension in the room.

"Max didn't walk out on your granddaughter, did he, Helen? You stupid, stupid woman. How many enemies have you made? Ruining weddings is a thing for you, isn't—"

"That's enough, Milicent."

Roberta heard Max speak in his normal voice, and then she heard Milicent screech, but the edges of their words were slurred, as if she were underwater and trying to listen to their conversation. Pain, both physical and emotional, was distorting everything. The tones were angry and threatening, and only every few words were clear, understandable. She closed her aching eyes and felt the heavy wetness of her mascara-laden lashes. Roberta pressed back hard against the wall and tried to follow the charged exchange. This was important, but her poor head was already reeling.

It was true. Max had told her the truth. Her grandmother had planned the whole thing. Her grandmother had hurt Prince. Nothing made sense anymore.

Max had to stop Milicent immediately, before Roberta took the next logical mental step and considered that Helen might be an old hand at manipulating her grandchildren's lives. This was not the time or place for Robbie to discover how their love had been destroyed.

"That's enough, Milicent."

"Max? You bastard!"

"I may deserve many epithets, Milicent," he said, tossing back the net and getting to his feet. "But that one is completely inaccurate."

"Shut up, you rotten pig! How dare you do this?" she hissed, flinging out her arms and stalking toward the screen. Max had to stop her again.

"I needed the truth. I needed an irrefutable record."

Milicent whirled in her tracks, planting her hands on her hips. The full skirt of her deep blue halter dress wound around her legs with the abrupt movement. Max prepared himself for the explosion, and then lifted the tape recorder he'd had on the bed the whole time.

Milicent paled, but didn't rage. What was she up to?

"This has really gotten to you, hasn't it, Max? I should have seen it Monday night, but I admit you had me running scared." She stepped toward him, letting her hands fall loosely at her sides. "Now I see it's very personal for you, Maximillian, and don't try to deny it. Look at the lengths you've gone to get my . . . confession." Milicent cocked her head and gave his disguise a slow perusal. She tapped a long, lethal-looking nail on her chin.

"The old woman has you by the, umm, under her thumb, too. Doesn't she, Max? That's why you want something on her. Hmmm. I wonder what it could be? I wonder if your secret is worse than mine?"

The beautiful blonde arched her million-dollar eyebrows and smiled. Ruthlessly. Max did not want or need another battlefront on his hands, so Milicent needed to be neutralized and pacified into believing she had a balancing hand. *Mon Dieu.* What must Roberta be thinking? Max knew he had to hurry, and feeding Milicent's incredible ego was the best way to control her.

If he needed to, he would, of course, reveal everything. And if she retaliated? *Qué será, será.* His mother was dead and he didn't give a damn about what the world thought of him. Let her shout it from the rooftops.

"All right, Milicent. Since we both know where we stand, here." Max opened the tape recorder, took out the cassette, and handed it to her. "But I suggest you follow your own advice and get all your ducks in a row. Time will no doubt shortly force our hands and we'll have to play the cards we're dealt."

She moved closer and reached for the tape, then tossed

her hair over her shoulder. Max couldn't help but notice her nostrils flare as she ran the edge of the cassette along the low-cut neckline of her sundress, back and forth over the rise of each breast.

"You know, Max, on occasion I've wondered why you never made love to me. But now I think I know. I'm too strong for you, aren't I?" She gave a little wave with the tape. "Wouldn't that surprise a host of people? Your clever plot had no punch. This was too easy."

Milicent shook her head as if he were a simpleton and walked to the door, opening it with a quick jerk.

Max followed, holding his tongue until she was almost through. "And who better to judge the easiness quotient of a given thing than you, Milicent. After all, you've had so much experience in that area."

Max turned the lock just as Milicent's smug, superior expression faltered. A muffled string of offensive expletives immediately bombarded the door, punctuated with a thud that sounded suspiciously like a kick. He waited for what seemed like endless minutes to make sure the witch had gone. Waited until an unusual sheen of sweat gathered across his forehead. It was too damn quiet. He started forward and stumbled on the long gown.

"Dammit!" Max jerked the stupid thing over his head and wiped the wad of cotton fabric across his damp chest and face before tossing it on the bed. "Roberta, you can come out now," he said, padding toward her wearing only his pants and socks.

Nothing. No response. No movement. Max strode to the screen and pulled it away, revealing his sweet woman hunched over like a ball, slumped on the floor. Her arms had a stranglehold on her knees, clutching them close to her chest. Two green pools of misery watched him hunker down and pry away one of her white-knuckled hands.

"Robbie, *chère*. I'm so sorry it had to be this way. Come, *mon coeur*."

He tugged on her fingers, but her eyes only filled with

tears, and so he scooped her up and carried her over to the bed. The weight of her small body on his lap and nestled close to his heart was exquisitely painful. If they could ever be together like this with joy between them! Max ran a hand up her spine and kneaded the back of her neck, then tucked her head under his chin. What should he say? Now that her heart was shattered, what should he do? What if his little mouse simply couldn't deal with this? *Mon Dieu*, he would have to call Prince and . . . no. That might not be safe.

"I want . . . to call Prince . . . but I'm afraid," Roberta whispered with a few watery hitches, then swallowed. "I'm afraid somehow my grandmother will answer or find out what I know." Max's whirling brain careened to a stop. This woman was amazing. A tiger. "I don't deserve it, but there's no one else to ask. Please help me, Max. My head hurts so bad and I have to do the right thing. Prince doesn't know where I am. He doesn't know any of this. . . . And something must be terribly wrong with my grandmother."

A small, cold hand unexpectedly skimmed up his arm, which lay across her lap. It rode the curve of his shoulder; then soft fingertips slid gently over his collarbone, and her palm descended until it stopped in the valley between his pecs. Roberta had never touched him like this before, and Max was vividly aware of every hair under her hand. He briefly wondered if she would comment on the violent pounding of his heart.

"I'm sorry, Max. I'm sorry for all of us." She lightly pressed the spot, then dropped her hand and leaned more heavily against him. "This is my job. It's why I came and now my darn head is—" Max felt her face turn further into his chest. Short, irregular breaths soughed over his skin, and the dampness on her cheek burned like a brand.

"I seem to be one of those people who can never get it right. I have headaches that flatten me when I want to be my strongest. Care for people who say they love me, but really don't. I rush off to help my brother and end up leaving him with the very person determined to ruin his life. And you know what's the worst, Max? Even if you had tried to tell me at the reception, I wouldn't have listened. I wouldn't have believed it. There was no choice. It had to come to this."

Max felt Roberta's jaw brush against his skin as she spoke with a strange mix of logic and despair. Too much was tearing apart inside her, and he flattened his hand wide across her back, trying to give support without giving in to his own feelings of love and desire screaming to be released. Roberta was drowning in a pain-filled haze of crushing revelations. Until she slept off her migraine and had a little time to come to grips with her grandmother's problems, his declaration would have to wait. She needed some time before she heard the next installment of Helen Chalmers's sick manipulations.

"Maybe that's what happened with our wedding, too."

Max slammed his eyes shut. Oh, God. She was too quick.

Roberta's voice wobbled, but she kept speaking. "I didn't think I could ever talk to you about that day. But, I-I guess I hurt so much right now, and in so many ways, this is the perfect time. I don't have a free nerve to be embarrassed with."

She leaned her head back into the hollow of his shoulder and looked up at him through half-closed eyes, her forehead furrowed and makeup smudged on her cheeks. Robbie mustered a small self-deprecating smile, and Max didn't think he was going to be able to take another breath.

"It hurt, Max. What you did hurt. I finally need to say that to your face. But I see now, if you'd just tried to tell me it was all off, it's very possible I wouldn't have believed you then, either. I might have made you feel you had to marry me and then just think how stuck we would—"

She stopped abruptly and stared. Max tried to call up his famous poker face, throw up a screen. But the longer Robbie talked the more impossible it became. He wondered if she could see his distress, because he had completely lost his ability to hide his feelings from her. There was no way to keep it out of his eyes. Could desperate longing and loss be translated into a look?

"Oh, Max. It hurt you, too. I can see it," she murmured, her eyes forlorn. "It had gone too far, hadn't it? We were truly just meant to be friends. Once or twice I've wondered if that might have been it. Maybe when this is all over and Prince and I have—have worked the problems out . . . maybe we could be friends again."

Max lifted his hand and pressed two fingers against her lips, praying the fine tremor shaking his body was imperceptible. After denying himself for so long, he was a hairbreadth away from breaking. Roberta's fine, cinnamon-colored brows lifted at his touch.

"I think that could be arranged," he managed to say. A slight smile curved against his fingers; then she grimaced. "You need your migraine medication, Robbie. Where is it?"

"Oh, Max, everything's packed in my room. I was going to check out, but now . . . I don't know what to do first."

"Hush, now, *chère.*"

"Max."

Max gently tipped up her chin with a knuckle and then rubbed his fingers in small circles against her temple. "We have just agreed to be friends, yes?" he asked in his most urbane tone, heavy on the accent.

"Well."

"We must start somewhere, *n'est-ce pas?* Now you will stay in this room and I will bring your bag here. While you sleep and get better, I will . . ." Max hesitated and took his hand from Roberta's head. He absently stroked his mustache. "You're right, a direct call to Prince could be unwise."

"I know!" Roberta rallied, patting his chest as if trying to get his attention. Oh, she had it, all right. Max grabbed her insistent little hand and pressed it flat against his skin to stop the torture, but not quite end it.

"Prince's security chief, Frank Henson, will know what's going on, I'm sure. His card is in my purse. Call him, Max, and then if we need to make plans, wake me no matter what."

Max carefully stood, cradling his love, and turned around to lay her on the bed. He slipped off her sandals and pulled the comforter up over her body. With the lightest touch he combed through her hair and she closed her eyes, relaxing as if he had truly comforted her.

"I'll be right back, *chère.*"

"Mmmm, fine."

Max took a few steps toward the door.

"Max?"

"Yes, *mon amour.*"

"You dressed up like an old lady."

"Yes."

"There's something . . . funny. I can't remember."

"Good. I hope it's all a blur." Max quietly shut the door, mumbling under his breath. *Mon Dieu,* after two hopeless years he'd finally had the chance to come to his lady's aid and he'd done it wearing a nightgown. Ah, but he had never claimed to be a storybook hero.

A very soft chuckle trailed unnoticed behind him.

Chapter Five

Max sat on the chair next to Robbie's bed and scrubbed a hand down his face. She'd been sleeping for about seventeen hours and he was going to have to leave her. He had no choice. Yesterday, after he'd given Roberta her medication, he'd planned to stay with her until she woke up. He'd canceled both other rooms, had all their belongs transferred to the new one, and left word with the staff to reach him here. He was not about to let Robbie fend for herself when she couldn't even stand up.

He leaned forward, propping his elbows on his knees, and rested his forehead on the tips of his fingers. At about six in the morning he'd been so worried he'd tried to rouse her. Roberta had asked for water and another pill and Max had forced her to let him help her to the bathroom. He closed his eyes and smiled at the memory. She'd stayed in there so long he'd finally pounded on the door and announced he was coming in.

He'd heard the muffled groan just before the door opened and there she stood, leaning against the sink with a towel clutched around her waist. She couldn't get her pants back on. She didn't have the strength. And she was so angry all she could do was cry and that made her even angrier. Max had scooped her up again and put her back to bed. He'd dozed off himself, until an hour ago when the message had come from the front desk.

He sat up and slid the small envelope off the end table. Could the phone call he'd made last night to Henson Security be behind this, or was it Milicent? Max tapped the paper on his chin. He hadn't been able to reach Frank; it seemed the man was unavailable, although the employee he'd spoken with had been very thorough and promised Mr. Henson would contact him as soon as possible. The question was, could he afford to miss this lead even if it came from the same seedy bar Milicent had used as a rendezvous spot?

No. He needed all the answers he could get. The sooner things were resolved the better. But he hated to leave her here. Damn. Max stood and moved to sit on the edge of the bed.

"Robbie, *chère*. Wake up. I have to go out for a little while." He leaned over her and patted her cheek. Slowly her eyes fluttered open.

"Max? What?"

He slipped a hand under her neck and brought a glass of water to her mouth. "Do you feel better? I'm sorry to do this, but I have to leave and I didn't want you to worry."

Roberta blinked and tried to focus. She felt as if she'd been on another planet. What was he saying? Leave? Leaving? Well, of course. He never should have stayed here.

"Leave, yes," she muttered. "I'm fine. Little more sleep and fine. Sorry you had to stay." She struggled to sit up and Max's strong arms supported her as she shifted and weakly kicked at the covers. He seemed to read her mind, steadying her with one hand and standing to pull the comforter back with the other. Roberta focused her spinning vision and thrust her legs over the side.

"Slow down, Robbie," Max warned.

"No. See?" She smiled, planting her hands on her trembling legs and taking a deep breath. "I'm fine. You don't have to babysit me now."

"*Chère*, I'm here with you because I want to be." Max hooked the chair leg with the toe of his shoe and dragged it closer so he could sit in front of her. This way she could feel as though she were functioning on her own power, and he could catch her in an instant if she started to fall. *Mon Dieu*, at last she was really awake. Was she ready to hear the words he'd been rehearsing all night long?

Max watched his stubborn little tiger try to stay upright. She closed her eyes and flexed her hands on her thighs. A second later the eyes flew open.

"Max? Where are my pants?"

"Robbie," he scoffed in a teasing tone, "they were too uncomfortable. Remember last night and the towel?" A fiery blush burst into flame on her cheeks. He knew exactly what she was thinking.

"Well." Roberta paused and tugged on the twisted bottom of her shirt. "I'm sure that was a first for you. Sorry, Max. Hell's bells, but I'm saying that a lot." She blew out a short, disgusted breath and looked away from him. "Have you heard from Frank Henson? Just fill me in and I can take it from here. If you'll just check in a little later, I'll let you know what my plans are and if Frank needs any more from you or if Prince needs—"

Max leaned forward and cupped her face in one hand, his palm covering her mile-a-minute mouth. "Stop, *chère*, or you will be flat on your back again." He waited until she gave a slight nod, and dropped his hand. Maybe she wasn't ready to hear everything yet, but he was damn well going to leave her with a whole lot to think about.

"I'm leaving, yes. But only for a few hours and only because you seem to be feeling much better. I spoke to one of Henson's men last night when I was informed the 'boss' was unavailable. They are working on this, but I couldn't get many details. I'm not sure what Prince knows, although Henson's man told me not to try to contact him, but wait for Frank's call. They have our number, so if he calls while I'm out, you tell him what we know. I'm going to check on a few concerns and then I'll be back."

Max hoped Roberta would still be woozy enough to miss all the shadow and smoke about his purpose and destination. She didn't need another thing to worry about. He watched and waited, the whirring of her poor, overwhelmed brain almost audible.

"Ah, Robbie. Now, my little fiery, flame-haired woman, you must rest until I get back. I promise we'll work everything out."

Roberta blinked and stared owlishly into his eyes, their faces about three inches apart. Her gaze lowered to his mouth. Max didn't move. She lifted a hand and with one shaky finger she stroked his mustache. Oh, so slowly, as if the feel of it gave her great pleasure. *Mon Dieu*. Max knew just how she felt. Then she rubbed his lips and he nearly came up off the chair.

"Max. You said *chère* was because we're friends. But *love* is too much, okay? Don't say that one." She dipped her chin and gave him a scolding look, but before she could drop her hand, Max grasped the back of it and kissed the palm. He never took his gaze from her as he kissed that soft skin again and rubbed his mouth back and forth in the hollow of her hand. Roberta's eyes went as round as her mouth.

"Robbie, what if I want to use both words?" His body, his soul, so desperate for her touch that he knew it was good he had to leave soon.

She slowly drew her hand away and curled her fist up tight as if she didn't want to lose the feeling he'd left there. Her other hand climbed the twisted buttons on her shirt, until she slid it underneath her collar and next to her skin.

"But that . . . that would mean—and you don't. You changed your mind. Remember? Do you like my hair?"

Max winced at her doubts as he watched her fingers fumbling with the twisted fabric. Suddenly he wished he could paint her a picture of his feelings, but he was not a painter. Yet in the next few minutes he could show her just the tip of the iceberg, the barest tip of his love and desire for her beauty and goodness. As clearly as if it had been whispered in his ear, he knew her artist's eye would understand his actions more deeply than any words.

Once Upon a Tangled Tale

She was confused when he stood and firmly sat her back on the bed. Max stepped quickly to one of his bags and found a T-shirt, the kind he sometimes worked out in. Robbie didn't speak, but her gaze never left him. He clenched the soft cotton in his hands and came back to sit in the chair, scooting up until their knees touched.

"Later, when I come back, I have some important things to tell you, *chère*. I'm afraid that part of what I say will hurt you, but I-I hope, I pray, that you will hear me out. I want to take the pain away, love. I want you to trust me again. I want you to feel safe with me. Friends and more. Much, much more. At long last, I want to speak the truth. And here is one to start with. I love your hair. It makes me think of glowing red-gold embers, ready to burst into flame with just the right touch."

Max lay the shirt in his lap and slowly lifted his hands to Robbie's top button. Her thoughts were unfathomable and he, who prided himself on his ability to read the most inscrutable of faces, swallowed hard and clenched his jaw to keep from begging for her secrets.

One by one he found the buttons and released them until his hands reached the knot at the bottom. Never once did Max break eye contact with her, and never once did Robbie try to stop him. She seemed to be waiting for something. Perhaps this was a test for her, too.

Roberta felt Max untying the knot and knew she had delayed as long as she could, as long as she should. But what did he want to show her? What truth? Her heart hammered in her chest. It seemed a lifetime ago that he'd dared her to come with him and find it. Should she? Should she?

Try again . . .

Her shirt fell open the instant those familiar, hopeful words echoed in her head yet again. Was it magic? Was it foolishness? Roberta closed her eyes, afraid to go forward, afraid to go back. She held her breath and felt the strong hands of the man she loved push underneath the fabric and cup her shoulders. Her eyes shot open as all the insecurities and fear about her body's inadequacies flooded her mind. Too thin, too small, too flat, too unlovable.

But Max's eyes were there, watching as if he knew exactly what she was thinking. His dark gaze held hers as he ran his hands up from her shoulders to her neck and back again. Once, twice, three times until the tension in her body softened like heated wax. Then he used his hands and pushed the top further down until her arms were caught in the blouse and nothing was hidden from him. Roberta felt a surge of heat stain her cheeks. She rarely wore a bra. She didn't really need one.

Max lifted his hands away from her and brought them to her face, his palms against her cheeks, his fingers threaded in her hair, his thumbs brushing lightly over her lips.

"No matter what happens after this moment, my love, no matter what you hear, no matter what we finally unravel, I want you to know how beautiful you are. How lovely. I-I stopped touching you when we were engaged because I was ready to break. Please believe me. You are worthy of anything you can dream, *chère*. You are more priceless than all the great art in the world."

Roberta felt the growing pressure in Max's hands. His eyes burned and his soft words were spoken with such intensity and so close to her face, that small puffs of air touched her lips where his thumbs didn't. She loved him and for the first time in her life she truly felt beautiful. She believed, she hoped, she wanted to try again.

"Max," she breathed against his thumbs and he stopped. His hands slid deep into her hair. He kissed her then. Just a chaste meeting of lips. Her eyes must have spoken her disappointment, because he smiled, that deadly smile that left women faint at his feet, and dropped his hands back to her shoulders. Then, with one finger, he traced the prominent ridge of her collarbone from one side to the other and came back to the dip at the base of her throat.

"Your eyes say too much, love. Too much to a man who has waited too long to see that answer."

Roberta felt a path of fire ignite beneath his finger as he deliberately drew it down between her breasts. Her heart was pounding so hard she was probably shaking, and nothing would make her look. Max startled her when his hands suddenly curled around her rib cage, each thumb riding up under a modest swell of flesh. She froze. She couldn't lift her eyes to his.

"Roberta," he murmured. "Roberta, love. Look at me." He gave her a gentle shake and she took a deep breath and raised her head.

"I love you. I've never stopped. You'll never know, woman—you'll never know until I can show you how exquisite you are. *Mon Dieu*, what you do to me! To have had just this much has been sweeter than I ever dreamed. But I can't kiss you again and keep the promise. Sleep now, and when I come back we'll make plans."

It took every bit of Max's control to gently pull his T-shirt over Robbie's head. He smoothed the butter-soft fabric down her back and across her shoulders. Those deep pools of green were still rimmed with fatigue, but there was a glimmer of hope in them now. And . . . the glow of desire. Max could not stop his greedy hands from one last touch. Just before he laid her down, he ran the backs of his knuckles over the delicate crests he dreamed of devouring.

Robbie's soft gasp nearly undid him and, minutes later, after Max closed the door, a howl as wild as he'd ever imagined hovered at the back of his throat. Perhaps there *was* something mystic in his name. Wolves mated for life. He would do nothing less.

Roberta stepped out of the shower and wrapped up quickly in a thick white towel. She sat down on the edge of the tub for a minute and tried to gauge her coherency. Her head still felt a bit like a mushy melon, with the usual postmigraine tenderness, but the pain was gone and her foggy recollections were clearing as quickly as the mist on the mirror. She looked up and stared at her pale, washed-out reflection. Maximillian Wolfe had said he loved . . . that woman. He'd said she was beautiful. He'd said he'd never stopped loving her. It wasn't a dream and it wasn't the medication. And he'd pretty much seen all there was to see. Roberta watched a scarlet flush climb up her neck and spread across her face. The redhead's curse was really going to get a workout if what Max implied actually happened. Plans. Plans? Had he really remembered their promise and what it meant?

Well, she'd best be ready to find out when he returned. Just thinking of the contrast between her new look and the half-drugged stupor Max had last seen buoyed her erratic thoughts. Roberta grabbed the blow-dryer and fluffed her hair into a wreath of curls the way Lucinda had shown her and then followed that with makeup. The woman surely had to be part magician, because Roberta couldn't believe that this version of herself had really been there all along. It was a present she should have given herself years ago.

Of course it was nice that Max approved, but darn it, she had judged herself to be lacking, and that had robbed her of all kinds of things. Robbie knew that externals simply didn't bother some people, but she was a living, breathing example of how individuals like herself could stunt their whole lives because they didn't feel good in their own skin. Because they couldn't accept themselves.

A swift heat suffused her face once again, and Roberta stepped back from the mirror. Deep inside, a tremulous flicker brought back the feel of Max's hands on her bare flesh and his eyes caressing what she thought to be her greatest flaw. How could she be the woman for a confident, devastating man like Maximillian Wolfe unless she thought she deserved him? Just the thought of turning into a simpering, whimpering woman every time someone like

Milicent or Miss Honeysuckle came on the scene made her sick. Her body, her face, could never compete with hundreds of women, so there had to be something else. If she really loved the man, if he really loved her, she had to believe that they saw some special, intrinsic beauty in each other.

Roberta took a deep breath, closed her eyes . . . and dropped her towel. Hesitantly she cracked open one eye and made a quick perusal. Gradually the other eye joined in and she tried to see what Max had seen. Good skin. Well, more than that. True it turned red at the drop of a hat, but in its normal state, it was smooth and clear. No beach-bunny look, ever. But if tall, tanned, buxom blondes weren't your idea of a ten, then small, delicate, peaches-and-cream redheads might hold up pretty well. Beauty had so many different definitions.

For just a minute she stared at her chest. All her life she'd thought she was inferior because her breasts weren't the size of casabas. And she wondered how may women did that to themselves. How could you ever freely share what you felt you had to hide? Max was about as male as the species got and he'd said he loved what he saw. Her unique, delicate femininity. An individual beauty that no one else could duplicate in quite the same way. What she was was enough. Inside and outside. Roberta snagged the towel off the floor and hurried into the other room to dress.

There was no question that a part of her life was about to fall apart. It hurt and it was frightening and Max told her they'd have to talk about it. But he'd promised he wouldn't leave her. He'd said he never stopped loving her and he wanted her. He wanted Roberta—the wallflower—Chalmers.

And as she stood up and twirled around in her new full-skirted dress made of crisp white eyelet, Roberta acknowledged the depth of the change in herself. The wallflower had been the disguise and she hadn't realized it. Now, because of Max, she'd found the key that had unlocked the complete woman that had waited, literally, just out of sight. Perhaps it was yet another truth. Every woman had to find her softness and her strength, her beauty and her intelligence, her power and her need.

Roberta fingered the fitted bodice that laced up the front and tied with sky blue ribbons. It made her feel like an island girl of two hundred years ago. A girl who might have been swept away on the arms of a dashing pirate. She smiled at her new ability to imagine herself as an object of desire, but she also knew how lucky she was, because her adolescent dreams of happily ever after had combined with the knowledge that she could stand on her own, too. That she was strong enough to face hard things and not run. That she had somehow managed to find a man who had loved her even before she had fully come to love herself.

And then the truth of it hit her. Another slicing truth that cut through her euphoria like a knife through butter. Roberta dropped onto the bed and fell back on the mattress. If Max had never stopped loving her, then why had he left? Why had he been so cruel? A cold, churning knot tightened in her stomach. No. Oh, no. Two years ago it had been her grandmother.

Max held his damp, monogrammed handkerchief to his left eye and tried to appear unhurried as he race-walked across the nearly deserted lobby to the elevators. Damn, he'd thought he'd be back in the early afternoon and now it was late evening. Roberta was probably frantic. She'd still been groggy and reeling from the truth about her grandmother, and the only way he'd been able to leave her had been to finally declare his love and give them both a taste of the feast that awaited.

Perhaps he'd gone too far, but she'd damn near killed him Tuesday with the forgiving and understanding conclusion she'd drawn about the end of their engagement.

So once she'd been coherent he simply couldn't let the woman believe that friendship was all there was between them. Not for another minute. But now, *mon Dieu*, she'd had too much time to wonder why, if he loved her, he'd left her the way he had. She'd had too much time to put two and two together.

The elevator chimed and as soon as Max ascertained he was alone, he removed his hanky and ran a finger around his aching eye. Frank Henson was a tall man, but hadn't looked like a fighter. Then again, when Max found himself pushed up against a wall, he fought back, no matter what the assailant looked like. Now he was going to have a black eye to explain. He gave the torn sleeve of his cashmere jacket a glance and winced. The man who'd done this to him could have posed for a demented Club Med poster, but what a left hook.

Max heard the mumble of voices just as the elevator came to a stop, and he quickly put his hankie back in place. Of course he'd gotten in a few good punches himself, before they'd both had the sense to listen to what the other one was saying. Frank had been the one who'd sent the message to his hotel room. Apparently he and Lilith had trailed him to St. Thomas, and when he'd surprised Max and then tried to detain him outside the bar for a few questions, things had gotten out of hand.

Frank had grunted that he was helping Prince, and Max had done the same, and they'd both finally collapsed against the wall while Max had spun out his slightly edited story about romancing Milicent Smythe and playing along with her in order to help Prince. Frank had been speechless when Max had mentioned that Prince and Milicent had dated. The lanky man with the Robbie-like glasses had become silent as stone.

Max was still confused about what had happened next. He'd been just about ready to tell Frank everything he and Roberta had discovered, when he prefaced it with a warning about the Smythes being in residence on the island.

Frank had gone rigid, his hands fisted at his sides. He'd demanded that Max repeat it, and Max told him he'd already seen Milicent and that she was denying any responsibility. Then, before he could continue, Frank had cursed Lilith Smythe to hell and back, which prompted Max to ask what he'd been using for a brain. Lilith Smythe and her sister were like peas in a pod. She had to know about the whole thing. He'd barely finished his sentence when Frank Henson had abruptly stalked away without another word.

Max had waited for a few minutes, but the man hadn't returned. And the hell of it was, he'd never even had the chance to tie in Helen Chalmers. Max raked a hand through his hair and exited the elevator, heading down the hall to their room. Just as soon as he and Roberta had things between them straightened out, he'd hunt down Prince's security chief and explain it all for the man. Frankly, if Henson had stalked off to deal with Lilith, well, a little cool-down time would be wise.

Which brought him back to his own immediate problem. Roberta had already had too much cool-down time. Max put his card in the locking mechanism, shut his eyes, and took a deep breath, trying not to think about the fact that Robbie hadn't said a thing about loving him.

Or staying until he returned. The room was empty.

Max's heart kicked into high gear as he rushed to the bathroom just in case. Nothing. He dragged both hands down his face, groaning at the accidental pressure on his eye. Wait. Wait. Think. She hadn't seemed afraid. She seemed to understand about waiting to reach Prince when it was safe. Max whirled around and pounded on the wall. Immediately someone pounded back. Damn thin walls! God, Robbie was so fragile and too weak. She couldn't have run again.

Max sank onto the end of the bed and dropped his head in his hands. *Mon Dieu*, his face hurt, he was exhausted, and he didn't know where to begin to look. *Please. Some-*

where there must be someone to help me. He rocked forward in a turmoil of thought. In the last few years he'd lost everyone he'd ever loved, and he could not bear to lose Roberta again. Max opened his eyes and stared at the floor in despair. And then he saw it. A faint, incandescent light seeping from under the bed. A flashlight? He fell to his knees and tore away the bedspread. Robbie's bag. He snagged it and pulled.

She wouldn't have left it behind. Max yanked it open. Yes, all her ID was still here. He rummaged around and then, with growing alarm, Max realized what was wrong. There was no flashlight in the bag. None under the bed. In fact, the strange light was completely gone.

Max lurched to his feet. Staggering out onto the small balcony, he braced his hands on the metal railing and let his head hang down between them. Almost immediately a breeze kicked up and Max threw back his head, glaring at the heavens. How would he be able to stand the loneliness again? It wasn't fair, dammit! A bright, shimmering light suddenly streaked across a velvet swath of sky. Max couldn't help but watch it. The tail of the falling star was longer than he'd ever seen before, and he wondered if it was this particular spot in the world making it appear so.

His gaze was oddly locked to the light, as if he had no will of his own. Down, down the glittering trail came until Max nearly shouted out a warning. The star seemed to be crashing to the earth. He blinked, his hands curled so tightly around the railing that his fingers ached. And when he looked again . . . the majestic tail of silver dust was gone. But it had landed on the rise of the hill behind the hotel.

Max held his breath and let it escape very slowly. The same light he'd seen under the bed was shining in a small, distinct circle about halfway up the shadowy hillside. And he knew. He knew as surely as the hairs were lifting on the back of his neck . . . that Roberta was there.

He didn't analyze. He didn't think. It was a gift and he ran to claim it.

By the time Max reached the bottom of the hill carrying a blanket for Robbie, the cosmic glow was fading. The creamy slice of moon didn't afford much light, and Max squinted against the darkness, searching for a shimmering sign. Tufts of shrubbery and ankle-high grass snagged the bottom of his pants as he climbed higher. Where was she? The spot had been so clear from the balcony. Max tried not to think about his illogical certainty and instead took a deep breath to calm his racing heart. But the sweet, tangy smell of flowers and the sea reminded him of something his American mother had once told him.

Her family had been longtime wealthy landowners in Tennessee, yet she was more than proud of that legacy's modest beginnings from simple hill people. People who believed in more than what they could see and hold. When he'd been about twelve, she'd had him close his eyes and try to tell her, without touching, what she had in her hand. So he'd used his nose and knew his mother held a gardenia. When he'd looked and seen he was right, she'd put her arm around him and told him to confidently use the brain power he had, but not to forget that there was more. Power that came from other than logic and book learning. Power as real as a flower's scent and just as impossible to see.

Magic? Perhaps. Right now he believed.

"Robbie? Robbie, where are you?"

"Max?" About ten yards ahead, a small, indistinct shape rose up before him. He reached her in seconds, breathing hard.

"Roberta, what are you doing here? Good God, woman, it's dangerous to be out at night alone. Even though they bill this island as paradise, you have to be damn careful." He caught her body and drew it close to his. *Mon Dieu*, she was shaking. The evening air was pleasant, but her arms were bare and chilled. Max wrapped the blanket around her and took a step back toward the hotel. Robbie didn't budge.

"Max? What did my grandmother do to you?"

Hell. She was too smart for her own good. Was she even strong enough to hear it all now?

As if reading his mind she answered, "I need to know, Max. I need to be as prepared as I can be, because very soon Prince and I are going to have to confront her. Please. It must have been terrible and I'm sorry if it's difficult. I'm sure you've wished you had never gotten involved with my family. But I have to know." Robbie reached through the opening in the blanket and curled her fingers around one of his wrists. "I-I meant to come back sooner, Max. I just couldn't sit there. I had to do something."

"All right, *chère*, but let's go back inside. I need to see your face and you need to see mine." Max tipped up her chin and bent his head until they could each look into the other's eyes, even in the dim light. "This injustice was done to both of us, love. I think you're missing that. Come on."

A few minutes later Roberta was sitting on a small sofa next to the room's sliding-glass door. Max had been purposely keeping the swollen side of his face turned away from her and, with the darkness outside and Robbie's distress as they walked to the room, she hadn't noticed it. Now it was unavoidable. He opened the sliding door for a bit of fresh air and faced her.

Roberta looked at him with big sad eyes, her arms folded, and then she gasped.

"Max! Your eye! What happened?" she demanded. "Who did this? Oh, God, I feel like I've gone down the rabbit hole and I can't find my way out."

Max quickly sat beside her and caught one of her hands, anchoring it between both of his.

"Frank Henson's here and we just happened to . . . run into each other."

"Prince's Frank Henson? Here on St. Thomas?"

"You should be happy, love. He's going to help us

straighten this out even faster."

Roberta tilted her head and pursed her lips. "If he's helping us, why do you have a black eye, Max?"

Max rubbed her hand between the two of his and carefully couched his response. No need making her worry over every single detail that had or hadn't been resolved. "Ummm. He and I had a small misunderstanding about whose side I was on. But it's resolved now and this"—he lifted a finger to his eye—"will be gone in no time."

Roberta tugged her hand out of his and scooted closer, her gaze intent. The corners of her lips turned down and she feathered her fingers through a shock of hair that had fallen across his forehead. "My grandmother is responsible for this, too, Max. Isn't she?"

Chapter Six

Max took a deep breath. "Robbie, your grandmother was not pleased when we were engaged. I don't know why, but it's obvious she doesn't want either you or Prince to find that kind of happiness. About a week before our wedding day she discovered that my father had been accused of and fired for embezzling." Max tightened his hold on her hand and tried to keep the dread out of his voice. "She came to me and told me that if I didn't leave you, she would expose my father's crime, even though his company had never made formal charges because of his heart attack. You knew he had died, but I hadn't told you about what he'd done."

"Oh, Max. I wouldn't have cared. You should have told me. We could have left . . . done something," Roberta whispered, tracking the pain radiating from Max's eyes.

"If it had just been me, *chère,* I might have done so, but there was another I couldn't let your grandmother hurt. Helen knew that only too well and used it against me. You see," he said, bending forward and bringing her hand to his cheek, "my father made a terrible choice. I wish he had come to me, but my mother was so sick and doctors had promised with more money she could be helped. Neither of us knew what he'd been doing. I—"

Max stopped and pressed her palm to his lips, and Roberta could feel his mouth trembling against her skin. She lifted her free hand and threaded her fingers into his hair, trying to comfort them both. Mercy! Her grandmother had a heart of stone.

"I couldn't let your grandmother destroy my father's memory and I could not let my mother suffer more than she already was. Helen told me exactly how I was to leave you, *chère*. That I was to wait so you would have to face all your friends at the church. *Mon Dieu*, I have never wanted to hurt another human being as badly as I wanted to hurt Helen Chalmers. God, Roberta, I knew how awful it would be for you. I knew you'd think I'd used you and there was nothing I could do about it. For a while, just after I tried to see you . . . remember in the garden . . . I didn't think I was going to be able to live with the pain.

"But then my mother had a turn for the worse, part of it, I'm sure, because she'd seen how happy I was and couldn't understand why I'd changed my mind. I had to go to Helen and secretly start paying back my father's debt. Helen had been very clear about my trying to contact you. There were no options, so I just stopped caring and tried to keep living. Then, months ago, she sent me a letter and tipped her hand about Prince. I knew in my bones that she was about to ruin his life, too, and I just couldn't let that happen. She'd dropped Milicent's name and I had a place to start. Of course she mentioned how happy you were. Every now and then she liked to mail me a little reminder of what I'd lost."

Roberta sat silently, letting her tears fall, struggling to hang on to her shredded emotions. She ran her fingers deeply into Max's hair and curled them tight against his skull. "Oh, Max. She lied. I missed you so terribly and she told me over and over again that you needed so much more in a woman than I had to offer."

Max pulled away from her touch and sat up, a grim expression on his face. "It's only been in these past few days that I've fully realized how she poisoned your mind, love. She wanted to keep you with her so desperately, she stripped away all your self-esteem to cripple you. I don't know how you feel about her now, Robbie. I agree she must be very sick, but I hate her for what she did to you, what she did to us."

"And your poor mother. I still have the letter she wrote to me after we got engaged." Roberta clasped her hands in her lap and hunched her shoulders. "I knew she was too sick to come to the wedding, Max, but I had hoped to meet her. I-I feel awful because I never tried to communicate with her at all afterward and— Wait! Max, what will this do to her now?" Roberta looked up at Max and cringed at the hooded darkness in his eyes.

"Nothing can hurt her now, love. She died almost a year ago. That's why I was free to come."

A soft, sorrowful moan seeped out of Roberta, and she closed her eyes and laid her head on the back of the sofa.

"I knew it was more than likely that you and Prince would still hate me, and I expected it. But the thought of facing him and the possibility of seeing you made my blood run cold. I'm telling you, Robbie, there are people who would love to see Maximillian Wolfe break, and I could have pleased them immensely a number of times over the past few days. But any more personal pain meant very little. I knew what Helen did not: my father's debts were cleared and my mother was dead. She had no more power over me."

Roberta felt as though she'd aged a hundred years. She forced herself to sit up and stare at the face of the man she loved—the man she'd thought was without a shred of decency. A man who had loved his parents so much that he had given up his own happiness and, in a way, his own good name, to protect them.

"Oh, Max, I wish I had been stronger then. We were both hurting so badly and all alone." Roberta shuddered and brushed the tears from her cheeks. "I'm so sorry for everything my grandmother took away. I wish we could have stood up to her together. It could have all been so different."

"Then let's stand together now, love." Max said, his voice

deep and unyielding. He went down on one knee, leaning against Roberta's legs.

"But, Max—"

Max grasped her around the waist and tugged her slightly forward. Robbie's face was pale and drawn and he couldn't stand to see her lingering self-doubt and misery another second.

"This time we can do it, *chère*. You are strong, and I'm so proud of all you've accomplished. My debts to my family are paid and nothing will keep me from having our dream, Robbie. Marry me this minute, love. Let's take back what was stolen." Max slid one palm down low on Roberta's stomach and brought his mouth a hairbreadth from hers. "Have you thought, even once, that we might have had a baby by now, *chère?*" He saw the tears well again in her eyes and he knew she had.

"So have I, sweetheart. God, Roberta, say yes," he whispered urgently against her lips. "It can all wait a day. This time we can't let anything stop us, unless . . ." Max reared back. "Unless there's been too much pain. Unless you don't love me."

The look in his eyes was so bleak, Roberta's reaction was instantaneous. She took his face in her hands and kissed him. Kissed him as he had kissed her on the plane, her mouth first soft and clinging and then lifting and pressing again and again until she heard a groan rumble deep in his chest. Max's hands flexed at her waist and then yanked her off the couch and against his body. With slow deliberation, he slid her down until she straddled his lap. His hands rubbing and roving over her back and sides filled Roberta with a primal surge of feminine power—a feeling she had never known.

She was hungry for his taste, and she opened her mouth over his as he let her inside, meeting her stroke for stroke until they were both desperate and breathing hard. Max rocked her against him, and Roberta could feel how much he wanted her, feel it in every way. The wide circle of her pooled skirts left very little between them, and she was determined to tear away the rest. Roberta reached for the buttons on his shirt and Max had her sitting on the couch in an instant.

"I—" Max held on to Roberta's knees and stopped talking to take a few huge gulps of air. He tried again. "I take that kiss to mean you love me."

Roberta lifted two fingers to her hot, puffy lips and smiled. "Maximillian Wolfe, I have never stopped loving you. I want to marry you and I want your babies, and no matter what happens, I would rather have you than anything else."

"Thank God," Max murmured; then he smiled, too. "Together we'll get through this, Robbie. I'm just sorry you have to marry me looking like this."

"Max, you have always looked wonderful to me."

"As you have to me." Her cinnamon brows lifted, and Max went up on his knees, sliding his hands up to the tops of her thighs and resting his thumbs over the heart of her. Roberta shivered and Max smiled as wolfishly as he ever had. "I speak the truth, woman, and just as soon as I'm able to walk we're making this legal. And then, as I once told you, I will show you very slowly and very thoroughly exactly how beautiful you are. First we keep the promise, love. Then we give the gifts. Tomorrow we'll deal with the world."

"But, Max, it's the middle of the night."

Max managed to drag his hands away and get to his feet.

"Well, my lady. I will simply roust the authorities on the end of me trusty blade as they did so often here two hundred years ago. A sharp sword or a wallet of cold cash, it'll work the same way."

"Perfect." She laughed, and Max realized he hadn't heard that happy sound in what felt like forever. "I'll get you a pirate patch in the gift shop, Captain Wolfe."

He wrapped his love up snug in his arms and whispered

before he opened the door, "And you, my lady, had best prepare to be ravished."

Max was as good as his word. Three long hours later they were married. Of course he'd had to throw his weight and money around, but it was done. He'd been as cunning as his animal namesake and as clever and determined as Francis Drake. And he'd sworn he would not leave until the deed was done. Roberta wasn't even sure what time it was, only that it was very early Thursday morning and she was both exhausted and wired.

They'd agreed to make one short call to Prince's private office phone, leaving a brief message. Max asked Prince to call, gave the hotel number, and added a cryptic comment about protecting what he should have two years ago. It was the safest way they could come up with to make contact, and both hoped Helen would never even know about it. Roberta felt that something had to be done to speed things up, and Max felt he could risk it now that they were officially man and wife. Almost. He'd smiled and left to shower first.

Then, when it had been Roberta's turn, he'd asked her to put her dress back on after she'd finished in the bathroom. At the time she'd been too nervous to ask him why, but now Roberta's hands were shaking so badly she could barely put on her lip gloss. No need for color if they were going to just kiss it off. Or whatever? She flattened her palms on the counter and looked at her reflection.

This was her wedding night. The night she'd dreamed of and then mourned for so long. And Max loved her and she loved him and in a few minutes they would make love for the first time and Roberta—her new, complete self—was ready.

Oh, she was scared, too. But she gave herself a thumbs-up in the mirror. Roberta took a deep breath, retied the ribbon on her dress, and opened the door.

"Ah, *chère*. I thought I might have to come get you out of the bathroom again."

Max had left only one low light on in their room, and he was framed with the island netting draped from the old-fashioned poster bed. A soft golden glow gilded his bare chest and shoulders, emphasizing the white sheet low across his hips. His dark eyes gleamed and one corner of his chiseled mouth was lifted, as was one black brow. He stretched out a strong, corded arm, and Roberta felt the bottom drop out of her stomach. Had there ever been a more perfect man? Everything she could see—the ebony hair brushed back from his face, the dark curls on his chest, the tanned, long-fingered hand—every part of him made her body hum and her heart race and her knees weak and her soul rejoice.

"Robbie, sweetheart, come here before you faint on me."

"Max." She swallowed and took a few steps. "I think you should know—I've never done this before."

Max closed his eyes and then sought her face again. "*Mon Dieu*, it makes this all the sweeter. Come here." He patted the bed. "I have a few confessions of my own, woman, and I need to hold you before I shake to pieces."

"Max?"

"Yes, *chère*." He nodded as she put her hand in his and sat on the edge of the mattress. "I'm as nervous as you are." Max elbowed himself up, careful to keep the sheet in place. "And I wish I had kept myself for you, too, Robbie, but I want you to know that since the moment we made our promise, all those many months ago, I have kept it. I have never been unfaithful to you."

He smiled at the wonder in her glorious green eyes. Max carried her hand up and placed it over his heart, holding it there. The pounding was more than obvious. "You must know, though, that I had to kiss Milicent Smythe a few times when I was trying to get information. It was less than honorable, but it had to be done, and your grand-mother is sure to blow it out of proportion if she gets a

325

chance. But please believe me."

"Max," Roberta said, lifting her other hand to touch his face and soothe his poor eye, "even if she gets a hundred chances I will never believe her, not ever again. I'm just so moved, so happy, and, I'm embarrassed to say, relieved. It means more to me than you can ever know to hear this." She hesitated and dropped her eyes, biting her bottom lip, then squared her shoulders and looked up. "Sometimes I'd wonder where you were and who you were with. It was horrible. I don't ever want to doubt you, Max. I don't ever want to worry. . . ."

"Ah, like on the plane, yes?" Max waited for her reluctant nod and leaned forward, catching her chin on the edge of his hand. "Robbie, I can only tell you that your memory alone shut down both my body and my heart for more than two years. In fact, woman, it wasn't until I saw you again and then that kiss on the plane that I was even sure my poor . . . manly endowments knew how to . . . ummm . . . respond."

She blushed a delicious strawberry pink, but Max would not let her pull away. She needed to hear what he had to say and see the truth of it in his eyes. "My soul, my heart, my body are pledged to you, Roberta Hood Chalmers Wolfe. There may be other women in the world who see me, but I do not see them. Do you understand?"

A bright, glassy sheen filmed her eyes, and her trembling mouth parted into a huge, heart-stopping smile. "I do understand and I know exactly how you feel. I don't see anyone but you, either. I love you, Max."

He leaned over, covering her mouth with his, and Roberta felt his hands tugging at her ribbons. He smiled against her lips. "Ah, *chère*, if you knew how this dress has tortured me. I have never seen such a beautiful bride, and I have thought of nothing else"—the bow came free—"but untying these laces."

Roberta drew in a light breath as his nimble fingers made lingering, deliberate passes over her sensitive breasts. Then when the bodice at last fell open, it was Max who sucked in a far more audible gulp of air. And she could not stop the provocative smile that spread slowly across her face. Max's black eyes grew even darker and he ran a single finger along the edge of her new strapless peach-lace bra.

"So," he murmured, a feral gleam pulling the skin over his cheekbones taut. "My little mouse has, indeed, become a little tiger." He rubbed one finger in the shallow valley between her breasts and then over the hook that seemed to be holding her together. Max came close again and spoke with his mouth brushing hers, feathering her lips with short, labored breaths. "Remember you once told me you had discovered very sharp teeth, *chère?* I will want you to show me."

He flicked open the fragile barrier and she did gasp this time, but Max boldly filled her mouth and stroked her tongue with the same primal rhythm that she knew awaited her body. He pulled back and for the first time ran his hands over her bare breasts, and she shuddered under that exquisite sensation.

"Ah, wife, how you please me." Then he covered her aching flesh with his palms and whispered against her mouth, "Your courage pleases me, your body pleases me, and your spirit pleases me. Now touch me, Robbie, and see how much I want you . . . only you."

He pulled her hand down, and Roberta knew that the woman in her had called up his love and need, perfectly combined in this undeniable response. Max moved against her touch and she reveled in the power of the gift they were about to give each other. Unsure but eager, she let her mouth tell him she was more than ready.

Max lifted her hand away and broke their kiss. He laughed softy at Roberta's disgruntled frown and laughed again at her round eyes as he pushed the rest of her dress off her shoulders and gathered the sheet in one hand to follow her to the edge of the bed. He swung his legs over the side and pulled her between them, using both his hands to ease the lovely white fabric over her slight hips.

"Sweet heaven," he muttered when she stood there so still, all peaked pink delicacy in just a small pair of lacy peach underwear. Max pressed his face to the smooth round curve of her stomach and closed his eyes as he swept Robbie's brave new feminine indulgence away. He felt her arms come around his shoulders and her fingers run deeply through his hair.

"Ah, love, you smell of lemons and springtime and hope," he breathed against her skin, and cupped her soft bottom in his hands. "I don't want you to be afraid, but it's been so long, sweetheart, and I'm not sure how smoothly the great Maximillian Wolfe will be able to perform."

"Max," Robbie said tenderly, pushing his head back with her hands still tangled in his hair. "Knowing that just makes it more perfect. Don't you see? I feel like this is new for both of us. Just love me, husband. We have so much time to make up for and I don't want to waste another minute."

Before she could even think to squeak, Max lifted Robbie in his arms and rolled her onto the bed and under him. Her eyes were huge as he shifted and tugged the sheet away, then settled into the cradle of her thighs. With his forearms tucked alongside her, he leaned down and lightly nipped at her bottom lip. "So you think we've been wasting time?"

He kissed her again and her mouth opened immediately, her arms coming tight around his back and her body lifting against him. Deep, wet kisses sent them both soaring, and he nearly lost himself when she purred and sighed at the magic his hands worked on her body. Her legs shifted restlessly, and Max licked her lips and then drew them into his mouth, sucking the tender flesh until she struggled and whispered raggedly, "More, Max. Please show me—show me now."

And he did. For a moment he felt the proof of her innocence and felt her instinctive withdrawal, but he framed her face with his hands and looked into her uncertain eyes and kissed her gently. "Be brave, now, little tiger. I love you so much."

And in one powerful move she was his and he was hers. The bond was sealed, the barrier broken, and slowly he felt the breath she'd been holding seep away. Her body relaxed and her palms once more pressed flat against his back. Roberta opened her eyes and smiled and Max began to move.

His eyes unflinchingly held her gaze, just as her body unflinchingly held his. Soul-deep looks of love took the place of kisses, and soul-deep touches wiped away all the pain and called up a wild, yearning need Roberta had never dreamed of. Faster and faster he urged her on until the feelings became flashes of glittery sensation. The scent of warm sandalwood and warm male skin surrounded her. Max loved her. Max lifted her. Max hurled her up to the stars, and Roberta shattered into a thousand silver shards.

"Nothing can part us now, love. Sleep," Max whispered, drifting on a wave of sweet satisfaction with the greatest treasure he'd ever won snug in his arms. The dice had finally turned to gold in his hands, but a hazy, niggling detail hovered in his exhausted mind. There was something he'd forgotten. What . . . ? Later. Later he'd remember.

A dull but insistent sound finally pulled Roberta out of her delicious, love-induced sleep. Max had his arms wrapped around her and she suddenly felt ridiculously shy about being naked in bed with a naked man in what had to be the middle of the day. She blinked her bleary eyes and ran her gaze over her husband's beloved face. He did indeed look like a pirate, all dark slashing brows, dark bristling whiskers, and, of course, his black eye. The man made her heart flip-flop and her stomach clench, and just watching him sleep triggered a few scorching flashbacks.

Roberta blew out a deep breath that ruffled her bangs. What would Max think if she woke him by—

A soft series of knocks jolted her awareness and abruptly fixed the sound that had woken her. Someone was at the door. That was what she'd heard. Roberta snagged the T-shirt Max had given her out of a dresser drawer and yanked it on as she scrambled to answer the rumble. How embarrassing, but she supposed that in such a romantic setting the hotel staff had seen pretty much every behavior under the sun.

She went up on tiptoe to spy through the peephole. Nothing. Maybe it had been her imagination. Roberta cracked the door and shot a quick look out into the hall. There, on the sandy-colored carpet in front of their door, was a beautiful basket tied with clear cellophane and a big purple bow.

Roberta finger-combed her hair into a semblance of order, cautiously leaned into view, and snatched the surprise. By the time she dashed back inside and shut the door, Max was standing at the bathroom door with a towel around his waist.

"What is it, *chère?*"

"I don't know," Roberta answered, setting the gift on the desk and working at the ribbons. "It looks like a goody basket. Rolls, juice, fruit." She turned her head and smiled at her sexy husband. "Oh, Max, did you think of this? I mean you must have known we'd be starving and . . ." Roberta stumbled off into silence and rolled her lips together.

Max threw back his head and laughed, then walked slowly toward her, deliberately letting his towel slip lower and lower with each step. "I was feeling worn down. But seeing you in my T-shirt has given me a surge of strength." Max reached out and rubbed his knuckles over the tip of Roberta's breasts and felt a jolt of pure desire run from his body into hers.

Max loved the way she responded to him: so quickly, so

freely. He bent over and pressed his lips to the side of her neck and then whispered, "I think I have just enough strength left for one more—"

"Wait! Wait!" Roberta choked, swaying backward and waving a card. "Let me read it." She tore open the envelope and held up a hand palm-out to halt her heavily breathing husband. *Much happiness, Miss Roberta. You see, love is all the magic you need.* "Oh, Max, it's from Lucinda, the woman you had the hotel send to fix my hair and all. How sweet."

Roberta picked up a big blueberry muffin and took a bite, while Max reached for the card and read it again. Hmmm. Hadn't he asked for Monica? And he was pretty sure he hadn't mentioned their marriage, either. But maybe when they'd returned early this morning, somebody had guessed. He'd have to thank the woman, whoever it had been. Max smiled and tucked the towel a bit more securely around his waist.

Yes, he'd definitely have to thank her, for as he turned his attention back to his little wife and watched her face grow rapturous over her muffin, Max grew a tad rapturous himself. He moved closer and captured Robbie's hand and carried her treat to his mouth for a bite.

"I think refueling is a very good idea, *chère*. First we eat, then we shower, then we practice? Until Prince or Henson calls we might as well enjoy our honeymoon." Roberta gave Max a saucy wink and in a few quick moves she had a good portion of Lucinda's thoughtful gift spread before them. She swung out a chair next to the desk and waved Max into it with a flourish. "Eat fast."

Two very satisfying and informative hours later, Roberta rested drowsily against Max, her head pillowed on his shoulder. The air conditioner filled the air with a low, comforting hum, and the late-afternoon sun reached through the balcony glass and bathed the room in a soft, mellow light. Pushed way to the back of her mind was a

331

simmering slew of worries and what-ifs she was trying to ignore. Roberta gave them another nudge and snuggled closer to her husband, rubbing her face over the silky hair covering hard muscle and breathing deeply of sandalwood and Max. Soon it would all have to be dealt with. But right now she needed a little more happiness to offset what was coming. She needed to laugh and love. She needed to dream.

"Max, whatever happened to your wine? Your dream of vineyards? Or has swimming with the sharks driven it out of you?"

Max shifted, rolling Roberta onto her back and propping his head up on his hand. "You remembered."

"Max," she said solemnly, resting her palm over his heart. "I remember everything."

A loud, blaring *brrring* shattered the moment, and Roberta swung her head to the phone screaming from the desk. Max caught her chin between his thumb and index finger and pulled her face to his. "We're together now, *chère*. We can do this." He dropped a quick kiss on her mouth and rolled to his feet, striding to the insistent ring.

"Hello . . . Yes, it's Max. . . . Wait, listen, Prince! . . . Yes she's here. . . . We're married. . . . Roberta, of course . . . Dammit, man! Shut up and listen."

Roberta crawled to her knees on the bed, hands clasped, praying her brother would calm down and believe her husband. As succinctly as possible Max outlined what Helen Chalmers had done to Roberta and what she was trying to do to Prince. He slumped in the chair and rested his forehead in his hands while Prince responded. Roberta felt as if she were sitting on a mattress made of nails. She had to know what was happening. She scooted off the bed and Max turned to her, holding out the phone.

"Prince and Cindy are okay, sweetheart. But we've got a problem with your grandmother. Prince and his wife have just gotten home from bailing out some other people your grandmother has involved, Cain Devlin and Belinda

Brown, but Helen was gone, love. Your brother said Ms. Brown had confronted Helen about framing Devlin and when Prince confronted her, too, she'd admitted she tried to get rid of the man. They'd left her to go to the police station and somehow she sneaked out of the house unseen. Now Prince is afraid she may have gone to the office to destroy any lingering evidence and that she may hear our message. He's going to start tracing her right now, but he wants you to be prepared. She could come here, and if that happens he wants us to try to stop her."

Reality crash-landed with deadly accuracy.

She stared into Max's concerned, caring gaze and took the receiver. "Prince?"

"Rob, honey. I don't know what to say. Everything has gone crazy. Are you all right? Have you really married Wolfe?"

"I'm as fine as can be expected, I suppose, and yes, we're married. We've never stopped loving each other, Prince."

"I have to believe that, if I believe what Max just told me. And God help us, honey, between him, Belinda, Cain, and Grandmother herself, I have to. But, dammit, it's just so hard to wade through all the confusion. As soon as I know what Grandmother's doing I'll call. If she's heading for St. Thomas, Cindy and I will follow as soon as possible. Just sit tight and follow the instructions I gave Max. I'll be in touch. She needs real help, sis."

"I know. Just think how many years it's been since Cain's accident. Oh, Prince, she caused all the trouble between the two of you, didn't she?"

"Yes, honey. But he and I are going to straighten it out. I'm not going to let her sickness hurt the people I care about ever again. If she's really on her way to the island, I believe there's an excellent doctor in residence who might be able to help us until we can get her back to California. I'll do some checking, but hang in there, Robbie. I love you. Wait for my call."

"I love you, too."

Max waited for Robbie to continue, but she just sat there hunched up on the end of the bed. He got to his feet and went down on his haunches in front of his heavy-hearted little tiger. Max could almost feel the weight of the worries piling up on those narrow shoulders. She needed some tender loving care and a good block of uninterrupted sleep. Both of which he could and would provide.

"Robbie, if it helps, I know a little of what you're going through right now. I know how it feels to discover that someone who loves you can also do things to hurt you. My father wanted to help my mother so badly that he never stopped to consider the long-term effects of his stealing. It's even possible the extra stress played a large part in triggering his heart attack. Sometimes love gets twisted, *chère*. Sometimes people become so desperate they lose all sense of reality."

She heaved a shuddering sigh and cupped his cheek in her small palm. "It more than helps, Max. You see inside me and understand. No matter how hard this is, I don't feel alone. I love you."

"Come, *chère*. Come let me love away some of this sadness." He rubbed a fingertip over her lips and brushed the tumble of short copper curls back from her face. Slowly he got to his feet and tugged her with him, deftly maneuvering them both back under the sheet. Max tossed away his towel and turned his wife toward him, trailing his fingers over her smooth thighs as he caught the edge of his T-shirt and pulled it up over her head.

Her wide, solemn eyes held his as he drew his thumb over one creamy cheek, down her small nose, and then up the long line of her neck.

"Now, my little redheaded Roberta Hood Chalmers Wolfe, I thought you were opposed to wasting such precious time."

"You're right, Max." She sighed again. "I just wish happily ever after wasn't so hard to hold on to."

"Ah, *chère*," Max growled, wiggling his eyebrows and

resting his chest gently on hers. "I think I can prove that wrong if you'll just let me."

"Oh, Max," she sputtered with a weak laugh. "You're such an irresistible wolf." Her genuine smile was like a ray of sun breaking through a stormy sky.

"All the better to make you happy, my dear."

"Max!" She gasped, her hands flying to his shoulders. "Have you ever thought about our names—our names together? It's so weird and I never realized it until this minute. Little Red Riding Hood and the—"

"Oh, ho," Max scoffed, nudging her legs apart and settling himself onto the woman he loved so desperately, wanting more than anything else to chase away the sadness for a little while longer. "Are you implying that *I* am the big bad wolf?"

"Well . . ." she teased, dragging her hands down his back and lower.

"If that is so, sweetheart, I will happily huff and puff . . . if you will let me come in."

"Max!" she snickered, slapping at a very sensitive part of his anatomy. "Besides, you've got the wrong story and the wrong wolf. Little Red Riding Hood is the 'what a big something you have' version, you know." Max flexed against her and Roberta's laugh hitched and stuttered.

"Ah, yes. That will work just as well, will it not?" Max murmured, his mouth hovering above hers just as his body was. With his one smooth move to her breathless sigh, he brought them together and took her soft mouth in a long, ravenous kiss. Max managed to lift his head for a moment, and Roberta's happy, shining eyes warmed his heart.

"Now, my very own fairy-tale authority, tell me. Isn't my line *'All the better to love you with, my dear'*?"

Max had never before heard a woman giggle and moan at the same time, but his woman was magic.

Part Four

"Happily Ever After"

Chapter One

The call from Prince came early Friday morning. Helen was indeed on her way to St. Thomas. And two, almost unbelievable strokes of good luck had given them the information. First, a longtime family friend, Mabel Anderson, had called Prince Thursday afternoon to report an odd visit from Helen. His grandmother had exuded an almost brittle happiness and then asked Mabel if she could use the Anderson home on St. Thomas for a week or so. Mabel had agreed, but as Helen was leaving, she'd sighed and added how good it would be to get away with the children. Mrs. Anderson had stewed for a couple hours and then called Prince worried about Helen's state of mind.

So, they'd known where she was probably headed, but not when. That was lucky stroke number two.

Prince got a call from the L.A. airport about a lost bottle of medication, and after a few more questions he'd had a flight number. But he'd remarked to Roberta on the phone how strange it was that their grandmother would have been carrying those pills in her purse. Normally she locked all such items in a special bag.

Whatever the reason, that one mistake had given Prince Helen's arrival time and set everything in motion at the airport. Roberta shifted uncomfortably on the hard plastic chair, and Max sympathetically reached over to squeeze her hand. Any minute now her grandmother would be walking down the converse, and Robbie didn't know what to expect. Prince had told her to play along with whatever flight of fancy Helen displayed. She was to stall for just a little while since, barring any unseen calamities, he and Cindy would be only an hour behind her.

"Oh, gosh, Max. There she is."

The diminutive white-haired woman stopped in the middle of a human river and looked around as if she couldn't imagine how she'd arrived at that particular spot. The red-and-gold Caribbean sunset streamed through the long walls of windows, painting a gorgeous, postcard-perfect welcome to paradise. Roberta bit her lip and rubbed her hands on the soft cotton of her culottes. She couldn't help thinking that paradise had a very poor track record with snakes.

"Are you okay, love?" Max said quietly, close to her ear.

"Let's just get it over with." Roberta forced a sliver of a smile. "Hold my hand?"

"Forever, *mon amour.*"

Most of the living wave had trickled away, and Roberta and Max started to walk up behind Helen Chalmers. Max tightened his fingers around the small ones that had begun to tremble and noticed a mismatched pair of men stop and speak to Helen as if asking for directions. In seconds, she waved them off and turned unexpectedly, coming face-to-face with him and Robbie.

"Why, Roberta. You're already here. How wonderful. Where's your brother?"

Max caught his wife's stunned gaze and squeezed again. She nodded imperceptibly and stumbled into a response.

"Prince will be here soon, Grandmother. Let's go sit down and wait a minute. Okay?"

"I need my bags first, dear. I can't relax until I have my bags."

Robbie shot Max a pleading look and he pointed a finger at himself and then down the wide walkway toward the baggage claim. Helen hadn't looked at him once, and he knew his wife was growing increasingly more anxious at her grandmother's bizarre behavior. He tried to pull away, but Roberta wouldn't let him go. Max held up his free hand curled into a fist and silently counted off his five digits. He tugged again and she released him, then steered Helen over to a row of molded chairs.

It took fifteen minutes to get Helen's bags. Moving at a double-time pace, with a good-size suitcase swinging from each hand, Max could feel the muscles pull across his arms and back. His shirtsleeves were rolled up, and he ate up the ground with long, determined strides. Robbie was a strong, smart lady, but Max knew only too well how difficult it was to deal with the onslaught of emotions that came when a child was suddenly catapulted to the role of parent.

He dodged and wove through a maze of people and halted abruptly at the empty chairs. Max whirled around. There wasn't one green-and-white-striped shirt in sight. Not one. *Mon Dieu!* The bags dropped like lead weights.

They were gone.

Forty-five minutes later Max was a raving wild man. No one knew it, of course, but his fuse was short and burning fast. He was ready to explode. For the first few minutes he'd tried to talk himself into believing the women had just gone to the bathroom or to get something to eat. Fool! Max sat on the low edge of a planter, uncharacteristically rubbing his hands up and down his stonewashed jeans. Earlier that morning Robbie had insisted on giving him a new look, too, and he'd been willing to do just about anything to distract her. Now he stared at his Reeboks and felt a sick wave of fear roll through his twisting insides. Where the hell was Prince?

Oh, how his business rivals would love to see him now, the unemotional, bottom-line Maximilliar Wolfe, refusing to face the hard, cold facts. Helen Chalmers might be delusionary, but she had more than proven she was coherent enough to be dangerous. Damn him for not hedging every bet. Damn him for not keeping Robbie with him every second, and damn him for not insisting his wife tell him where the Andersons' villa was. He checked his watch for the hundredth time and honed in on the gate Prince and Cindy would be coming through.

And after twenty more minutes, when they did, Max cornered his prey like a real wolf, almost growling out the turn of events. Helen had indeed arrived over an hour ago, and then disappeared with Robbie.

He didn't know how he looked, but it must have been bad because Prince told him to hold on until he could find them a private spot and then insisted he sit next to Cindy. Prince's beautiful wife patted his clenched hand and introduced him to Belinda Brown and Cain Devlin. Max tuned in enough to realize the huge man with the scars across his left cheek was the one Helen Chalmers's sick meddling had almost killed. Robbie had filled him in on her brother's friendship with Devlin and the mysterious explosion five years ago that had ended it.

Cain's pretty companion, Belinda, had a calm but determined look on her face and a firm grip on the man's hand. As upset as he was, Max could see the bond between the two of them and it made his anxiety and longing for Robbie even greater. Helen Chalmers was probably bombarding his love with every bit of garbage she had. Every slip he'd ever made. Every detail of his life that she could twist to her advantage. Max felt an icy chill shoot up his spine. *The money.* Dammit! That was the detail he'd forgotten. Hell.

Prince suddenly rounded a corner and motioned for them to come. In seconds he'd ushered them into a small employee lounge and shut the door.

"All right," Prince said, running a hand through his hair as he sat on the corner of a table. "Have introductions been made?"

"Yes, sweetie," Cindy answered with a nod and an encouraging smile.

The flow of love between Prince and Cindy was all but visible, and Max was reminded again of what he, too, had and what might yet be lost. His belly cramped. If Helen had told Robbie about the money, what could his love be thinking? Max closed his eyes and rubbed the bridge of his nose. They loved each other. He knew it was real, but he hadn't told her the complete truth and Roberta could be hurt by more of her grandmother's lies. Again. God! Pain rolled in his gut like broken glass. How deep had her forgiveness gone? How much did she trust their love? Had he shown Robbie enough of his heart for her to believe? Believe as he'd hoped for days ago when he'd remembered his mother's fairy tales of undaunted heroes?

"Max?" Prince waved a hand in front of Max's face. "Look, I've never seen you this way, Wolfe. Maybe you'd better explain what happened to your eye."

Max shrugged, barely able to sit still. "It has nothing to do with Helen. Frank Henson and I had a difficult introduction a few days ago."

"What!" Prince barked, jumping to his feet. Then he shook his head and raised a hand, palm up. "No, wait, you can explain that in the car. Right now I need to know if you're going to be okay. We've got to get out to the Andersons' and we all have to be under control."

Max clamped down on his fear and spoke through clenched teeth. "Sorry. I'm fine. Let's go."

"Prince, do you want Belinda and me to wait here?"

Cain Devlin's voice rumbled the question, and Max looked briefly into his laserlike gaze. He could tell at a glance that he and Devlin were of the same mind, as was Prince. The shadows of past battles echoed from the eyes of one man to another, and Max knew he would have all the support he needed.

"No, Cain, everyone needs to be there. I even took a chance on finding Frank at the Smythes' and called just before I arranged for this room. He's bringing the other destructive contingency. I think we might as well face the

343

whole ugly mess at one time and get it the hell over with."

"What are we waiting for, then?" Max thundered, striding to the door and pulling it open. "Let's go."

Ten minutes later they were riding up a narrow, winding road away from Charlotte Amalie and toward a final reckoning.

"Roberta, dear. I'm coming in. Please behave yourself or I'll have to call Mr. Bart."

Roberta sat on a leather wing chair in the Andersons' faithful reproduction of a turn-of-the-century English library. She'd been pacing and pounding for the better part of two hours and this was her grandmother's first response. Anyone's first response. Roberta wrapped her hands around her knees and drew in two deep breaths. She needed to stay calm just a little longer. Surely Prince had arrived by now and any minute he and Max would be here. Mercy, her husband was probably furious. Even more so because she'd put off his request for directions to the Andersons' very private residence.

The lock clicked into place and her grandmother stepped into the room. "Turn on a light, dear, it's too dark."

Roberta reached for the unusual lamp on the small mahogany table next to her. Within minutes of being incarcerated in the library, Roberta had started searching for a phone and noticed the brass base that looked exactly like her idea of Aladdin's magic lamp. It was the one bit of whimsy in the otherwise traditional decor. As her fingers felt for the switch in the semidarkness, she ran them over the cool metal, spinning a fanciful scenario about her next three wishes being granted.

Now, dearie, love is all the magic you need. . . .

Roberta's heart jumped into her throat and she swallowed hard, her hand trembling on the lamp. It was impossible that a voice almost like Lucinda's had just whispered through the murky darkness. She gulped a breath of air and flicked the button. It had to be her over-stressed subconscious, but somehow Roberta felt less alone.

"Good, now I can see you. I just wanted to tell you I'll be leaving for a while, Roberta. I need to take care of a few things, but Mr. Bart and his friend will be here, dear. So please act like a lady even though your attire is far too casual. We'll have to fix that later."

Roberta had the distinct impression that her grandmother was going to the Smythes'. Darn, she had to stall until her knights in shining armor arrived.

"Oh, Grandmother, please don't go yet. I wish you'd stay and talk to me first."

Unbelievably, Helen instantly sat down on the matching wing chair. "What is it, Roberta?"

Robbie covered her surprise by planting her sandaled feet on the floor and scooting to the edge of her seat, hands clasped. "Prince and I are both adults, Grandmother. We are both capable of making the right choices. We're both married and there's nothing you can do to change that."

Helen blinked and clutched at the purse resting in her lap. "Nonsense, Roberta. You and Prince aren't nearly ready for that and I must do what I think is best."

The unfocused look in her grandmother's eyes was eerie and frightening. Roberta had to try to make her see reality. "Oh, Grandma," she mumbled under her breath. "I wish I could get through to you for just a few minutes." She cleared her throat and tried again. "Grandmother, I know all about your plot to ruin Prince's wedding. I know what you did to me and Maximillian Wolfe and I'm beginning to put your hatred of Cain Devlin into the picture, too. What in the world were you thinking?"

Helen cocked her head, and Roberta swore she could see the awareness come back into blue eyes the exact shade of her brother's.

"When Prince got involved with that Devlin, I knew something had to be done. They wanted to change so many things your grandfather had started. I couldn't let that happen, dear. Don't you see? And once I fixed that, then you got mixed up with a foreign gigolo. I couldn't understand a man like that being interested in you, Roberta. But then I discovered what his father had done, and I knew why Wolfe was paying court. He wanted a good marriage to get the money he needed, and I had to set him straight. You can understand that, can't you? And then Prince completely lost his common sense by falling for that common woman. She would never have made him a proper wife. Prince needs someone with society polish."

"Like Milicent Smythe?" Roberta gritted out.

"Why, yes. You must encourage your brother to see her again, dear."

"Grandmother, Prince is already married to Cindy and I am married to Max. There is nothing, nothing you can do to stop it. Even your attempt to blame Cain Devlin has backfired. In fact, any minute Prince and Max will be here." Roberta slumped back against the smooth leather and plopped her hands on the armrests. "Mercy, but I wish they'd heard this whole crazy conversation."

"We did, *chère*."

For a second Roberta's head spun, and she felt as if her heart had stopped beating in her chest. Then her dark and dangerous husband stepped through the partially open door, followed by her battle-ready brother.

Roberta was so distracted she hadn't even noticed her grandmother's reaction. Suddenly Helen shrieked and scrambled to her feet, backing away.

"Maximillian, I warned you never to see Roberta again. How dare you! You'll be sorry—you know what I can do."

The frantic old woman snapped open her purse, and Max instantly crossed the room, shoving Robbie behind his body. Max could feel her arms slip around his waist and her soft breasts press close. Her beloved and beguiling lemony scent soothed his raw emotions, and for the first time in almost three hours, the beating of his heart throttled down to a tolerable pace.

"No, Helen. My mother is dead and my father's debt has been more than paid in full. There is nothing you can do to keep Roberta and me apart. You have lost on every front, Mrs. Chalmers."

"Max is right, Grandmother," Prince said, walking slowly toward her. "Cindy and I are both here and Cain Devlin is waiting in the living room. In fact our partnership may still be possible even after all these years . . . and all the tears. You should have trusted us, Grandmother."

"No, no! You're wrong. You'll see. I do have something. I do!" Helen's jeweled fingers flashed in the lamplight as she dug frantically through her purse. Her eyes were glazed, all the carefully made up lines in her face becoming clearly visible as if the paint had come off a once-shattered spot.

Max lifted a hand and wrapped it around one of Robbie's. Helen was too insistent for this to be a ruse. She was so close to cracking that she wouldn't even be able to reason through such a plan. It had to be something to do with the money. *Mon Dieu*, he didn't have a moment to prepare Roberta. A strangling mix of fear and dread climbed his throat. No! He tightened his hold on his wife's hand. No. If their love was truly strong enough this would not do a drop of damage.

"Yes! I knew it was here," Helen cackled with childish glee. "Did you know you're betrothed was bought off, Roberta? This is the proof that all he wanted was money, you foolish girl. I've kept this canceled check just in case I had to show you exactly how much you were worth to him."

Helen tossed the small square of creased paper and it floated close to Max's feet. He took Robbie's hands from his waist and bent down to pick it up. Without looking, he handed it to his wife.

Max heard a soft inhalation behind him and saw Prince step toward Helen and take her by the arm. He flexed his hand hanging at his side, then slid it into his pants pocket for his wallet. Max's felt his mouth press into a thin line and his gaze grow hooded and hard. The three others in the room were utterly still as he reached inside the hand-crafted leather and pulled out a gold key. Only then did he turn and face Robbie.

"Robbie, I—"

"Wait, Max. My grandmother made you take the check and cash it, didn't she?" Max nodded and he heard Helen moan. "She wanted one more tangible way to hurt me and keep us apart. You don't have to say another word about it. I love you, Maximillian Wolfe, and I trust you completely."

Max closed his eyes and then opened them, pouring his love into a brilliant smile while wrapping an arm around Robbie. He tugged her close, vaguely aware of Helen whimpering, "Nooo, Roberta," and slumping in tears against Prince's hold.

Max held up the key so Prince could see it and then placed it in Roberta's hand.

"That wouldn't be gold, would it, my new brother-in-law?"

Max smiled and nodded.

"Well, Robbie," Prince conceded with a bittersweet smile, "you shouldn't have to wait a moment longer to hear about this mysterious gift. You can tell me all about it and your lovely . . . transformation later. I can't deny I'm incredibly curious about both. You're beautiful, honey. I glad you've finally seen it."

Roberta looked into her brother's eyes while sending a silent message of thanks, he gently picked up the old woman who'd done so much to hurt them in the name of love.

"You two take a few minutes, but only that," Prince finished. "I'm sorry, but I left Belinda calling Dr. Clark's sanitarium about our emergency, and Cindy drilling Milicent and Barbara. She's insisting they either follow her and Lilith's example or go cool their heels in Switzerland. All hell has probably broken loose down there and we're going to need the two of you to help sort everything out."

"Oh, Prince," Roberta whispered.

"I know, sis. Don't worry, Grandmother will get the best possible care and we'll see her tomorrow."

As Prince quietly shut the door Roberta burrowed her head beneath her husband's chin and pressed her palms flat against his strong, wide back, breathing in the unique blend of warm Max and sandalwood.

"Oh, Max, I can hardly believe this. And I'm sorry I didn't tell you where the darn house was. But who would have guessed my grandmother would bring her own thugs along and snatch me from the airport? It happened so fast that I didn't even have the presence of mind to scream or anything. Wouldn't you know, my first real dangerous encounter and I didn't have my pepper spray."

Roberta paused. Was Max shaking? "Sweetheart," she questioned softly, lifting her head and studying his dark, turbulent eyes. "Do you mind if we sit down a minute?" In one abrupt move, Max collapsed onto a wing chair, bringing Roberta with him.

"Dammit, I knew something wasn't right when I saw those Neanderthals speaking to Helen. Forgive me, *chère*," Max implored, his eyes still burning with self-recrimination. He kissed Robbie's cheek and ran one hand up to her neck, tangling the other one with hers resting in her lap. "*Mon Dieu,* I must thank Cain for dealing both those bastards a telling blow when we first arrived. I suspect his lady, Ms. Brown, has been manhandled by those scum, too."

"Mercy, Max! Prince was right," Roberta exclaimed, sitting up and facing him. "Things sound like a madhouse out there."

"And they probably will for some time, so let me tell you about the key and then we'll face the storm together."

Roberta smiled and opened her hand. Max lightly traced a fingertip over the precious metal infinitely less valuable than the precious woman who held it.

"You were right, *mon amour*. Helen did contrive the perfect way to make it look as if I had been bought off. I was tormented for weeks thinking of what to do. If nothing else, I'd planned to send it back to you on her death."

Roberta felt one lone tear track down her cheek, but she didn't drop her gaze from the beautiful, anguished eyes of her love.

"Then I had a crazy idea. It made no sense, yet in my heart I felt it was the right thing to do. I bought a home and some vineyards—

"No, sweetheart. I didn't use your grandmother's money for that. But I needed someplace to make my idea a reality, and the vineyards helped me feel that all was not completely lost. Somehow, I think, I believed that if I could bring my dream and your dream together . . . Well." He paused and raked a hand through his hair.

"Some days, Robbie, the only thing that kept me breathing was seeing our dreams together, empty and hopeless as they were. Some days I would take your key and open the door and step into the painting loft I had built for you when I remodeled my lonely house. In some indefinable way, the bittersweet hope I found there would keep me sane for another few weeks."

The tears fell unchecked now, and Roberta brushed them away, then leaned forward to tenderly press her lips to his.

"Max, I love you so much. And as soon as we can I want to go to *our* house and love away every inch of loneliness and fill every ounce of emptiness with babies and wine and color and happiness."

"Ah, my love," Max murmured, smoothing a thumb over her damp cheek and cradling her back into the curve of his shoulder. "Surely the heavens are smiling. For us the dream begins now. No more loneliness. No more emptiness in the night without loving arms to fill it. No magic imaginings could ever be better than this."

Max covered her mouth with his and Roberta felt that new, delicious quickening catch fire deep inside. Warm, grateful passes of silky lips quickly became the hot, needy kisses of soul-deep relief. Max urged her to open to him and she did, welcoming the insistent slide of his tongue and meeting his intimate demand. For now it was as close as they could be, and both desperately needed the feel, the taste, the reality of what they had fought for and won.

Then, over the thundering in Roberta's heart, she thought she heard a distant voice flavored with a breath of island dialect and overflowing with happiness.

Ah, my dears. Never again alone. Never again apart. Love is the only magic that heals the heart. . . .

And Roberta knew they had found the greatest truth of all.

Epilogue

"Fern, I'm warning you. This is highly irregular. You've already pushed this assignment over the line. Or should I call you Lucinda?"

"Hush up, Esmerelda! I can't hear."

Fern Tatiana Goodwin held a finger to her lips and shushed her stern companion sent by the Fairy Godmother High Council. While it was more than possible that she had stepped close to a line or two, she wasn't about to leave . . . yet. Their invisible floating perch in the far corner of the Andersons' elegant living room was completely undetected by the people gathering below.

A short time ago, when Milicent arrived and began raving at Cindy, Belinda, and Lilith, the waves of emotion were so strong Esmerelda had almost zapped the whole lot of them into frogs. Luckily Fern, who had adapted her instincts to modern times, managed to calm her archaic companion. Besides, Cindy took care of the problem beautifully. Esmerelda had clearly been working on the administrative level too long. She'd completely forgotten the thrilling ups and downs of helping a life-tale come together.

Fern sneaked a peek at the tall, spare, bespeckled fairy and sighed with a shake of her head. Yes, it was true that she had been discouraged before her girls popped onto the scene, but Esme didn't even seem to think like a fairy godmother anymore.

"Listen, Esmerelda, my girls and their heroes have all

come through in the finest tradition. But I just want to make sure every loose end is tied up neat and tidy."

Esmerelda pursed her lips and harrumped disapprovingly. "Fern, the high council sent me to officially notify you of your nomination for Fairy Godmother of the Year and to give you your next assignment."

"Thorns and brambles, give me five more minutes! This is practically the best part."

Fern paused and drew in a sharp breath when the doors opened and Roberta and Max entered the room. Cindy jumped right up, oohing and ahhing her way to Robbie's side.

"Oh, Roberta, sweetie," Cindy said, giving her sister-in-law a big hug. "I'm so sorry about Helen, but we'll get through this, you'll see. Loving Max will help so much. In fact I can already see some wonderful side effects. You look beautiful."

"You really do, Rob," Frank added, he and Lilith joining the two women.

Fern elbowed Esmerelda. "Those two have learned so much, they don't even care they're still wearing wet, wrinkled clothes."

"Fern, come on now."

"Are you kidding? I've got to see how Max and Frank handle this." Fern eyeballed her insistent emissary and fisted her hands on her ample hips. "Esme, these life-tales have been tangled right from the start, and after almost blinking myself into a whiplash, I finally know why." Fern waved her hand in a wide arc. "The people in this room were meant to be friends. They were meant to love each other and help each other, but things got twisted and hearts were hurt and I have to be sure that any lingering ill will is well on its way to being mended. Why do you think I held off dealing with Helen Chalmers? I needed to get them all together to see how they'd react. Now watch this."

Roberta laid a hand on Frank's arm. "Thanks, Frank.

And by the way, the new me likes seeing a little of the *old* you, too," she quipped, flashing a knowing smile.

"Are you sure that's Frank?" Prince called out with mock innocence.

Frank raised an eyebrow, dipping his head in acknowledgment, and then turned to Max. "Listen, Wolfe, I'm sorry I came on so strong. At the time there was too much I didn't know. How's the eye?"

"It's a small price to pay for so much. Don't give it another thought."

Fern tapped a finger on her chin. Lilith needed to clear the air with Max also, but she was hanging back. Of course magic could fix things immediately, except Fern had learned that a quick fix often fell apart down the road. In the old days if things got a tad too violent or iffy, fairy godmothers sometimes waved their wands a bit prematurely, finishing with a big splash of magic—dragon-slaying and such. But mortals frequently lost the vision of their life-tale when living settled down to normal.

Truthfully, in the last hundred years or so, Fern had found that humans who worked out their own solutions held on to happiness much longer because they had paid such a price to win it.

So, Fern patted the wand secured in her iridescent sash. She did not reach for any fairy dust, but she did cross her fingers and smile when Max spoke.

"Why, Lilith, great new casual look," he teased in a cautious tentative tone, one arm snug around Roberta.

"Yes, well." She paused, glancing up at Frank and smiling when he winked at her. "My taste has changed a lot lately. I've kind of come out of my designer cocoon. You look a bit less . . . structured, too."

"You're right," he conceded with a wry grin. "I'm going to be a winegrower, and these clothes are just perfect."

Lilith glanced at Roberta and sighed. "Max, I was wrong about you and I'm sorry."

Max lifted his free hand and rested it on her shoulder.

"I was wrong about you, too. But that's good for both of us. I'll always be grateful that you cared enough about Cindy to get involved. If you hadn't pointed the finger at me, I might never have had a second chance with Robbie."

"See, Lil," Cindy said, giving her stepsister's hand a squeeze. "Max and Roberta, I'm afraid you missed an ugly scene with Milicent and Barbara. They've pretty much disowned me and Lilith, but we're going to stick together, aren't we, sis?" Cindy looked at Lilith, and the gorgeous ex-model hesitated, then smiled, and smiled even more confidently when Frank tucked her close to his body.

Cindy turned back to Max and Roberta. "Lilith's been worried that her confession at the wedding reception started this whole thing."

"I'm still shocked and hurting over my grandmother, Lilith," Roberta said. "But what you did also brought Max back into my life. And I've learned that sometimes, something really wonderful can come out of pain. Max is my silver lining in this storm. Thank you."

"And I might have never met my silver lining without this storm, either," Cain Devlin called out from his place on the period sofa next to a huge, marble-faced hearth. "I might never have known that Prince was still my friend."

The couples near the door moved closer to the ones sitting, and Belinda laid one hand on Cain's thigh and smoothed the other down his queue.

"I can't help feeling terrible for the heartache Milicent and Helen caused for so many of you, but if good coming from bad counts for anything, I think we've got a lot to be happy about. I know I do."

"Are you referring to me, my beauty, or getting rid of those gray sweats?" Cain murmured, leaning close to Belinda's ear and triggering a suggestive laugh that rippled through the room.

Fern was pleased as punch to see the man so open with this group of people. Love and friendship were going to completely change his life. She fisted her hand and pumped her arm once in the air, pointedly ignoring Esmerelda's prune-faced reaction. Instead she concentrated on Prince.

"Belinda, my friend, you are most certainly right," he agreed, getting to his feet and walking toward Cindy, standing near the mahogany mantel. "We do indeed have a lot to be happy about, but I think I have an idea that will give us a chance to relax and actually enjoy that happiness."

"What?"

"Prince, come on, tell."

"What are you thinking?"

The seven voices spoke and sputtered at once until Prince waved all of them except himself and his wife, to a seat.

"Okay, Esme, dear," Fern whispered, trying very hard to disguise her reverse psychology. "We can leave now."

"Wha-what?" The sober-faced fairy watched the mortals with rapt attention, and Fern knew her quarry was hooked and ready to reel in. Prince was just too sweet, and Esme was about to see it up close and personal. Once you remembered how wonderful it felt to help humans . . . well, it was mighty hard to resist.

"We want to thank you all for caring so much by giving a very special gift." Prince hesitated and took Cindy's hand. "We want you all to stay on the island and honeymoon with us."

Cindy laughed at the stunned silence. "Prince and I never really got ours started, so we're staying for sure."

"Of course," Prince continued, "that means we need to get some of you married, since it was my fault—"

"Hell yes," Cain interrupted, tugging Belinda to her feet. "I'm not sleeping in another bed until this woman is right beside me and legally mine."

"Cain!" Belinda blushed.

"That's how I feel about it, too," Frank added. "Let's go get married so the honeymoon can begin."

"But isn't it too late tonight?" Lilith offered, tugging at the drooping neckline of her dress.

"Forget it, woman," Frank countered. "You're not taking the muumuu off until we're married."

Max ran a knuckle along the edge of his mustache and Roberta nudged him hard. "Max knows how to arrange it. We got married even later than this."

"Wolfe!" cried the male chorus.

"Fine, gentlemen. Let me make a call and then we can be on our way."

"Wonderful," Cindy bubbled. "Just think, ladies, we can sightsee and shop and . . ."

Prince's mouth dropped open and he abruptly swept up his squealing wife. "Dinner in three days?" he asked, shooting a quick look at each man.

"Three days just might be enough," Max answered with such a serious expression on his face that Frank and Cain burst into gales of laughter. Soon everyone else joined in . . . and the laughter held soul-deep healing. Love and friendship were here to stay.

Fern dabbed at the corner of her eye with a shimmering swath of her sleeve. She couldn't help but notice Esmerelda's tears, too. It was now or never.

"My, those mortals were just so special I can hardly wait to jump into my next project. Where was that again?"

Esmerelda tipped her head and stared off into space, her hands twisting in the fine gossamer fabric of her flowing dress. Fern took pity on her.

"You know, Esmerelda, I'm a bit worried that I might not have the strength to do my best right now. I think you should take the next one, Esmerelda."

"What, me? Really?"

Bronwyn Wolfe

Fern could hear both the fear and longing in Esme's voice. She pinched a finger of fairy dust and blew it gently toward her. Every once in a while, even a fairy godmother could use a cosmic kick in the keister.

"You'd better hurry and get to your assignment."

Esmerelda shuddered with indecision and fairy dust fallout. She looked at Fern and then slowly pulled out her wand and squared her shoulders.

"Do you have any advice? I'm afraid I'm a little rusty."

Fern yahooed and clapped her hands. "Just remember, love is the greatest magic of all. And stay away from panty hose."

Friends,

I hope you have enjoyed my own fractured fairy tales. I loved that cartoon when I was a little girl, and it was fun to try my hand at a "what if" idea. I was having a blast until I got sick at Christmas. Believe me, I was hoping my own fairy godmother would appear with a whopper of a magic spell.

And speaking of magic...some of you legal eagles out there may have wondered how my characters were able to get married so quickly on St. Thomas. Actually, it takes eight days for an approved license. But, heck, these were not very long stories. I had to fudge on the time a bit. One of the fun things about writing is getting to wave your own magic wand and re-create your own version of the world.

I hope your day was a little brighter because of *Once Upon A Tangled Tale*, and I look forward to taking you with me on another romantic adventure. By the way, I really do believe that love is the greatest magic of all.

Best Wishes,
Bronwyn Wolfe

P.S. I love to hear from fellow readers. Write to me at P.O. Box 4926, Ontario, CA 91761, and include an S.A.S.E.

An Angel's Touch

Longer Than Forever

BRONWYN WOLFE

"A wonderful, magical love story that transcends time and space. Definitely a keeper!"
—Madeline Baker

Patrick is in trouble, alone in turn-of-the-century Chicago, and unjustly jailed with little hope for survival. Then the honey-haired beauty comes to him, as if she has heard his prayers.

Lauren has all but given up on finding true love when she feels the green-eyed stranger's call—summoning her across boundaries of time and space to join him in a struggle against all odds; uniting them in a love that will last longer than forever.

_52042-7 $5.99 US/$7.99 CAN

CORAL SMITH SAXE

A Faerie Tale Romance · The Mirror & The Magic

Bestselling Author Of *A Stolen Rose*

Sensible Julia Addison doesn't believe in fairy tales. Nor does she think she'll ever stumble from the modern world into an enchanted wood. Yet now she is in a Highland forest, held captive by seven lairds and their quick-tempered chief. Hardened by years of war with rival clans, Darach MacStruan acts more like Grumpy than Prince Charming. Still, Julia is convinced that behind the dark-eyed Scotsman's gruff demeanor beats the heart of a kind and gentle lover. But in a land full of cunning clansmen, furious feuds, and poisonous potions, she can only wonder if her kiss has magic enough to waken Darach to sweet ecstasy.

__52086-9 $5.99 US/$7.99 CAN

An Angel's Touch

Forever Angels

TRANA MAE SIMMONS

Tess Foster is convinced she has someone watching over her. The thoroughly modern woman has everything: a brilliant career, a rich fiance, and a glamorous life. But when her boyfriend demands she sign a prenuptial agreement, Tess thinks she's lost her happiness forever. Then her guardian angel sneezes and sends the woman of the nineties back to another era: the 1890s.

At first, Tess can't believe her senses. After all, no real man can be as handsome as the cowboy who rescues her from the Oklahoma wilderness. And Tess has never tasted sweeter ecstasy than she finds in Stone Chisum's kisses. But before she will surrender to a marriage made in heaven, Tess has to make sure that her bumbling guardian angel doesn't sneeze again—and ruin her second chance at love.

_52021-4 $4.99 US/$5.99 CAN

An Angel's Touch

Time Heals
SUSAN COLLIER

Tired of her nagging relatives, Maeve Fredrickson asks for the impossible: to be a thousand miles and a hundred years away from them. Then a heavenly being grants her wish, and she awakes in frontier Montana.

Saved from the wilderness by a handsome widower, Maeve loses her heart to her rescuer—and her temper over the antics of his three less-than-angelic children. As her angel prods her to fight for Seth, Maeve can only pray for the strength to claim a love made in paradise.

_52030-3 $4.99 US/$5.99 CAN

An Angel's Touch

D.J.'s Angel
Lori Handeland

D.J. Halloran doesn't believe in love. She's just seen too much heartache—in her work as a police officer and in her own life. And she vowed a long time ago never to let anyone get close enough to hurt her, even if that someone is the very captivating, very handsome Chris McCall.

But D.J. also has an angel—a special guardian determined, at any cost, to teach D.J. the magic of love. So try as she might to resist Chris's many charms, D.J. knows she is in for an even tougher battle because of her exasperating heavenly companion's persistent faith in the power of love.
_52050-8 $5.99 US/$7.99 CAN

An Angel's Touch

Daemon's Angel

Sherrilyn Kenyon

"Sherrilyn Kenyon is a bright new star!"
—Affaire de Coeur

Cast to the mortal realm by an evil sorceress, Arina has more than her share of problems. She is trapped in a temptress's body, tormented by untested passions, and doomed to lose any man she desires. Yet even as Arina yearns for the safety of the pearly gates, she finds paradise in the arms of a Norman mercenary.

The villagers say Daemon is the devil's son, but he is only a man plagued by strange dreams—visions of a tantalizing beauty who enchants him like no other. Then the enticing stranger appears in the flesh, and he vows nothing between heaven and earth will keep them apart. But to savor the joys of his very own angel, Daemon will have to battle demons—within and without—and risk his very soul for love.

_52026-5 $4.99 US/$5.99 CAN